KU-727-784

THE WRONG CASE

JAMES CRUMLEY

EAST SUSSEX COUNTY COUNCIL
WITHDRAWN
17 AUG 2024
17

BLACK SWAN

TRANSWORLD PUBLISHERS
61–63 Uxbridge Road, London W5 5SA
www.penguin.co.uk

Transworld is part of the Penguin Random House group of companies whose addresses can be found at global.penguinrandomhouse.com

First published in the United States by Random House, Inc., and Canada by Random House of Canada Limited in 1975
First Vintage Crime/Black Lizard edition published 1986
First published in Great Britain in 2016 by Black Swan
an imprint of Transworld Publishers

Copyright © James Crumley 1975, 1978, 1983

James Crumley has asserted his right under the Copyright, Designs and Patents Act 1988 to be identified as the author of this work.

This book is a work of fiction and, except in the case of historical fact, any resemblance to actual persons, living or dead, is purely coincidental.

Every effort has been made to obtain the necessary permissions with reference to copyright material, both illustrative and quoted. We apologize for any omissions in this respect and will be pleased to make the appropriate acknowledgements in any future edition.

A CIP catalogue record for this book
is available from the British Library.

ISBN
9781784161941

Typeset in 11/14 pt Sabon by Jouve (UK), Milton Keynes
Printed and bound in Great Britain by Clays Ltd, Bungay, Suffolk

Penguin Random House is committed to a sustainable future for our business, our readers and our planet. This book is made from Forest Stewardship Council® certified paper.

1 3 5 7 9 10 8 6 4 2

Praise for *James Crumley*

'The Hemingway of the detective novel . . . a big bearded bear-like man who loves to drink and raise hell and talk about literature' John Williams, author of *Stoner*

'Resonant and lyrical' Ian Rankin

'The stunner that reinvigorated the genre and jacked up a generation of future crime novelists' George Pelecanos

'Crumley is the singular reason that a lot of today's forty-something writers headed straight into crime fiction' Laura Lippman

'The first-person style, the author's sound, is bigger than life, satirical, and it lets Crumley get away with murder' Elmore Leonard

'Reading Crumley is like hurtling through an assault course . . . funny, salty and ruthless . . . one of the marvels of contemporary crime writing' *Literary Review*

'The pleasure of Crumley's writing has always been in the characters, dialogue and incidental delights' *Independent*

'The themes of nightmarish madness, betrayal and survival will glue readers to the page. Crumley remains one of the finest writers in the Raymond Chandler tradition' *Publishers Weekly*

'If you like Crumley's attitude, his cool view of human nature, his love of the drinking life and the West, and his scorn for authority, there's no one quite like him. He takes it to the limit' *Washington Post*

'The poet laureate of American hard-boiled literature, superior even to James Lee Burke in his ability to evoke extreme melancholy, gruesome violence and an acute sense of landscape . . . Deeply compelling' *Guardian*

04427923

James Crumley was born in Three Rivers, Texas and spent most of his childhood in South Texas. He served three years in the US Army before teaching at University of Texas at El Paso, University of Montana and University of Arkansas. He passed away in 2008.

His private eye novels featuring Milo Milodragovitch and C. W. Sughrue are regarded as masterpieces of contemporary crime fiction, praised by Dennis Lehane, Ian Rankin and George Pelecanos. He was awarded the Dashiell Hammett Award for Best Literary Crime Novel and the CWA Silver Dagger Award.

By James Crumley

ONE TO COUNT CADENCE
THE WRONG CASE
THE LAST GOOD KISS
DANCING BEAR
THE MEXICAN TREE DUCK
BORDERSNAKES
THE FINAL COUNTRY

For Peggy

and with special thanks to Lee Nye
for the loan of his faces
and to Gil and Jean Findlay
who provided shelter

Never go to bed with a woman who has more troubles than you do.

Lew Archer

1

There's no accounting for laws. Or the changes wrought by men and time. For nearly eight years the only way to get a divorce in our state was to have your spouse convicted of a felony or caught in an act of adultery. Not even physical abuse or insanity counted. And in the ten years since I resigned as a county deputy, I had made a good living off those antiquated divorce laws. Then the state legislature, in a flurry of activity at the close of a special session, put me out of business by civilizing those divorce laws. Now we have dissolutions of marriage by reason of irreconcilable differences. Supporters and opponents were both shocked by the unexpected action of the lawmakers, but not as shocked as I was. I spent the next two days sulking in my office, drinking and enjoying the view, considering the prospects for my suddenly very dim future. The view looked considerably better than my prospects.

My office is on the fourth floor of the Milodragovitch Building. I inherited the building from my grandfather, but most of the profits go to a management corporation, my first ex-wife, and the estate of my second ex-wife.

I'm left with cheap rent and a great view. At least on those days when the east wind doesn't inflict the pulp mill upon us or when an inversion layer doesn't cap the Meriwether Valley like a plug in a sulfurous well, I have a great view. From the north windows, I can see all the way up the Hell-Roaring drainage to the three thousand acres of timber, just below the low peaks of the Diablo Range, that my grandfather also left me. And from the west windows, if I ignore the junky western verge of Meriwether, the valley spreads out like a rich green carpet running between steep rocky ridges. On the north side of the valley, Sheba Peak rises grandly, holding snow until the heart of summer, as white and conical as the breast of a young woman, a woman conceived in the tired dreams of a dirty miner, a dream only gold or silver might buy.

Unlike my prospects, the view was worth toasting, which I did. Since I assumed dissolutions of marriage would arrange themselves without my professional assistance, my prospects were several and unseemly. I could take up repossession full time, taking back the used cars and cheap appliances so sweetly promised by the installment loan, pursuing bad debtors as if I were a hound from some financially responsible hell. I could do that; but I knew I wouldn't. No more than I could live on the forty-seven bucks and odd change left each month from my office leases, no more than I could cut my timber, or no more than I could convince the trustees of my father's estate to turn loose any of his fortune before my fifty-third birthday. At least I could have another drink out of the office bottle, another drink and another glance around my office to search for hidden assets.

The large old-fashioned safe in the corner, left from my grandfather's days as a banker, was empty, except for two thousand dollars of untaxed mad money. The three file cabinets were full of the records of failed marriages, not even worth anything to those unhappy folks recorded there. The portrait of my great-grandfather had been painted by a famous Western artist and drunk, and might be worth something, but it seemed unkind to consider selling my great-grandfather. Surely, I should sell my timber first. Or the old desk and Oriental rug, which looked shabby enough to pass for antiques, scarred with cigarette burns and gritty with the detritus of grief and outrage that had scraped off all the husbands and wives who had trembled through my office. Age and sorrow, those were my only assets, my largest liabilities.

But like most men who drink too much, I had spent most of my life considering my dismal future, and it had stopped amusing me. So I had another drink and walked over to the north windows to look down on the happy, employed folk of Meriwether. Once, we Milodragovitches had been big stuff in this town, but now the only way I could look down on anybody was to climb up to my office, stare down from the windows. Lunch hour was done; people were hurrying about their business, driving back to office and store in air-conditioned cars, even though the air seemed more like spring than summer. I had never owned an air-conditioned car, so I could feel vaguely smug. Until August anyway.

Directly beneath me, a gray-haired woman, dressed in modern elegance, stepped out of the side entrance of the bank that leased the ground floor, and as she was fussing with her open purse a long-haired kid jerked the purse out of her hands and fled clumsily across the street, pumping his legs and swinging his elbows wildly, like a heavy bird longing for flight. He dodged the eastbound traffic on Main, gathering speed, but he ran into the side of a car as it slowed to make a right-hand turn north on Dottle; bouncing back, he turned, grinning dreamily like a man who has just had a final fix, then stepped into the westbound lane. The car that hit him never touched brake shoe to drum but drove right through him like a good solid punch. The kid rolled up the hood, throwing the old woman's purse straight up in the air. As the contents of the purse scattered in the air, the kid fell off the hood into the center of the intersection. Another old woman, who obviously hadn't seen any of this, turned her giant sedan illegally left on to Dottle and ran over the kid with the two right tires. He rolled, stuck beneath the rear bumper, and she dragged him half a block up the street before she could stop.

I had never realized that purse snatching was such a dangerous crime and I wondered what the kid needed badly enough to take up petty theft. Meriwether didn't have much street crime, perhaps because we still suffered from some frontier idea of justice: shoot first, apologize to the survivors. Whatever the kid had intended, he was obviously dead, crumpled under the rear of the car like a road-kill carcass at the end of a broad blood spoor. The old woman whose purse had been stolen was wandering around the intersection gathering up the debris from her purse, carefully checking each item. The man who had hit the kid was walking around his car, examining it for damage. Up the street, the other old woman was being helped from her car like an invalid.

It was a lovely summer day, smogless and fresh, and below me the flies struggled against their violent amber. But when the first siren split the air, they slipped free, went quickly about their business. Except for the kid, squashed into place, and one woman standing across the street from my building. She held her own small pink purse to her open mouth as if it were a secret message she'd devour before she'd divulge. From where I stood, she looked good. Nice legs, a trim body. Red hair that seemed aflame above the pink dress. The sort of woman who stayed out of bars and away from the likes of me.

When the light changed, she stepped off the curb, stumbling slightly, breaking the spell. I went back to my desk, had another sip of whiskey, and opened a carton of blueberry yogurt. I watch my weight; I wouldn't want to look like a drunk.

As I ate I concentrated on the small decisions, letting the problem of my future take care of itself. I knew that if I had another drink I would probably get drunk instead of driving out to the university to play handball with my friend Dick Diamond, but I had another hit at the bottle just to prove that I could handle it. Have the drink, fight the drunk, play handball anyway. That was the plan. But somebody rapped timidly at my office door. Private investigators always have somebody rapping timidly at their doors, so I didn't leap out of my chair and spring into action. Back in the days when I still had a business, I would have hidden the bottle and the half-finished yogurt, slipped into my boots, and answered the door as if I knew what I was doing. But not this day. I left things as they were, didn't even answer until the light tapping resumed.

'Go away,' I said. But not loudly enough.

The lady in the pink dress opened the door and peeked around it like a kid who hopes the dentist is still out to lunch. But as she stepped into the office I could see that she wasn't a kid. A well-preserved thirty-five perhaps, maintained not by working at it but by saving it. And she'd saved it fairly well. A slim, firm body beneath the pink knit dress. Thick, dark red hair tucked away from a sweetly freckled face. Slightly myopic eyes that had that dreamy contact-lens blur about them. A mouth, daubed half-heartedly with a color that nearly matched the freckles, that seemed mobile and generous in spite of the prim way she pursed her lips.

'I'm sorry,' she said softly, as if she had failed to meet my standards, still standing at the door. I decided that the lipstick, which would have looked bad on any other woman, gave her just the right touch, as if she were still young enough to be foolish about a lipstick, choosing a color because she liked it, not because it went well with her face. 'I'm sorry,' she repeated, as if it were the password.

'So am I. The dentist's office is four doors down. We have the same name because we're cousins. I'm famous, but he's rich.'

'Oh, but I'm not – I wasn't looking for the dentist,' she said, flustered, then held the pink purse, which looked as if it had come in a set with the summer flats she wore, back to her mouth.

'Surely you aren't looking for me,' I said. 'Don't you read the papers? They don't have divorce in this state anymore. Just dissolutions of marriage. You can do it yourself. Thirty-four-fifty. I charge a hundred a day, plus expenses. A three-day minimum.'

'I'm from out of town,' she said, as if that explained everything. 'And I'm not married.'

'That's nice.'

'What?'

'That you're not married. Marriages can be messy. And expensive. I should know.'

'I'm sorry,' she said again. 'Do you mind if I sit down? I've just seen a terrible accident. In the street. Some poor young man was hit by a car. Then run over. It was awful. I'm quite shaken.'

'Certainly,' I answered, standing up, wishing I had put my boots on. 'Please sit down.'

She shut the door quietly, then walked over to the chair I was holding for her. She stepped on my foot, then nearly knocked the chair over as she sat in it.

'I'm sorry.'

'It's all right,' I said, retreating behind the desk to safety, slipping into my boots and sitting down. 'Well, what can I do for you?'

'I've interrupted your lunch, haven't I?'

'It's all right.'

'Please go ahead. I'll wait.'

Rather than argue with her, I had a spoonful of

yogurt, then took out my note pad, asking her again what I could do for her.

'Well, an old friend of mine recommended you. Said you might be able to help me.'

'Who?' I asked, not telling her that she didn't look like the sort of woman who needed my sort of help.

'I'd rather not say, if you don't mind.'

'Why should I mind?'

'I don't know,' she answered, as literal as a child.

'We're not getting anywhere, you know?'

'I guess not,' she said.

'Let's try the easy questions first, okay?'

'I'm sorry. I've been under quite a strain. And when I saw that young man . . . killed, I nearly went to pieces. I'm sorry. If you would just bear with me for a moment.'

'Certainly. Take your time. Would you like a drink?'

She shook her head quickly, as if she had a bad taste in her mouth. Feathers of red hair, tidily pinned back, began to drift across her face. She brushed them back, sighed, then changed her mind.

'Yes, I think I will. Perhaps it might help. And it *is* after lunch, isn't it? Do you think I could have a whiskey sour?' she asked shyly, then leaned back in her chair, fluffed her skirt, and stared at me expectantly, as if I were her favorite bartender. She looked at me silently, smiling so sweetly that I knew I must seek whiskey sours wherever they might be.

I had had some strange requests in my office. Husbands who wanted me to do obscene things to myself when they found out that their wives were exactly the sluts they supposed them to be. Or when they found out how expensive my services were. And wives had made their share of indecent requests too. Usually concerning my fee. They tried to take it out in trade, and sometimes became angry when they discovered I'd take it out but wouldn't trade it for anything. Some of the ideas that hurt and angry wives had in my office were damned strange. But I'd never been asked to whip up a whiskey sour.

'Okay,' I said, 'one whiskey sour coming up.' She smiled and crossed her legs, managing to kick my desk and expose a trim thigh at the same time.

I dialed Mahoney's, which is forty quick steps south of my office, and told Leo to whip up two whiskey sours in go cups and to send Simon up with them. Leo grumbled a bit, grousing about fancy drinks and my running tab, but he said he'd try to remember how to make a whiskey sour. Mahoney's is a wino bar, and anybody who asks for anything fancier than soda with their whiskey was either a sissy or a stranger.

'The drinks are on their way,' I said after Leo hung up on me.

'Is that legal?' she asked, concerned.

'Sure. This is the great American West. Where men came to get away from laws. Almost everything in this state is legal. And a lot of things that are illegal are done in spite of the law. You can order ten whiskey sours in go cups, then get into your car and fly up and down the highways at whatever speed you can call reasonable and proper. You can murder your spouse and the lover in a fit, preferably of passion, and the maximum sentence is five years, and even that is usually suspended. And it's all legal. If you prefer gambling or drugs, which are still illegal, you can find any sort of game or machine you'd like within three blocks of my office, or buy all the drugs you want, except heroin, right on the street. So don't worry about two little drinks coming up the street.'

'All right,' she said. 'I won't worry. Please go ahead with your lunch.'

As I finished the remains of the yogurt, she tried very hard to sit still and look unworried. Her hands were clasped tightly around the small purse and crammed into her lap, but her fingers kept plucking at the ragged cuticles of her thumbs. At close range she seemed more girlish, nervous and giggly, like a teenaged girl on her first date. And scatterbrained and clumsy. The sort of woman who would need help to find her clothes afterward, who would always be losing things – gloves and glasses, hairpins and ribbons – then would prance around the room, smiling coyly as she looked in all the wrong places. I thought I might like that. It had been a long time since I had been with a woman who could seem innocent and vulnerable. Not that I mind strong, self-reliant women, but most of the women I knew were so tough they could chip flint hide-scrapers with their hearts. I decided that I liked this woman. Perhaps more than I should on such short notice. Whatever her problem, I intended to console her until she discovered that there wasn't much I could do to help her. Two drinks in the office as we discussed her problem, an early dinner at the Riverfront, martinis as we waited, brandies afterward as we watched the river flow into the setting sun, then home to my little log house by Hell-Roaring Creek to smoke a little dope and watch the long mountain dusk become night, to listen to the creek rumble in its rocky bed.

What the hell, I wasn't above taking advantage of a woman, running out the tired trappings of romance, even drugging them to have my way. We could make up the morality afterward in that sad time when passion has degenerated into a quick cigarette, a slow drink, silence.

'So what can I do for you?' I asked one more time, hand poised over my pad.

'I'm . . .'

'Wait a second,' I interrupted, reaching into the bottom desk drawer for the cassette recorder, which I'd bought from Muffin when I'd had to sell the fancy Ampex reel to reel. Muffin had assured me that the cassette recorder wasn't hot, but I didn't believe him for a moment.

'Do you mind?' I asked as I switched on the recorder. 'My secretary went to lunch and hasn't come back yet. I like to have a record of these things. I assure you that everything that passes between us will be strictly confidential.'

She hesitated, then nodded. I didn't tell her that my secretary had gone to lunch four years ago, and that the reason she hadn't come back was because she had run away with a dope dealer from Portland. It had been a successful match. They were living in Mazátlan now; she sunbathed, he financed dope deals.

'Where shall I begin?' she asked, a nervous tremor in her voice.

'How about name and address? That sort of stuff.'

'Oh,' she said, somehow surprised, as if she had expected to hire me without telling me her name. 'All right. My name is Helen Duffy, and I live with my parents,' she said, her voice unnaturally high and loud for the benefit of the recorder.

'Listen,' I said, 'just speak normally. You don't have to shout or anything.'

'Oh, I'm sorry. Those things make me nervous.'

'They make a lot of people nervous, but don't let it bother you. Just tell me where you live. More specifically than "with my parents," okay?'

'All right,' she whispered, then steeled herself to begin again. 'My name is Helen Duffy –'

'A little louder than that, please.'

'– and I live with my parents at Rural Route Number 4, Box 52B, Storm Lake, Iowa, Zip Code 50588, and I am an assistant professor of English at Buena Vista College in Storm Lake.'

'Isn't that where they had the massacre?'

'What? Oh, no, that was Spirit Lake. MacKinlay Kantor wrote a rather good novel about it.'

'Yeah,' I said. 'I read it a long time ago.' She looked so surprised that I added, 'I went to college too. Not very successfully but for a long time.' I didn't add that I went until my GI Bill ran out, along with the patience of the trustees of my father's estate.

'Where did you go?' she asked politely, her voice normal now, which was what I had been after.

'Here at Mountain States, Mexico City College, USC, a couple of junior colleges in California.'

'What did you major in?'

'Booze, broads, and various water sports,' I said, hoping to turn her back to the business at hand.

'Oh.'

'Who do you want me to find? Whom?'

'How did you know I wanted you to look for somebody?'

'Easy. You're not married, so you don't want a divorce. You don't look like the sort of woman who wants me to repossess a used car or a color television or hassle some guy for a gambling debt, so I assume you want me to find somebody. Let me guess,' I said, showing off. 'Your sister came out West –'

'Brother.'

'Younger?'

'Yes.'

'Okay, your younger brother came out West to work this summer and –'

'Two years ago. To work on his master's in history. Raymond always loved Western history,' she said, as if that too explained everything.

'– and dropped out of school into radical politics or into the drug scene –'

'To finish his research for his thesis on criminal justice on the Western frontier,' she corrected me.

'– and the family hasn't heard from him in several months, and you've come West on your summer vacation to find out what's wrong.'

'Three weeks. We – I had a letter three weeks ago.'

'Three weeks isn't very long,' I said, glad to be right about something.

'In his last letter, he seemed worried about something, under some sort of strain.'

'What about?'

'He didn't say,' she said primly.

'Then how did you know he was under a strain?'

'He's my brother,' she stated flatly.

'Sometimes parents don't even know their own children.'

'That isn't the case here.'

I managed to keep myself from saying, 'Well, what is the case, lady?' It was a beginning. In the book it says to let the client talk, to listen carefully and take copious notes, and making certain that, when you do speak, to be sure to reveal your perception and intelligence, your deep understanding of human behavior, and that way the client will have the utmost confidence in your abilities, etc. But I always seemed to do it this other way: stagger them with wit, ply them with romance and whiskey sours, and convince them that I wouldn't be able to eat that night unless they paid me a large retainer. Sometimes it worked.

'Okay. Did the letter have a return address?'

'Yes. A hotel. But when I went there, it had burned down.'

'The Great Northern?'

She nodded sadly.

'What the hell was he doing living there?'

'It had something to do with his research, I think.'

'What was he researching? Cockroaches and bedbugs?'

She didn't bother to answer.

Once, the Great Northern had been a fine Western hotel, where prospectors who had hit it and ranchers who could afford it came to raise hell in Victorian splendor. Even after its heyday, it was a good hotel, somewhat run-down but still holding on to enough elegance to make a person feel comfortable. But an Eastern corporation had bought it, and in order to show a profit they had subdivided the rooms; made it into a flophouse for winos with a steady income and a hot-sheets home for Meriwether's few prostitutes. It had burned down about three weeks ago, burned down in about fifteen minutes because the sprinkler system was rusted shut.

'A terrible fire,' I said.

'You don't think . . .'

'No chance. I was there when they sifted the ashes. Everybody got out, except for two winos. Petey Martinez, who was deaf and wouldn't wear his hearing aid except on formal occasions, and the old man who started the fire, smoking in bed, drunk probably. Your brother wasn't in there. At least not when it burned down.'

She didn't seem relieved, so I tried another question.

'Was your brother – Raymond, isn't it? – into the drug scene or radical politics?'

'No.'

'Are you sure?'

'Of course I'm sure. He was a decent middle-class young man. Well-mannered, considerate, intelligent. Somewhat timid, I suppose, but then that seems to run in our family. He was opposed to the Vietnam war, of course, but he certainly wasn't a radical, and he wouldn't have had anything to do with drugs. He had hobbies.'

'Hobbies?' I guess I said it as if I wanted to know what they were. She took it that way.

'Yes. He was a fine horseman, and his gun collection was the finest in the state. He was also a regional fast-draw champion.'

'Some hobbies.'

'He enjoyed them, yes. He was kind to his horses and he never killed a living thing with his guns.'

'Okay,' I said, not knowing what else to say without making her defense of her little brother even stronger. I had the distinct feeling that her little brother wasn't quite the angel she had in mind, and I knew we wouldn't get anywhere if I told her that. So I changed tactics: 'Have you ever smoked marijuana?'

'Of course not. Why do you ask?'

'Just trying to see how reliable a source of information you are,' I said. 'Sometimes people who aren't familiar with drugs don't know when –'

But she burst into tears before I could finish. After all that had happened, she chose to fall apart over that.

'I – I may not know anything about – about drugs or radical politics or anything like that – but I do know my – my little brother,' she sputtered, trying to hold her face together. 'Know he wouldn't do – do anything awful.' The *awful* nearly became a scream. Her pain and worry were real, and they dangled between us like a frayed empty sleeve.

'Excuse me,' she blubbered, coughing to cover the tears. 'I – I have to take out my contacts . . . I haven't had them very long, I'm not used to them.' So she removed her contact paraphernalia from her purse and started prying at her eyes.

I switched off the recorder. Some things didn't need

recording. As I watched her face tilt over her open palm, I tried to think about her missing brother. I almost told her that it was senseless for us to go on like this, since the chances of me finding her little brother were less than slim. Runaway children are almost impossible to find, even for people who are trained in missing-person work, which I wasn't, and the only lost children I'd ever found had been lost in the woods. But I didn't tell her. I still wanted her, so I didn't tell her. She seemed like a woman from a simpler, better time, a small-town time when sprinklers graced neat lawns and screen doors smelled like rain or dust instead of plastic, when the seasons changed as gracefully as scenes on greeting cards, when snow was never dirty, when fall leaves were never soggy and damp, and when children never cried, except for brief moments, and then were so gently comforted that they didn't mind crying at all. She did that to me, made me homesick for a childhood I'd never really had, the one I sometimes constructed in odd drunken moments to make me forget the real one. And she made me hope, something I hadn't done for years, made me believe in a better, cleaner world where a man and a woman could raise a family in peace. I decided then that she deserved better than my tired version of comfort; she deserved my help, such as it was.

So I didn't have another hit off the office bottle, but capped it and set it back in the bottom drawer, trying to think seriously about her little brother. But she dropped one of her contacts, and we spent the next few minutes crawling around the faded and scarred carpet, searching the charred spots for her contact. She had one eye closed, and I acted like I could really see after drinking most of the day. I cursed silently, cursed Simon and the missing drinks, which I knew he had slipped into an alley to drink, hating himself even as he drank them but already constructing the lie he would tell Leo to get two more and another free shot for his grief. And I cursed vanity: hers for the contacts, mine for refusing to wear my glasses. The longer we searched, the more it looked like she was going to need a drink. She snagged her panty hose twice; she bumped heads with me only once, but so hard that she sat back on the carpet, her knees folded under her, her hand to her forehead. For a moment it seemed as if she was going to wail like a hysterical child, but she caught herself when I found the lens in the chair. At least I found something. She put it away, took out the other without incident, and we went back to business.

As I switched the recorder back on, I said, 'I know this must be a strain, but if I don't ask hard questions, I'll never be able to help you. Okay?'

'I'm sorry,' she answered, slipping on rimless glasses that made her look more her age. 'I'm not usually this sensitive. But sometimes . . . sometimes, as my mother says, I'm a ninny. I never know when it's going to happen. Sometimes the tears just start. Sometimes when I lose things, I just can't . . .'

'That's all right. Don't worry.'

'How can I help but worry? I just know Raymond is in some sort of difficulty. Otherwise he would have been in touch. Raymond and I are very close.'

'Okay, I'll take your word for that. Let's start over. What sort of trouble do you think he might be in?'

'I don't know,' she said quickly.

'You won't even guess?'

'I thought you were supposed to do that.'

'Yeah. I guess so. Who referred you to me?'

'I told you I'd rather not say. If you don't mind,' she answered, folding her hands around the purse and arching her neck. Then she suddenly began to giggle and blushed very nicely, the warmth rising from her bare shoulders to her slim neck. I tried to blush back, but there are some things not even I can fake. After the giggles rattled away into the summer afternoon, she straightened her face and hair, then said, 'I'm afraid I lied a moment ago. I *have* smoked pot a few times. When I was in graduate school in the early sixties, but nothing happened.'

'What did you expect to happen?'

'Oh, something terribly sinful, I suppose. Don't look at me like that, please. I'm not as naïve as I may appear.'

'Whatever you say, lady,' I said, wondering where the blush and giggles had come from. 'But back to your little brother and his trouble.'

'Oh, I don't know that he's in trouble,' she said gaily, 'I mean I don't know it for sure. I think he's in trouble but I don't know it for a fact, and as my mother is always telling me, thinking isn't knowing. Perhaps he's just angry at the family and is staying out of touch to hurt us.'

'Why should he be angry with your family?'

'That's rather personal. I'd rather not go into it, if you don't mind,' she said quietly, her gaze dropping back to her lap, where her fingers were busily mauling each other, her voice no longer gay at all.

'Why should I mind,' I said, but she missed the irony. *Family life*, I thought, *wonderful family life*. There ought to be a law against families, or, at the very least, children should be given a choice of families or colors of their Skinner Boxes. Families are always a mess: everybody always wants to fuck everybody else and usually finds a particularly vicious substitute. And love doesn't seem to matter either. Too much, not enough – somehow the same unhappy family life comes out. Her family was probably a nice middle-class, ordinary group. My family had been a nightmare. My father a rich, worthless drunk; my mother an insane drunk. So here was Helen Duffy coming to me for help, when I probably needed help more than she did. And her little brother probably wanted nothing more in the world than to be left alone by his family. But help I intended to give, and for that help I intended to be paid in kind. Long days looking for a kid who didn't want to be found, short nights with his big sister.

But as I thought about it, I suddenly didn't like myself very much. I'd never been really fond of myself anyway, but now I disliked myself so much it made me feel old and tired, deceitful and dirty, the drunk in the gutter unworthy to even touch the shoes of the passing lady.

'Miss Duffy – Helen. Do you mind if I call you Helen?'

She sighed rather than answering, keeping the night-watch on her frantic fingers.

'Miss Duffy, I'll be frank with you, if you don't mind. I haven't been frank with anybody in years, not since I started this grimy racket. In the ten years or so since I started this crap, I've done almost nothing but divorce work. A little repossession work, but I don't like it. Every now and then somebody comes into my office wanting me to find somebody else – a runaway kid or a husband who decided to become somebody else – and what usually happens when I look for a runaway is that I find them really quick because I bribe some creep at the power company or the telephone office or the post office, which costs my client three bills plus the bribe and which makes me feel worse than the creeps I have to deal with. If that doesn't work, and a lot of times it doesn't, then I never find the runaway, and that costs my client a small fortune and makes me feel even worse than when I find somebody. It makes me feel like warmed-over shit, if you'll excuse the expression.

'And if I'm looking for a kid who has slipped into the street scene here, I never even get close. Not even the hometown freaks who've known me all their lives, who deal me dope, they won't help me find somebody in the street scene. They know that nobody wants to go home – that's why they ran away – so they won't talk to me, and I can't find my ass with either hand when people won't talk to me.

'So save your money. If you want somebody to look for your little brother, go to the police. The bastards are corrupt but they're cheap. I'm expensive and corrupt. And not very good at my job. I can find a naked woman in a dark room, but not if she runs . . . Shit,' I said, trying one of her sighs and discovering that I was standing up, leaning heavily on my desk, shaking slightly like a man who needed a drink more than he needed frankness. So I reached in the drawer and had one.

Her hands had fallen still, and she looked up at me blankly, then said quietly, 'You're rather a profane and unhappy man, aren't you?'

'Lady, I'm worse than that,' I said as I sat down.

She stared over my shoulder into the blue slopes of the Diablos, her clear blue eyes reflecting the peaks and the mountain sky.

'Oh, you're probably like most men,' she murmured, a sad authority in her voice as she looked past me, 'not nearly so terrible as you think. Men are always so hard on themselves. Morally, I mean. My friend, who recommended you, says you're a good man. Unhappy but good. And he warned me that you would be profane. I really don't mind. I just can't talk that way, you know, the words feel dirty in my mouth.' Then she giggled faintly but not happily. 'My friend said you knew – knew whenever anybody farted in Meriwether County –'

'His opinion is too high,' I said.

'And he said that if anybody could find Raymond, you could, and I'm so afraid that – that something awful has happened to him – he was such a lovely child, so kind and gentle. Not like other boys. And he left home too soon; he wasn't ready for the world just yet. But my mother – my mother . . .'

But she had stopped talking to me. Her words were directed somewhere else. Inside her perhaps, or into her past, or maybe off into the mountains where she saw herself living in a quiet, sheltered cabin, mate to a pious man who might help.

'And if you don't help me, I don't know where to turn. I'm so afraid – I must find him, you know.' The eyes she turned toward me were glazed with a fear approaching madness.

'What are you afraid of?'

'I beg your pardon?'

'What are you frightened of?' I asked again.

'That something awful has happened to Raymond, of course.' She picked at her cuticles again, digging at them so hard that I could hear the thrum as thumbnail ripped flesh, even over the sound of the afternoon traffic drifting up from the street below. She bit off a piece of cuticle as neatly as my grandmother used to snip thread with her store-bought teeth, then spit the skin sharply onto my carpet. I expected her to apologize, but she didn't seem to know that I was in the room. Her glazed eyes turned misty and sorry with some unexplained loss.

'Hey, let's start over,' I said.

'What?'

'Let's try again, okay?'

She touched her face with her hand, her fingers moving like a blind woman's across an unfamiliar face. Then she came back, saying, 'I must apologize for taking your time, Mr. Milodragovitch. You've been very kind and patient. But somehow I thought – thought it would be different somehow –'

'Like on television?'

'No. Easier somehow. I don't know. But I can see now that you can't help me, can see that this was a mistake from beginning to end, so if you'll just tell me how much I owe you for your time, I'll pay you and be on my way,' she said, her voice carefully controlled. Then she giggled again. 'Be on my merry way,' she said lightly, taking a sheaf of hundred-dollar traveler's checks, so thick that she couldn't fold them, out of her purse. In another time I might have thought, *Hey, this dame is loaded!* And since I'm an old-fashioned guy, that's exactly what I thought. She had come prepared to look long and hard for the little brother, had come burdened with the family hopes and fortune.

'Hey, put the money away,' I said, taking a quick hit off the whiskey, making myself talk without thinking. 'Hey, listen,' I began again, then had one more drink, that drink that frees the tongue. She neither looked at me nor stuffed the checks back in her purse; she sat there at my command like a child waiting to be punished. 'Hey, listen for a minute, will you? I'll make a deal with you. My life hasn't been too grand these past few years. Shit, my life was never grand. And the thing I liked best of all about divorce work was that I never had to see anybody whose life was any better off than mine. The people who came asking for my help convinced me that the world was just as stupid and filthy and cruel and corrupt as I thought it was. And maybe I still think that, I don't know. It doesn't matter what I think, I guess, because that part of my life is over. I'm out of business. The Robin Hood of the Divorce Courts has slung his cameras and mikes and dirty pictures behind him . . . and I've got nothing to show for those years but bad debts and grief, I've not done a single thing in all that time I could be proud of, so maybe here at the end I should do something nice for a change, something for free, and maybe this shitload of misery I call myself will feel better instead of worse for a change. Maybe.

'So I'll make a deal with you, okay? I'll make your little brother my last official act as a private creep, I'll look for your goddamned little brother in the daytime, if you'll . . .'

But when it came down to it, I didn't have the guts to say it.

'I'm not sure I understand,' she said into my pause, and she didn't sound as if she cared to understand either.

So I said it: 'I'll look for your brother in exchange for your nights . . . my days for your nights.'

So what if I was half in the bag, lonesome and dumb with self-pity, left with a life that had become all hang-over and no drunk. I wanted to feel human again, and the only way I knew was with a woman, and the only women I knew were gay divorcees, stoned hippie chicks, and tired barmaids whose emotions were as badly man-gled as mine, and I wanted more, wanted this squirrelly, oddly virginal English professor from some goddamned crossroads in Iowa, wanted her like I hadn't wanted anything in a long time, too long. So I said it again, 'My days for your nights.'

She glanced up coldly, her face composed and prim.

'I'm afraid I don't know what you mean.'

'Fuck it then,' I said, finding myself standing again. 'Just fuck it, okay?'

She didn't seem particularly angry. She just slipped the checks back into her purse, snapped it shut, then left my office without another word. As she walked she held her back very erectly, moving her legs as if she had envied too many models. It was an exit, but she tripped over the sill, stumbled down the hall, leaving my office door open. I didn't feel much like laughing but I tried one anyway. It sounded like the croak of a crushed frog, so I turned back to my bottle and my northern view, shut off the recorder and sat there without thinking about anything.

A light haze shrouded the Diablos, not smog yet but the hot afternoon sun vaporizing the pine pitch, drawing moisture from the needles and the bark. When the trees were dry enough, lightning or a careless smoker would start the first fire, and my timber would finally burn all the way down. Again I considered selling it, maybe even selling the land to some rich tourist. Recreation land, they called it, better than gold or silver. I thought of selling and taking the money away with me to some foreign land where I could live cheaply until my fifty-third birthday made me a rich man, but even as I thought about it, I knew I wouldn't leave. Not yet.

Traffic north of Dottle Street was still stalled by a fire truck. Two firemen washed the blood off the street, leaving a larger, darker stain that steamed on the hot asphalt. The man with the hose worked very intently; his partner stood with his hands on his hips, his cap tilted back, the smile of an untroubled man wide across his face.

When I went to shut the door, the smell of her was thick in the cool air of my office, a fragrance of spring, flowery and untainted, then old Simon shuffled sheepishly through the open door, bringing the drinks and the smell of stale cigarettes and whiskey sweat with him.

'Sorry, sorry, Milo, sorry to be so long, sorry, but these two kids, Milo, these two kids took, sorry . . .' he babbled in his usual drunken manner as he sat the drinks on my desk. Then he began to pound his clothes so hard that dust puffed from his shoddy suit. 'Cigarette, Milo, sorry, Milo, cigarette, Milo, please, just one.'

'She's gone, you old fart, so you can act human again. The cigarettes are right where they always are.'

He filched a whole pack of Camels from the drawer where I kept them since I quit. After he lit two, he gave me one, then sucked on his so hard that he nearly choked to death. As soon as he caught his flimsy breath, he said, 'Thank you, Milo. You're a real gentleman.'

'Fuck you, old man,' I answered as I had the single drag I allowed myself. I flipped the long butt out the window, hoping it landed on a tourist. 'What took so long with the drinks, huh?'

'You know how it is,' he said, not even bothering to lie. He was drunk but maintaining. He could still rub his hands together as if he were just about to freeze to death, could still revolve his cigarette in the corner of his mouth as he spoke, and he still spoke in a normal voice, which meant that he knew who I was and spared me the string of foolish chatter which he used like a shield against the sober world. 'Who was that lovely bit of fluff on the stairs, Milo?'

'Fuck you, Simon.'

'Since you don't care to confide in an old and trusted friend – who's saved your dumb ass more times than can be counted – perhaps you'll share these as yet untasted drinks with an old man in great need of a taste.'

'Weren't the first two enough? And the two shots?'

'Milo, my boy, there's never enough.'

'Yeah,' I said, stepping over to the desk to get the drinks, since Simon obviously wasn't going to. I handed him one, then looked at the recorder. I started to erase the tape, but the sound of her voice was there. I thought I might want to hear it sometime, might want to hear my own foolishness, so I took the cassette out and slipped it into my hip pocket. Then Simon and I snapped the lids off the Styrofoam cups, left the office and sipped the drinks as we strolled the forty easy steps down to Mahoney's, sauntering like lords through the summer afternoon buzz of shoppers and gaping tourists, down to Mahoney's Bar and Grill, where I had unlimited credit and willing friends, grease to ease the squeaking wheel of a summer afternoon.

'Did you hear about the tragic purse snatcher?' Simon asked. When he said it, it sounded like the first line of a dirty joke, but I told him I'd already heard it.

2

During his more lucid moments, Simon often said that when I grew old enough to become a full-time drunk, he and I would have a worthless contest, and he maintained that I would lose because I lacked the necessary character to forgo the last vestiges of middle-class morality. 'When I'm so soused that I defecate in my trousers,' he would confide in his rich, rolling, private voice, 'even in your deepest stupor, boy, you will turn away in disgust. However mild, still disgust. And the man who would truly discard his life lacks that fatal disgust. And prides himself upon that lack.'

Simon and I had been friends for years, ever since the night I had taken him home in my deputy sheriff's unit instead of heaving him into the county drunk tank, which had been filled with its usual Saturday-night complement of outraged Indians, collapsed winos, and downright mean drunks. I'd fed him bacon and eggs, coffee and whiskey, and talked to him, I guess, as if he were still a man, and we'd become friends. It had been on his advice that I'd become a private investigator after resigning from the sheriff's department. He told me that if I didn't have a job I'd drink myself to death before I really had time to enjoy it. He added that being a divorce detective was about all I was good for. Like most of his advice, it sounded good, so I took it. But in all those years, he never told me why, out of all the people in Meriwether's bars, he had chosen to allow only me behind his drunken mask. Perhaps he did it in memory of my father, who had been his friend and drinking companion too, or perhaps simply on a drunken whim. When I asked him why, he would only say lightly, 'Even the foulest drunk needs a friend. One dependable friend. Any more than one confuses the issue. When I die, I'm assured one mourner.' Then he would laugh until he choked, adding, 'And that's more than you can say, boy.' I never asked myself why I let him choose me.

Like me, Simon had been the scion of an old Meriwether family, and until he was in his early forties had been a damned successful criminal lawyer, perhaps the best in the mountain West, feared by prosecutors in seven states, beloved by assorted murderers, rapists and bank robbers. Then one spring day he lost it, lost his belief in the law, in justice, in the court system. He said that anything that easy to best couldn't be any good. So he closed his office and opened a bottle, drank from that bottle seriously for ten years, long enough for people to forget who he had been and to see only what he had become. With whiskey he destroyed their memories, then settled down to steady drinking, his thirst strong but not suicidal, and joined that fair brigade of peripatetic drunks that makes Meriwether such a fine and pleasant city, the best little town in the West, a small city that could boast of the highest per capita ratio of bars in America.

(It could but it doesn't. Instead it chooses to boast of mountain vistas, trout streams and the most highly speculative land values in the West. Sometimes I think the Chamber of Commerce and the tourist office should tout the bars: at least they aren't filled with strangers.)

Although he worked on it very hard, Simon didn't quite qualify for the honors of town drunk. They were reserved for a young man who had appeared in the local bars one day wearing an old Brooklyn Dodgers baseball cap and claiming to be able to repeat the radio broadcast of any Dodger game within the last twenty years. When he was sober, that is, which was never. Nonetheless, Simon was a character of some renown in his own right. He lived in the discarded clothing of other men, possessed nothing except those clothes, a pencil and a child's notebook for his letters, and whatever might lurk in the dusty pockets of other men's suits. Year round he slept where he fell or wherever people dragged him afterward. I never saw him buy a drink or a meal, although he had a small monthly income from his father's trust. Surely sometime during those years he must have bought a meal or a drink, but I never saw him do it. A matter of pride, he maintained. There were a few things that he wouldn't do for a drink, though. He wouldn't humor a fool, if he recognized the fool beforehand, and he wouldn't change his political opinions, which were dangerously violent and radical.

Periodically he was arrested for threatening the life of some political figure, and only because he was Simon

Rome he spent two or three months drying out at the state mental hospital at Twin Forks instead of two or three years in a federal slammer. Almost daily, he wrote long, rambling letters of protest to Washington, letters that must have given many a sweet laugh to poor secretaries dulled by the Capitol atmosphere. During the days of antiwar protest marches, Simon could always be found at the head of the line, dancing and shouting the most vile threats against the government. The freaks and college students who came into Mahoney's at night, looking for a *real place*, loved Simon. They could cheer him on in his idiot act, buy him drinks just to hear him shout for presidential blood. Simon was our only radical wino and he played his role day and night. Except with me. With me he could be ordinary, normal, and even sad, if it suited his mood.

As Simon and I reached our favorite booth in Mahoney's, I waved at old Pierre, who was sitting like a stone at the back table next to the jukebox and the shuffleboard machine, watching each new customer as if he dared him to activate either electronic obscenity. I didn't offer Pierre a drink because his brain was so whiskey-soaked that he didn't bother to drink much anymore; he just sat around and thought about being drunk, which usually worked. Sometimes he would clutch his head and curse in his unintelligible French, squeezing his head as if that would put the taste of whiskey in his mouth. After he had awoken one morning to discover that he had completely forgotten the English language, he cut down his consumption, but he still spent his days in Mahoney's, watching the shuffleboard machine and grunting with a French accent. Sometimes, though, I suspected that like Simon's idiot babble this was the ruse with which old Pierre kept the world at bay. It certainly simplified life, and on certain days, such as this one, I envied that simplicity and wondered what sort of guise I would wear when I made that final retreat. When I waved at Pierre, he seemed to smile slyly.

When Leo brought the shots and beers, he mentioned that he had added four whiskey sours and two shots to my heavy tab.

'You mean you didn't buy Simon's story of robbery and near murder?' I asked, but Leo just sneered. The only person more cynical than a drunk is a reformed drunk.

After he left, Simon checked to see that nobody was close enough to hear his normal voice, then he asked, 'And what did that lovely lady want, lad? Not a divorce, I venture.' Then he cackled softly. The ruin of my business amused him greatly.

'I'm not sure what she wanted. A better man than me, I guess.'

'That wouldn't be hard to find,' Simon said, sipping slowly at his shot.

'Off my ass, old man. Let's get drunk and be somebody.'

Simon nodded sagely, sipped again, then started to say something, but Fat Freddy, whom Simon hated passionately, waddled slowly past our booth, picking his teeth and sucking the last juices from the debris of his Slumgullion lunch. Simon hated Freddy because he had been a corrupt cop, fired from the force of a large Midwestern city for running a string of whores. The passion came because Freddy had taught me to shadow by following Simon everywhere he went for three weeks. Simon had never seen us but he had felt us behind him somewhere, dogging his tracks like a pair of patient but lazy hounds. After a month or so, Simon had forgiven me but he had never forgiven Freddy.

'Good afternoon, Milo. And how are you today, Mr. Rome?' Freddy said as he loomed past our booth, presenting his enormous belly as if it were a treasure of great worth, a leg of lamb with mint jelly, perhaps, or a crown roast engulfed by oysters.

I nodded, but Simon went berserk, sputtering, 'Fa-fa-fat ba-ba-bastard bastard bastard.'

'Don't have a fit,' I said. 'Not at my table anyway.'

Simon hushed and Freddy moved on to dock next to Pierre, where they would wait out the afternoon, Pierre watching for the fool with a coin who would destroy his peace, Freddy plying his toothpick with a devotion my cousin the dentist would have admired.

When he finally settled down, Simon went back to the lady, saying, 'That was a truly fair maiden, boy. I would have thought that you would have done whatever she asked.'

'I tried.'

'A really lovely lady,' he whispered, pausing to stare into his shot glass. 'Something sweet and lovely about that lady. I remember the ladies. Vaguely . . .' Then he chuckled at his self-pity. Though there were rumors that Simon had been hell on the ladies in his youth, he had never married, and after the years of drinking, he had become as sexless as an old woman. He didn't even indulge in the bitter, helpless comments of the other winos when they would appraise the body of a young woman in the bar. Just passing Helen Duffy on the stairs, he had been caught like me by the special nature of that woman. 'Lovely,' he repeated, as if the word would bring back the vision, then he smiled sadly, lifting his small red notebook and pencil from his coat pocket as carefully as if they were deadly weapons. He began to babble and scrawl, forgetting me completely.

He wasn't long for the world, I feared, wasn't going to survive many more winters. He would freeze in a dark doorway some night or stumble in front of another car or forget which role belonged to which time. He would die soon, I knew that, and dead, have a tiny gold star pasted into the corner of his portrait, which shared the walls of Mahoney's with those of his compatriots, the living and the dead and those still trapped in between. And that was nearly as sad as losing the lady.

Leo had been a hack photographer in upstate New York, shooting weddings and smarmy babies and beaming old couples whose bland lives had blurred their features into the same characterless mold, using his camera to support his painting and drinking. He had a good eye but no hand, so he gave up painting for drinking. His wife and family finally left him, and he couldn't find many customers who wanted their sentimental memories recorded by a drunk. He sold his business and equipment and fled into a long, down-spiraling drunk, heading West to die in a strange place where he wouldn't shame his family. But he didn't die; he broke the pattern and dried out. He didn't miss the drunks or the drinking, but had been at home in bars so long that he missed them – so he bought Mahoney's. I co-signed the note, putting up my timber land to secure it, and Leo made a success of the old bar. Then after he was sure he was going to stay dry and successful, he took up the camera again, seriously this time. His eye found the lost history in ruined cabins and old mines, the poetry in spare winter landscapes, and the dignity and pride in the battered faces of his patrons. He caught them in brave laughter and elegant sad loss and then hung the portraits on the walls of his bar, as if to remind them what they could be. The large pictures reminded us of hope, reminded us that we weren't social drinkers, and the gold stars in the corners of the dead were like medals.

Unfortunately, I hadn't been shot and hung yet. I meant to speak to Leo as soon as I finished my drink, to suggest that my time might have arrived.

But I never finished that drink. My friend Dick Diamond, my handball partner who taught English out at Mountain States University, came bounding into the tranquil and languid afternoon to harass me about missing another match.

'Thanks, old buddy. Had a great game. Really great. Played with two kids who were learning the game. Slowly. Only one was blind, though. And the other only slightly crippled. Both retarded, though. Don't have any idea how they ever passed the entrance exams. But thanks for the game, old buddy,' he said as he walked toward the table. Dick had never recovered from a strong dose of college basketball. He had been both too short and the only Jew on the team, but he made up for it by believing that death was preferable to losing. Sometimes I thought he only liked to play with me because he could beat me eighty percent of the time.

'You're welcome,' I said as he grabbed a chair and straddled it at the end of the booth.

'Know you're a busy man, Milo – dark corners and high transoms and all that – but can't you make it one time a week?'

I raised my shot glass at him, and he nodded. 'Understood, old buddy.'

'Is Marsha still mad at me?' I asked.

'Marsha?'

'Your loving, devoted, forgiving wife,' I said.

'Oh, you mean that woman who lives in my house, mothers my children, but who hasn't spoken to me in several weeks, not since my best friend ruined not only my marriage but also my career?'

'Yeah, her.'

'She forgives you, sure, she loves you more than your mother did, loves you because you're such a dear, lonesome man. But me? She hasn't gotten around to forgiving me. I've been sleeping in the study again, old buddy.'

'It wasn't my fault,' I said as Leo arrived with a mug of beer for Dick. 'I'm innocent.'

'Sure, man, innocent,' Dick said.

'Everything's your fault,' Leo said.

Simon nodded wisely.

'Couldn't you at least have found a fetid corner of the

bathroom or gone out on the lawn like any self-respecting dog? Jesus H. Christ,' he said, then was silent long enough to drink half his beer.

'Want a divorce?'

'Wise ass.'

'Look, it wasn't my fault, how did I know . . .'

'Sure, man,' he said, 'she drug you into the wardrobe – Jesus, man, my antique cherrywood wardrobe – forced you in there at gunpoint, right?'

'I didn't know what she wanted in there,' I said, grinning at the memory of Hildy Ernst. 'I didn't know until it was too late. And what sort of gentleman would I be if I stopped in the midst of the act? Besides, it wasn't my fault the damned thing fell over. That's your fault for having unstable antiques.'

'Jesus, man,' Dick said, gunning the rest of his beer as if in a race. He waved to Leo for another round, but I told him to leave me out, since I still hadn't started yet.

'Who shouted "Earthquake!"?' I asked.

'Who do you think?'

'That's what Marsha's mad about, huh?'

'Right. Who gives a rat's ass? Sleeping in the study has certain advantages,' he said.

When the wardrobe hit the floor with Hildy and me engaged within and Dick shouted 'Earthquake!' the departmental chairman's wife was in the upstairs bathroom, drunk as a sow, and she believed it. She had fled down the stairs like an avalanche, her enormous white panties flapping about her feet like a small but very angry dog. After she had been laid to rest in the guest bedroom, six men lifted Hildy and me and the wardrobe off the floor, and we sauntered out the doors, grins on our faces and jism on our clothes like icing on the cake.

'Well, I'm glad you're happy about everything,' I said.

'Jesus. Every time I see the chairman, he harrumphs like a bull moose with terminal phlegm because his chubby, lovely wife has fled to Indiana and may never return,' Dick said, 'but I can't tell if he's happy or sad. And when I meet Hildy in the halls of Academe, she giggles like some monstrous child bride. I hope to hell it was worth it, Milo.'

'It was,' I said. 'It surely was.'

It had been one of those moments. Hildy and I had been talking politely about nothing. She looked at me, I leaned over and kissed her, and we fled into the wardrobe beside us. Wonderful. I didn't care. I had made a small career out of breaking up Dick and Marsha's parties, either by getting too drunk or fondling some faculty wife in the kitchen. Hildy had tenure, so she didn't care. We left the party hand in hand like young lovers, vowing loudly to do it again. Which we did, whenever and wherever we found the energy and room. It was a brief but athletic affair, fun while it lasted, but Hildy had an aversion to beds. Beds were for sleeping, she said, not balling. Which I found tiresome. Then she wanted to make the affair a crowd scene, so I moved aside, bowed out. But it had been fun.

'I wonder if all German ladies are like that?' I asked Dick. 'Have you ever been to Germany?'

'Are you kidding, man? Jesus.'

'Maybe I should go to Germany for these golden years while I await my fortune.'

'You'll be too old to ball by the time you're rich,' he said, grinning. 'Maybe that's what your sainted mother intended when she persuaded your old man to tie up the trust.'

'I think she had something else in mind,' I said.

'What?'

'To keep me from being a drunk like my old man. A heart as big as all outdoors and a liver as big as a salmon,' I said, raising my whiskey.

'Didn't work, did it,' Dick said, then casually added, 'Did Helen Duffy talk to you yet?'

I set the shot glass down without spilling a drop. 'Who?'

'Helen Duffy. She's, ah, an old friend of mine. From graduate school.' So I wouldn't mistake his meaning, he said, 'We were, ah, pretty close.' Sometimes Dick and I competed for women too, and part of his mock anger about Hildy was real because I had and he hadn't. But that didn't make up for Helen Duffy.

'She's lost her little brother, or something, and I told her you might be able to help,' he said. 'Told her you're great at finding lost people. Thought maybe you could use the business too.'

'Thanks,' I said, more shortly than I meant to.

'I didn't think he'd gotten too lost, maybe just a little misplaced, and you have enough contacts among freaks to handle that – don't you?'

'Sure.'

'No, man, seriously,' he said, then glanced at Simon, who seemed so busy with his bourbon and political complaint that he wouldn't have noticed an earthquake.

'Listen, man, we were really close for a long time. She's something special.'

'Wonderful.'

'No, really, man, I nearly left Marsha for her –'

'It's a good line, Richard, but don't waste it on me. Hell, man, I'm easy,' I said.

'What the hell's wrong with you, man?'

'Nothing, man.'

'Come on. So I fuck around, so what? Everybody fucks around. But this was different. It might have worked out. But Marsha caught us. She drove over to Helen's apartment one afternoon after somebody called her and told her what was going on, that there wasn't a Victorian seminar on Tuesday and Thursday afternoons. Marsha was six months pregnant, man, but she hammered the shit out of me. A terrible scene. Helen felt so bad about it that she left school right after that. Never even finished her degree.'

'How tragic,' I said.

'You saw her, huh? She does that to men, particularly the old and corrupt, the young and lonesome. How did you two get along?'

'Just great.'

'That bad, huh,' he said cheerfully. 'You couldn't help her, huh?'

'We couldn't agree on a fee.'

'That's strange. She's loaded, man. Her father sued the New York City Police Department a few years ago – false arrest and brutality, something like that – got over a hundred thousand in the settlement.'

'We weren't exactly bickering over money,' I said.

'You bastard. You propositioned her the first time you met her, didn't you? You bastard.'

'Didn't you?' I asked.

'Goddammit, Milo, sometimes you piss me off. You've got the moral fiber of a – a baboon.'

'Didn't you?' I repeated.

'All right, so what if I did?'

'Then get off my ass about "moral fiber." You know as much about morality as you do about baboons. So get off my case, man.'

'Okay,' he said, 'you're right. For a change. I'm sorry, but just talking to her on the phone brought it all back, man. She showed up at a bad time. Marsha is really pissed; I'm really sleeping in the study. No joke.'

'You know where she's staying?'

'She didn't say; I didn't ask.'

'Afraid?' I asked.

'You're damned right. That woman does things to me, man.'

'I know,' I muttered, remembering her face all over again, remembering the awkward walk and the torn hands. 'Say, man, if you hear from her, tell her . . . tell her I'm sorry. Tell her I was drunk or something, distraught over . . . over business failures. Tell her I'll seek her little brother all over the county, find him and put him safe and sound in her arms. And no fee. Okay?'

'Sure, man. If I hear from her.'

'You and Helen Duffy,' I said quietly, holding up the shot of pale Canadian whiskey, staring through it into the bars of afternoon sunlight that fell through Leo's front blinds. 'I can't get over it . . .'

'Say, man, I think Simon wants something,' Dick said.

Simon was rolling his eyes dramatically, flapping his tongue, and shaking his head like a palsy victim. He was so excited he couldn't talk. When I shook my head like a man who didn't want to be bothered, he nearly fell out of the booth, so I relented, got up and followed him into Leo's empty poker room. But that wasn't good enough for Simon; he wanted to go into my other office. We went into Leo's walk-in cooler, where he kept case and keg beer and enough smoked trout and whitefish to feed most of the drunks in the county, then I unlocked the door to my other office.

Unlike my regular office, a man could live in my other office. There was a double bed, a small table and chairs, a hot plate and sink, a fridge and shower, and a tiny Japanese color television, which was hot as a fresh muffin. All the comforts of home and as secure as a prison cell. It was my interest on Leo's note, my hiding place, except that everybody in town knew it was there. Drunks can't keep secrets. But Simon liked it; the room suited his sense of the melodramatic and made him feel as if we were as important as a detective and his trusty sidekick in a movie. He wouldn't tell me anything he thought really important anyplace else. And as part of the cinematic ritual, he always made me pay him for the information.

He wanted to talk now so badly that he had to hop from foot to foot just to stay quiet, but still he rubbed his fingers rapidly together, his sign for money.

'Come on, Simon, I've been buying shit information from you for years and I'm in no mood for games today.'

'You wouldn't be nothing without me, boy, nothing. And this is something you really want to know, so come up with some scratch,' he said adamantly. 'Or find out for yourself.'

Since I didn't have any money in my pocket, I had to go back into the bar and borrow two dollars from Dick, who gave me a very odd look, then I carried the two bills back to Simon, who held them up as if they were scraps of used toilet paper.

'Goddamn, Milo, this is hot stuff and you come up with two lousy bucks. What sort of friend are you anyway?'

'A two-dollar friend, Simon. What the hell do you want?'

'Ah, what the hell. You really liked that lady, didn't you?'

'So?'

'Well, I know who her little brother is. You do too.'

'Who?' I asked.

'He's that kid who used to hang around with Willy Jones.'

'Who the hell is Willy Jones?'

'Ah, for Christ's sake, Milo. Willy Jones was that old fart who claimed to be Henry Plumber's son, the old man who burned up with the Great Northern. Remember?'

'Vaguely,' I lied.

'And this Duffy kid, he also hangs around with that large and ferocious faggot, Lawrence what's-his-name, the one that affects leather pants and purple eyeshadow.'

'Reese, Lawrence Reese. Shit, you mean the Duffy kid hangs around with that bastard? Jesus.'

'Absolutely,' Simon said. 'Absolutely.'

'I'll be damned.'

Nothing Helen Duffy had said prepared me for this. Reese was a bad dude, giant glitter queen of the Northwest. He dealt drugs and seduced young boys. Or maybe raped them. He was large enough, as big as a professional defensive end and probably even meaner. When he found the heat oppressive, Reese also taught one of those esoteric, violent but dutifully spiritual Eastern combat arts. And he was hell on bare feet. Once, in a north-side bar, I'd seen him destroy three sawyers who made fun of his eyeshadow. Reese chopped tables and bit the necks off beer bottles between rounds as he waited for the sawyers to get up. When it was over, the sawyers went to the hospital, and when they got out of the hospital, they left town. And Raymond Duffy must have been his buddy, a tall, skinny kid in cowboy clothes leaning against the bar, watching the fight with what looked like a mad sexual excitement. He had a heavy black beard that grew high on his cheeks like a mask, and the eyes above the beard were as hard and opaque as marbles. If that was Raymond Duffy, Helen had a sick little brother. Really sick.

'This Duffy kid, Simon, tall, dressed in cowboy clothes, a black beard –'

'That's the one,' he said.

'He hangs around with nice people.'

'He's a creep, Milo.'

'But he shouldn't be hard to find.'

'Just hope you don't find Lawrence what's-his-name at the same time,' Simon said, shaking his head. He was so afraid of Reese that he wouldn't even stay in the same bar with him. Truth was, neither would I.

'But if you're really looking for the kid, I'd bet money that Muffin knows where Lawrence lives,' Simon said.

'Why?'

'They've had dealings in the past,' he muttered mysteriously.

'Well, I'll ask him,' I said. 'That should be a paternal right, right?'

'Hell, Milo, Muffin don't give anybody any rights.'

'I've noticed. Listen, thanks, Simon,' I told him as we walked out, but he didn't answer. He seemed worried about something. 'What's the matter, old man?'

'That kid, that Duffy kid. Milo, how could a lady like that have a brother like that . . .'

'I know what you mean,' I said, patting him on the shoulder as we stepped out of the cooler.

'Save your goddamned sympathy, Milo,' he said roughly, waving the two one-dollar bills. 'Two lousy bucks, Milo, two lousy bucks . . . Lemme alone. Needa taste.' He pushed past me and hurried toward the booth for his drink, but somebody had drunk it while we were gone. Fat Freddy was grinning broadly when Simon looked at him, and Simon shouted at him, accusing him of all sorts of incoherent crimes. He made such a fuss that Leo came around the bar and ran both of them out of the bar.

'Dick said he had to go,' Leo said when he came back, still puffing with outrage. 'Goddamned drunks,' he sighed. 'Dick said he'd call if he found out where the lady was staying.'

'Thanks,' I said as I walked away from the booth.

'Hey, Milo, you didn't finish your drink,' Leo said.

'Yeah, well, give it to old Pierre.'

'Sure. Say, did you hear about the colonel?' he asked. The colonel was a retired mustang who lived upstairs in the Dottle Hotel, which catered to those members of the wino brigade who received monthly checks from the government.

'Nope.'

'Some crazy kid jumped him last night. Right in the hallway. Nearly killed him for six lousy bucks. He's in a critical condition. The kid threw him down the stairs. Broke some ribs. One punctured his lung. He ain't got a chance in hell. Six bucks. Christ.'

'They catch the kid?'

'Naw. All them long-haired kids look alike. Dynamite had a look at him but he couldn't catch him,' Leo said, looking like the sad father of too many wild children. 'Freddy said it was probably a junkie, but what the hell does he know.'

'Well,' I said, 'if he's seen one street junkie, he knows more than any of us.' There had always been lots of dope in Meriwether. It came in from the West Coast in large and frequent lots. But there had never been much heroin in town. The only addicts I knew were either doctors or nurses or rich old women. 'Maybe the kid was just freaking on speed or acid.'

'Maybe,' Leo said.

'Sorry about the colonel.'

'Yeah. Say, Milo, who's the lady?'

'What lady?'

'The one Dick said he'd call about.'

'Just a client,' I said.

'Sure, Milo, sure.'

'Cynic,' I said as I headed for the street.

'Fool,' he muttered behind me.

As I went out, thinking to drop by Muffin's, I found myself hoping that Helen Duffy would forgive me if I found her little brother, but I knew better than to think that she would fall into my arms in appreciation. Not many women like to feel beholden to a man. But at least it was a way to get to talk to her again, and I was sober and had nothing else to do, so I got my old Toyota four-wheel rig out of the bank parking lot and went looking for my adopted son, Muffin, who was the local electronic fence. As I drove across town, I tried to avoid being crushed by the summer horde of lumbering campers plying the hot streets like large, tired animals searching for a place to lie down.

3

'Don't ask me, man,' Muffin said for the tenth time. 'You don't need to know where that dude lives, man, you don't need that kinda trouble.'

'Muffin, you owe me.'

'What the hell I owe you, man? I don't owe you shit,' he muttered, stepping behind one of the four stereo color television consoles that divided his large one-room apartment. As he stood there glaring at me, his small black face nearly lost beneath the spread of his huge Afro, he looked like a gnome hiding under a giant black mushroom. He had a bottle of Ripple in one hand and a joint in the other and he took alternate hits of each, still trying to come down from two years of amphetamine frenzy, which had left his veins and nerves humming like wires in the wind. 'Don't owe you nothing, man,' he said.

'Four years' room and board, nearly three thousand in hospital bills, a shitload of grief –'

'Didn't ask for nonna that shit, man.'

'You took it, Muffin.'

'What the fuck, man. Just money. Shit, I got plenty a

money. Pay you cash right now, man. Just tell me how much.'

'How much you reckon Tern's worth?' I asked. She was my second wife, who moved out when Muffin moved in. The marriage hadn't been made in heaven – she was a lady bartender, and I was her best customer – but it gave both of us somebody to drink and fight with. Three weeks and a day after the divorce decree was final, she and an airman from Nellis were killed in an automobile accident outside Tonopah, Nevada, leaving me the support payments for two children of hers from a previous marriage. 'Come on, Muffin. How much you gonna pay for Terri?'

'That's low, man, mean.'

'You're the man with the money.'

'Yeah. What the hell you want with that Lawrence dude. Man, he's bad. And I don't mean good.'

'Business,' I said.

'You ain't got no business no more, Milo, and the only business that Lawrence got is dealing dope and handing dudes' asses to them. Which you looking for, man?' he asked, then skittered away through the maze of stereo gear.

'You owe me.'

'Fuck off, man.'

'Please,' I said.

'Damn, you must be getting old, Milo. Never heard you say no "please" before,' he said, then began to laugh and flap his arms. He stopped long enough to switch on one of his sound systems, the music blasting so loud that the walls of his apartment began to shake. Muffin hit the bottle, then the joint, dancing to ignore me.

It was more habit than anger that sent me after him, the habit of making people talk to me because they were somehow guilty, and I was somehow the law. I walked around the consoles, slapped the joint and the wine bottle out of his hands, grabbed his loose sweatshirt, and slammed him against the shelf of receivers and tape players and record changers until the music stopped.

'You owe me,' I said, then dropped him to the floor. Before he got kicked off the team for coming to practice stoned and started shooting speed, Muffin had been a first-string defensive halfback for the MSC Vandals, but now he neither weighed any more nor felt any stronger than he had when I'd jerked him out of a wrecked, stolen Corvette when he was fourteen. He hadn't touched the speed in nearly four years, but his body had never recovered. I felt as if I'd been roughing up a mummy, and the dust of decay tickled my throat.

'Go ahead, Milo,' Muffin said from the floor, 'you the man. You just ain't the bad man. You might hurt me but you ain't gonna kill nobody. That faggot'll kill me, man, if he finds out I had my mouth on him. So go ahead.'

For a moment my head filled with familial rage, and I started to kick him. But I stopped myself. I told him I was sorry.

'What's the matter with you, man?' he asked, standing up. 'You gone crazy? What the hell's wrong?'

'Nothing. I'm sorry. I'll see you around,' I said, starting for the door.

'You ain't gonna see my ass, man, you just stay off my case for good, you hear, off it.'

'Okay,' I said. 'I'm still sorry.'

'That's for sure, Milo. You one sorry mother,' he said to my back, then added, 'And one sorry father too.'

When I looked back from the door, he was grinning.

'See you around,' I said again, grinning too.

'Right,' he said. 'But don't be looking for my ass over on the north side, not on Lincoln Street, man, not two houses west of that abandoned church house.'

'Okay. I won't look there,' I said. 'Take care.'

'You take care, Milo. You the man with the trouble.'

'What's new,' I said, and he laughed.

Most of Meriwether's freaks, dopers, hippies and assorted young folk lived on the north side of town in an old blue-collar neighborhood, which the earlier residents had deserted in favor of tacky developments on the south side of town, but the neighborhood was still pleasant in a small-town way – inexpensive but fairly well-built houses that aged nicely, like a handsome woman, the yards shaded by old trees and overgrown with evergreen shrubbery and flowering bushes. Except for the psychedelic glare of an occasional headshop and the studied humility of several natural-food stores and the long hair and bright clothing, it could have been a working-class neighborhood of twenty or thirty years before. And in its own way, it was still working-class, since most of the freaks had manual-labor or service jobs, living quietly except for the occasional too-loud party or family fight, living peacefully with the few original residents who had stayed to grow old with the neighborhood.

In the past few years, as more houses with possibilities of elegant restoration came on the market, young professionals moved into the neighborhood, which made the police careful about hassling long-hairs, so they patrolled it just like any other neighborhood, and unless they saw somebody balling on the front porch or smoking a joint in the street, they left the young people alone to live whatever life they chose, as long as they lived it inside their houses.

After two years and three months as an infantryman in the Korean War and ten years as a deputy sheriff, I knew how to be scared. It took a long afternoon and about five whiskeys for me to find the nerve to go over to the north side to ask questions about the whereabouts of one Raymond Duffy. I didn't have any foolish ideas that I could make Lawrence Reese talk to me if he didn't want to, which he probably wouldn't, but along with the drinks, I took large doses of the memory of the lady. The way her trim hips moved beneath the knit dress, the sound of her hose as she crossed her legs, the eyes so easily hurt. Then I drove over to the north side, just as afternoon eased into dusk.

The house that Muffin said Reese lived in was slightly more dilapidated than most of the others around it, and some former tenant had added a large porch, which looked like a heavy afterthought about to collapse in the light of reason. On that porch, Simon was standing, gesticulating madly at a slim young girl wearing cut-offs and a gray T-shirt that claimed to be the property of the athletic department of the University of Connecticut. I didn't know they had either a university or an athletic department, but then my only vision of the East had come from the phony gentility of my mother.

I parked my rig in front of the house, locked it, and set the alarm. I always carried about a thousand dollars' worth of crap clattering around in the back. Two rifles and a shotgun and a .38 revolver, a tape deck and a toolbox, fishing rods and gear, a pint of brandy and a partial lid of Mexican grass, and assorted junk. As ready as I'd ever be, I turned around and walked up the buckled sidewalk.

'What the hell are you doing here?' I asked Simon as I stepped onto the rickety porch and leaned against one of the fake frame pillars.

'I live here, motherfucker. What the hell are you doing here?' the young girl asked angrily, switching her hollow eyes across me like a curse.

'Not you, honey,' I replied. 'Him.' And jerked my thumb at Simon, who was locked in a paroxysm of flying arms and spittle.

Her anger passed as quickly as it had come, and she was stoned again, sinking gracefully to her rump on the wooden floor, where she sat, smiling happily and chipping the tired brown paint with her fingernails.

'Him?' she asked in a small, concerned voice. 'I don't know what he's doing here. He don't make much sense. I think he thinks he lives here, but I've been crashed here for weeks, and I don't think he lives here.' Then she giggled. 'But I don't know why not. Every other crazy mother in this creepy town thinks he lives here, so maybe he does. Who knows? You gotta cigarette?'

As I searched Simon for my pack, I whispered, 'What

the hell are you doing here?' But he was trapped between roles, struggling like a man caught halfway into his pants and trying to explain to an angry husband why he was halfway out of them. He finally gave up, shrugged vaguely as he muttered to himself.

'Go away,' I said to Simon as I lit the girl's cigarette.

He didn't move, but she answered me again, pleasantly this time. 'Sorry, man, but I live here.'

'Not you, goddammit. Him.'

'Oh, him. He doesn't live here,' she reminded me, hitting the cigarette so hard that she flashed deeper into her stone.

'Does Raymond Duffy live here?' I asked quickly, hoping to catch her before she faded out of my reality.

'Who?' she asked, moving away.

'Raymond Duffy. A tall skinny kid. Black hair, big beard. Dresses like a gunslinger.'

'Oh, him. You mean El Creepo,' she answered, giggling again.

'Is he here?'

'Who?'

'Raymond Duffy.'

'Oh, him. Haven't seen El Creepo in a *long time*.' *Long time* sounded like forever.

'How long?'

'Who knows? Just a long time.'

'A week? Two weeks? A month?' I asked, leaning over her, pressing.

'Yeah.'

'Shit,' I said, standing back up. Simon looked like a man doing his income tax on his fingers. 'That long, huh?'

'Yeah,' she said, smiling up at me prettily. She had a narrow, ordinary face, but when she smiled she was pretty. 'Want to go inside? We're doing some bad hash, man.'

'No thanks,' I said, smiling back with a dry mouth. 'How do you know I'm not the man?' I asked, nearly giggling.

'I'm fucked up, man, but I ain't crazy,' she said by way of explanation, then touched me on the calf with her small hand as our smiles turned into grins. 'The man don't get contact highs,' she said, and we giggled.

'Is Lawrence Reese here?'

'Lawrence?'

'You know Lawrence?' I asked.

'Man, everybody knows Lawrence. It's his hash. Do you know Lawrence?'

'I'm afraid I haven't had the pleasure,' I said, grinning with her.

'It ain't always a pleasure,' a voice said through the screen door. Then Lawrence followed it outside, strolling across the porch, his bare, heavily callused feet gliding across the warped floorboards, his large body all muscle and fluid motion and threat.

'What's happening?' he asked the girl, ignoring whatever wisecrack I might have made.

But he was large enough to ignore anybody, broader and taller than I remembered, harder and older, nearer forty than thirty. His face seemed to hang off his skull in a hard, grainy mask, as if it were all scar tissue. The lavender eyeshadow didn't make his eyes look a bit feminine or soft. They just looked bruised and wary.

Shoulders ax-handle-broad and arms like logs jutted out of his black leather vest, and in the tight leather pants his legs rippled and flexed as he raised his right foot, the toes pointed like a dancer's, to touch the girl's bare arm. His foot stroked her arm very lightly.

'What's happening, Mindy?' he asked again.

'Jesus,' she said, 'I don't know.' She stood up, wandered back to the front door, her slim hand drifting, intimately casual, across Lawrence's groin and hip.

As she slipped through the door I caught a glimpse of the Arabian nightmare within the room. Oriental rugs covered with plush pillows and slight bodies hid the floor, carelessly circled around a brass water pipe. The bodies were caught in the tender mold of pan-sexual adolescence, the faces blank, waiting to be formed out of youth, but the eyes were as dark and empty as burial caves etched into chalk bluffs. A ringlet of smoke curled slowly above the pipe, and the sharp, bittersweet stink of blond Lebanese hash hovered in the cool, heavy air.

'Having a party?' I asked, trying to be pleasant.

'Do I know you?' he asked in a slow, hard voice that went more with the ball-point pen and needle tattoo, which had faded into a blue smudge on his right forearm, than with the eyeshadow and the tailor-made leather clothes.

'Milton Milodragovitch,' I answered, holding my hand carefully toward him. 'I'm a private investigator and –'

'I know damn well I don't know you,' he said softly, disregarding my hand introduction. He spun slowly on the ball of his left foot toward Simon, who hadn't moved since Lawrence came outside. Lawrence lifted and cocked and extended his right leg so quickly that I only saw a black blur. The foot stopped so close to Simon's nose, quivering like an arrow shaft driven deeply into a tree, that Simon must have been able to smell it. Simon didn't have time to move, but his viscera flinched, and a loud fart escaped him, and the stench quickly filled the porch.

'Jesus Christ, that's disgusting,' Lawrence said, putting his foot down. 'Get outa here.' Simon went.

'Are you still here?' Lawrence asked.

'My name is Milton Milodragovitch,' I said, 'and I'm a –' But I couldn't finish because I was stumbling down the porch steps. Lawrence's right hand had snaked out and shoved me lightly off the porch.

Though I carry fifteen or twenty pounds of whiskey flab, I don't look like the sort of guy most men would casually shove off their front porch, but Lawrence didn't seem too worried about it. As I got up off my butt, he sat down on the steps and began rolling a huge joint.

'Get your dander up, cunt?' he asked pleasantly, then licked the number and stuffed the makings back in his vest pocket.

'I think so,' I said, rubbing my hands together.

He lit the joint and took a hit off it large enough to paralyze an elephant. 'Flake off,' he said, holding the hit.

'Listen,' I said, 'I'm a private investigator and I'm looking –'

But he laughed so loudly that the smoke came roiling out of his lungs. 'Don't do that, man. Made me lose the hit. Just get the fuck outa here, okay?'

We stared at each other for a few seconds, then I looked around the yard for a big stick, relieved that I couldn't find one among the tangled high grass and blooming weeds. Lawrence smiled; I tried. In the house to the right, an old woman with gleaming white hair and a faded black lace dress stood at her side window, waving coyly at me. The dress belonged to another time, as did the neatly marcelled hair. Her cheeks bloomed hopefully with rouge, her mouth smiled beneath a contusion of dark red lipstick.

'Listen,' I repeated as I walked toward him. He stopped smiling.

'You want more, man. I got more than you can handle.'

'I've had plenty, thanks. You can throw me off your porch all night long, but it's no big deal. I just want to ask you a few questions about a friend of yours,' I said, still walking.

He kicked the inside of my right thigh, and when I turned sideways the foot hit me again, on the left shoulder, and I hit the sidewalk. I kept most of my face off the sidewalk by getting my hands in front of me, but the heels of my palms didn't feel too good about it.

'Hit the road, cunt.'

When I stood up, my left arm felt like it had been hit with a billy club, and there was blood and gravel in my hands.

'I never hit anybody wearing purple eyeshadow,' I said, picking at some of the smaller stones embedded in my flesh.

'Don't start now, friend,' he said, holding the joint in front of his mouth. 'Not now.'

We smiled at each other again, but I quit when my face started hurting.

'You're probably right,' I said.

'You know I'm right, cunt.'

'Don't go away,' I said. 'I'll be back.' But it was a weak and empty threat.

'I live here,' he answered as I walked away.

I wasn't mad, and the whole thing suddenly seemed a foolish waste of time better spent in a mellow bar hustling cocktail waitresses, so I was willing to leave it that way. But I forgot to switch off the alarm before I fumbled the key into the door lock, and the fancy air horns started blaring and the lights blinking wildly in the crepuscular air. And Lawrence laughed too loudly behind me. Enough is enough. So I unlocked the door and reached into the back and unracked the twelve-gauge automatic, wishing it loaded with goose-loads but knowing they were just skeet-loads. It wouldn't matter, though, even loaded with rock salt, the three-inch magnum loads would blow down a house.

'All right,' I shouted over the horns as I walked back up the sidewalk, 'you cocksucker, we're going to talk now!'

He didn't even stand up, but I sensed rather than saw movement away from the living-room windows, small animals slipping off into the dusk. In an upstairs window, a faceless voice said 'Jesus' between the bleats of the horns.

'I don't think so,' Lawrence said. 'I don't talk to people who call me dirty names.'

'Either we talk, asshole, or you're going to be damned

unhappy,' I said, keeping the shotgun barrel pointed at the ground.

'I'm already unhappy, cunt,' he said, flipping the joint away, the bright spark glittering as it arched toward the grass.

'Wonderful,' I said. 'I'm looking for a kid you used to hang around with –'

'I don't hang around with anybody.'

'– named Raymond Duffy.'

'Never heard of him.'

'Talk to me, you son of a bitch!' I shouted, raising the barrel at his face.

He looked at it, then at me. 'You're not going to kill anybody, cunt,' he said, then stood up and headed toward the door, his back toward me.

I'd never known that the ability to kill people was such a necessary asset in my business, but I didn't like being accused of it twice in one day, so I pulled the trigger. The left porch pillar exploded into a cloud of splinters and dust. A window crashed behind it. Lawrence flinched but he didn't run. He glanced up as the porch roof sagged toward him, creaking loudly.

'Missed,' he said, facing me. 'I'll send you the bill.'

So I blew up the other pillar, which turned into dust and splinters even more nicely than the first one. That made him mad. He started for me, and either I would have blown his leg off or he would have torn my head off, but the decision was taken out of our hands.

As the second pillar buckled, the porch roof creaked again, mightily, old nails squealing like lost souls and joists cracking like dry bones, as the porch roof swung down like a trap door, ripping off most of the front of the house and slamming shut on him. It knocked him right through the screen door. Suddenly, alert faces appeared in the void upstairs, then vanished. Two bare butts vacated the downstairs bedroom, bobbing and bounding away toward the back of the house. A disembodied voice tolled through the debris: 'Far fucking out.'

'Amen,' I said, grinning so hard that my cheeks cramped. The day hadn't been completely wasted.

4

By the time Reese recovered from the blow his porch roof had given him and began wading through the wreckage, the police had arrived, and, considering the reception he had given me, he was amazingly polite to them, which made me certain that he was an ex-con. I had thrown the shotgun on the grass as soon as I saw the flashing lights, raised my hands and tried to stop grinning. One patrolman cuffed me while the other put the shotgun in their unit and called Lieutenant Jamison, who I knew would be glad to hear that I was under arrest. Because the patrolman knew who I was, he cuffed my hands in front, but he still locked me in the back seat of the unit. Then he kept the crowd of spectators moving down the sidewalk, and his partner questioned Reese, who was busy dusting his clothes and combing splinters out of his long blond hair. Once he glanced over at me, shook his head and seemed to grin. The patrolman moving the crowd paused long enough to open the hood of my rig and rip off the horn wires. In his absence, the people bunched like cattle in a storm until he came back and prodded them along.

Even though Meriwether is a city of nearly fifty thousand, it often seems like a small town. Almost every face that passed was familiar, and I could put names to most of those. There were a few long-haired kids I had never seen before and one retired brakeman whom I had known by sight for years but whose name I'd never learned. Most of the crowd knew my face, too, and some my name, but only the strangers were crass enough to stare at me, cuffed like a killer, in the back seat of the police car. One came back several times, glancing covertly into the car as if to make sure that it was really me. His face was mostly hidden behind a thick black beard and dark glasses, but in spite of the shoulder-length black hair he was obviously middle-aged and too well dressed to be a working-class hippie. He smiled once, I thought, and seemed vaguely familiar, perhaps a professor from the college I'd met at Dick's, drunk, or an undercover policeman working narcotics. But before I could hang a name to the oddly familiar face, Jamison pulled in behind the patrol unit.

Jamison and I, as they say, go way back. We had been raised in Meriwether – same age, same grade in school, all that – and even when we were children, I had been his project: he intended to make me a better person, no matter what. And for years I'd paid him back with small nips and little jokes at the expense of his implacable seriousness, his elevated sense of morality. Small but mean things. Wintergreen in his jock the night he was supposed to lead the homecoming queen onto the football field before the game. His socks wrapped in condoms and soap in his rifle barrel on our first inspection in basic training at Fort Lewis. He owed me lots of small pain, and one big one. He had married my ex-wife, and she made more money off my settlement and child support than he brought home at the end of the month.

But instead of being amused at my predicament, he seemed damned serious as he tugged me out of the back seat and trundled me back up the sidewalk. Lawrence was slapping shoulders and explaining that he didn't want to press charges because it had been as much his fault as mine.

'I'll decide that,' Jamison said grimly. 'What happened here?'

One of the patrolmen started to tell him, but Jamison hushed him and repeated his question to Reese.

'A private beef,' Reese said.

'How would you like to take an obstruction fall, Mr. Reese? Or maybe have me walk into your house to search for injured occupants?' Jamison asked.

'Okay,' he answered. 'It's no skin off my ass.'

'Thanks, Lawrence honey,' I said. 'I thought we were buddies.'

'Shut up, Milo,' Jamison said, and I did. 'What happened?'

'This dude,' Reese said, pointing a thumb as big as a shotgun barrel at me, 'came around looking for somebody –'

'Who?' Jamison asked, taking out his notebook.

'He didn't say.'

'Who?' Directed at me.

'A kid named Raymond Duffy,' I said.

'Runaway?'

'Nope. His family just hasn't heard from him in a while,' I answered.

'How long?'

'Three weeks.'

'Then what's the fuss about?' he asked. I shrugged, then he asked Reese if he knew the Duffy kid.

'I knew him. He used to hang around the house. Crashed here for a while –'

'How long?' Jamison asked.

'Who keeps track?' Reese answered.

'How long?'

'I don't know. Five, maybe six months.'

'And where did he crash-land after he flew away from here, Mr. Reese?'

'The Great Northern Hotel. He was shacked up with an old faggot, Willy Jones.'

'What's the matter, Reese? The kid leave you for a better piece?'

'No, sir. I asked him to split,' Reese said softly.

'What's the matter? Too butch for you?' Unlike me, Jamison didn't seem frightened of Lawrence Reese.

'No, sir. I got tired of him. I get tired of people, you know. Some people quicker than others.' Reese didn't like being pushed around, either.

'I hope you don't mean me, Mr. Reese. I hope you aren't getting tired of me.'

'Lieutenant, sir, I been tired of the man all my life but I ain't ever been able to do anything about it,' Reese said, almost sadly.

'Just don't forget that I'm the man, Mr. Reese. Don't forget that.'

'I'm sure I won't.'

'Good. What happened after you wouldn't talk to this creep here?'

'I asked him to leave, he wouldn't leave, so I helped him. He came back, so I helped him harder. I guess I pissed him off,' Reese said, smiling. 'He got a shotgun and offed my front porch.'

'Did he threaten you with the shotgun at any time?' Jamison wanted to know.

Reese glanced at me then smirked. 'No, sir,' he said. 'If he'd threatened me, I'd have gotten pissed off.'

'And what would you have done, Mr. Reese, if pissed off?' Jamison asked sweetly.

'Stuck it up his ass and pulled the trigger,' Reese said flatly.

'Too bad you didn't. Two creeps with one shot,' Jamison said as if he meant it. 'Uncuff him,' he added, and the patrolman did. 'Behind.'

'Thanks,' I said to the patrolman as he tugged my arms behind my back and snapped the cuffs. 'I was thinking of escaping and I'm glad you took the idea out of my head.'

'Shut up,' Jamison said. 'Mr. Reese, if you don't mind, I'd like you to come down to the station in the morning. Let's say nine o'clock. We'll find somebody to take your statement.'

'You're the man,' Reese said.

'Let's go,' he said to me, jerking on my arm so the cuffs could grind merrily against my wrists.

'Where?' I asked, smiling.

'Duck Valley,' he said. 'Two to five maybe, you dumb son of a bitch.'

'I've been needing a vacation,' I said.

'Ah, Lieutenant,' one of the patrolmen said behind us. 'Ah, we didn't read him his rights.'

'That's all right,' Jamison said. He read them to me on the way to the car. I didn't have any.

Jamison had forgiven me for years, had even gone to the trouble to make up excuses for all the things about me that he couldn't understand. Like not having school spirit and not playing for the team. He forgave me because I thought both silly. And in Korea, when he discovered that I didn't think night patrols or frontal assaults on Communist-held ridges were life or death matters, he thought I was joking, and he kept volunteering the two of us. While I was tending to important matters, like staying alive and keeping warm and hustling booze, he tried to kill us. No matter how much I goofed off, he kept believing in me. The only time I'd ever known him to lie or even slightly bend a rule, he covered for me one night when I was too drunk to go on patrol, reported me present when I was three miles behind our lines, passed out in the back of a wrecked ambulance.

In college after the war, I got away from him because we lived in different worlds. He was at the heart of things, an honor student working his way through school, student body president and all that. I was usually in a fraternity house, drinking beer and watching television, or drinking beer and reading, or drinking beer and playing poker. And I thought he had given up on me, but the day I joined the sheriff's department, Jamison showed up at my house with all sorts of great affectionate ambition. Together, arm in arm, city and county, we would make Meriwether a decent place to live. I told him that I'd become a deputy because the sheriff was an old crony of my father's and I sort of liked the idea of tooling around the county in a three-quarter-ton, four-wheel-drive pickup and carrying a gun.

'Listen, Milo,' he had said, 'being a law enforcement officer will get into your blood, just like it has mine. You'll love it.'

'You see too many movies,' I said.

'Hell, I've been so busy that I haven't seen more than two or three movies since I joined the force,' he answered, his pride slightly damaged.

'That's too many,' I said, but he laughed and slapped me on the shoulder.

I don't know which was harder for Jamison: finding out that Meriwether didn't care to be a decent place to live, or discovering that I was on the take, like every other deputy in the county, from the local boys who controlled the electronic slots, the pinball machines and punchboards, and the sports pools. Whichever, he never forgave me. And he nearly worked himself to death trying to clean up Meriwether.

Sometimes I felt sorry for him. He had boy scout ideals in an adult world, and after it became clear to him that there were certain laws that were never going to be enforced, he began to look slightly dazed – like a Thermopylae freak without a pass – then old and tired. He had become, like most policemen, adept at selective enforcement of the law, but not corrupt. He couldn't be bought for love or money. I didn't have either anyway.

'How's Evelyn?' I asked from the back seat as we drove downtown. 'And the kids?' One mine, two his.

'What the hell do you care?' he answered without turning around.

'It costs me a lot of money every month to run your household. The least you can do is give me an occasional report,' I said, knowing he was willing to live like a pauper to stay out of my money – but Evelyn wasn't.

'You're a real bastard, you know that.'

'At least I don't gloat about my old friends doing time,' I said. Maybe he'd feel sorry for me.

'You'll be back on the street in an hour,' he said, then laughed. 'But it will do my heart good just to see you behind bars for a little while.'

'Glad I could help.'

'Who's this Duffy?'

'College dropout,' I said.

'Look, Milo, I'm tired and I'm busy and I got no time for your bullshit.'

'That's straight. The kid was a graduate student out at the college, and he dropped out of sight.'

'For how long?' Jamison asked.

'I told you once: three weeks.'

'Right. Got other things on my mind, Milo. What the hell's he doing hanging around with scum like Reese?'

'Love at first sight, I guess,' I said. 'Criminals and ex-cops are a heavy trip this year.'

'Did it ever occur to you not to be a smart-ass?'

'I don't think so,' I said.

'The kid ever been in trouble?'

'As far as the family knows, he's an angel.'

'I'll bet he is,' Jamison said. 'I'll just bet he is.'

At the station I was booked and relieved of my personal effects and allowed my telephone call. Everything polite and perfect, by the book all the way. I called Dick, but Marsha told me that Simon had already called and Dick was on his way down to bail me out. On the way to my cell, I waved at all my old buddies in the drunk tank, and those who could still see waved back gaily.

'Well, you look okay, old buddy,' Dick said as the desk sergeant gave me back my effects, 'but you ought to see Simon.'

'What's the matter?'

'He's sober.'

'Must be a frightening experience,' I said, checking the manila envelope, but the tape cassette wasn't there. 'Goddammit,' I said. 'Back in a minute.'

Jamison didn't complain when I didn't knock on his office door. He just looked up from the recorder on his desk and shook his balding head.

'Enjoy yourself?' I asked.

'If you weren't so sad, you'd be funny,' he said as he snapped out the cassette and flipped it to me. 'And you're gonna be sadder.'

'What's that supposed to mean?'

'Get out. Drop by and see your son sometime. He's a nice kid, in spite of you. That ought to make you feel better,' Jamison said, tilting his chair back and rubbing his eyes.

'He's not my kid,' I said. 'He's been around you too long – his head's too big for his halo.' Jamison was right, though. He was a nice kid, but his face was already pinched with the same sad seriousness that crumpled Jamison's. I don't know which was more painful: for me to see my innocent face on the kid, or for the kid to see his face old and corrupt on me. Whichever, we stayed away from each other. 'Hell, he's even wearing your name.'

'That's something, Milo. You ain't got nothing.'

'I got a case,' I said, and for some reason that made me feel better.

'You ain't got nothing,' he said as I went out the door. 'You poor sad fucker.'

Simon was a pitiful sight. Sober, yes, but trembling wildly, and he seemed to have aged ten years. Somewhere he had found an ill-fitting sleazy suit, an iridescent gray that shimmered like an oil slick beneath the mercury vapor lights, cheap colors rippling across the fabric as his skinny old frame quivered. His face was so pale and hollow that he might have been dressed for a burial.

'What the hell were you doing at Lawrence's house?' I asked. 'And where the hell did you get that suit?'

'Don't, don't be mad, Milo, Milo, don't – I just – asked around . . . that's all.' Without whiskey, his voice seemed as thin as his suit.

'What the hell are you doing here?'

He flinched, ducked his head and, muttering, backed away from me as if I'd slapped him.

'What?'

'Advice, Milo, legal advice. I've been . . . disbarred,

but I can – can still give legal advice,' he whispered into the gutter.

'Oh, for Christ's sake, go have a drink and stop this crap,' I said. 'You look terrible.'

'Yes,' he answered vaguely, 'yes . . .' Then he turned and drifted slowly down the street like a scrap of wrapping paper in a night wind, lurching and hitching the hip that had been broken the year before when he stumbled into the path of a pickup. I started to shout after him, but sober he was just too pitiful, so I let him go.

'What's wrong with him?' Dick asked as we got in his van.

'He just needs a drink.'

Being nasty to Simon had ruined the good feeling I had when I decided to find the Duffy kid, and the arm and the buttock that Reese had kicked were beginning to throb. Not even the sight of the ill-fated house cheered me. It had been deserted, and in the dim streetlight looked as if it had been bombed.

'Did a job on it, huh?' Dick said, but I didn't bother to answer. 'Remind me not to piss you off, old buddy.'

'I wasn't even irritated. It just happened.'

'And what happens now?'

'You find out where Helen Duffy is staying?'

'No. Why?'

'Because I'm going to find her goddamned little brother.'

'Good luck,' he murmured, not sounding too happy.

'Don't worry,' I said. 'I'm not after anything. I'm just going to find the little bastard, that's all.'

'It's none of my business,' he said lightly.

'Don't try to shit your friends, Richard.'

'Okay. Like I said, good luck. You going to stop for a taste?'

'Don't I always?' I said.

'See you at Mahoney's,' he said, then drove away as I stepped out of the van.

I started toward the rig, but the lights were still on in the old woman's house next door, and she was standing at the front door looking out. Thinking she might be the sort of Nosy Parker who might have seen the Duffy kid, I cut through the brambles and weeds and climbed up on her porch, but she wouldn't open the door. She just stood there, smiling and waving through the glass as if we were on opposite sides of the street. When I knocked on the door, a large, angry woman came to the door, looked at me, shook her head, and took the old woman away before I could explain that I wasn't selling anything.

When I got to my rig, I discovered that I had been, as the kids say, ripped off. Everything was gone but the seats. Everything.

'You forgot the fucking seats!' I shouted at the silent, dark houses, then drove back down to the police station to report the theft in the hope that I could collect the insurance. If the premiums were paid.

Publicly I bemoaned my lack of desire to hunt animals and blamed it on the Army and the Korean War, but the truth was that I'd never really liked to hunt. It seemed a great deal of hard work, both before and after the quick excitement of making a good shot. But I liked guns, so I took up skeet and target shooting and promised my friends that I'd go hunting next year for sure. Driving down to Mahoney's, the inside of my rig as empty as a church on Saturday night, I thought about hunting low-life bastards, the sort who would steal a man's guns.

When I got there, Dick had already left. I had a quick drink by the door, then shoved my way through the frenzied melee of freaks toward the back and my other office. They didn't seem like happy flower children that night; their fragrance was that of the unwashed, and they were no nicer drunks than any other type of people. I bounced off a tall girl, made her spill her beer, and she snapped at me, her long, pointed breasts rearing like the muzzles of two Afghans. I shouted at the night bartender helping Leo, told him to give the bitch a beer on me. She ran her fingers through her kinky blond hair and asked me why in the hell I had done that. I replied that I was afraid she would bite my head off, then walked away, into the quiet sanctuary of my other office, grabbing a can of beer as I passed through the door.

Inside, I switched on the television, flipped around the cable stations until I found a movie on a Salt Lake station. I sat down to watch it while I loaded clips for my Browning 9-mm automatic pistol. Harry Carey and Ben Johnson were riding Roman style, standing on two horses each, as they circled the parade field. John Wayne had a mustache and a cavalry officer's uniform. His face twitched, as if the mustache made his face itch. Victor McLaglen looked as if he had a hangover, and Maureen O'Hara like a good Irish girl who needed a drink. I remembered the title, *Rio Grande*, but couldn't remember the actor's name who played John Wayne's son by Maureen O'Hara. He was riding with Harry Carey and Ben Johnson – that is, his stunt man was riding. Also, I couldn't remember who got killed in the movie.

'The old fart looks good in a mustache,' Leo said as he came into the office.

'Did you see Gregory Peck in *The Gunfighter*?'

'Think so. Why?'

'He had a mustache. Remember?'

'Oh, yeah.'

'He looked really good. You think I ought to grow a mustache, Leo?'

He laughed for a moment, then stopped and said, 'I just came from the hospital. The colonel just died.'

'That's too bad,' I said, filling my mouth with empty words.

'The old fart survived two wars and some goddamned punk pushes him down the stairs and kills him. What the hell kinda life is that?'

'I don't know, Leo. The kind we have, I guess. I don't know.'

'The kind a fella needs a drink just to survive,' Leo said, his hand holding his little gray beard. His mouth moved silently, as if pleading for a drink. 'I don't know if I can handle that mad-house tonight. Why don't you lock me in on your way out?'

'Why don't you just go home?'

'Can't be a success staying at home, Milo.'

'You want me to stay with you?'

'Ah, hell, you wouldn't be any help, Milo,' he said,

then glanced at me. Maybe he thought he had hurt my feelings because he added quickly, 'I didn't mean that. You'd just get drunk, then I'd have to tend to you.'

'Might keep you busy.'

'I ain't up to tending drunks tonight, Milo. Not even myself.'

He left slowly, unable to face the business of his life, but going anyway. I turned off the television without looking to see what John Wayne was doing. From the old trunk beneath the bed, I took a .41 double-barreled derringer and a handful of rounds, then a shoulder holster for the automatic, and stuffed my armaments into a paper sack. I needed a quiet bar and a slow drink, a large sandwich and a telephone, more than I needed the guns, but they were important too.

Occasionally, in my line of business, I had to cause a small scene at a local motel to obtain evidence for divorces. As a result, I wasn't too popular with motel management. If a switchboard operator or night clerk recognized my voice on the telephone, they wouldn't give me the correct time, but by the time I started calling around I was so tired that nobody knew my voice. I found Helen Duffy registered at the Holiday Inn, and just after midnight had the switchboard ring her room. She answered on the first ring, sounded expectant instead of sleepy, almost cheerful, but I broke the connection, and leaving the remains of my coffee and cheeseburger, drove out to the east side of town, where the better motels lined the highway – large buildings discreetly lighted, looking like a government installation or the campus of a shoddy junior college.

When I knocked, she came quickly to the door, asking who it was. I told her. She opened the door abruptly, warm and flushed from her bath. Streaks of dark-red hair lay across her cheeks and forehead like smears of dried blood, and her eyes, reflecting the dark green of the velour robe, were wide and empty, like the eyes of an accident victim. She fell against me, throwing her arms around me as if she had been waiting for me all day, her shoulder banging heavily into my sore arm. But the groan came from somewhere deeper inside. I held her, wondering how she could cry when I was so happy.

As she cried, she scattered tissues about the room, and they seemed to surround us like a flock of little pink animals. Between her sobs, she told me that her little brother was dead. He had been found in the Willomot Hill Bar men's room, an Indian bar north of town, and the deputy had told Helen that it looked like a drug overdose. Raymond Duffy had been found with a shoelace around his biceps and the needle still hanging from the bend of his elbow. Helen had gone down to the morgue and identified the body. Her grief, seeking a safe object for displacement, had centered upon her little brother's hair and beard; she accused the morgue attendant of cutting his hair short and shaving off his thick black beard.

'I didn't believe it,' she murmured, dabbing her eyes, 'not even when I saw the body, and I didn't cry until you came. I've been taking showers, one after another. I used all the hot water in the motel . . .' She began to giggle faintly, but they quickly changed to sobs. This time she fell into a chair, out of my arms.

'But now I've accepted it,' she said, drawing a deep breath, seeming almost calm. 'However, I do not believe he – he died of a drug overdose. The young deputy seemed to think that Raymond was an addict; he didn't come right out and say it, but I could tell.'

'How did they find you?'

'Who?'

'The sheriff's department.'

'Oh – I don't know . . . they – didn't say,' she said brokenly. 'I didn't ask.'

'I'll ask,' I said, taking a pad and pen out of my pocket.

'I'm sure it isn't important,' she said, so I put the pad back.

'Did they mention the autopsy?'

'No. They can't do that . . . Can they? I mean I didn't sign anything. I can't – couldn't bear – that.'

'I'm sorry,' I said, 'but in a case like this, they don't need your permission.'

'Oh my God,' she wailed, the sobbing about to begin.

'If you don't believe he died of an overdose,' I said, reaching out to touch her shoulder, 'then an autopsy will prove it.' My fingers stayed a second on the warm, damp cloth of her robe, my thumb gently kneading her fragile collarbone.

'I'm sorry,' she said softly, moving away from my hand. 'I'm just not thinking – the shock, I guess . . . you're absolutely right.'

'Just don't think about it,' I said, which, of course, made her think about nothing else.

'How . . . He looked so frail – lying there – like a child – so young . . . innocent . . .'

'You must have been awfully close to your little brother,' I said, hoping she might remember happier times, and in the memory ease the grief.

She glanced up at me, staring for a long moment, then in a very calm voice said, 'Yes.'

'That's unusual,' I said. 'The age difference –' I stopped because she seemed angry. Her eyes, abraded by tears, flashed a hard green and fired with anger. Then, as if heavy shutters had fallen inside her, the eyes became opaque with control.

'My father,' she said, 'is a wonderful man but somewhat – distracted and not the outdoors type at all. My mother – works. Raymond and I were very close.'

'Have you called your parents?' I asked, and for the second time said exactly the wrong thing.

'Oh my God,' she whispered, her hand flying to her mouth, her eyes suddenly frightened. 'Oh my God.' Sobs jerked her body, and she jammed her fist into her open mouth as if she could hold them back with physical force.

I reached for her, but she jumped out of the chair, stumbled across the room and threw herself across the bed, moaning about kindness and suffering, youth and innocence, and dreadful grief, both hands holding her face. She cried so hard that I almost envied her the grief. Nothing had ever touched me that hard, not since my father's death years before. She wept among the disarray of hurried packing or unpacking, slips and brightly colored dresses and dark hose scattered as if by the wind across the bedspread. An empty suitcase, wide open like a hysterical mouth, leaned against the headboard. As she sobbed and rocked, like a mother thrown across the body of her child, a cosmetics case slipped off the side of the bed and emptied itself on the carpet, glass and metal clinking, a heavy gold chain slithering out of its niche like a sigh. But she heard none of it.

Beside her now, I pressed my hand into the small of her back, finding in the raw palm another bit of tiny, sharp gravel, and I rubbed her back until she finally fell asleep, whimpering and flinching in the uneasy sleep. I cleaned off the bed, folding her soft scraps of clothing, then covered her with the blanket from the other bed, my fingers caressing once more the slim reach of her waist, then, knowing that my comfort wouldn't be enough, I called Dick.

'Did I wake you?'

'Of course not, old buddy. I'm never asleep at – one in the morning. Especially when I have an eight o'clock freshman comp class. Christ, I can explain illiteracy to the little bastards in my sleep –'

'Helen Duffy's little brother is dead,' I said, stopping him.

'What?'

'Helen Duffy – her little brother is dead.'

'Jesus Christ, what happened?'

'Doesn't matter. Can you come over?'

'Jesus, Milo, I don't know.'

'She's in pretty bad shape.'

'Okay. Be there as soon as I get my pants on. Where?'

'Room 217. Holiday Inn.'

I hung up before I could overhear the beginnings of Dick's excuse to Marsha, then went back to the bed to tug the blanket higher about Helen's shoulders. I nearly pulled it over the top of her head. An old habit from the days when most of the bodies I covered with blankets were growing cold beside steaming, mangled automobiles, hunks of meat quivering in the pulse of red lights. Sometimes I thought that the accidents had finally driven me out of a deputy's uniform and into the wreckage of the divorce courts. I slipped the blanket back from her neck, felt lightly for the pulse in her warm, soft throat. She groaned slightly, turning, but the blood ticked merrily along beneath my fingertips.

Our bodies betray us constantly. In grief and confusion that should still its beat, the heart murmurs on about its business. Cells wither like ash with every beat, but never from sorrow. And desire remains. As I held a handful of her thick hair, as I leaned over and buried my face in the smell of her, clean and unscented, my body, ignoring my pleas, wanted her, a fierce unbidden desire rising. I wanted her then, wanted to lie next to her, to stroke that bare damp skin beneath the green robe, to bury myself in her.

But I moved away, picked up the room, putting things in their proper places, until Dick rapped softly at the door.

While he sat with her, I went down to the lobby and called Jamison at home. Evelyn answered but wouldn't wake him.

'He's tired, Milo, damned tired. He works too hard,' she said quietly, sounding much older than I remembered her.

'If you don't wake him, babe, I'll come over and kick the goddamned door down.'

'You bastard,' she hissed, but she went to wake him. We hadn't lived together in years, but she remembered.

'What the hell do you want?' Jamison grumbled. He didn't sound sleepy, just tired.

'You knew about the Duffy kid, didn't you?'

'Yeah,' he sighed, 'I knew. I didn't know you were gonna wake me up in the middle of the night to tell me what I already knew.'

'Why didn't you tell me?'

'It wasn't any of your business, Milo. She wasn't your client anyway.'

'I'm going to take this personally,' I said.

'Thought you might. The Duffy lady – is she taking it hard?'

'That's none of your business.'

'Ah, get the fuck outa my life, Milo,' he said, then hung up, banging the telephone.

Dick and I spent the night watching over her, drinking coffee and talking about nothing in whispers, as she started and muttered through her restless dreams. Once she sat up, her wild eyes staring through us, then she laughed in short, hard barks. Before either of us could rise, she fell back on the bed, tumbled back into her dreams. Just after sunrise, she woke, sat up again, rubbing her eyes as if she were trying to gouge them out. Then she remembered and let her hands fall into her lap. Her robe gaped open, revealing small, freckled breasts with dark, heavy nipples. I looked away. She saw Dick, and with a moan that sounded as if it had been wrenched from her chest with a steel hook, she launched herself at him, nearly knocking his chair over. She wept against his shoulder. He glanced at me over the top of her head, his arms away from her body, his palms open as if in explanation or making a plea, his face drawn and confused.

I left, walked out into the summer morning, into birdsong and air as light and pleasant as children's laughter. The sun came up, as they say, like thunder, topping the eastern ridges, raining golden fire into the valley. It was a morning for youth and rosy cheeks, but I was old and tired and needed a shave, so I went home, up to my log house on the bank of Hell-Roaring Creek, on the northern verge of Milodragovitch Park, which had been the family estate and my front yard until my father died and my mother gave the land to the city, cut the family mansion into sections, had it moved east of town to be reassembled as a country club house.

The sun wasn't high enough over the east ridge to reach the creek or the house, but the tops of my tall blue spruces shimmered like blue flames above the cool, shaded air. Inside, I drew the drapes to capture the shaded morning. My father had solved his life with whiskey and the full-choke barrel of an LC Smith hammerless double. The police had my shotgun, but I still had his. And a case of Canadian whiskey. I switched the telephone to the answering service, then laughed and jerked it out of the wall, sat down at the kitchen table to work on my own suicidal drunk.

5

Since I've never been what they call a thoughtful man, I didn't spend much time worrying about why I only had one drink that morning. One drink and an omelette, then a shower and to bed. Maybe I was just bored with being drunk. Not that I tried anything quite so drastic as quitting. I drank; I didn't get drunk. For a change. Living very peacefully, working out at the gym and playing handball every morning, fishing in the afternoons but without ambition, watching the light ripple across distant mountains without thinking of it as scenery. In court, I pleaded nolo contendere, and paid small fines for disturbing the peace and discharging a firearm within the city limits. I persuaded the judge not to suspend my license, though what I needed it for wasn't clear, but failed to convince the telephone company that vandals had destroyed their property. I paid cash for that damage but had to sign a note to the real estate agency that owned Lawrence Reese's former house. And I thought about Helen Duffy more often than I meant to.

After the inquest, which attributed Raymond Duffy's

death to a misadventure with drugs, she flew the body back to Iowa for burial. Dick went with her on the next plane. Whatever he told Marsha, she accepted it more gracefully than I did. Simon fell hard into the bottle again, going on a binge that put him back in the hospital. Muffin went to the Coast for a few days and drove a rented truck back loaded with thirty thousand dollars' worth of hot stereo gear and televisions. Fat Freddy was on his way to the hospital to harass Simon when he was mugged by two kids. They flattened him with a piece of pipe for four bucks and change. Freddy ended up in the bed next to Simon in the charity ward, and Simon recovered immediately.

Freddy's mugging was only one in a rash of petty street crime that began to plague Meriwether. Our mayor, who was running hard for Congress, attributed the crime wave to the heat wave, which had socked Meriwether in a frenzy of 100-degree heat and blinding smog. He began orating about the long, hot summer of Meriwether, finding urban problems and previously invisible ghettos primed for a riot, by which he meant the local Indians, freaks and winos. Perhaps he had visions of them attacking City Hall to demand free whiskey, cheap dope and a thirty-day party. The mayor might have been a fool, but this new street crime had made the citizens edgy. The streets emptied at night. Except for Indians, freaks and winos. The mayor made speeches about Meriwether making the transition from town to city – with a city's problems, a city's pride to solve them.

He was an ass and an idiot, but only corrupted by

ambition. And he had a point. Meriwether had problems, problems that had existed even when it was smaller. Perhaps it was the hard, long winters, months of Canadian fronts falling upon the valley like wolves, howling winds sharp with ice and snow; or maybe the sort of rootless people who drifted into the valley from the urban East or Great Plains, looking for paradise and mad as hell when they didn't find it; or perhaps it was Meriwether's vision of itself as still part of the wild and woolly West, the last, lawless frontier. Whatever the cause, Meriwether had divorce, suicide and alcoholism rates that embarrassed the national average. And the dope, which for years had just been another way to get high, had become serious. The kids had moved away from marijuana and had begun to kill themselves with pills and speed. After four eighth-graders died from horse tranquilizers, the police shook down the junior high lockers and found a wealth of pills, speed and needles. Grass wasn't very profitable to deal anymore, so dealers turned to other, more profitable drugs. Even the police department became involved when two officers lifted twelve thousand ten-grain dextroamphetamine whites out of the evidence locker, then dealt them to a wholesaler right in Meriwether. They were fired but never indicted.

Some of the people who had either been raised in Meriwether or had lived there for years were beginning to drift on, seeking that place they remembered, trying to find it again in British Columbia or Alaska or Australia. I wished them well but stayed on, sitting in my office a few hours each afternoon, enjoying what I could see of the view through the smog, but not answering the telephone, watching my prospects become dimmer. And it seemed a fine way to live. Until Dick and Helen came back from Iowa after two long weeks.

They found me in the other office, stoned out of my mind and sharing the last of my smoked whitefish with the lady with the fuzzy hair and the pointed breasts. We had come to terms the night before, both of us showing up late on Saturday night, both being sober and bored by the party drunks. The next morning we got stoned again and attacked the whitefish. Somebody had been pounding on the office door for what seemed like hours, long enough to convince me that Leo had given my position away, so I answered it.

'What the hell you want?' I shouted through the door.

'It's me, goddammit!' Dick shouted back. 'Open the goddamned door! It's freezing out here!'

'Go get your own girl,' I said as I opened the door, grinning because Dick had maintained that the girl was too mean to bed. 'Oh, you've got one,' I added, then tried to act as if I'd spent most of my life naked in front of Helen Duffy. She blushed, glanced over my shoulder, then excused herself.

Dick wasn't amused; guilt and love had driven the amusement right out of his life.

'What's happening, man?' I asked, cheerfully blasted but not amused either.

'Don't you have any decency at all?'

His face flushed with anger when I laughed. I stopped to ask him what he wanted.

'Business,' he said curtly.

'Go find somebody decent to do business with.'

'She wanted you. For some reason,' Dick said.

'Fine. Tell her I have a business office.'

'What do you call this?'

'Go to hell.'

'Sure,' he said, leaving. He came back before I could close the door, and muttered unhappily, 'She wants to talk to you.'

'Today?'

'Today.'

'All right.'

'How long will it take you to straighten up?' he asked.

'There must be forty wisecracks in that answer,' I said.

'Try to resist them, old buddy, if you can,' he said bluntly.

'Don't hard-ass me,' I said, feeling very foolishly naked.

'How long, old buddy?'

'Couple of hours. In my office.'

He nodded, then left again. Friendship hadn't survived love. I went back to the table and the nude lady, who was carefully licking her greasy fingers with the happy greed of a child.

'Who was it?' she asked, as if she didn't really care.

'Adulterers. Fornicators. Lovers. Fools.'

'Jesus, what a crowd.'

'Yeah.'

'What'd they want?'

'Me to straighten up.'

'What an outa-sight idea. Where'd they get it?'

'Who the hell knows?' I said.

Now that I wasn't stoned anymore, the girl had nice breasts and a splatter of freckles across her shoulders, but her feet were dirty and her hair smelled of smoke.

Two hours later, which I spent alternating between the steam room and the sauna at the Elks Club, with occasional forays into the whirlpool and the bar, I made it to the office, slightly tipsy but functional, red as a boiled lobster. The dark glasses I'd borrowed from the Elks Club bartender felt silly. I left them on my desk, then wandered down the hall to harass my cousin the dentist for a heavy vitamin shot. He wasn't there. That's how I found out it was Sunday. I was back in the office, hitting the bottle, when Helen came in the open door.

'Lady, I get double-time on Sundays and national holidays,' I said, 'and it started forty-five minutes ago.'

'I'm sorry,' she said softly, 'I was – was occupied.' She shut the door and came over and sat down without turning over the chair.

'Where's your boyfriend?'

'Dick went home. I think.'

Except for her muted gray suit and her hands, which looked as if she had been forming concrete for the past two weeks, she didn't seem to show any signs of heavy grief. Her slim neck might have been a bit loose on her shoulders, and she shifted uneasily in the chair when I stared at her, but I thought the cause was guilt, not grief.

I switched on the recorder without asking her permission, and asked her what she wanted. After a long pause, she answered in a slow, measured voice.

'I would like to engage your services – employ you to look into the details of my brother's death.'

'Why?'

'Is that important?'

'This time I'll decide what's important.'

'I see,' she said, watching her hands. Then she folded them, sat up straight in the chair, saying, 'I'm not satisfied with the coroner's verdict. I suspect something must have happened.'

'You or your parents?'

'My father doesn't know how Raymond died. He hasn't been well for some time.'

'What does your mother think?'

'Oh, she agrees with me.'

'Or you with her?' I asked, thinking that the grief-stricken mother had sent Helen back out West.

'I suppose you could say that,' she answered slowly.

'And what is it you and your mother suspect?'

'Some sort of – foul play.' The old-fashioned phrase seemed proper in her mouth.

'Murder?'

'Something – like that.'

'What does Dick think?' I asked.

'Does it matter what he thinks?'

'He knows you better than I do,' I said, 'and he's a pretty bright guy. I'd like to know what he thinks. If you don't mind.'

'You're awfully sarcastic today.'

'I don't feel well. What's he think?'

'He thinks I'm a fool,' she said calmly. 'What do you think?'

After a moment's stammering, I managed to sound fairly sincere when I answered, 'I would guess that you're a fairly sensible young woman, but between your grief and certain sorts of family pressures, you didn't have any choice but to come back. But then, I'm not paid to think.'

'And I'm not so young, either,' she said, smiling pertly. 'Will you look into his death?'

'I don't know that I should,' I answered. 'I'd like to help, but right now I'm not too popular with the police. Your brother died in the county, but he lived in town, and that's where I'd have to ask questions. They might not like that.'

'Aren't you an ex-policeman?'

'Ex-deputy. But that doesn't buy me anything. I don't have any sort of working arrangement or good buddies on the force. There are a lot of guys over there who don't care for me, and a few who hate my guts. So there may not be much I can do. Why not try to get them to reopen the case?'

'I tried,' she said, trying not to smile, 'but they refused. The state police and the sheriff's department too. Everybody refused.'

'And I'm your last resort?'

'Yes,' she admitted, letting the smile come.

'It's nice to be in demand,' I said, the anger gone now, my face distorted in a goddamned boyish grin. 'I'm not busy now, so if you want me to poke around for a few days, I will. But you should know up front that I don't have much experience with this sort of thing.'

'I understand,' she said, staring over my shoulder.

'Better than nothing, huh?'

'What? Oh, I wouldn't have said that.'

'Thanks. What do you see out there?'

'I'm not sure. I thought I saw lightning in the mountains, but the smog . . .'

'Let's hope not,' I said, 'I've got some property up there. How long do you want me to look into this?'

'As long as necessary.'

'Lady, I charge a hundred a day. Plus expenses. That can cost.'

'I remembered your fee; I can afford it.'

'It's your money. I'll look until I dead-end, okay?'

'That will be fine. I'll trust your judgment.'

'Okay, but this time you answer all my questions.'

That was harder than the money, and her answer didn't come so quickly.

'I'll try,' she said, bowing her head.

'That's not good enough.'

'All right,' she said, 'but please understand that – that sometimes it's difficult – painful . . .' She settled herself into the chair as if I were about to extract her wisdom teeth. 'I'll do my best.'

'I guess that will have to do. I suppose Dick mentioned your little brother's living arrangements prior to moving to the Great Northern?'

'Yes,' she answered, sighing so deeply that I thought she might faint.

'You knew he was a homosexual?'

'It wasn't – his fault.'

'You knew?'

'Yes.'

'Since when?'

'I don't know exactly. I suspected it for some time, then found out for sure when he was a senior in college.'

'How?'

'Raymond was a dormitory counselor at Buena Vista, and he and another boy were caught smoking marijuana in a dorm room. During the interrogation, the younger boy claimed that Raymond had seduced him.'

'What happened?'

'The other boy was expelled. Raymond was allowed to graduate *in absentia*. As a personal favor to my father and me.'

'Your father teaches there too?'

'He did. For nearly twenty years. Until his accident –'

'Accident?'

'I suppose you'd call it that. He was beaten and robbed in New York City some years ago, as he was returning to his hotel after reading a paper at a conference of English professors. Two young men, drug addicts probably, beat him rather severely, then left him in the gutter. He lay there for some time in the cold and snow, and the people who walked past him must have assumed he was drunk. He's absent-minded about some things, like clothes. Mother packed his good suit, but he forgot to wear it, so he was dressed rather shabbily. Anyone who looked carefully would have realized that he wasn't a drunken bum. But no one cared. Not even the police. His identification was gone, he was incoherent and smelled of the single drink he had with an old friend after he read his Twain paper . . .

'So the police threw him into a drunk tank, where he was beaten again, where he stayed without assistance until he began to vomit blood the next afternoon. He never mentioned it, but I think he was also – molested somehow – sexually . . . Oh, this is so sordid . . . I'm sorry – I can't seem to stop . . .'

She cried quietly for a few minutes. I let her, remembering how badly I'd comforted her the night Raymond died. Then she stopped, saying, 'I told you it would – would be hard.'

'There's no other way.'

'I guess not. After he got out of the hospital, my mother sued the city of New York. They settled out of court for a rather large sum of money, but by then it didn't matter. My father never recovered. After all that had happened, this was just too much. I had to quit graduate school to go home, and the college hired me to replace him. I suppose I've been replacing him ever since –'

'You said, "after all that had happened?"'

'Oh,' she sighed. 'From the outside, on the surface, we look like such an ordinary middle-class family, but so much has happened . . . We had no luck . . .' Her fingers were scrambling at each other now, and she was gazing out the window. 'We were happy – once, but we had no luck . . .'

The tears came back, flooding out of her open eyes and coursing down her cheeks. I handed her the box of tissues I kept in the desk for despondent wives, and she grabbed them and fled into my bathroom.

I didn't follow her. I did the necessary things. Erased the tape, switched off the recorder. Had a drink. Thought about families and luck.

When I lived in a family in the big house with overgrown grounds, we hadn't had much luck either. My father had blown his head off with a shotgun, but nobody ever discovered if it was an accident or a suicide or bad luck. He and my mother had been drunk, fighting as usual, breaking things to show their disgust for each other and their lives. Since I seemed somehow the center of their anger, I tried to listen, usually, but that night had fallen to sleep. The two springer spaniels woke me, barking excitedly downstairs, as if they were ready for the hunt. When I walked to my window to see if it was near dawn, the night sky was black, except for a slice of the moon. In the verdant spring air, I smelled a skunk, then heard the shotgun go off downstairs.

My mother never told me why he was going for the shotgun. Her or the skunk or himself. Perhaps she really didn't know. Perhaps it doesn't matter. When he reached into the hall closet and pulled out the shotgun, the trigger caught on the open bolt of a Remington .30–06 rifle, and the full choke barrel discharged a load of number four shot just under his chin.

I remember the stink of the skunk, the dogs yapping in circles, my mother still shouting at the body, his heels rattling on the hardwood floor. I was ten.

When I was twenty, during the long and stupid truce in Korea, the Red Cross informed me that my mother had died in a fancy alcoholic retreat in Arizona and her body had already been shipped back East to her family for burial. They offered me a leave, but I didn't need it. After the war, I found out that she had hanged herself with a nylon hose, but by then it was too late to feel anything, to do anything except curse the bad luck.

Helen came back from the bathroom, the make-up scheme of her face washed away, her skin pale and eroded with sorrow. She apologized quickly, then continued: 'We moved to Storm Lake when –'

'Let's skip the family history, okay? Concentrate on Raymond.'

I had confused her again.

'But – but how can you understand about Raymond, that he couldn't have – caused his own death?'

'Wouldn't it be better for me to have an open mind about it?'

'I'm not sure. You don't believe me either, do you?'

'You're not paying me to believe you,' I said, 'you're paying me to find out what happened. Right?'

'I guess so,' she said, her mind working at it. She seemed to be having her first doubts, to begin to consider that perhaps her little brother had died by his own hand, either accidentally or on purpose. But the concept was too hard. She shook her head like a dog with a mouthful of porcupine quills, then spit the idea out. 'He couldn't have killed himself!'

'Maybe it was an accident,' I said, not asking her why not suicide.

That seemed more repugnant. She continued to shake her head, a silent *no* falling from her lips each time her face reached the apex of its denials.

'Look, you want me to find out what happened? Or console you with lies?'

'Find out what happened, of course,' she said primly, but neither of us believed her.

'Okay. Let's start over. Why did he come out West?'

'What?'

'Why did he come to Meriwether?'

'I told you before,' she said, irritated now. 'To take a degree in Western history. He was quite a good student. He had finished his course work and was a graduate teaching assistant; he was writing his thesis when he dropped out of school. I know because I checked.'

'Did you think he might have been lying?'

'I doubted him, yes, but I shouldn't have. Raymond would never lie to me. Not even about the money – oh . . .'

'What money?' It was normal; my clients usually lied as often and as badly as politicians.

'What money?' she echoed.

'Come on, lady.'

'Oh, all right. The last time he wrote, he asked me for money . . .'

'Why not your parents?'

'Because I was sending him to school.'

'Why?' I asked, knowing we were back into family history.

'After the trouble in his senior year, my mother threw him out of the house. His clothes, his books, his guns, everything. Told him to never come back. She sold his horse and tack, she drove him away from the front door. She – she can be a hard woman. She didn't mean to be cruel; she just couldn't stand any more – any more grief and trouble. She even said she regretted adopting him.

That was the – cruelest thing of all . . . she regretted being his – mother.'

'Raymond was adopted? I didn't know.'

'There's no need to be nasty. After the other boys had – had died, my parents adopted Raymond.'

'Others? How many?'

'Three.'

'I'm sorry. How?'

'One of the twins was killed in an automobile accident when he was four. My father hit a bridge abutment on the way to Chicago. My mother miscarried with a male child in the wreck. The next baby choked to death on a button. The other twin drowned in our pond when he was nine,' she said so matter-of-factly that I expected her to count them off on her raw fingers, but her eyes had found their way to my north view again, hoping perhaps to see lightning in the hills.

'I am sorry. I didn't need to know that.'

'It doesn't matter.'

'Let's go back to Raymond. You were sending him to school. But he wasn't in school, yet he wrote asking for more money?'

'Yes. He did that sometimes. Unexpected expenses,' she said.

'What was it this time?'

'He wanted to buy – some papers – or something . . .'

'What?'

'Some historical papers, letters and diaries that some old man had. I think he was one of those who died in the hotel fire. Raymond had become his friend, and the old man told him that he wasn't really the son of the outlaw he said he was . . . Something . . . The old man claimed in public to be the bastard son of that bandit the vigilantes hanged in Montana, the leader –'

'Henry Plummer?'

'That's the one,' she said hurriedly. 'But it wasn't true, it was just a way to get people to buy him drinks. He was really the son of a less famous bandit, here in this state, a Dalton – something-or-other. I'm sorry. I've forgotten the name.'

'Dalton Kimbrough.'

'That's it. Raymond said nothing had been published on this Kimbrough and that anything he did with the old man's papers would surely be published. Publication is very important in an academic career.'

'How much did he ask for?'

'Five thousand dollars. Two thousand for the papers, three to live on while he checked their authenticity and worked on the thesis.'

'Did you send it?'

'Yes, of course.'

'Where did you get that sort of money?'

Her face said that was none of my business, but then she remembered and answered, 'I have quite a bit in savings – I live at home.'

'And you believed this story?'

'Absolutely. I told you: Raymond wouldn't lie to me.'

'Maybe he needed the money to support his drug habit? Or maybe for a deal? Sometimes addicts deal too?'

'He was not a heroin addict,' she said.

There didn't seem to be any room for argument, so I

paused, then said, 'You see that old bastard in the Cossack uniform hanging there on the wall?'

She turned so quickly that her chair nearly fell over, as if she expected to see a man swinging from a gibbet.

'That's my great-grandfather. He's the man who killed Dalton Kimbrough.'

'Oh, really,' she said. She didn't seem to share her little brother's interest in outlaws.

How fleeting is fame, I thought, laughing to myself. My great-grandfather had parlayed the death of Dalton Kimbrough into a fortune, and if he hadn't started wearing that damned phony Cossack uniform and carrying a knout, he would have been the first governor of the state. I knew how quickly they forget too, how fleet the foot of fame, how easily it tramples. Five months after I became a deputy sheriff, I had become momentarily famous. I captured a mass-murderer. A soft, fat honor student who had killed his mother, his grandmother, his aunt, and the four other women in the beauty shop his mother owned. All the law enforcement officers in Meriwether County surrounded the shop with shotguns and bull horns. I knew the kid and thought he had probably killed all the people he wanted to. Besides, I wasn't a woman. So I went through the rear of the house, through the jungle of doilies and knickknacks, and brought him out the front of the shop, cuffed and leaning heavily on my shoulder. The picture made the wire services and newsmagazines: intrepid young deputy captures mad-dog killer. *Time* even mentioned my splendid combat record.

What nobody knew except the two of us was that when I'd walked into the shop, he had stamped his foot petulantly, chunked his .22 pistol to the tile floor, then burst into tears. He nearly knocked me down, trying to get his head on my shoulder. I cuffed his wrists while they were around my neck. By the time we went outside, my shirt was wet with his tears. In the news photo, it looked like a bloodstain. The angry crowd outside was much more dangerous than the sad, fat kid. My great-grandfather had made a fortune off the hero role, but I didn't even get a raise.

'Really,' I said to Helen Duffy. 'He killed Dalton Kimbrough with a rock in the winter of 1866.'

'What?'

'Nothing. What made you come looking for your brother after only three weeks without word?'

'I'm not sure – I just felt that he might be in trouble . . .'

I had let her sit too long while my mind dabbled in my own past, so I said, 'It's been fun talking to you, Miss Duffy.'

'What's that mean?'

'It means that if you won't talk to me, there's no sense in going on. Save your money, I won't find out anything. Hell, I can't even find out anything from you.'

'Well – dammit, it's hard answering all these questions. Can't you understand that?' Grief had become anger; I was glad.

'Sure. But that doesn't tell me where to begin.'

'You're supposed to know that.'

'I do. I begin with you. Why did you come looking for him?'

'Oh – because – because my mother made me,' she answered impatiently, throwing her head back like an angry little girl. 'That's why. She found out I'd sent him that much money and she insisted that I come out to see what he was doing with it. She didn't believe him, she didn't believe me, and she made me come, and when I got here the damned old hotel was burned down. Can't you understand how frightened I was? I walked down the street checking numbers and looking for the sign and there was this gaping hole full of scorched bricks and twisted pipe and I didn't know what had happened or what to do . . . So I called Dick because he's the only person I know in this whole damned state and he suggested that you might help.'

'Okay. Take it easy.'

'Sometimes – sometimes I get damned tired of taking it easy.'

'Okay.'

'Well, I do.'

'Okay.'

'Raymond had been in that trouble before, and it hurt him so, and I was afraid he was in trouble again, this time with nobody to help him, and I was afraid to go to the police –'

'Why?'

'You know – how they treat – people like Raymond.'

'Did your mother make you come back?'

'What?' She was the most beautifully confused woman I had ever seen. 'What?'

'Your mother. Did she make you come back this time?'

'No.'

'Then why?'

'You've never loved anybody, have you?'

'What the hell difference does that make?' I asked.

'Then you wouldn't understand what I felt when I saw Raymond's face, when that man pulled back the sheet and showed me Raymond's face . . . Oh, I know you don't believe me, I know you had a fight with that terrible man Raymond was – seeing, I know you don't believe me, but it's all true . . . When I saw his face . . .' She paused, then gave me a helpless look. 'Why did they have to cut his hair and shave his beard? Why? He had such lovely black hair, and his beard was so full and fine, and in the sunlight sometimes it would look almost red, sometimes I could –'

'Almost believe that he was your natural brother?'

'What?'

'The red in his beard – it made you think he was your natural brother.'

'Oh, I don't know. He was such a lovely child, such a fine young man. Nobody knew him like I did. Nobody.'

'Okay,' I said. 'I understand.'

'No you don't.'

'Okay, I don't.'

'Then don't say you do.'

'Jesus Christ, all right!' I shouted. It took two tries to get the cork out of the bottle, but I made it and had me a long drink.

'Is that really necessary?' she asked, as snottily as she could.

'Asking you questions is hard,' I said. 'Can't you understand that?'

'I'm sorry,' she said quietly.

I reached across the desk, placed my hand against her cheek. She leaned her face into my hand, holding it against her shoulder. Her skin was warm and slightly damp. With forgiveness instead of grief.

'You're a troublesome woman.'

'I don't mean to be. Besides, you're a troublesome man.'

'I know.'

'But you don't mean to be,' she said. In that soft way that good mothers forgive their children, letting them know that they are better children than they know. 'Dick told me all about you. He's really fond of you, you know?'

'We were good friends,' I said, withdrawing my hand.

'Were? And now you won't be anymore? Because of me?'

'It doesn't matter.'

'I am truly sorry,' she said gently, then reached and took my hand back. And I understood what I had only sensed before. The woman behind the fluster, the dread and sorrow, the fog of tears and pink tissues – the woman that Dick had called something special – bloomed, blossomed forth like a nightflower under the new moon. The compassion, fine and lovely; the forgiveness, eternal. A woman so strong that she could believe in hope and trust and families and love, a woman who had survived without luck.

'I can understand,' she whispered, 'how you could think Raymond was on drugs, why you think he might have killed himself, but believe me, he didn't. And if you can find out anything at all about his death, I would greatly appreciate it.'

'I'll do what I can.'

'Thank you.' She had become as placid as a night pond, patient and calm. She needed to care as much as I needed to be cared for. 'Thank you very much.' Then she released my hand and took out the sheaf of traveler's checks.

'That's not necessary,' I said as she began signing them.

'Don't you want a retainer?'

'You watch too much television.'

'There isn't much else to do in Storm Lake,' she said lightly, scribbling at the checks. 'And if your other offer is still open, I'd like to take you up on that.'

'What's that?'

'Oh, you know,' she answered, perky now.

'No.'

'Your days in exchange for my nights,' she said, very businesslike about it, then she ripped out five one-hundred-dollar checks and laid them on the desk. 'Is that enough?'

'Why?'

'Why what?'

'Don't be coy.'

'Sometimes it's fun.'

'Not now. Please.'

'Oh, all right. I need to get over Dick. I've needed to get over Dick for an awfully long time. I must have been mad to let it start again. Although I've ended it – that's why he was so angry earlier – I'm not over it. If I hadn't been so frightened the first time, I would have taken your offer then. You did look so desperate, and I was such a . . . so nasty to ignore you completely, and I know it's terribly unkind to ask – to use you like this, but I think you're probably a kind man, and perhaps as frightened of all this as I am. Well?'

Her smile was only partially strained, the rest happy and willing, and her face was solidly determined. She was serious. She wasn't exactly desperate, but she would do it. But I wouldn't. Or couldn't. And I didn't think about why.

'I'll work day and night.'

'Oh,' she said, the smile limned with white as she held it gaily on her face. 'You mean no, don't you?'

'I'm sorry.'

'See? I told you that you were a kind man, that you weren't as bad as you thought.'

'Who is?'

'Oh, anybody who really wants to be,' she answered, chattering as brightly as a hysterical squirrel, lonesome upon the high limb where I had left her. She didn't hate me for the rejection, but she didn't like the rejection either. We were back to business again.

'Do you have a picture of your little brother?'

'Yes,' she said, dipping back into the purse. 'I had these made up the first time I came out here.' She handed me a stack of three-by-fives. 'They're copies of his graduation pictures.'

The young man in the photographs had a narrow face with sullen eyes and full lips arched in a sly smile, longish hair but not to his shoulders, and the beard was only a shadowy potential. He didn't look like a young outlaw, but there were hints of arrogance and bravado about the eyes and mouth; my great-grandfather might have called him a back-shooter, but to me he looked like an unhappy punk.

'Of course he didn't look like that when he was living here,' she said.

'I know.'

'You know?'

'I saw him around the bars a few times.'

'You did? Why didn't you . . .' But she didn't finish. Whatever it was that I had failed to do, she blamed me for it now.

'Did he look like this when he came to Meriwether?'

'Yes – no.'

'Which?' I asked.

'Yes.'

'Then how did you know about the long hair and the beard?' I asked, not interrogating, just curious in an aimless way.

'I didn't,' she blurted out, then covered her mouth with both hands and her purse. 'I did . . . I don't know anymore.'

'How did you know about the long hair and the beard, lady?'

'I – ah – Raymond sent a picture.' The lie stood between us like a wall.

'And don't tell me you'd rather not say if I don't goddamned mind.'

'Oh.'

I handed her back the checks. As she stared at them

blankly I had another drink, this one more necessary than the last, the whiskey doing its job, flowing in, washing out the bad taste of my life.

'He did,' she said meekly.

'Don't fucking lie to me.'

She stood up, tried to look shocked as she grabbed the checks and headed for the door. There she paused, slapped the checks against her thigh, then came back, hissing: 'All right. I came out last summer too. I live at home, and nothing ever happens at home, nothing. My mother still switches on the floodlights when a man brings me home, and nothing ever happens. So I came out last summer to see Raymond, and to see Dick, I hoped I'd see Dick, and, oh, damn you and your questions. Are you happy now?'

'Damn right. What happened last summer?'

She slammed the checks on the desk.

'What happened?'

'Nothing that has anything to do with this.'

'I'll decide that.'

'Really,' she pleaded, 'nothing.'

'What?'

'Oh, damn, if you must know. Raymond was living with a young history professor, who had left his wife for Raymond, and she kept coming around, dropping by or calling at all hours, threatening to *sic the law* on Raymond, and it was just awful. I never had a chance to call Dick. Really. And one afternoon she caught me coming out of the apartment and followed me down the street, screaming obscenities at me, holding this tiny baby out at me like a club and shouting about who was going to provide for her children, and suggesting that – that I was somehow involved, somehow to blame – sexually involved – and she got right in my face and screamed that she was going to take a needle and thread and fix my – faggot brother so he couldn't – couldn't – I can't say it.'

'You want me to?'

'No! Damn you, no!'

'What do you want?'

'I don't know!' she screamed, then fled the office, her shoes ringing down the hall, all the way down the stairs, oddly confident in flight.

I didn't know what I was mad about. Her handwriting on the checks was as sorry as mine. I needed the name of the errant history professor and of Helen Duffy's motel, but that I could handle without her. Unlike my life. I needed Simon to drift into the office to tell me what a fool I was. I had a drink instead, toasting the heroic form of my great-grandfather. His dark eyes glittered above his large, defiant nose; his huge mustache shadowed what must have been an arrogant mouth. He seemed to be smiling, but I didn't like it.

6

The lady was gone, but the money was still on my desk. Thinking the money small recompense and wondering what I thought I was doing, I endorsed the checks and filled out a deposit slip. She hadn't signed a contract, but money had changed hands, so I had a client. I started a file and an expense sheet. My expenses were already immense but, unfortunately, unclaimable: my auto insurance had lapsed, so all the gear stolen out of my rig was just another lost cause; the two bruises Reese gave me had faded into large yellow stains, but the indignity hadn't eased at all; I'd lost an old friend and handball partner; and I had a feeling that Helen Duffy wasn't going to be a fond memory. I left the expense sheet blank and printed her brother's name at the top of a new legal pad, but the information I had about him was both vague and confusing. Praying that ignorance wasn't going to be a fatal handicap, I left the legal pad blank too.

As I pushed away from my incipient failure, I glanced into the Diablos. Summer thunder showers lurked about the peaks, shot with hairs of lightning and trailing transparent veils of rain too light to dampen the vigor of a lightning fire. By morning there would be fires, but not enough rain, and the valley smog would fill with the odor of pine pitch and smoke. On the ridges and timbered slopes, gray clouds would rise, writhing with flames, the animals would move nervously downhill, and in Meriwether the people would look into the hills, some hoping for small things – hoping the fires wouldn't frighten the tourists or ruin the fishing – others hoping that the fires might grow too large for the Forest Service crews so that civilian crews would have to be hired, hoping for a few days of work in hell to buy a few drunk nights. Since some of that timber was my last ace in a deep and empty hole, I hoped for a front off the northwest coast, for long steady rain, easy showers without lightning, clouds to cut the sun, cool air to slake the heat.

Some hopes aren't foolish, some prayers are answered. Just as I had decided to write off my timber, the shades on the western windows, lowered against the afternoon sun, darkened and rattled in a rising wind. I raised them; the front waited just behind Sheba Peak – a broad thick blanket of blue clouds heavy with rain, already lapping at the late afternoon sky behind the peak. Even as I watched, the gray cone of Sheba fell prey to the vaporous arms. Once again, by the grace of those infamous gods, who tend to fools and drunks, the long bitter summer was eased.

The wind kicked up a notch, rattling the shades in a dry brittle clamor that sounded like a soothsayer's bones being cast. And the wind moaned in the hollow Sunday streets below me, lifting cheap cowboy hats off the sun-baked heads of tourists, tilting the random shirt, hurrying the pedestrian on his way. I lifted my head into the wind, tilted my face.

Simon, who sensed rain and cool air in his bones, who could forecast the weather better than ants or barn swallows, was heading north over the Dottle Bridge, scurrying and scuttling and limping like a sorely wounded crab intent on the safety of his hole – wrapped loosely in a tweed overcoat, surely purchased only moments before from the Salvation Army store south of the river.

So he has it now, I thought. The overcoat. It had been my father's, a heavy Harris tweed overcoat, purchased in Winnipeg on a binge; a coat he loved and wore at the slightest excuse, as a woman might a new mink. Ensconced within the coat, his thick unruly black hair set above like a fur cap, my father was prepared to weather any storm. At home he used it in preference to whatever robe my mother might buy him. Outdoors it became his shield, his cloak against the world's expectant daggers. Sometimes, wearing the coat, if his hair hadn't yet been tangled by the wind or his thick fingers, if his whiskey flush still resembled a tan, sometimes he might have been taken for a successful businessman instead of a rich drunk. After his death, I stayed wrapped in it, unafraid in the solid odor of wool and sweat and whiskey, curled like a sleeping pup on the study couch, until my mother took it away, gave it away, along with all his other clothes, to the Salvation Army.

So the drunks and bums could have them, she said, so the whole town could know for certain and remember forever what a drunken bum he had been. I didn't even know how to protest, how to stand before her hate and rage, which poured off her like heat from a burning house. I did ask why she had married him, and she answered '*Because of you!*' so vehemently that I flinched. But I didn't understand what she meant until I was older, and after I understood, I became very nervous when people talked about abortions upon demand.

I grew up as my mother meant for me to, watching my father's clothing parade up and down the streets of Meriwether, warming the backs of whatever dispossessed came into them. A retired NP engineer had been buried in his favorite tweed suit. His Russell snakeboots wore to greasy decrepitude on the feet of a local garbage man. Once I saw his Malone hunting pants on a drunken Willomot squaw, dirty and worn, the fly broken and a scrap of pink panties bulging out like a coil of gut. As I grew up, I saw my father sodden in doorways, urine snaking across the sidewalk toward the gutter, saw last rounds poured into him like *coups de grâce*, then saw the stumbling body disgorged like a walking corpse from two o'clock bars, saw brains and eggs shoveled into his toothless mouth, saw a brigade of fallen men falling to their death in his clothes.

Over the years I bought up what I could, haggling my allowance away to the Salvation Army, the Goodwill store, the second-hand dealers of Meriwether. On the streets and in the bars and skid-row hotels, I sought his clothes, bought and burned them. Once the winos found me out, I bought more clothing than my father had owned in his life, and if I had had enough money, the winos of our fair city would have been rich but naked.

But in the haggling, I learned that they were men also, that they had had lives full of chances too, not all of which had gone begging. And they still had dreams, dreams and lies enough to live with them. Unlike my mother, they were honest drunks, not too often ashamed. In their odd moments, drunk or sober, they knew who and what they were; they had looked at the world for a long steady moment, and found it wanting. As they took on individual faces and histories, I began to see them, both in the bars and at work – many did work, shoveled Meriwether's shit like white niggers – and the more I saw them, the more I preferred them to sober citizens. And I understood the defiance in the pathetic motto: I ain't no alcoholic, Jack, I don't go to no fucking meetings. And they needed no army for their salvation.

Just before I went to Korea, I thought I had found all the clothes except the overcoat, which I assumed had been garnered on the sly by a tall, portly professor or trundled out of town on the warm back of a railroad bum. When I came back from the war, it was back on the street, but I didn't care anymore. The war taught me that I wasn't the heroic type, and my childish notion of slaking my grief by burning his clothes had always seemed vaguely heroic. So I stopped. When I saw the overcoat around town, I tipped my hat and said hello, let it cover whatever back needed warming. It had endured so long, I knew it wasn't about to wear out in my lifetime, thought it might outlive us all.

Once later, I thought I had found his red felt crusher hunting hat on the head of a dead Assiniboin buck who was in a carload of breeds that had missed the last curve coming down Willomot Hill. Even in the ragged light of my unit, I saw the name inked into the felt, black as blood through the sweat and grease of countless men. But it was my childish scrawl on the name, not his firm hand, darkly smeared where the buck had tried, like a cowboy in a B Western, to wear his hat all the way through the fight.

That was when I cried for my father. Or perhaps for myself. And I quit the sheriff's department. No more car wrecks, no more bar fights, no more lost children whimpering at the dark mouths of canyons, no more family disturbances. No overcoats, no hats.

And now the overcoat had passed from deathbed to second-hand store to Simon. The coat wasn't an omen of death but of life; Simon had been dying for years. I leaned out the window into the deepening dusk, shouted and waved at him in the rising wind as the first splatters of rain shattered against my face. He didn't hear me; he turned into Mahoney's as if it were home.

My past exhumed and worn ragged, I gave it up and went back to work. I called Dick, hoping he could tell me where Helen was staying and what history professor had had the delight of living with her little brother, but one of his little girls answered the telephone. Usually children are death on telephone conversations, but Marsha, with her infinite patience, had taught their children to cope, and the child went obediently to fetch her father.

She came back shortly, saying carefully, 'He's busy, sir, and can't come to the telephone. Can I – may I take a message?'

'Honey, would you please go back and tell him that it's Milo and that it's important.'

After a longer wait, she returned, her small voice full of wonder and apology, 'Hello?'

'Yes.'

'I told him – but he didn't say anything.'

'Well, thank you, honey,' I said, but before I could hang up, I heard a clatter of footsteps and Dick's muffled voice, but I couldn't make out what he was saying.

'What the hell do you want?' he asked.

'Two things, old buddy. Helen's motel and the name of the guy in the history department who lived with her little brother last summer. Okay?'

He paused, his breathing harsh against the mouthpiece, then said, 'Why don't you do your own fucking work for a change?'

Behind him, in her shocked stage whisper, I heard Marsha saying, 'Richard! Not in front –'

But then the line went dead. I hung up, then dialed the first two digits of Dick's number, thinking to mend fences, but then I realized that I didn't know what to say, so I hung up again. Then I picked it back up and called Hildy Ernst.

The telephone rang until my ear started to ache, but she finally answered breathlessly, as if she had just run up the stairs to her apartment.

'Hello,' she said. Hildy had one of those voices that rub women the wrong way and men the right. My knees were suddenly weak. But there were odd noises behind her, grunts and groans and thumps. It sounded as if she was holding the NCAA wrestling championships in her living room.

'Hildy. This is Milo.'

'How nice. Where have you been, love?'

'Recovering. How have you been?'

'*Comme ci, comme ça.* You know how boring summer can be, darling.'

'Right.'

'Then why haven't you called me, you terrible man?'

'I meant to. But every time I tried, my hands shook so badly, I couldn't dial.'

'You're sweet, Milo.' There was a thud, then cheering.

'What the hell is going on?'

'Oh, some friends dropped by. We're playing charades, darling. You want to come over?'

'No, thanks,' I said. 'Crowds make me nervous. Besides, I'm working. But I need some information. Last summer a history professor left his wife to live with one of his male students –'

'How tragic.'

'– and I wondered if you knew who it was.'

'Of course.'

'Who?'

'If I tell you, will you stop by?'

'Some other time?'

'Promise?'

'Sure, Hildy.'

'I don't believe you, darling, but his name is Elton Crider. He's one of those hillbilly types, all bone and Adam's apple. You will stop by soon?'

'Sure.'

'You bastard, Milo.'

'Say, Hildy.'

'Yes?'

'What did you ever see in me?'

'I get bored with younger men, Milo. They all expect me to be grateful,' she said, then laughed in her husky voice.

'Thanks,' I said, then hung up, laughing. Hildy was the sort of woman an older man could fall in love with – if he could keep up. I couldn't.

Elton Crider wasn't listed in the telephone book, and when I drove over to the address listed in the university directory, another family lived there. They had no idea where the Criders had moved, except that it was somewhere in the country. So I called my telephone-company creep, and for fifty bucks, his weekend price, he went down to the office and got me the unlisted number and the new address.

At ten o'clock and fourteen miles up the Meriwether River, I found a dark house and an empty garage. I rang the bell anyway, standing close to the door under the narrow eaves of the tacky new house, trying to stay out of the soft rain. The door flew open so quickly that I nearly toppled into the dark hole of the doorway.

'You son of a bitch,' a shrill voice rasped from the darkness. Then an angry hand whipped back and forth across my face as the voice cursed me with each swing. I backed off the low concrete stoop, but the hand followed me.

'Hey, lady, I give up,' I said, trying to hold my hands in front of my face.

'Elton?' she asked, her raised hand somewhere above my hot face.

'No, ma'am.'

She stepped back to switch on the porch light. In the yellow glow of a bug lamp, we considered each other. She was a tall woman wrapped in a faded pink chenille robe. An angular face with a broad mouth and a large straight nose and a sharp chin jutted out at me. She might have been a handsome woman once, but the softness had been eroded from her face, and the yellow light wasn't flattering. Sallow skin stretched tightly over her facial bones. Then she giggled slightly, and her face softened.

'Ah'm sorry, mister. Ah thought you's my husband,' she said in a Southern voice that twanged like an out of tune E-string, which was an improvement over her shout, which sounded like a ripsaw in a pine knot.

'You always wait in ambush for your husband?' I asked, but she didn't answer, so I rubbed my cheek, playing for sympathy. 'I guess I'm glad I'm not him. You nearly took my head off.'

'Ah didn't even double up my fist,' she said, smiling as if she had made a joke. The fist she held out to me was large, heavy, with knuckles like stones.

'I'm glad,' I said, shrugging and smiling.

'Well, Ah'm sorry Ah hit you,' she said, wrapping her long arms around her spare chest. 'What was it you wanted?'

'To begin with, you could let me in out of the rain.'

'This'll do fine,' she said quietly.

It was late on a dark rainy night and the nearest house was five hundred yards away, but she wasn't a bit frightened. She was a hell of a woman.

'Is your husband home?' I asked, then remembered that he wasn't. 'Sorry. Silly question,' I said, rubbing my cheek. 'My name's Milodragovitch. I'm a private investigator.' I showed her my photostat. 'I'd like to talk to your husband. Do you know where I might find him?'

'Why?'

'Business.'

'In the middle of a Sunday night?'

'I work strange hours,' I said. 'I've got to catch an early flight tomorrow morning, so I thought I'd try to catch your husband tonight.'

'What's Elton got business with a private investigator for?' she asked in a hard voice, as if I were the law.

'I'm looking for a missing student, and somebody told me that your husband knew her quite well.'

'Who?'

'Elaine Strickland,' I answered quickly. Elaine had been my childhood sweetheart; she had beaten me half to death with a rag doll in the third grade.

'Never heard of her. Who says Elton knew her?'

'Ah, her parents. She mentioned Professor Crider in several of her letters.'

'What did she say?'

'That she'd had several classes under him, that he had helped her with some research. That sort of thing.'

'Oh. Why don't you leave a number, and Ah'll have Elton call you tomorrow or the next day.'

'I won't be in town for a week or so. I'm flying to Seattle to follow another lead,' I said importantly. 'If I could talk to him tonight, I'd really appreciate it. If you know where he is.'

'Ah damn sure know where he ain't. Ah'd have to guess where he was.'

'A good guess is better than nothing.'

'Yeah. Lemme see that thing again.' I handed her my license. She examined it carefully as I stood in the rain. 'Milodragovitch, huh?' she said as she gave it back to me. 'Ain't that the name of that park in Hell-Roarin' Canyon?'

'Yes.'

'Kin a yours?'

'Used to be my front yard.'

'That so?'

'Yes.'

'Ah'll be damned. What happened?'

'Family fell on hard times,' I replied.

'Some folks don't never have no good times to fall onto hard from,' she said, her voice shifting closer to the rhythms of the Southern hills, full of hardscrabble farms and lost chances, failed crops and good hounds ruined by mean coons. She stared into the rain over my head as if she could see all the way back there to the dim hollows flanked by steep, sharp ridges.

'Kentucky?' I asked. 'Tennessee?'

'Don't matter none,' she answered. 'Don't live there now.' She shook herself like a lanky dog just awake, brought herself back to this new place of young mountains and old strangers. 'Elton is probably drinkin' at the Riverfront. He hangs out there some. We had a little fuss, and sometimes he goes there to sip whiskey and gnaw on his liver. You might find him there.'

'Thank you very much, Mrs. Crider,' I said. 'I'm sorry for the trouble.'

'Me too,' she whispered, 'sorry as hell.' Then as if the apology made her feel better, she brightened and smiled. 'Ah've been impolite to make you stand in the rain. Why don't y'all come on in? Coffee's on the stove. Warm yourself up.' Then she paused and added, 'May be that Elton will come on home 'fore the bars close this once.'

We looked at each other, both knowing he wouldn't. I didn't know what the invitation meant, and I decided that I didn't want to know, so I declined.

'Thanks, but I've got to be going. Thanks for your help,' I said, then turned to trudge out to my rig.

'Take care,' she said, her voice warm and vibrant through the easy fall of the rain.

After the divorce business went bankrupt, I thought I was finished with the long signs of dead marriages, but as I backed out of the driveway, she stood framed in the saffron glow, a tall woman, her long hair growing lank in the damp air, her strong hands strangling her waist with the cord of the ragged robe.

With the rush of affluent tourists in the 1960s, the mountain West had suffered a blight of shoddy motels, built, like mining camp saloons and whorehouses, strictly for profit. Cheap and fragile lodgings, buildings just waiting for the rumor of another strike to collapse into permanent vacancy and decrepitude, instant ghost towns, as frail as dead neon signs.

But the Riverfront Motor Inn had obviously been designed in protest, in the vague hope of permanent opulence. The carpets were thicker and the furnishings ached to be tasteful, but the cedar shakes and natural wood and stone trim covered the same old plywood and profit motive. When credit cards slipped through their imprinters, they came out shaved, like crooked dice. The dining room had an elegant menu; the bar, fancy drinks; but the food was tasteless and the liquor spurted niggardly from a speed gun. They did a fine business in tourists, but the local people, except for lovers on an illicit tryst, stayed away.

Rumors persisted, too, that the Riverfront had been built with Syndicate money and was used to wash money skimmed from the gaming tables of Nevada, rumors aided and abetted by the fact that a local Italian, Nickie DeGrumo, had returned from World War II with an Italian bride from New Jersey, an ugly, hawk-faced woman who came West with money from unidentified sources, money that had started him in the bar business that had culminated in the Riverfront Motor Inn complex. This in spite of the fact that everybody in town knew him to be the worst sort of fool about business, the sort who leapt into each new venture at exactly the wrong time and in the wrong way. He built a drive-in movie theater just in time to be ruined by television, a pizza place that lasted a year before the franchised pizza companies moved into town, and a putt-putt golf course so easy that even the children were bored with it. He bought a fleet of soft-icecream trucks before the machinery was perfected, and he only missed an Edsel dealership because his wife refused him the money.

It became apparent that she and a series of cousins from the East ran the business, that Nickie was just a name on the liquor license, a local front tethered by a small allowance like a child. He was the only bar owner in town who never set up a round of drinks when he visited other bars, and his was the only bar in Meriwether that never bought its regular patrons a drink. Like Simon, Nickie always seemed to have a drink in his hand that somebody else had bought. Around town he was known for being slow with his wallet but quick with his mouth. 'I'll get the next round, boys,' he'd say, but he so seldom did that the drinkers around town tagged him Old Next Round, and called him so behind his back and to his carefully smiling face.

Just after midnight, I parked in the nearly empty lot next to the dining room and bar, then poked around the few cars until I found one with an MSC faculty sticker, a battered blue Ford station wagon, paint so faded that it didn't even glisten in the rain, looking more abandoned than parked, listing on ruined springs like a tired horse, but it was registered to Elton and Martha Crider, so I opened the hood and lifted the rotor out of the distributor, slipped it into my pocket, then wandered into the Riverfront lobby – tired, lonesome, sodden as a drowned cat.

The building was fairly new but badly maintained. The ornate metal handles of the double doors showed the effects of pushing hands, the red carpet the marks of passing feet, and the night clerk, in spite of his razor cut and nifty gold blazer, had the sharp feral face of a cornered rat. His beady eyes, which checked the empty lobby around me, weren't happy; he had lost his last job because I had bribed a look at his guest register, then made a large fuss when I kicked down a room door to take pictures.

'I'm sorry, sir, but all our rooms are taken,' he said in a new voice, warm and rich, the split ends trimmed. Then he glanced around the lobby once more, and added in his old voice, 'Get the fuck outa here, Milo.'

I bared my fangs; he subsided into a whine.

'Any trouble, man, I call the law.'

I had stopped to consider what sort of trouble to give him, when Nickie came bouncing out of the darkened dining room. Nickie bounced because he affected expensive cowboy boots, but even with low walking heels, his heels bounced and his soles flapped against the carpet. On a hard surfaced floor, Nickie's walk sounded like slow ironic applause.

'Milo, Milo,' he greeted me, glad hand extended and inane smile pasted on his face. 'How's the boy, Milo? How you been? It's been too long. What's happening? You're looking great. Haven't seen you in a coon's age.'

I shook his hand and mumbled something before he flayed me with clichés.

'Business or pleasure? Business or pleasure?' he asked, pumping my hand. His sun-lamp tan failed to cover the drinker's flush of his face, just as the expensively tailored Western jacket refused to drape his paunch. His thick black hair hadn't grayed, but it looked painted on his round head.

'A drink,' I answered, trying to move away from him, but he followed me toward the bar.

'Let me buy you the first one,' he said.

'That's okay, Nickie. You got the last one. I'll get this one.'

'Sure, Milo,' he said, clapping to a halt. 'I'll get the next one.' His face colored – anger, perhaps, or shame – then he looked very tired and gray when the flush faded, standing in his wife's lobby like a clown whose antics have failed to cheer the crowd, and rubbing his chest beneath his string tie.

'Sure,' he said again, trying to smile.

'Vonda Kay tending bar?' I asked.

'Huh?'

'Is Vonda Kay tending bar?'

'Oh, yeah.'

'I'll tell her the first one is on you,' I said.

'Sure,' he said. 'You do that.' A hard nervous edge sharpened his voice, as if he wanted to pick a fight with me, which would have been funny if it hadn't been sad.

'Thanks,' I said, ignoring his uneasiness, then walked into the dimly lighted bar.

Like the parking lot, it was nearly empty. Sunday night was for hard-core drinkers, and they didn't care for the California cocktail lounge decor of the Riverfront. The prices were too high for the serious drinker anyway. Their clientele that night was made up of occasional drinkers and refugees from love. In a corner booth, a drunken foursome mauled each other at random, two middle-aged men waxing prosperous, two middle-aged women waning, chipping and putting and hacking at lust, replacing divots in their chests. Another couple sat at the rear of the lounge, holding hands across the table and whispering seriously above the watery drinks – a younger couple, who, when they troubled to glance around the empty room, did so with lovers' disdain.

Vonda Kay, who had the biggest breasts and the sweetest disposition west of the Big Muddy, stood behind the bar as peacefully as a saint, working slowly at her nails, a serene smile lighting her face. Her only bar customer sat hunched on a stool, as lonely and wasted as a man who has just discovered how bleak the shank of his evening is. When he raised his glass to his mouth, his Adam's apple rose, then fell with the trickle of whiskey.

Elton Crider, I guessed – taller but as angular as his wife. He might have been her brother, but her bones were hickory, his rubber.

When I stepped up to the bar and ordered a Canadian ditch from Vonda Kay, the tall man turned toward me with a bright smile as phony as that of a trained horse, a forced grin so desperate that it went beyond the sexual domain, into that desert where any sort of human contact – the touching of fingers over coins, shoulders briefly wedged in a doorway – stood like a distant, shimmering oasis, the burning green toward which he loped, dry and sore-footed.

He should have been looking at Vonda Kay, who, if she was between boyfriends and if she felt sorry for a man, was the most comfortable one-night stand in town, as warm as freshly baked bread, as loving as a puppy. But it seemed obvious that he wanted something more, something spiritual and clean as a blue flame. An undying love, perhaps, a consummation of souls. Feeling sadder than I wanted to be, I remembered his wife framed in the wan light, twisting the frayed cord.

Vonda Kay handed me the drink and heaved her breasts on the edge of the bar like a man loading sacked feed. She took my hand in hers, said kindly, 'Long time no see, lover.'

When it rains, it pours, just like they say. I wished there were a mirror over the bar so I could look at my face to see if it was bright with love or lust or desperation. But there was no mirror, just Vonda Kay's shining eyes.

'How're you doing, lady?'

'Without, Milo, without,' she murmured. 'I've just worn out another occupation.'

'What this time?'

'Rock-'n'-roll singers.'

'Where the hell did you find a rock-'n'-roll singer?'

'Where the hell do I find anybody?' she said, glancing around the bar.

'What's next?'

'Old friends, I hope.'

'All right,' I said. Even a man of stone can be tempted to get out of the rain. 'You're on, lady.' As we laughed together the tall man down the bar coughed loudly. 'Who's your customer?' I asked.

'Don't really know, Milo. Comes in now and again and drinks till closing time. Never says much. What happened to your face? Looks like somebody slapped you good. Now, who would do a thing like that?' she said, teasing, touching my cheek with her hand.

'A chance encounter,' I said, 'in a dark alley.'

'Sure.'

'What's he do?' I asked, nodding toward her customer.

'Don't know. Somebody said he teaches at the college.'

'Sure,' I said loudly, 'I thought I knew him.' Then turning down the bar: 'Aren't you Professor Crider?'

He nodded hesitantly, as if he didn't want me to know, then grinned so widely that I thought he was about to whinny.

'I'm sorry,' he said. 'I don't seem to remember your name.'

'Milodragovitch. We met at a party a few years back,' I said. He looked confused, like a man who had good reason to remember every party. 'Can't remember where, though. I remember talking to you. Aren't you from the South?'

'Tennessee,' he offered slowly.

'Right. Didn't we talk about Nashville and the Opry? I told you about the time when I was stationed at Fort Bragg and a bunch of us drove over to see the Opry but got so drunk in the Orchid Lounge or whatever that place is called that we never made the show.'

'You did?' he asked, wanting to believe, to establish contact even with my lie. 'Must have blanked it. I did go to school in Nashville – Vanderbilt – but we never went to Ryman except to watch the rednecks queue up in the afternoon . . .'

'Right,' I interrupted. 'You told me about the Jesus Christ fans and the women standing there in flats, holding their high-heels in one hand and a drumstick in the other.'

'That's right. How did you know that?'

'You told me, remember?' Actually, it came from my second wife's first husband.

'Oh . . . yes . . . I seem to have some faint memory . . . certainly. It was at Frank Lathrop's spring bash two summers ago. Of course. Oh, Lord, was I loaded that day. That punch he made, my God,' he wailed, gleefully recalling the day, locking the false memory into his mind so tightly that I'd have trouble convincing him it was a lie.

'That's right,' I said, wondering who Frank Lathrop might be.

'Oh, Lord, Ryman Hall. I haven't thought about it in years. Of course, I never cared much for hillbilly music, or Country and Western, or whatever silly name it goes by today. Always seemed too shrill to me. And distressingly mawkish . . .'

He went on about Country music, now that we had shared experiences, occasionally shifting his hips on the red stool as if he were about to slide gracefully across the three that separated such good old friends. His accent was Southern-educated, genteel and effete, so languid that he might have brushed his teeth with sorghum molasses, but beneath it rang the sharp bite of a nasal hill accent, so much like his wife's that he sounded like her echo, and it crept under his assumed accent like a whining hound beneath a ratty porch. He was so damned snobbish about Country music, holding it up in such contempt, wrinkling his long nose as if he held a dirty diaper, that even though I wanted to pump him about Raymond Duffy, I nearly started to argue with him. So I bought a round of drinks instead, invited him to the stool next to me, hoping he would stop. He didn't.

'Say,' I said, breaking into his spiel, 'don't you teach history?'

'What? Yes, I do. Why?'

'I used to have a good buddy who was a graduate student in the history department and I haven't seen him in a long time. Maybe you knew him? Raymond Duffy?'

His eyes narrowed, and he looked at me in a frankly sexual way, thinking perhaps he had found a kindred soul, but he couldn't make himself believe it.

'No, I don't believe I know the name,' he said carefully. 'I don't teach graduate courses very often. Would you excuse me?' he said, pushing away from the bar.

'Hey, buddy,' I said. 'You haven't finished your drink.'

'I'll be right back. I'm just going – to the john,' he answered, pawing at the carpet with a scuffed loafer.

'Hope everything comes out all right,' I said heartily as he reared past me, blushing so hard that tears came to his eyes.

'Okay, Milo, what's going on?' Vonda Kay asked as Crider lurched toward the rest rooms.

'Working, love, working.'

'We don't need that kinda business in here, Milo.'

'Don't worry,' I said, standing up to go after him. I had gotten coy and lost him, so we would have to talk in the john. He looked as if he might have some experience with toilet communications.

'This is a good job, Milo. I don't need trouble.'

'No trouble, love, no trouble at all.' I gunned my second drink and went after Crider.

The rest room looked more like an operating room – white porcelain, beige tile and a soft green carpet. Crider was manfully trying to make water and ignore me. Thanks to modern technology, there was a hot-air blower instead of paper towels, so I jammed the swinging door with my handkerchief. Nobody was going to come in, and Crider wasn't going to get out quickly. He had a tall man's reach and thick wrists, and I wanted to immobilize him quickly. I stepped behind him and jerked his faded windbreaker over his shoulders to pin his arms. He reacted violently, not to get at me but at his fly to zip it up, and the London Fog gave up the ghost, splitting right up the middle of the back.

Zipped up, he spun around, anxious and confused, his teeth chattering and his lower lip trembling. 'Hey,' he stammered, 'hey, what's, what's happening, whatcha do that for?' He held up the two halves of his windbreaker. They dangled from his wrists like distress flags. 'Dammit, I've had this jacket since college, dammit, why, what . . .'

'It seemed like a good plan,' I said calmly.

'What?'

'I didn't want you to get excited. See? You're excited now.'

'What?'

'Now, don't get excited. I want to talk to you about Raymond Duffy.'

His eyes grew wide and wild, but I didn't hit him because they also filled with tears. I knew I could handle him, and he knew it. After the brief spurt of anger, his shoulders slumped like a man ready to take a beating. He looked as badly used by life as his wife, and somebody was huffing outside the door, so I shouldered the door and jerked my handkerchief out. Nickie, red-faced and breathing hard, came rushing into the rest room, saying, 'Goddamned door. Hi, Milo. Wonder what the hell's wrong with that door? You have any idea what those goddamned things cost?'

'No, Nickie, I don't,' I said, then walked out, went back to the bar to have another drink.

'What was that all about?' Vonda Kay asked as she handed me the drink.

'I don't know. Did you send Nickie back to the john?'

'Are you kidding, Milo? I don't send Nickie anywhere. He's useless as tits on a boar hog. Anytime there's trouble, I holler for one of the bar managers, then there's no more trouble.'

'Hard-asses, huh?'

'Nope. Just quiet and mean as hell. They even scare me,' she said, then laughed as if she weren't really afraid at all.

'See you later,' I said as I finished the drink.

'Want one to go?'

'Sure. Why not.'

She made one in a go cup, then said, 'See you about two?'

'If I can make it.'

'It's too cold for maybes, Milo.'

'Best I can do, babe. I'm working.'

'Then come back some night when you aren't.'

'You know me, love, I work twenty-five hours a day.'

'That's not what I hear,' she said, but I didn't laugh.

Outside the rain had eased to mist, which shifted dully across the black gleaming asphalt and the empty cars.

Elton Crider was hunched over his engine, busy with a flashlight. I walked up behind him, took the rotor out of my pocket, and said his name. He didn't hear me, so I said it louder.

His head whanged against the open hood as he stood up and dropped the flashlight. The lens broke and the light went out when it hit. It rolled across the asphalt, and I stooped and picked it up. He rubbed the back of his head and moaned.

'Is it broken?' he asked. He had taken off the pieces of his jacket and disposed of them somewhere. His shirt was soaked, and he looked so pitiful that I almost offered him my jacket.

'Looks like it,' I said.

'Damn. That was a new bulb too. Damn. What the hell have you got against me,' he groaned. 'What do you want?' Beneath the thin white shirt, his bones thrust out of his flesh like those of a concentration camp prisoner. 'What do you want?'

'To talk to you about Raymond Duffy.'

'He's dead. Don't you know that? It was in the papers. He's dead.' Then he began to blubber.

'I know he's dead. I want to know why. I want to know whatever you know about him.'

'No,' he moaned, 'no.'

I handed him his broken flashlight, but he flinched, falling back against his car, whimpering. 'Go ahead and kill me. I don't care, I just don't care anymore. He was the only person I ever loved and he's dead and I just don't care anymore.'

I shoved the flashlight into his hands, and he crumpled

to the asphalt, wailing and cuddling his flashlight, rocking back and forth. A car full of drunks hissed over the Ripley Avenue bridge and down the ramp above us, fleeing through the night down black and wet streets, heading home or to another gaily lighted bar rife with music and dancing and sweaty women with bright eyes and lips like faded rose petals. As the driver down-shifted, the exhaust belched, the tires snickered across the slick pavement, a girl's shrill laughter flew out, abandoned like an empty beer can in the skid. The colored lights from the discreet Riverfront sign reflected off the dark asphalt, wavering as the wind sifted the rain, glowing distantly like the lights of a city beneath a black sea. I replaced Crider's rotor and slammed the hood, listening to his mewling, then squatted beside him, offered him my drink and handkerchief. He sniffled and took both; he snorted into the cloth, sipped at the drink, then asked, 'Why do you want to know about Ray and me?'

'His sister is in town –'

'His sister?'

'Right.'

'She's a nice lady. I was concerned when Ray asked her to stay with us last summer, but she was very nice, never judged us, never complained about – Ray and me – living together. She mothered Ray a bit, you know, and he didn't like that very much, but she didn't smother him. Say, why is she in town?'

'She doesn't believe that Raymond's death was a suicide –'

'Well, of course it wasn't,' he interrupted.

'– and she asked me to look into it.'

'Why didn't you say so?' he asked, wide-eyed again.

'Habit,' I said. 'People don't usually tell me what I want if I tell them what I want.'

'Oh.'

'Why don't you think he could have committed suicide?'

'Oh, Ray just wasn't the type. He had come to terms with his . . . his predilections. And though he was a wild man sometimes, he had enough sense not to mess around with heroin. That's what it was, wasn't it?'

'So I heard.'

'Well, Ray just wouldn't have. He was happy, in his own way. He thought he was bad, you know, tough, but he wasn't really. Just shy and quiet, a really sweet boy beneath his wildness.'

'So I keep hearing,' I said, thinking perhaps that I should begin to believe it. He offered me the drink, but I shook my head. 'You have a cigarette?' I asked. He shook his head sadly, his eyes shining with trust. He patted me on the leg; we were old buddies now. He told me about his love affair with Raymond Duffy, and it was properly sad, but nothing seemed to have anything to do with those cruel blank eyes I had seen glowering above the beard as Lawrence Reese destroyed the three sawyers, nothing to do with a kid dead on a toilet seat, the nail locked into the fatal vein. Nothing.

'What about friends? Who were his friends?' I asked, stopping Crider before he mourned his lost love into hearts and flowers.

'We didn't have any friends. We didn't need them,' he declared proudly.

'What about Lawrence Reese? Or Willy Jones?'

'Who are they?' he asked, gazing into my eyes with absolute innocence.

'Willy Jones is a dead drunk and Lawrence Reese is the world's largest faggot, complete with leather pants and purple eyeshadow,' I said, not hiding my disgust.

'Oh, I've heard of him.'

'Who?'

'The giant glitter queen.'

'From the Duffy kid?'

'Oh, no. Ray wouldn't have anything to do with trash like that,' he said.

'They were shacked up.'

'I can't believe that. But then . . .' He stopped, licked the rain off his lips, shaking his head.

'But then what?'

'Nothing.'

'What?'

'Oh, well, I guess it doesn't matter. I don't like to criticize the dead, but Ray did have one problem.'

'What was that?'

'He really was quiet and shy, you have to believe that, but he also wanted to be – an aggressive gay. A mean faggot, as he used to say. He used to stalk around the apartment, flashing his guns – his sister told you about the guns? – and threatening the straight world. He had the idea that he was going to be the last great faggot gunfighter or something – I mean, for God's sake, whoever heard of a faggot gunfighter in this day and age?

But Ray was determined that nobody was ever going to make fun of him for being gay.'

'I thought you said he was happy with his life.'

'Oh, he was. Very happy. Very manic and almost never depressed, except around other people. Sometimes, you know . . .' He paused.

'Sometimes what?'

'Well, frankly, sometimes he scared me when he was happy. He liked to do that Yul Brynner trick from *The Magnificent Seven*, you know – draw and pull the trigger of his pistol before you could clap your hands. He had won all sorts of prizes in quick-draw contests, or whatever they're called, you know –'

'I know,' I said. Crider wasn't any help at all; his image of the Duffy kid was as confused as mine had become. Maybe it was true love and blindness, the old routine. So I changed directions. 'When did you see him last?'

'Several months ago.'

'What did you talk about?'

'Oh, we haven't talked since – since we split up last summer. We took a vow,' he said, bowing his head. Then he added apologetically, 'I've got a family. But every time I saw him on campus, it was so hard, you know, not to run over –'

'I know,' I said, patting his shoulder, wondering what warm bed Helen Duffy slept in while I hunkered in the cold rain. 'Do you know anybody who might have talked to him lately?'

'No. I don't know. Maybe.'

'Could you ask around?'

'I guess so. Around the department.'

'I wasn't exactly thinking about academic friends.'

'Oh. Well, I don't see those people much anymore, you know.'

I knew, but I didn't think he wanted to hear about it. I stood up, my old legs quivering under me, and wiped the rain out of my face. I said, 'Could I, ah, pay for your jacket?'

'Oh, that's not necessary.'

'I'm sorry.'

'Oh, it's not important, you know,' he said, clambering awkwardly to his large feet. He handed me my wet handkerchief and the empty plastic cup. 'Not important . . .'

'I, ah, fixed your car,' I said.

'Oh, thanks.'

'Take care,' I said, remembering his wife's voice and wishing them a better life than they had had so far, then I climbed into my rig, my wet pants sticking to the seat as I settled behind the wheel.

'So long,' he shouted as I drove away. I glanced back to wave. He was standing hesitantly at the door of his station wagon, staring back toward the bar, like a man who had left something behind. He shut his car door and walked back toward the lighted lobby.

I cruised the motels on the east side with no real purpose in mind – just an aimless, habitual shifting about – thinking perhaps I'd find Helen Duffy to tell her not to waste her money. These transient rooms were my haunts. Bribed night clerks and bugged rooms. The muttering plaints of illicit love, the refrain of muffled springs. Startled faces and scurrying bodies frozen in the explosion of the flash. Penises as flaccid as ruined breasts. Then the dull courthouse routine: professional testimony, shamed faces.

Tired of myself, I made one last swing through the Riverfront lot, hoping to see Vonda Kay venturing out into the rain. We could go home, have breakfast, smoke a little dope, and sleep comforted by the sound of the creek, the soft brush of the spruce needles, the placid warmth of two old veterans, our nerves ruined in the front lines of love and failure. But she walked out of the bar with another man.

As I drove away, my headlights swept across the line of cars stalled in front of the rooms. Dick's van was there. The lights of 103 were still on; dark upright figures hovered behind the drapes, measuring the room with strides and outflung arms – shadows that merged, then flew apart. At least I knew her room number now. I drove home to my empty log house, where the creek complained and the spruce needles rattled harshly against my windows.

7

By morning the rain had moved on, and at nine o'clock, when I knocked on Helen Duffy's motel room door, the puddles were retreating before the hot glare of a summer sun, the cool, damp respite destroyed with a vengeance. I was dry again, and Dick's van was gone.

She came to the door, keeping the safety chain fastened, but she peeped through the open crack as if she didn't feel safe at all. The same green robe, clutched to her neck, glowed at me, her red hair draped across her shoulders, and the same horde of pink tissues huddled about the carpet. But she was different this time; she didn't seem to know who I was.

'Remember me?' I said. 'I'm the one who loves you.'

'Wonderful,' she muttered. 'Can I go back to sleep now? I've had rather a long night.'

'Sure,' I said, full of cheer and energy. 'I just wanted to be sure I was still working for you before I deposited your checks.'

'I don't seem to have any other choices.'

'I'll take that as a vote of confidence. Are you going to stay here?'

'Yes,' she answered, daubing at her galled nose with a scrap of toilet paper. 'Why?'

'If you want me to call you, when and if I find out anything, you'd better leave word at the desk.'

'Whatever for?'

'They aren't very fond of me here.'

'I can imagine that,' she said. I couldn't tell if she was smiling. She blew her nose fiercely. Her face, pillow-wrinkled, and her hair, ruffled by the toils of sleep, hadn't spent the night cradled by any fond lovers, which is why I felt so good. 'Why aren't they fond of you?'

'This is a classy motel. They don't want no second-rate peepers or transom-sneakers to bother their guests.' Or breaking down doors and snipping safety chains with bolt cutters to take dirty pictures either.

'I see. All right, I'll inform them. Have you found out anything yet?'

'I've only had one night, but I'm still working on it.'

'Wonderful,' she said again, pursing her soft, tired mouth.

'You look like a woman who needs a good-morning kiss,' I said brightly, but she had already closed the door in my face.

A family of tourists filed past, glancing at me from the corners of sleep-swollen eyes – vacationers escaped from some suburban hell – the leading demon festooned in electric-blue curlers, the imps draped with pistols and leather vests, and the poor devil caught between, sagging toward a lower, more ulcerated circle. And they were no more startled than I was, when the door opened again and a vision of swift red and green slipped out and blessed me with those soft, tired lips, then flew back inside before my arms could encircle her.

'Don't gawk, Leonard,' the witch growled, but Leonard gawked his heart away.

'Who are those guys, Leonard?' I asked the little boy. But he didn't know either, so he drew and fired, shooting now but facing years of questions later, his cap pistol flashing with smoke and flame. I clutched my chest, reeled against a parked car, groaning, 'Ya got me, Leonard.'

He grinned like little boys should: ear-to-ear toothless gaps. It was probably the high point of his vacation until his mother jerked him away, whipping him along behind her like a banner, grunting, 'Come on, Leonard.'

'Hey, lady,' I shouted from the sidewalk. 'What kind of world is it, when the only fun left for little boys is shooting old men?'

'Drunk,' she hissed at me, then scurried down the sidewalk toward a well-deserved breakfast.

'Fucking-A!' I shouted, laughing. Leonard grinned as he disappeared, and the poor devil tried gamely not to.

I rose, still laughing, the gentle kiss still warm on my mouth, not having to fake my morning cheer anymore. Thirty-nine wasn't too late to begin. So I went to work. Just as if I knew what I was doing.

The county coroner, Amos Swift, had been a long-time friend of my father's, and he owed me four hundred dollars from a poker game so far in the past that neither of us really remembered the circumstances. Amos tried to like me, but he never made any bones about how he felt about my divorce work. I'd never had occasion to ask him a professional question, so I had no idea how he might react. But he owed me money, and if I couldn't make sense out of the Duffy kid's life, maybe I could of his death.

'How the hell are you, Milo?' he grumbled happily as I walked into his office. 'Say, I haven't forgotten the markers, lad, but I'm just a little short right now. If you're strapped, I can let you have some of it, but if you're not, I can sure make better use of it. Some of us are heading for Reno this weekend, and you know how it is, you can't win without playing.'

Amos was one of those fat, jolly pathologists who acted as if violent death was a chance everybody took, as if the song of the bone saw caused him shivers of delight. But he and I both knew that he smoked cigars to keep away the antiseptic stink of the morgue, that he had become county coroner because he preferred to take his chances with the dead rather than the dying. He was a better autopsist than Meriwether County needed or deserved.

'But, lad, if you're down on your luck, I'll do my damnedest to come up with some of it, and, hell, I know you're having hard times but, dammit, it's hard times everywhere nowadays.'

'Let me have a cigar, Amos,' I said, sitting down, 'so I can stand yours.'

He did, but with great reluctance, as if it were money.

'Treat it sweetly, lad, that's a real Havana. And, say, if you run into Muffin, let him know I'm down to my last two boxes and smoking slow. Don't know where that boy finds them, and don't want to know, but it saves me a trip to Canada and maybe a bust. God, this is a sweet berth, lad, and I sure as hell would hate to lose it next election for smuggling Communist cigars.'

'I'll tell him,' I said, starting to bite off the end of the long cigar.

'Goddammit, boy, don't bite it,' he huffed, handing me his clippers. 'Look at that,' he added, waving his fuming cigar at me, the end of it as immaculate as when it had left the wrapper. 'Be gentle, dammit. Hate to see a man mangle a good cigar. How much do you need?'

'Don't worry about the money,' I said, drawing smoke and blowing it toward his relieved face. 'I'm here on business.'

'What business could we have, boy? You ain't dead and I'm already divorced.'

'I'd like some information about an autopsy you did a few weeks ago.'

'Has the inquest been held?'

'Yes,' I said.

'Then it's a matter of public record.'

'I know,' I said. 'I looked at the record before I came downstairs, but it didn't tell me what I want to know. I want to know what you think, not what went into the record.'

'Who was it?'

'A kid named Raymond Duffy. An OD up at the Wilomot Bar.'

'I remember,' he said, waving his thick hand through a cloud of smoke. 'A clear overdose.'

'Of what?'

'Well, hell, as I remember, everything. Alcohol, barbiturates and heroin.'

'Suicide or accident?'

'Who the hell knows? Some of both. The kid probably tried to settle down while he was waiting for a fix, then got hold of better junk than he was used to. We called it accident, but an insurance company would make suicide out of it, and who knows what really happened?'

'No marks of foul play?'

'Depends what you call foul play. He had a recent contusion on his right shoulder, which looked like a hickie, and there was evidence of anal intercourse recently, plus a sore throat.'

'A sore throat?'

'A dose of the clap, Milo. The kid was a fruit.'

'So I hear,' I said. 'How long had he been an addict?'

'Just guessing, I'd say around a month. Certainly not much longer.'

'Any other interesting facts?'

'Not that I can remember. I can dig up the report, if you want to see it.'

'That's okay,' I said. 'Thanks.'

'Sure. Say, what was that last hand anyway?'

'You tried to run four spades at a pair of sevens.'

'That's right, kid. I remember now. Dammit, boy, what kind of fool stays in against a broke man, four spades, and a four-hundred-dollar bet?' he asked, pinching his nose.

'You pinch your damn nose sometimes when you run a bluff, Amos.'

'I'll be goddamned,' he exclaimed, sitting up and staring at his thumb and index finger. 'Who knows about that?'

'Everybody in town, Amos.'

'I'll just be damned. Thanks, boy, I'll remember that. By God, you might be as good a player as your old man, and that son of a bitch was so good drunk that I wouldn't even play with him sober.'

'No sweat,' I said, 'he wasn't ever sober.'

'That's for damn sure.'

'Besides, he didn't have to worry about losing money.'

'That's for sure. Say, boy, don't forget to tell Muffin about those cigars.'

'Sure,' I said from the door. 'Say, one more thing. Why did you have his hair cut and his beard shaved?'

'Wasn't us, lad. When he came in, he was slicker than a preacher's kid. Say, Milo, what's this all about?'

'The sister doesn't believe the death was either suicide or accident.'

'Well, I'm sorry for her,' Amos said quietly. 'Damn sorry. Either she's blind or crazy.'

'Neither,' I said.

'Hell, boy,' he said, rising and walking around the desk to pat me on the shoulder, 'if you believe that, you're both. Sorry I wasn't much help.'

'Join the crowd,' I said, handing him back the dead cigar. 'Throw that away for me, will you?' I left him staring down at the cigar as if it were the corpse of a favorite son.

'Goddammit, boy,' he said as I closed the door.

I stopped at my office to check the calls and think about what Amos had said. The trouble was, though, that I believed Amos. The Duffy kid had either died of an accident or a suicide, died by his own unhappy hand. I didn't want to tell Helen Duffy just that. I thought perhaps I could shed some light on why, but Reese wouldn't talk to me and Willy Jones was dead. As I pondered that, Simon wandered in, still draped in the overcoat, stooped as if the burden might collapse his spine, his second-hand wing-tip cordovans ruffling the hem of the coat as it flittered behind him, almost touching the floor. I held up my hand so he would wait quietly while I returned the single call the answering service had given me. It was from Nickie DeGrumo. As I dialed I wondered what he wanted. But only briefly. I really wondered if Helen Duffy would kiss me again when I told her about her little brother.

When I asked the Riverfront switchboard operator for Nickie, she rang the bar, but Mama D. answered the telephone. Even though she had been out West for years, her accent was still thickly East Coast Italian. If she was a daughter of the family, I assumed that she had had a very protected youth, and I wondered how Nickie had managed to ferret her out of her father's house. Her papa mustache accent wasn't endemic, though, since her cousins all sounded like television announcers. Over the telephone, I could hear her heavy breathing, then Nickie's distant voice saying that he would take the call in his office. Instead of saying 'Hello' when she picked up the telephone, he told Mama to hang up, which she did after a long silence.

'Milo,' I said. 'What's happening, Nickie?'

'How's the boy, Milo, how's the boy?'

'Fine,' I sighed. 'What can I do for you?'

'Oh, drop around for a drink,' he said, trying to sound cheerful, but his voice still had an edge to it. 'On me, Milo, on me.'

'Okay. I'll drop in sometime.'

'Now would be better, Milo. Right now if you can make it.'

'I'm on my way to lunch, Nickie.'

'Listen, Milo, this is important. I'll spring for the lunch.'

'What do you want, Nickie?' He must be desperate to offer a free lunch.

'Got a job for you.'

'What sort of a job?'

'Can't discuss it over the phone, Milo. But hell, boy, I know you can use the business, and this might be worth two or three grand.'

'Who do you want me to kill?'

'Huh?'

'Just a joke. What's the job?'

'Not over the phone,' he said melodramatically. 'Just come on out.'

'I don't know, Nickie.'

'Hell, Milo, I'll pay for your time even if you don't take the job. How's that, huh? Pay you for the day.'

'That's expensive.'

'Ah, how much?'

'Hundred and a half,' I said, raising my fee for Nickie.

'Christ, Milo, I didn't know . . . What the hell, it's only money. Come on out. That's fine if you come out now.'

I didn't like to be pushed, but for that sort of money I

guessed I could stand having lunch with Nickie, so I said I'd see him shortly.

'And, Milo . . .'

'Yeah?'

'If you could act like you just dropped in for lunch, I'd appreciate it. Understand?'

'You don't want Mama D. to know, right?'

'Oh, no, nothing like that. It's just that . . .'

'I understand,' I interrupted. 'See you in ten minutes.'

'Great,' he said, trying on the happy voice again, but I hung up before he could get started again.

'I wonder what he wants?' I asked myself, but loudly enough for Simon to hear.

'Who?' he asked, pausing in midshuffle.

'Nickie DeGrumo.'

'Whatever it is, boy, don't take a check from that cheap asshole.'

'Yes, sir,' I said.

'You going out there?'

'I guess so.'

'Can I go?' he asked, his weathered face cocked. 'Just for the ride. This is one of those goddamned boring days, so why don't you take me along?'

'I'll meet you at Mahoney's when I come back. Tell you all about it. How's that?'

'Goddammit, boy, you ain't got no respect for me, do you? You're so smart. Think I'm just an old drunk, don't you? Well, just g-go on out there and make a fool of yourself. See if anybody gives a shit.'

'Easy, you old fart. You'll have a stroke. I got something else going too. Maybe you can help.'

'Don't patronize me, boy,' he said grandly, then shuffled out the door.

'Stay sober,' I said, but Simon didn't look back.

Nickie met me in the lobby with a barrage of greetings, which I ignored, asking him what he wanted.

'All business and no pleasure, huh, Milo? Makes for a hard life,' he said, squeezing my arm. If it hadn't been Nickie, I might have thought he was being condescending.

'That's right,' I said. 'What's the job?'

'Come on, I'll buy you a drink,' he said.

I followed him into the nearly empty bar, to the booth in the corner occupied by the sensual foursome the night before. As I waited for Nickie to order the drinks from the day manager, I found myself checking between the vinyl cushions for change, a habit left over from following my father through the bars. I expected to find a used condom or a pecker track, but discovered sixty cents in change and a bobby pin.

'CC ditch, brandy soda no ice,' I heard Nickie tell the guy behind the bar. Somebody had told Nickie once that cold drinks caused stomach cancer. No ice in his drinks was Nickie's single gesture toward good health. At the other end of the bar, where she perched eternally, Mama D. rang the drinks, and the register obediently coughed up the ticket.

'Sign it for me, will you, Mama?' Nickie asked.

Without stirring her obese body, she turned her head toward him, her fat face haughty with aquiline disdain, her eyes like obsidian chips. A slight smile, like a knife mark in fresh dough, cut her face, and I expected cachinnations, but she answered in an oddly pleasant voice, 'You sign, Nickie. The books.'

And he signed. Walked all the way down the bar and signed the ticket. Her pudgy hand caught his, patted it once, then turned him loose. He carried the drinks over to the booth, unable to hide the disgust on his face from me, but Mama D. smiled like a happy mother as she watched him walk away from her.

'Listen,' he said, handing me my drink. 'I need a big favor, Milo, really big.'

'I thought you said a job.'

'Oh, yeah, it is. The favor is – to start right away, this afternoon.'

'Doing what?'

'Well, listen, this is kind of complicated, Milo,' he said, patting his dyed hair carefully, as if he didn't want to dirty his smooth hands. 'I, ah, got this friend, Milo, you know, and this, ah, friend has a friend, a lady, you understand, kinda like a practice wife.' He smiled at his own joke. 'And he had to leave town suddenlike, you know, and he sort of wants to know what his lady friend does. While he's not around, you understand. And my friend is a very important man, you know, ah, can't afford to have lady friends who – who mess around, you know.'

'I know, Nickie. That's how I made my living,' I said.

'Right, right. That's why I called you, Milo boy. You're a professional,' he said, smiling broadly. 'Listen, money's no object, so my friend wants you to handle this, you know. Twenty-four hours a day.'

'Nickie, I have to sleep sometimes.'

'Oh, yeah, I understand. But full time, you know, whatever you usually do – in a case like this.'

'Sure,' I said, already thinking that I could hire Freddy and Dynamite, charge the rented car and mobile phone to Nickie, and still make a nice price without turning a finger. 'How long?'

'Two, maybe three weeks. Till my friend gets back, you know.'

'That's going to cost a pretty penny,' I said.

'Like I said, Milo boy, money's no object.'

'Must be nice.'

'What's that?'

'For money not to be an object.'

'Oh, yeah,' he said, smiling again. 'Yeah, I'll bet it is.' Then he finished his drink in one gulp. 'Another?'

'No, thanks,' I said, but he had already gone toward the bar. While he was gone, I dumped the change into the ash tray for the waitress next on duty. When he came back, I said, 'Thanks. I'll go out to the rig and get a contract.'

'Oh, no, Milo,' he said quickly, then lifted his drink, gunned half of it. 'Nothing written down, boy-o.' Then he rubbed his chest and muttered, 'Goddamned soda.'

'What?'

'Goddamned soda give me indigestion.' His smile was gone, his face old and tired again. 'But, listen, no contract, huh? You understand? Nothing written down. My friend wouldn't like that, you know.'

'I don't like that, Nickie. If there's any trouble, my ass is left hanging out.'

'Trouble? What sort of trouble?'

'You never can tell, Nickie, not with a deal like this. Suppose the lady sees me following her and decides to call the cops –'

'Don't worry about that, Milo, she ain't the type.'

'Okay, what if I catch her in the sack with some dude, and your friend decides not to pay?'

'Don't worry about that,' he said.

'It happens.'

'Listen, I'll – I'll guarantee your fee, Milo, you know. You trust me, don't you?'

How do you tell a guy you don't trust him?

'It's just not good business, Nickie. You understand?'

'Yeah.'

'So either sign a contract or pay me up front.'

'How much?' he asked hesitantly, looking very unhappy.

'Let's see, two weeks, say twenty-five hundred.'

'Christ, Milo, I can't . . .'

'Then let's forget it, Nickie,' I said, standing up to leave.

'Okay,' he said, grabbing my arm. 'Okay. Just wait a minute, let me think a minute, you know.' Thinking involved finishing his drink and rubbing his belly to ease the indigestion. 'All right, Milo, all right. Be right back.'

As he walked away I watched him. Unlike his wife, I didn't have any fond glances for him. Nickie walked like a scared man, lost in his own house. His friend must be big stuff, I thought, if Nickie was going to front twenty-five hundred bucks. Then I began to worry. What if

Nickie only came back with part of the money? What if he wanted to give me a check? But before I could worry too much, he came back to the table and slipped a white envelope out of his inside coat pocket.

'It's all there,' he said, handing it to me. 'No need to count it.'

'Sure,' I said, not counting it but peeking. Nickie's money was as old and worn-out as he was. I thought he must have hit his mad-money stash. 'Want a receipt?'

He wanted one but shook his head. 'Nothing written down, right? You don't even write down reports, you understand. You come tell me, you know, casual like. Okay? I trust you, Milo boy.' Being that close to money seemed to restore some of Nickie's lost confidence, so I tried for icing on the cake.

'Listen, Nickie, for an extra three bills a week, I can put a mike in her telephone that will pick up a fart in the next room.'

'My God, Milo, no bugs. Jesus, my friend . . . he wouldn't like that at all. Jesus,' Nickie blurted, scared again.

'Okay. I'll just tail her, watch the house. No more.'

'Perfect,' he said, touching my arm. 'Just right.'

'Okay. Who's the lady? Where's she live?'

'Huh?'

'What's the poop on the lady?'

'Huh? Oh, the poop. Christ, Milo, I haven't heard that since the war. God, that seems like a long time ago.'

'It was.'

'Yeah. Remember what this town was like then? A good town, Milo, a goddamned good town. Not so many tourists, no fucking hippies or dope or any of that crap. Kinda makes me glad I . . . we never had kids, you know.'

I nodded politely. For that sort of money, Nickie could tell me his life story, and I'd even act interested.

'Yeah, but, Christ, I used to really like kids, you know. Remember when I had those goddamned icecream trucks? I used to follow them around sometimes. At first I was just checking to see how much the drivers were screwing me, but later it was just to watch the kids. Damn, it was great to see them scooting out of their houses when they heard those goddamned bells. And when I lost my ass, I put in that little golf course, you know. Everybody told me it was easy, but, goddammit, the kids loved it. Everything doesn't have to be hard, does it? I mean, for Christ's sake, things don't have to be so hard.'

I nodded again, wondering if I should offer him my handkerchief, but he had something better. He went for two more drinks. It was strange to see Nickie boozing harder than me.

'Who's the lady? Where's she live?' I asked again, reminding him of business when he came back with the drinks.

Nickie stared at me for a moment, swallowed air and belched quietly, then said, 'Goddamned soda.'

'Yeah.'

'Back to business, huh, Milo?'

'Right.'

'Okay. Her name is Wanda.'

'Wanda what?'

'Oh, Wanda – Smith.' He waited for me to object, but I didn't care if her name was Smith. 'My friend has a house on the slope south of town, in that new development, Wildflower Estates, the last house on the circle at the end of Wild Rose Lane.'

'What's the number?'

'Christ, Milo, that's such a classy development that they have names instead of numbers, you know. Wish to hell I could afford a place like that, but I got every loose penny tied up in this place,' he said sadly.

Not every penny, I thought, and none of them his.

'What's the name, then?'

'I'll be damned,' he said, looking very confused. 'I . . . my friend told me the name, but damned if I can remember it. You can't miss it, it's the last house on the street.'

'Okay,' I said. 'I guess I can find it. What's the lady look like?'

'Oh, Milo, she's something else. A real looker. A real lady,' he answered, his eyes glassy with the vision.

'That's a little abstract, Nickie.'

'Huh?'

'What color's her hair?'

'Kinda blond, strawberry blond, I think they call it.'

'How old?'

'Oh, Milo, just right. Not too young, not too old, you know. Just right.'

'Okay, Nickie, I'll handle it from there,' I said. It didn't matter to me what she looked like. I wasn't going to tell some Mafia fat cat that his lady was messing around, not even if I caught her giving head to the grocery boy. 'Just leave everything to me.'

'Huh?'

'I'll take care of everything.'

'Great. Great.'

'And won't write down a word.'

'Huh? Oh, yeah, right. And listen, Milo boy – my friend, he likes the people who work for him,' Nickie said carefully, 'he likes them to just work for him, you know. So if you got anything else going, maybe you ought to – to think about dropping it. I think I can get my friend to cover what it costs you.'

'I don't have anything going.'

'Huh?'

'I said I'm free. Say, Nickie, are you going deaf?'

'No, of course not. Why?'

'Because you don't seem to hear me too well.'

'Yeah, well, I've got this goddamned ringing in my ears, you know. Been working too hard, I guess, need a vacation, you know. Maybe I can – get away soon . . . Goddamned soda,' he said, belching again.

'How's business?' I asked, tired of Nickie's friend and his practice wife.

'Huh?'

'Business. How is it?'

'Oh, couldn't be better,' he said, glowing now. 'I'm making so much money that it's making me feel young again, you know.' He paused for effect, then winked. 'Maybe I'll get me one of those practice wives, huh.'

What a pathetic creep. Of course business was great. Illegal whiskey, hijacked beef, and dirty money. I had never liked Nickie very much, just pitied him occasionally, but now that I was working for him, I gave up even the pity.

'This friend, Nickie. Is he family?' I returned his wink.

'Oh, no, he's . . .' Then he realized what the wink meant. 'Christ, Milo, don't do that. Why the hell does everybody think I'm – I'm in the Mafia or something, some kind of goddamned gangster, just – just because I'm – I'm Italian,' he sputtered, his face red and hurt. 'I mean, Christ, Milo, don't kid me about that.'

'Sorry, Nickie,' I said, no longer angry at him, just sorry again, almost sorry enough to tell him why everybody thought he was Family. 'People see too many movies, I guess.'

'Christ, Milo, you don't know how much – how much I hate those goddamned slick East Coast bastards. I'd like to fix those bastards, you know, those bastards,' he muttered pathetically, a child's threat. Then he stood up, adding, 'Stay on this thing, okay, Milo?'

'I said I would.'

'Huh?'

'I got it, Nickie.'

'Yeah,' he said, then loosed a short bark of laughter. 'Yeah, you got it.'

'Sure,' I said, holding back the renewed anger. Once again, I had the feeling that Nickie was condescending to me, that there was some sort of antagonism seeping out of him. But I had always known that Nickie was unhappy behind all his smiles and gladhands. As he stood up, trying to look calm and self-assured, his shoulders slumped beneath the weight of his coat, his neck bowed under the weight of his dyed hair, and his fingers kneaded belches out of his sunken chest. He couldn't hide the fatigue of a long life of being nobody, a fatigue I understood more than I wanted to. To be childlike might keep a man young, but to be treated like a child makes him old too soon.

'Say, Nickie?'

'Huh?'

'Want some free advice?'

'What's that?' he asked, not wanting any advice from me at all.

'This afternoon, call up Meriwether Vending and order a couple of punchboards. They'll even tell you which cops to pay off.'

'That's illegal,' he said righteously.

'No shit. But you've always had the only bar in town without at least one punchboard. Makes the local people nervous. They think you're up to something really illegal, if you're afraid to have a few punchboards.'

'I'll be damned. I wonder how come Ma – how come I never thought of that?'

'Because she's still a stranger here,' I said quietly.

'Huh?' But he had heard me.

'Nothing.'

'Keep in touch, Milo,' he said, then walked away, muttering to himself, his boots slapping the carpet.

When I finished the first drink, I remembered the lunch that Nickie had beat me out of. It could go on the expense sheet. I left the other drinks untouched. As I walked through the lobby, Nickie was engaged in a serious conversation with an expensively dressed man. The motel manager, I thought, another of Mama D.'s inevitable cousins. He listened politely to Nickie, nodding his head without interest, as if he were being told a very boring story by a child. He was listening to Nickie but he was watching me.

On the way back to the office, I drove by Wildflower Estates, down to the end of Wild Rose Lane. Wanda wasn't visible, but there was a new Mustang parked in the garage. Poppy-red or something like that. I wrote the licence number down, then poked around the neighborhood, looking for a place to stake out the house. On the next street up-slope, a house was under construction. I knew the builder, so Freddy and Dynamite could hang out there without calling attention to themselves.

Back in the office, I called the builder, and after I reminded him that he had borrowed the money for his first house from my father, he agreed that he could use an extra hand in the daytime and a free nightwatchman. Then I started to make out another deposit slip, my second in two days, which didn't happen too often. I stopped, looked at the roll, thought about the IRS. The money was mostly twenties and fifties, with only a few hundreds, and the bills looked like they had been carried around in a wino's pockets, stuffed hither and yon, then ripped out at a wild moment and scattered across a damp bar. I wondered if Nickie had taken to rolling winos, but he was such a coward that the idea was ludicrous. Nearly as comical as the idea of paying taxes on unrecorded cash.

I took out five hundred and put the rest into the large safe in the corner which said CATTLEMAN'S BANK AND TRUST, MERIWETHER COUNTY, MILTON CHESTER

MILODRAGOVITCH, PRESIDENT. That had been my grandfather. My great-grandfather wanted his son to have an American name. There was also a sign hanging from the handle which claimed that the safe was an antique and asked prospective safecrackers not to use dynamite or a crowbar or acid. A combination was printed at the bottom of the card. The wrong combination. It wasn't much of a joke, but then it wasn't much of a safe either.

When I leaned out the window to see the bank clock, it was only eleven, but I thought I'd have lunch anyway. On Nickie.

8

So Nickie had a friend who had plenty of money and a practice wife. Nickie, with his little boy's allowance and too real wife, must have been furious with envy. Perhaps that explained the odd flashes of hostility. But it was too lovely a day to worry about it.

As I strolled down to Mahoney's, careful not to jostle the tourists who clotted the sidewalks as if they owned both the streets and the summer morning, I begrudged them the day. But I only lived there; they were the paying customers, rubbernecking and crowing and snapping endless color slides of the cobalt sky and the peaks – white hot with new snow above the dark cool reaches of pine – and the lower slopes, which blazed with new grass, bright yet tender, yellow-green beneath the clean rush of sunlight.

I wondered if Nickie's friend was among the vacationers, out West for two weeks of expensive fun. Somehow, I'd never thought of gangsters on vacation, thinking perhaps that they enjoyed their work more than some poor slob condemned to an eternal salesman's smile, more grimace than grin, or spot-welded next to an assembly line, slapping door handles on Gremlins as they trundled endlessly past in mechanical cortege. But perhaps not. What did I know about the rigors of organized crime? The nearest I had been to it was an occasional hard look from one of Mama D.'s cousins when my voice was too loud or my tip too small. Maybe organized crime was hard work – all that corruption and graft and worry, the discreet violence undertaken with an air of urbane toughness. Hell, I had been corrupted on the local level, and the paltry payoffs I had received to overlook the punchboards and electronic slots were so small that they seemed almost moral in a world that made folk heroes out of airline hijackers and box-office successes out of Mafia dons, with never a mention of the Mafia to avoid legal action; a world where politicians were for sale but overpriced; where giant corporations shouted the ideals of capitalism, then fixed prices; where even the President shaved without looking in the mirror.

Maybe I shouldn't have been so smug, not when I was walking down the street with a pocketful of dirty money, money I had lied to obtain and would lie to keep and would spend without a single twinge of conscience. But then, that's one of the great things about living in America: moral superiority is so damned cheap.

So I could saunter into Mahoney's, out of the sunlight and the dark clusters of vacationers, a smile on my face, no guilt in mind, and wish Nickie's friend a grand time out West, lots of fun and summer adventures and jerky home movies. Shots of him feeding candy to a surly sow bear with cubs. Or walking into a swollen creek in brand-new chestwaders. Or traversing a glacier in sparkling white sneakers. Or roasting his weenie in Old Faithful.

But in the cool shade of Mahoney's, the regulars were always on vacation, patiently waiting for their turn at that great trout stream in the sky, where the fish are always rising from deep clear pools to take the fly snugly in their mouths, where the women wait quietly on the banks, lovely and kind, where the nearest bar is only a cast away, and when you go in, your friends greet you with fond jokes and the bartender never mentions your tab.

'By God, boys, this is the life,' I exclaimed to three of the best as I joined them. Simon, Fat Freddy, and Stone-faced Pierre. They greeted me in dulcet tones – a belch, a grunt, a soft murmuring babble.

'Where did you get the goddamned fish, boys?' I asked, pointing at the mound of bones, as clean and white as cat's teeth, heaped in the center of the table.

Freddy leaned back, intent upon his toothpick. Simon tilted forward into his open notebook. Pierre glared at me with marbled eyes. They ignored, as if it were a corpse, the remains of the last of the smoked steelhead, which Leo and I had brought back from Idaho and which, all things considered, only cost thirty or forty dollars a pound to catch.

'Well, hell, boys, if it was one of mine, I hope you enjoyed it,' I said, then waved at Leo for a round of drinks, circling my finger in the still air. A torpid fly tried to land on it, but missed and buzzed aimlessly away. Leo brought the shots and beers with a sheepish grin, so I knew who had divided the fish among the loafers. I handed him a twenty anyway, told him to put the change against my tab. He muttered something snide about the change being only a drop in some cosmic bucket. I told him to set them up for the house. On my tab.

When he rang the bell behind the bar, three sleeping winos rose from their stools, grinning, and two slipped in from the street. A small band of long-haired kids drifted toward the bar like calves at milking time. Everybody waved at me as if I were a movie star – one of them was the slim girl from Reese's front porch – then fell upon their drinks eagerly, ignoring me.

Once things had settled down, I gave Freddy a handful of Nickie's bills and told him to round up Dynamite, a rental car and a mobile telephone, setting my wino hounds loose on Wanda of Wild Rose Lane. I had used them before; they made a great team, cheap and carefully sober when working for me and oddly invisible. They were both local characters, recognized winos, and downtown they faded before the eyes of the good, sober folk. In the suburban developments, they used part-time jobs for cover, and looked like winos drying out or working a few days to support another binge. Their obvious failure to deal with life was a more effective means to cloud men's minds than any secret of the East.

Freddy was so happy to be working again that he discarded his frayed toothpick, replacing it with a brand-new one that smelled faintly of mint, then he rose and strode out of the bar, his shoulders back, his spine mightily erect, his stomach as rigid as a barrel. Pierre also rose, but more slowly, like a statue coming reluctantly to life, and headed for the john at a furious totter, where he would lean against the wall and wait for his tired bladder to empty, staring at everybody who came in, waiting until somebody, usually Leo, helped him rebutton his pants. Simon, who had overheard my talk with Freddy, scribbled madly in his red notebook.

'Bastard,' he muttered when he glanced up.

'What?'

'Let that fat bastard work for you, Milo. You must be crazy.'

'Hush, Simon.'

'I could have done it, I could have.'

'Simon, you can't drive a car.'

'That doesn't make any difference,' he said, then stared at me for a minute. 'I hear the lady is back in town.'

'What lady?'

'Don't be a wise ass, Milo. What's she doing back in town?'

I told him.

'What have you found out?' he asked.

I told him that too.

'What are you going to do now?'

'Well, goddammit, Simon, I don't know, but when I get through, I'll give you a written report.'

'I don't like the smell of this whole thing, Milo,' he said, disregarding the irony. 'Let me help.'

'Why don't you take that goddamned overcoat off before you have a heat stroke?'

'Hell, boy, it's cold.'

'That was yesterday, Simon.'

'It's always yesterday in here, boy.'

'It's at least a day behind, but I'm not sure if you have the right yesterday.'

'This was your old man's coat, wasn't it?'

'Looks like one he used to have.'

'Looks like it, hell. It is.'

'Okay, so what?'

'Wanna buy it, boy,' he said slyly, then grinned. 'Make you a good deal.'

'You old fart.'

'If you're going to sit there and call me names, boy, you have to buy me a drink.'

I waved at Leo, and he brought the drinks.

'To your old man,' Simon said, raising his shot glass. We drank, then he asked, 'So what's in your mind?'

'She paid for three days, so I'll give her three days. Try to find somebody who knew him, I guess, and ask some more stupid questions.'

'Reese knew him,' Simon said, smirking. 'Ask him.' Then he giggled like an old woman.

'Maybe I'll just do that,' I said, but my threats were as empty as Nickie's. Simon laughed so hard that I thought he would choke. To death, I hoped. 'What's so funny?'

'You, boy, you.'

'Thanks.'

'Anything for a friend. Want some help?'

'What did you have in mind? Fart and hope he faints?'

'That's not funny, Milo,' he grumbled, falling into a sulk. 'Goddamned faggot.'

'Yeah, but don't tell him,' I said.

'Maybe if you took Jamison along,' Simon said thoughtfully, 'Reese might behave.'

'Jamison wouldn't help me across the street if I was an old lady. Besides, I don't know where lovely Lawrence lives now. His old house is empty,' I said. 'And the neighborhood kids are tearing it down, stick by stick.'

'I'll bet Jamison knows where Reese is holed up.'

'Probably does,' I said, meaning to walk over to the police station to ask him just as soon as I finished my drink.

'Want me to help? I could ask around. Like before. I found him before you did,' he said.

'I don't know, old man, you might get hurt,' I answered, which made Simon so mad he lost his small connection with reality, spitting and sputtering curses. He became a foolish, tired old drunk, unruly gray hair and liver spots, his horny fingers knotted so tightly around the pencil stub that it seemed the lead must squirt out, spraying like ash across the empty glasses and fish bones.

'All right,' I said, 'you can help.'

'Thanks,' he managed to say. But not as if he meant it.

'Anything for a friend.'

'Sure.'

'You remember the old lady in the window? Next door to Reese's?'

'Yeah, sure. Why?'

'Why don't you go by and talk to her. See if you can get a description of some of the people who were living there. Maybe it will give us somebody to talk to who won't try to kill us.'

Simon nodded his head so furiously that he banged

his chin on the rim of his beer mug, then held his mouth as if he had a rock under his lower plate.

'I'll do it,' he mumbled, pounding his notebook as if he intended to make notes in iron. 'You can count on it.'

'All right. But promise me you won't go anywhere else. And stay sober.'

He nodded again, lifting his beer in agreement, but when he felt it in his hand, he set it down quickly, grinning.

'I'll finish my letter, Milo, then go see her before it rains.'

'It's not going to rain, you old fart.'

'Wanna bet?'

'Not with you about rain, old man.'

'What are you going to do?'

'Try to find Reese.'

'Be careful, boy.'

'You be careful, old man.'

'Sure,' he said. 'You care if the kid died on purpose or by accident?'

'Not really.'

'You got no curiosity, boy,' he said, turning back to his letter. 'And you don't care about nothing but the lady, huh?'

'Who are you writing to?'

He glanced up in disgust.

'What are you complaining about now?'

'Somebody ripped off my Social Security check. Right out of the mailbox.'

'What the hell can the government do?'

'Replace the son of a bitch!'

'You don't need the money.'

'What the hell difference does that make? I deserve it!' he shouted. And maybe he did.

'Take care,' I said, standing and patting his shoulder. Beneath the heavy tweed, his body felt as feeble as an old woman's. Stringy flesh on the verge of corruption, bones nearly dust. But he didn't look up, busy now with his protest, flailing at the political system with scrawled words. In the tranquil bar, among the wrinkled faces on the walls, secure from time, his nattering murmur was as peacefully eternal as a creek's plaint to stones, a hushed and wisely gentle sound, a finer silence, as much a part of my life as the rising and falling cycle of Hell-Roaring Creek. I ruffled his hair for luck, touched the parchment scalp, the fragile skull, making my amends, then I left him there in his repose.

On the way out, I glanced at the girl, Mindy, thinking to ask her about Reese, but she and a young boy were watching a fly circle the inside of a foam-encrusted beer mug, watching it with the vapid concentration of the perpetually stoned, so I left her alone. Outside, in the brilliant summer noon, among the creep of traffic and bedizened tourists, I realized that I hadn't had a vacation in years. They seemed too tiring to chance another. But I wondered if Helen Duffy needed a vacation, wondered where we might go, how tired we might be when we came back, and I smiled benignly at the frantic tourists.

As I walked over to the police station, I thought about what Simon had said about the Duffy kid. He was right about one thing. I didn't care about the kid. What little

I'd seen of him around the bars hadn't filled my heart with joy, and what I'd learned about him hadn't convinced me that my first impression was wrong. He might have been confused and unhappy, but he was still a bad kid. But I didn't think I'd tell Helen Duffy that.

I took a shortcut through an alley to avoid the crowded sidewalks, and at the far end a freak walked up to a large man dressed in logging clothes. The kid held his hand out shyly, as if he were panhandling, but the man hit the kid in the face, knocked him across the alley into a pile of garbage cans. I ran up, grabbing the man from behind as he advanced on the fallen kid to work him over with his boots. The kid didn't move, except to touch his swelling eye and brush away yesterday's garbage.

'Police!' the man shouted. 'Police!' He struggled in my grasp, swinging and kicking backwards with his high-heeled boots, catching my right shin. I changed holds and threw him against the wall, then hobbled over and kicked the fight out of him.

'Okay,' he groaned, clutching his gut as he rolled out of the garbage, lettuce pasted to his hair with Thousand Island dressing.

'Take the goddamned money,' he grunted, then tossed his wallet at my feet. 'You guys leave me alone, okay?'

'You guys? What the hell were you picking on the kid for?'

The kid tried to stand up, but slipped in the slops, falling to his hands and knees. I stepped over to see how he was, and the man lurched to his feet and ran down the alley, his heavy boots thudding, shreds of lettuce scattered behind him like dollar bills. I picked up his wallet and started after him, shouting, then the kid stood up again and ran off in the opposite direction, leaving me the alley and the wallet.

'Town's getting too goddamned nervous to live in,' I said.

The desk sergeant who accepted the wallet and my explanation looked vaguely familiar, but behind the bulletproof glass and his professionally calm policeman face, I couldn't place him. On the wall behind him, a platoon of riot helmets hung in rows, their dark plastic visors gleaming like the eyes of some fearful machine, and below them rows of gas masks sagged like empty faces. After the first protest march in the late sixties, during which only marchers were hurt, our local police officers had been hurriedly trained and equipped to handle riots up to the size of small wars, but nobody had been able to arrange one for them. The smoked plastic of the visors looked expectant, though, and as lethal as the racked shotguns.

When he had finished his report, I asked the distant, barricaded face if Jamison was in.

'Yes, sir,' came the metallic voice. Then he shut off the outside speaker and called Jamison's office over the intercom.

'He wants to know what you want?'

'To talk to his exalted lieutenancy,' I said. My shin was throbbing, and I wished I had kicked the logger one more time.

'About what?'

'Oh, goddammit, lad, just tell him I need to talk to him.'

'About what?'

'I want to report a crime.'

'What sort?'

'Against nature.'

'What?'

'Down on Main Street there's a pig fucking a goat.'

'Aren't you ever going to grow up?' Jamison asked after the boys in blue had conducted me to his office. Before I could answer, he asked, 'What the hell do you want? I'm busy and tired.'

He looked it, his clothes wrinkled and limp, his tie tangled at his throat. I didn't look like Cary Grant approaching forty, but Jamison looked ten years older than me.

'Yeah, well, you look tired,' I said, trying my best old-buddy smile. 'And, hey, I'm sorry about the trouble, but some of your help is a little arrogant. It was nice to see that dignified face get mad.'

'What do you want?' he repeated, having neither the smile nor the conversation.

'A favor.'

'You gotta be kidding.'

'Might help us both.'

'Get out. Get outa my life, Milo. Get outa town. Just get out.'

'Just listen a minute, okay? You owe me that.'

'I don't owe you the time of day,' he said.

'How many muggings and petty thefts you had in the last month?' I asked, playing it by ear.

'Read the papers, creep.'

'How many? How many kids arrested hooked on smack?'

'None of your business,' he said, but I knew I had guessed right for a change.

'Just go with me to see Lawrence Reese so I can ask him about the Duffy kid without getting killed, and maybe I can help you find out who's dealing smack in our fair city.'

He lowered his head as if thinking about what I said. His bald pate was damp and furrowed, his pudgy hands wrinkled with sweat. I nearly felt sorry for him. Being a cop is no fun, but Jamison looked as if he had never had any fun. Then he told me what he had been thinking, and I wiped the pity away like cold sweat.

'Milo, I've known you all my life, and you're a chicken-shit, corrupt scumbag, and I'm goddamned tired of knowing you. Get your ass out of my office.' He spoke quietly, which was worse than shouting, which gave me a glimpse of the depth of his disgust. Then he added, 'I'm sorry.'

I seldom get angry, but that did it – the pity and condescension in his apology.

'Let's drive out in the country, motherfucker, and talk about it,' I said as quietly as I could. 'Right now.'

Jamison stood up swiftly, then grunted and sank back into his chair, saying, 'You don't know how much I'd like that, Milo, but I don't have time for your kids' games. Just get out. I've got work to do.'

He went back to the reports on his desk. More sad than angry now, I left.

'What's going on?' the desk sergeant asked. He had been waiting just outside the door.

'No charge,' I said. 'The lieutenant is too busy to mess with scum like me.'

'How is he?' the kid inquired softly, as if we were standing outside a hospital room.

'Working too hard, but what's new.'

'That's for sure. Some goddamned crazy guy stopped two twelve-year-old boys on the Dottle bridge just after the movie let out last night. They didn't have any money, so he assaulted them. One's in the hospital; the other's in the river. They haven't found the body yet.'

'Catch the guy yet?'

'Nope.'

'Was it a junkie?'

'Probably, but who knows. They're sure making a mess out of my social life. We been on double shifts for a week now.'

'Yeah.'

'Say, Milo, how come you said that about the pig and the goat, huh? You were a law enforcement officer once.' The kid sounded honestly hurt.

'That was in another country,' I said.

'Yeah, it sure was. If things keep up like this, I'm moving to British Columbia.'

'Not a bad idea,' I said, moving around him.

'Hey, we recovered your property.'

'Great. How?'

'Two kids showed up at Deacon's store with all of it loaded in a wheelbarrow, and they got nervous when Deke started to check the hot sheet. When they ran, he pulled down on them with that .44 magnum he keeps below the counter.'

'Hit them?'

'Naw, they stopped too soon. Hell, even the wheelbarrow was hot. Kids had gall but no guts.'

'Yeah. Guess I ought to read the newspaper more often. When did all this happen?'

'Oh, a couple of days after you reported it. Hell, it wasn't even on the hot sheet yet.'

'How come it took so long to notify me?'

'Well, you know how paperwork is,' he drawled, scuffling the tile floor with his polished boot. 'We misplaced your complaint.' Then he grinned like a man who had more important things on his mind than paperwork. But I couldn't tell if it was Canada or crime.

When I opened the iron door between the administrative area and the front desk, my logger friend was standing there, examining his wallet, counting his money and checking his credit cards. I shut the door quietly and left by the back door. Out of the fluorescent gloom of the station and into the sunny afternoon. It should have been night. Or raining. Or something to account for the sudden lethargy of my legs.

9

Youth and strength might fail me and my sense of purpose be altered, but I knew how to get some of it back. I had a bag of whites in my other office; speed wasn't a good alternative, but it helped sometimes. I always had an odd notion that if amphetamines had been in vogue when I tried to play college football, I would have been an all-American guard instead of a bum. Speed reached inside me somehow, released the angry energy from its hiding place. It made me mean, but in my business that was sometimes necessary.

In Mahoney's, I ordered a plastic sandwich from Leo, then called my answering service, hoping Helen Duffy had called to take me off the case. But she hadn't. Mrs. Elton Crider had called and left word to call back, and Muffin had left a message, a song title: 'This is my year for Mexico.' I didn't know what it meant, so I returned Mrs. Crider's call. We had a brief conversation. Her husband hadn't come home the night before, but I didn't know where he was and told her so.

'Doesn't he ever stay out all night?' I asked, the fatigue making me more cruel than I meant to be.

'Sometimes,' she answered, 'but he usually goes to work.' She hung up curtly.

I sat down at the bar, since Simon had already left our booth, and had a beer with the packaged sandwich, wondering what Muffin had meant by his cryptic message.

'You shouldn't eat this kinda crap,' Leo said when he brought me the sandwich.

'You shouldn't sell it.'

'*Caveat emptor*, Milo,' he answered. But he didn't charge me for the sandwich.

I finished half of it, half a beer, then left the mess on the bar. When I came out of the cooler with enough whites in my pocket to start a small riot, Pierre was watching a long-haired kid and his little boy playing the shuffleboard machine, laughing and banging the chrome puck against the back of the machine. They were happy; Pierre wasn't. As I walked past him, I laid a hand on his shoulder, telling him not to worry, but I might as well have stroked a brick wall. His terrible glower had found focus. I waved at the freak and his kid, their matching ponytails bobbing with glee, and wished them love and luck.

In our state, children are allowed in bars. It's one of the few laws of which I approve. My warmest childhood memories were forged in bars. Not in zoos or camps, not on family outings or at church picnics, not with gracious gray-haired lady English teachers helping me love Shelley and Keats. All those things happened, but the bars counted more. Country bars with bowling machines and little balls that seemed to fit my hand and an endless supply of quarters. Cowboy bars, where all the men wore boots, and all the boots had stirrup scuffs. Darkened cocktail lounges and hushed conversations that had to be important. That's what I remembered fondly. And an old man, over eighty, whose withered arms were still strong from the years of farming, strong enough for me to chin myself on one of them. And a retired lady trick rider who taught me how to spin a loop, how to dance in and out. And all the stories, the bars and the drunks, and my father carrying me through them as if I were his good-luck charm, his familiar, his pride and joy.

After his death, I missed the bars just as hard as any alcoholic drying out. Perhaps my long quest after his discarded clothing was just an excuse to hang around the bars. Whatever, I guess I'm glad that children can be in bars here. It keeps them off the street, keeps the family together, and shows the children a world where the natural accidents of life can be forgiven with a shrug and an 'Oh, hell, he was just drunk.'

As I watched the father and son plumb the depths of Pierre's infernal machine, scattering lights and mechanical noises across the afternoon like golden coins on a table, I felt happy. But confused too. I'd seen the other side. I hoped nobody ever had to cover their torn bodies with a gray blanket or explain to a befuddled drunk driver that he had just killed somebody's son. Maybe there should be laws against automobiles, not drunks, but . . .

And the confusion stayed with me, a fierce muddle of mixed emotions and memories that gave me absolutely contradictory propositions. I wondered if only the simple-minded could keep one thing in mind, the simple-minded and the purposeful. To hell with it. I went to the bar for a whiskey. My hand trembled slightly as I raised it.

'How did you get to be a drunk, Leo?'

'Oh, Christ, Milo,' he answered, then stomped away on the duckboards as if he couldn't stand the sight of me.

I glanced at my tired face in the old muddy mirror behind the back bar. I didn't like it any more than Leo did, but I watched it, working on my drink, trying to think through things. It was difficult. I'd never spent much time thinking, depending usually on action akin to instinct – act instead of think. But now I was out of my depth; action wasn't enough. I needed a theory about Raymond Duffy, right, and a plan, a plan of action, right. Wasn't that how the world was conquered? With plans and theories, right? Decisions arrived at after due consideration of relevant data, right? But I didn't even know what constituted relevant data. I could, however, turn around to see Mindy, who was watching a brigade of flies march through dried beer foam.

'Mindy,' I said rather loudly. She looked up. 'Mindy, do you know where Lawrence Reese is living now?'

'Sure, man. He's crashed up at the Holy Light Hog Farm,' she answered quickly, not so stoned anymore. The Holy Light Hog Farm was a capitalist commune up in the Stone River Valley about forty miles north of Meriwether – a real, live, working hog farm, where pigs lived as daintily as princesses on acres of immaculate concrete. 'You going up to see him? Can we catch a ride?' she asked, nodding toward the boy sharing her table.

I wanted to talk to the girl and didn't need the boy along, but then I wondered if he knew Reese.

'Does he know Reese?'

'Naw, man, he's new in town.'

'Then he can't go,' I said. They shrugged and accepted it without a moment's rancor, just as if it had been a command from their guru. I wondered how far I could carry it.

Mindy stood up, I finished my drink, and we left. It wasn't a theory or a plan, but it was movement. Out of the bars and into the real world.

'You gonna kill him?' she asked calmly as she lit a joint on the outskirts of town.

'Hadn't planned to,' I answered, chuckling like a jovial insurance salesman. 'I just want to talk to him, that's all.'

'Well, don't ask him no questions, man,' she said, holding the hit and passing the joint to me. 'He ain't a bad dude, really, but he don't like questions worth a shit.'

I looked at the joint, then took it, had a small hit, just to relax. I could stop at the Willomot Hill Bar for beer, wash down two whites, smoke some more grass, and dope my way into courage. A noble American tradition.

We smoked the number silently, then I asked her if she lived at the Pig Farm.

'Hog Farm,' she corrected. 'No, man. I thought I'd crash up there for a few days, get some meals, then hit the road.'

'Where you headed?'

'Just on the road, man, outa this crazy place. The freaks out here are weird, man. Everybody into speed and pills and smack and pure damn meanness. I been lotsa places, man, but I ain't never been no place like this. There ain't no grass in town but homegrown, all the acid is cut with speed, and I ain't seen so many smack freaks since I left the East Coast.'

'Yeah,' I mused, either stoned or drunk, trying to be casual. 'Does Lawrence Reese deal smack?'

'Man, he'd deal pigshit if you could get off on it,' she answered, giggling. 'And there's loads of pigshit up there. I went up with Lawrence, but the dude who runs the place wanted me to work, and I told him I didn't leave the farm to end up shoveling pigshit for some god-damned hayseed freak.' She giggled again. 'Burned the hair right off his ass – he got mean around the eyes just like my old man, and I thought he was going to try to whip me, but he just threw me off his wonderful fucking farm, right off, no dope and just the clothes on my back, but then, that's the way I showed up. I used to travel with a lot of shit, man, back when I first split, but now, man, I don't carry nothing but the clothes on my back –'

'I've got a friend like that,' I said, hoping to slow her babble. It didn't work.

'Hey, man, I kinda like Lawrence, and I wouldn't want to give him any grief. I ain't scared of him, or anything like that, but I wouldn't like it if you were going to shoot him or something,' she jabbered, twisting on the seat to face me, the white rims of her thighs above the tan slipping out of the legs of her cut-offs. She had an inflamed mosquito bite on the inside of her right thigh and she scratched at it with a dirty, broken fingernail. 'He's sorta silly sometimes, but he ain't a bad dude. Just unhappy a lot, man. He's so goddamned big and strong, sometimes it's hard to remember he's got feelings just like anybody else, man. He's an ex-con, you know. That's where he got hooked on dudes. He says he can't get off too good no other way, and what the hell, man, I don't mind dudes getting it on, if that's what they like – like they say, different strokes for different folks – but I don't think it makes Lawrence happy, you know, not very happy. That's why he got into that glitter crap, I bet, and started hanging around with creeps – that must be amazing, man, balling in make-up. I ain't had make-up on since I was eleven, that's weird, man. I balled him a few times, and he kept wanting to do silly things, you know, tie me up and make me give him head, which is okay, I guess, if you like that sort of crap, but my wrists always started to hurt and I like to move around some, man.' She bounced up and down on the seat to illustrate movement, the nipples of her small breasts scribbling around her T-shirt nicely.

'Yeah,' I said, no longer hoping that she would stop, just wishing she would slow down, but she went right on, rattling like a loose pebble in a hubcap.

'But he's all right, man, and I hope you don't shoot him or anything, but you can shoot that goddamned hayseed freak if you want to.' She grinned, pleased at the idea. 'You can blow his fucking head off for all I care, except let me know and I'll split because dead people are a hassle. I was at a party once, somewhere in the Midwest, and one of the dudes fell out of a tree – we were all wrecked and sitting in this big old tree, and this guy fell out and killed himself, broke his neck or something, and the pigs came and busted all of us, but I jumped bail and I'll never go that way again, man, if I can remember where the fuck it happened.' She wailed laughter, pounding the seat and my arm, bouncing and pounding and laughing harder and harder. 'What the hell,' she coughed, coming down, 'maybe I saw it in a movie, man, that happens to me sometimes, that's why I had to quit going to the movies, man, I had to give up dope or movies, man, I couldn't handle both, so I gave up movies.'

I looked at her. She was grinning widely.

'You're okay for an old man, you know. Lawrence is an old man too, maybe older than you, but sometimes he's a kick in the ass. Are you a kick in the ass, old man?'

'Right now, baby, I'm so stoned that I don't know,' I said, feeling as if I had been standing in a strong wind for hours. 'I just don't know.'

'Well, don't you go hurting Lawrence, old man, 'cause he's a kick in the ass.' She loved that, barely able to hold back the spurts of laughter. 'Sometimes.'

I sighed and promised that I wouldn't, under any circumstances, hurt a kick in the ass, which set her off again.

'You ain't all that bad looking for an old kick in the ass,' she said when she came back. 'Hey, man, you ever find old El Creepo?'

'Yeah, I found him,' I lied. 'But he was dead.'

'That's too bad, man, dead people –'

'Are a hassle,' I finished for her.

She sighed deeply, as if her wind was spent. She curled up on the seat, her legs drawn under her, her narrow head resting on the seat back, her face hidden in lank hair.

'Must be sad dying,' she whispered as I headed up Willomot Hill.

'Some people say that living is the sad part.'

'Well, that's silly,' she said, sitting up and brushing the hair out of her face. 'What the fuck is that?'

'Tourists,' I said.

A caravan of identical aluminum travel trailers occupied the right-hand lane, strung out up the hill like metallic sausages. I down-shifted the rig and roared around the laboring automobiles and their gleaming burdens in the passing lane.

'Goddamned tourists.'

'Be nice,' she said, shifting roles, flitting from stoned child to bemused adult as easily as I changed gears. 'I'm a goddamned tourist, man, into sightseeing and all that crap, I'm a tourist everywhere I go.' But the role slipped and the giggles came back. 'Let's give the bastards a sight,' she said, slipping out of her cut-offs. She hopped up on the seat and propped her naked butt out the window. But the slow trek of the trailers proceeded smoothly, the eyes in the cars fixed on some more distant and photogenic vista. Mindy was happy, though, grinning wildly, her eyes bright beneath spare brows.

'Put your clothes on,' I said at the top of the hill as I slowed to turn into the parking lot of the Willomot Hill Bar. 'I'm gonna get some beer. You want something?'

'Sure, man, a Coke and all the goddamned candy bars in the world,' she said, tugging up her cut-offs. A flash of white around the sparse pubic hair made me weak. But then I could always be tempted.

'Right,' I said, parking the car.

The bar was in a low building, windowless on both long sides, and it seemed to have been hacked out of the side of the hill behind it, then skidded down to rest slightly askew beside the highway. Blunt and unfriendly outside, it was like a cave inside, the lair of feral humans, dark and dank, the low walls lined with the mounted heads of deer and elk and mountain sheep and goats and bears, more like totems than trophies. At the very back of the long, low room stood an erect grizzly bear, dim and shaggy, frighteningly shapeless in the deep shadows, its glass eyes glowing like two embers. At night, filled with smoky yellow light and sullen drunks off the reservation, the bar seemed like some primeval ruin, a temple where human sacrifices had just been offered to the hirsute demon-god lurking at the back, an offering refused by the beast. I knew what it looked like at night because I had gone in too many times officially as peacemaker or arrester of vicious movements – roles the owner, Jonas, objected to. At night it looked like the sort of place Raymond Duffy might choose to die in, and in the day, empty except for the silent Indian woman behind the bar, it was no better.

'Jonas around?' I asked the woman bartender, whose face was so impassive and eyes so glassy that she might have been another trophy hanging behind the bar. I thought Jonas might remember the Duffy kid, but the Indian woman shook her head slowly, silently.

'Is he coming back today?' My voice sounded oddly reverent in the hushed bar. The woman shrugged, then nodded, then shrugged again. I didn't know what she meant, but it didn't matter. Jonas was easy to find: just look for the meanest, loudest, toughest runt in the county, and it had to be Jonas. I ordered a six-pack of beer, two Cokes, but she didn't have any candy bars. I took a package of potato chips instead, hoping they would suffice.

On the way to the door, I thought of bringing Helen Duffy up to see the place where her little brother had died. Perhaps it might explain something to her, then she could explain it to me. But there was no need to kid myself. If Helen walked into the Willomot Bar, she would only see a dingy, depressing bar, sadly degenerate, and even worse, she would be able to tell that I was right at home in the bar. I made foolish noises to myself about being disgusted by the Willomot and I didn't hang out there too often, but I seldom drove past without stopping in, and in an odd way I was fond of the bar. It was a Kamikaze bar, pledged to a divine destruction.

Outside, back under the rational glare of sunlight, the vault of blue sky resisted the advance of another front, Simon's rain, a reef of bruised clouds stealing in from the west. Over a ridge directly north, the stone peaks of the Cathedral Mountains spired, as clear as chimes in the summer air. The column of trailers still trundled slowly past, metallic worms on a fatal migration. And sweet Mindy sat cross-legged and naked as a jay bird on the roof of my rig, waving gaily at the tourists.

'What's happening?' I asked, trying not to let her know how delighted I was with her.

'Nothing, man, absolutely nothing,' she answered over her shoulder. As she twisted, the muscles of her narrow waist shimmered in the sunlight. 'I haven't caused a single wreck.'

'Too bad,' I said. 'Come on down. I've got work to do.'

'It's too nice a day to work,' she said, waving at a logging truck driver as he pulled his truck back across the road, just missing the last of the shining trailers.

'It's gonna rain,' I said, pointing behind us at the relentless gray front, from which thunder showers were breaking off like reckless children, slipping ahead of the clouds, splashing rain and cool wind down the mountain valleys. 'Soon.'

'You can work after it starts to rain,' she said.

'It's supposed to be the other way around.'

'That's silly,' she grumbled, but she climbed down as I watched. She was so casually naked that there didn't seem to be any point in looking the other way. Her legs were long and slim, her perky rump firm, and her breasts were small but looked as hard as green apples.

Once in the rig, she tossed her clothes on the floor and sat with her head hanging out the window, her hair fluttering in the wind. Then she faced me again, shaking out the wind tangles, and popped the top of a Coke can.

'Thanks,' she said. 'They didn't have any candy bars?'

'Nope.'

'Good. They still make my face break out, man, and that's my last shred of middle-class vanity.'

'Got some potato chips, though.'

'Yuk,' she grunted. 'Fried in animal fats, man. Yuk.'

She was so smug that I had a handful even though I didn't want them. She was wrong. They had been fried in used crankcase oil.

'Hey,' she said, poking me in the ribs. 'You wanna

ball?' she asked, not faking the casual nature of the question. 'I could use a little bread for the road, man. A little bread lets you choose who you have to ball for meals,' she added, grinning broadly as if she hoped to shock me. When I didn't answer, she said, 'Well, if you're in such a hurry to see old Kick-in-the-ass, I could give you some head while we're driving. I'm kinda skinny and don't have any tits to speak of, but I move around a lot to compensate, man, and I could use the bread.'

I wanted to ask her who she had been traveling with and how she had come up with the routine, but I asked her how much instead.

'I don't care, man, spare change or twenty bucks, it don't matter.'

'What if I just give you twenty bucks?'

'Outa sight. What if I ball you for nothing?' she answered quickly.

'I don't know,' I said, laughing. 'How old are you?'

'Who cares,' she said, reaching for my fly.

'I do,' I said, stopping her busy little fingers. 'I never ball a chick without a personal history.'

'That's weird, man. I ain't got the clap, so whatcha afraid of?'

'Balling strangers, I guess.'

'Everybody's a stranger, dummy, and you're puttin' me on,' she said, her fingers working again. 'So find a flat spot.'

'How old are you?'

'Nineteen going on forty, man, just like the rest of the world.'

She took my silence as criticism, which it wasn't. I had a momentary rush of sadness, but I didn't know if it was for me or her.

'Don't worry about me, man, I've been on the road since I was thirteen. My old man wouldn't let me go to Woodstock, so I split and I ain't been back. You grow up quick on the road, man, and I'm about as old as I'll ever be,' she said, defending herself against the years between us.

'How old will you be at forty?'

'Who cares. To get old, man, you have to remember things, and I don't even remember this morning. My old man told me all the time that I'd have to grow up someday when I got out in the real world,' she said, moving closer as she talked. Her fingers had opened my shirt, and her hands were stroking my chest. Her breath was hot against my face. 'Well, I'm all grown up and this is the real world, man.'

'Right,' I said. 'Let's find a sylvan glade.' Helen Duffy wouldn't understand, but my father would have.

'What's that?'

'A nice flat spot.'

Afterwards, we exchanged the polite and breathless compliments by which casual lovers maintain their dignity. Consideration touches more deeply and longer than passion. We began with spontaneous passion but finished with consideration, which surprised both of us pleasantly. And after the surprise came the sadness. She rose after a few still moments of holding each other and wandered aimlessly over to the small creek that stuttered past our flat spot. She eased her slim foot into the cold water, muttered a complaint, then rambled on to a large, smooth rock which lay partially in the water, where she lay down to sun. I walked over and sat beside her.

'A while ago I asked you if Reese was dealing smack, but you never got around to answering me,' I said softly, rubbing her firm thigh with the back of my hand.

'Working, huh?'

'Yes.'

'You make a lot of money?' she asked.

'I used to. But I spent a lot too, so it evened out.'

'I never balled a private eye, man.'

'Neither have I.'

She grinned and held my hand tightly for a second, then said, 'Lawrence used to deal, man, but I don't think he ever dealt smack. That's what he took his fall for, so he was kinda afraid of it.'

'Dealing smack?'

'No, man, smuggling it across the Mexican border. I think that he asked El Creepo to move out when he got hooked. I heard that. But I didn't hear it from Lawrence, so who knows if it's true.'

'How long ago was that?'

'I don't know, man. I didn't spend much time keeping up with that crap.'

'How well did you know the Duffy kid?'

'As well as I wanted to, man. He was a prime creep. I knew that the first time I saw him strutting around with his goddamned guns, quick-drawing and snapping the trigger in people's faces. Man, after that I wouldn't even stay in the same room with him, and I told him that if he ever did that to me, he damn well better have a bullet in his goddamned gun because I was gonna knock his fucking head off. And I'd have done it too, man, I ain't no goddamned pacifistic flower child or nothing like that.'

'Was he around a lot?'

'El Creepo? Naw, he paid the rent, man, but he wasn't around all that much. But he was around enough so that some people wouldn't even crash there for free.'

'It wasn't Lawrence's house?'

'Naw, man. He never has any bread. El Creepo paid all the bills.'

'Was he dealing?'

'I don't know, man. He always had dope and money.'

Dope and money, the trappings of new wealth, I thought as I gathered my clothes and dressed, cursing myself for quitting cigarettes, needing that blue swirl of thoughtful smoke. Dressed, I walked back to the rock and held her tightly for another moment, not thinking at all.

'Hey, man,' she breathed against my neck.

'Yeah.'

'Hey, man,' she repeated, leaning back to stare at me with her soft brown eyes, light brown like her hair, dry and shaken clean in the wind.

'Yes,' I said into her silence, the silence of the young, which ran like an underground river beneath the dope babbles and inarticulate riffs of their private language, the silence of frustration and anxious grief for nameless losses.

'Hey, man, don't be sad, okay? Sometimes older guys,

you know, they get down afterwards. I don't like to make guys sad when I ball them,' she said, sounding as lonesome as easy rain among stolid pines. 'Okay?'

'You don't make me sad,' I said, not telling her that youth was sometimes sadder than middle age, not telling her that she made me feel old, older than the mountains, more ruined than the gulleys jagged on sunburnt slopes. 'It's been too nice a day to be sad.'

'Great,' she said sadly.

And I lifted her in my arms, as light as a bundle of dry wood. She smelled of sunlight and stone, her limbs as smooth and limber as green sticks, and her mouth on mine, sun-warm and gentle, as soft as down, drove a stake into my tired heart. I wanted to break the spell, to heave her into the creek, to shout and splash water happily, to find some quick irony with which to resist, but the spell held.

'You're crying, you old fart,' she whispered sweetly, forgiving me, almost happy.

'I must be drunk.'

'You're crying.'

'Yeah, but I'm not sad.'

10

The Holy Light Hog Farm was one of those visions of paradise nurtured by dirt farmers going bust on the Great Plains – their faces implacable, sunburnt, wind-furrowed – a vision for which they would have gladly sold their souls. Lacking a market for souls, they did the next hardest thing: rose up from behind their plows and dragged their suffering families west out of that great bitter sea of harsh land that stretched to the bleak horizon in all directions, heading west to the promised land, rich wet valleys where the mountains broke the sharp thrust of the winter winds, land so fertile that fence posts took root overnight and cattle fattened like hogs. Not very many found their Edens, but the man who first owned the land and built the house now occupied by the Hog Farm did.

The house was yellow and square, three stories high, softened by a gabled roof and a broad veranda on three sides, and set on a shallow hillside at the foot of the Cathedral Mountains, which rise as grandly as the Tetons, overlooking the wide, fecund valley of the Stone River. Large and stately trees grew around the house, providing shade and dignity, and a deep lawn, broken randomly by flowering shrubs, flowed down the hillside from the house to the edge of the fields and meadows. It was a lovely place, a proper seat for a baron, an old man, tall and weather-honed lean, wrapped in faded, starched khaki, his collar buttoned loosely around his thin, stiff neck. So it was a shock to drive up and see a naked, pregnant woman stretched on the thick grass to catch the last of the sun and a bearded freak sitting on the veranda steps rolling a joint, to hear the dull thud of hard rock music rippling like thunder from the broad windows.

The young man who owned the place didn't have any illusions about the community of man. His land was posted, and nobody stayed at the farm unless he worked. He grew his own hog feed organically, so the fifteen or twenty young people living there had plenty of work. Since I have the average older American's theoretical attachment to work, I approved of his concept, but I had been up to the farm on business – once to bring back a runaway teenage girl and twice to verify that runaway wives were living in sin – and I didn't completely approve of the people. Not that they were bad people. They were suspicious of strangers and too damned self-righteously superior about their modern morality to suit me. But they didn't bother anybody and they worked. Probably harder than I did. And because of my previous visits, they didn't like me at all.

'You wait in the car,' Mindy said, patting me on the thigh. She had made me promise once more not to give Reese any grief, and she reminded me of the promise as she climbed out of the rig and trotted across the lawn toward the front door, pausing to say hello to the pregnant lady.

The kid on the veranda obviously didn't know me because he waved and smiled and shouted, 'What's happening, man?' but the pregnant lady recognized me. She rose, eased into a loose shift and walked over to my rig. A tall blond lady, as beautifully healthy as some expectant mothers are, she was the ex-wife of a real estate salesman in Meriwether. In my own small way, I'd been responsible for the paucity of her divorce settlement.

'My ex-husband send you up here to spy on me?' she asked in a hard, flat voice.

'Don't be paranoid, lady,' I said. 'You'll hurt the baby.'

'Fuck off. Did he?'

'No, ma'am.'

'Then get your ass off the property.'

'Oh, go to hell,' I said, not knowing if my irritation was from my memory or the two whites I'd taken when Mindy and I left the creek. The tall woman left, striding across the lawn so strongly that she could have pulled a plow. It had been a lovely divorce. The dude she was shacked up with had taken a swing at me when I came up to verify her living arrangement, and then I had to sue her ex-husband for my fee. But the woman looked so good walking away from me that I was sorry she didn't like me.

'Occupational hazard,' I said to myself, sipping beer and wondering what I was going to do if Reese didn't show up. Or if he did. I reached under the seat for the Browning automatic, looked at it, checked the clip and made sure there was a round in the chamber, then put it back under the seat. I wasn't going to shoot anybody. The whole idea was silly. I had learned the hard way that if you pull a gun on a man, you damn well better be ready to shoot him. Otherwise, he might get mad. I had pulled my service revolver on a huge gypo logger once, and he broke my wrist taking it away from me. Then he knocked me cold, stuffed me in the back of my unit, and drove himself to the county jail. It felt nice to have the 9-mm pistol under the seat, but that's where it should remain.

Mindy bounced out of the side door, her lean legs flashing as the sunlight failed and the front settled over the valley. She threw a wave my way, then ran toward the barn, kicking her legs like a child. The air tingled with ozone and the hammer of distant thunder. A light mist dappled my windshield. I wished I were as happy about seeing Lawrence Reese again as she was.

I thought about other weapons, the leather sap hidden in the crack of the front seat, a flat sap with a spring steel handle and a lead disk in the head. It worked really well on drunks and fighting families when you could get behind them, but I couldn't see Reese letting me behind him. I also had a good knife, a large Buck folding knife, razor-sharp, but I didn't think Reese would roll over and play dead if I jerked it out and shaved all the hair off my forearm. That left my intelligence and his generosity, neither very dependable weapons.

Just as I had almost decided to forget about the whole thing and get drunk, Reese came shambling out of the barn door, Mindy at his side talking earnestly. Country living seemed to have changed him. His swagger had become a country-boy barefoot shuffle, his face was slightly sunburnt, and his thinning hair had been cropped so short that his pink scalp glowed through. But he hadn't gotten any smaller; he was still a horse. His faded overalls would have fit a grizzly bear, his neck and shoulders done credit to a fighting bull.

I got out of the rig anyway, leaned against the fender, my arms crossed peacefully. I tried to look pleasant but unafraid. Reese stopped about three feet from me, his large hands hidden in his pockets, his bare feet scratching at the skim of dampness over the dust. We looked at each other without greetings. In the soft light, without the purple eye shadow, his eyes were pale blue and dim, almost watery, no longer arrogant. Mindy paused beside him, then hurried to my side, hooking her arm in mine. Her smile had gone ragged at the edges, but she wore it bravely, and she held my arm protectively. In the damp, cool air, her slim body began to tremble, but mine had become oddly still.

'I'm not too happy to see you, man,' he said quietly, almost apologetically. And I started feeling cocky. As he spoke, the veranda filled with people coming out of the house and barn, most wearing worried grimaces, but others aglow with happy expectancy. The tall blond lady especially; she wanted to see me hurt.

'I didn't come to make you happy,' I said. 'I still want to ask some questions about Raymond Duffy.'

'Why don't you just go away,' he said.

'Not this time.'

'This time ain't gonna be any different.'

'It won't be as easy,' I said. Reese took his hands out of his pockets, flexed them, then jammed them back into his pockets. Something I didn't know about was holding him back.

'Listen, man,' he said in a harsh whisper, 'I don't need any trouble. Just go away. These people don't like you, man, and they don't like trouble.'

'Just answer a few questions, and there won't be any trouble.'

He thought about it, shaking his head, glancing once over his shoulder, then he mumbled, almost pleading, 'Just go away, man.'

There it was. In the ashen light of a rainy afternoon, no dragon, just a large, tired man on the wrong side of forty, punch-drunk from his life. His pale eyes were afraid, not of me, but of his future. I might not think too much of the Hog Farm, but he wanted to live there so badly that he might do anything, even talk to me.

'Hey, man,' I said, 'let's go have a drink of whiskey.'

Reese smiled, as if he meant to say yes, and I shrugged my right arm out of Mindy's clasped hands, but he shook his head, saying, 'No way, man.'

He could have ducked the punch, or dodged, or tried to block; instead, he let me have a free one, leaving his hands pocketed. I assumed that if it was free, it had better be good, so I aimed a straight right hand at his throat. But he lowered his jaw and took it in the mouth. It split his upper lip and knocked him down but didn't knock any teeth out or make his eyes glassy even for a second.

'I guess that means trouble,' I said lamely.

Reese glanced over his shoulder again, and a thin-faced young man with a long beard nodded from the veranda, then Reese got up.

Afterwards, vaguely conscious but unable to stand up again, I remained where I had fallen.

'Enough,' I said, hoping he believed me.

Mindy ran over, knelt and held my head against her bare thigh. A long smear of blood and dirt stained her leg when I lifted my head, but I couldn't tell where the blood was coming from.

'Are you okay?' she asked.

'I don't think I'm dead,' I said, tottering to my hands and knees, 'but I'm not sure.' My tongue took a roll call of teeth and came up with a familiar number, and when I felt my nose, it seemed intact. I dreaded a broken nose as much as a dentist, so I couldn't complain too much. My eyes worked, if I concentrated on focusing them, and I could breathe without fainting, which meant that even if I had broken ribs, at least they weren't sticking into a lung. I tried standing, which worked, then tried not to weave, which didn't. The crowd was still arranged on the veranda, smiling gravely, as if for a family portrait. The light mist fell coolly on my tired face.

'Why didn't you make him promise not to hurt me?' I asked Mindy, trying to smile to let her know it was all right.

'She did, man,' Reese muttered from the edge of the lawn. 'You're not hurt, man, not permanently.'

'Could've fooled me,' I said, my hand following the

blood up my left cheek to a gash three fingers wide in my left eyebrow.

'Sorry about that,' he said pleasantly, 'but you bobbed when you should've weaved.'

'Someday I'm gonna get beat up by a guy who doesn't want to be my goddamned buddy afterwards.'

'Hell, man, I'm hurt worse than you,' he said, smiling broadly, as if he was happy about the injury, and holding up his right hand. The middle knuckle had been jammed halfway back to the wrist.

'You're a hard-headed son of a bitch,' he added, as if it were a compliment.

'You don't know just how hard-headed, buddy,' I said, then walked over to my rig and took the automatic from under the seat, keeping my body between the gun and the crowd. I went the rest of the way around the rig and stood behind the hood. 'Okay, Reese,' I said quietly, 'I don't want to scare your friends, so I won't show this automatic pistol to them, but I want you to know that it's here, and that no matter how hard you try, you can't get to me before I put a large and painful hole somewhere in your large and painful body.'

'Get it on, man. I been to the hard place where the real bad dudes hang out, and you ain't nothing. And that's what you get, nothing.'

'Does this mean we're not buddies anymore?'

'You guessed it, man,' he said, moving a slow step closer to the rig.

'Think about it, now, before you do something foolish. Whatever happens when I pull this trigger, it's all bad, it means the man has to come out here to disturb this bucolic tranquillity.'

'You won't pull that trigger, man.'

'You can find out the hard way.'

The crowd on the veranda began to mill about, craning their necks to see why Mindy had her hand over her mouth. I smiled pleasantly, Reese shuffled his feet and jammed his sore hands behind the bib of his overalls, and Mindy stood absolutely still.

'What do you want?' he asked.

'Let's go have that drink.'

'Okay.'

I climbed in the passenger door and replaced the pistol under the seat. Reese walked toward the rig, moving reluctantly.

'Where you guys going?' Mindy asked, taking her hand out of her mouth.

'Get a goddamned drink,' Reese said, 'before that crazy bastard kills somebody.'

'Can I go?' she asked, looking at me. I looked at Reese.

'It's your party, man,' he said, shrugging.

So I nodded at Mindy, and she slipped in the door in front of Reese and settled between us.

'You dudes are crazy,' she said. She sounded happy about it.

'Just him,' Reese answered. When I glanced over at him, he wasn't smiling. But he looked as if he wanted to.

'Violence makes strange bedfellows,' I said, 'but then you guys know all about that.'

Mindy elbowed me in the ribs, her hand trying to hold back the giggles, and if I hadn't known better, I would have sworn that Reese blushed. At least he grinned. And we drove away through the shifting rain as cozy as a newly-wed *ménage à trois*.

At the small infirmary in the town of Stone River, a clumsy doctor put ten stitches in my right eyebrow, then let a nurse clean the rest of the scrapes and scratches while he checked the X-rays and set Reese's hand.

'You guys have a fight?' he asked as he wound Reese's hand with an elastic bandage.

'That's right,' I answered.

'Who won?' he asked.

'You charge extra for jokes?' I asked, but he didn't answer. At least they weren't listed on the bill, which I paid.

'My treat,' I said to Reese.

'That's right.'

The bar in Stone River was just a bar, the only bar in town. Two old farmers, excusing themselves from the fields because of the light rain, stroked lazily at a ritual pool game in the rear of the bar, bitching patiently at each other like a couple married much too long. The resident drunk aimed his blind grin at us when we came into the bar, but we didn't offer greetings or whiskey, so he staggered past us to the door to watch the rain. At the bar, I ordered a shot and a beer, and Reese had the same, but Mindy took too long to make up her mind, and the bartender asked for her ID. Except for lint, her pockets were empty, so she had another Coke.

'I hate that crap, man,' she groused.

'You can't have civilization without laws,' I said.

'Oh, Jesus Christ,' she groaned, then took my change and walked over to the pinball machine. She played the first few balls without using the flippers or touching the sides of the machine, just letting the balls roll wherever they might, but soon she had her fingers locked to the flipper buttons, and she was hammering and twisting, fighting gravity and the stainless-steel balls.

Reese and I drank silently, watching her battle. When we finished the shots, I ordered two more.

'I'm flat, man, I can't buy back,' he said.

'No sweat.'

'It's your money, man.'

'Not exactly,' I said.

'After all the trouble you caused me, man, the least you could do is buy the drinks with your own money.'

'Trouble?' I asked.

'Trouble,' he said, smiling. 'Blew up my porch, man, hit me in the mouth, broke my hand, and got the man on my ass.'

'Jamison?'

'You guessed it, man.'

'Give you a hard time?'

'No shit. Daddy, that's one uptight man. I can't afford any felony hassles, but that dude scared me so bad, I nearly busted him and run. He may think he's a boy scout but he's as bad as any cop I've ever seen. And I seen a few.'

'He takes his work seriously,' I said.

'He's crazy. All you goddamned hick cops are crazy. In the cities, man, the cops are usually just dudes doing a job of work, and some of them like it and some don't, some are good, some bad. But none of them think they're gonna save the world from evil. Hick cops always think they're John Wayne making the frontier safe for decent, God-fearing folk. That's why we're having this drink, man, 'cause you're a crazy cowboy.'

'I'm not the man and haven't been for years,' I said, feeling some need to defend myself.

'But you think you are, man. It's all over you.'

I didn't ask him what that meant because I didn't want to know. Or maybe I knew but didn't like it.

'You mind answering some questions?'

'Of course I mind, man. Didn't you get that impression from me yet?'

'Sure.'

'But you're just hard-headed enough to keep after me, huh?'

'You guessed it,' I said.

'What's in this for you?'

'You want the truth?'

'Why not?'

'Maybe nothing. Maybe a lady.'

'The sister?'

'Maybe.'

'I told you you were crazy, man. Hell, if you want a lady, take that one home,' he said, nodding toward Mindy. 'Feed her a few meals and wash her back every now and then, and she'll follow you around like a puppy dog. For a while.'

'Maybe that's the problem,' I said.

'Christ, not true love, man. Not that. Yeah, that's it.

I can see it now. Well, daddy, if she's anything like her little brother, you're in one hell of a mess.'

'She's not,' I said. 'The kid was adopted.'

Reese looked at me for a moment, rolling the shot glass between his thumb and forefinger so smoothly that it was hard to think of his hand as broken. Then he shook his head, saying, 'He never told me that.'

'Maybe he was ashamed of it,' I said. 'Some adopted kids are.'

'Not the Duff, man. Whatever he was ashamed of, he threw it right in people's faces. Like the homosexual thing. To compensate for the guilt with aggression.'

'You learn that in prison?'

'Man, they got more shrinks than cons in the joint. Group therapy on every floor.'

'Must be fun.'

'It's a scam, man, a way to get out. You ever see a crib sheet for the Rorschach test?'

'That's where my tax money goes, huh?'

'You probably cheat on the returns,' he said.

'That's right. But don't tell anybody.'

'Man, I never tell anybody anything.'

'So I gathered. Which puts us right back at the beginning,' I said.

'Wrong, man, this is the end. You wanted to buy me a drink, you bought me a drink, we chatted, and that's it.'

'Three drinks,' I said, motioning to the bartender. 'And either we have more conversation or round two.'

'You're serious, huh?'

'You better believe it,' I said.

'This time you might get hurt.'

'Reese, old buddy, I think you're afraid to hurt me. How many falls have you taken? Two? Three? How many more before you take a habitual rap? So you can't afford to hurt me.'

'You're real smart, man, aren't you? A real bad-ass, right? Well, just swing away, old buddy. I won't raise a hand to stop you, and when you get tired, man, I still won't have nothing to say.'

'I guess you got me then,' I said. 'To hell with it. Enjoy your drink.' Then I picked up my beer and started over to watch Mindy.

'Hey, man,' he said behind me.

'What?'

'Come here. What the hell does the sister want to know?'

'She doesn't believe that her little brother committed suicide or died by accident. Of course, she can't believe that he was hooked on smack either.'

'Well, he was, man,' Reese said sadly.

'I know. But not too long, right? A month or so.'

'Whatever the coroner says, man,' he answered, his face going blank again. 'You tell the sister that the Duff killed himself, man.'

'And if she asks how I know?'

'Come on, man, get off my ass.'

'No way,' I said. 'You asked me to come back, Reese. You got something you want to say, I want to hear it, so let's quit farting around.'

'Okay, man, but let me tell you something first. I ain't never been straight. As soon as I could walk, I was boosting shit outa the corner grocery store, and I been in and out of every kinda joint there is, but I ain't never talked to the man. Never. And I pulled some hard time for it, man, but I never been a snitch. And that's a hard habit to break. Just like being bent. But when that crazy bastard Jamison had me in interrogation, man, I got scared. I don't want another trip to the joint. No more bars, man. I couldn't handle it. And if I tell you what I know about the Duff and you tell the lady, and she makes a fuss, then Jamison is going to want to know how you know. He'll turn the screws on your ass, you'll babble, and I'll go back to the slammer for one final engagement.'

'Nope. Won't happen like that,' I said.

'What?'

'I won't give Jamison the time of day.'

'You won't take an obstruction fall for me, man.'

'Of course I would.'

'Why?'

'I don't know. Maybe I just like you,' I said, then finished my whiskey.

Reese was silent a second, then he burst out laughing. He slapped me on the back and said, 'That's pretty damn slim, man, but what the hell. Why not?'

'So give,' I said, ordering another round.

'None for me, man.'

'I'll drink it.'

'It's your money.'

'It's your turn,' I said.

'Right,' he said, almost sounding happy. 'Sure. Absolutely, man. What do you want?'

'Everything.'

'You ain't gonna like it. The lady ain't gonna like it, so you still gotta come up with a good lie, man,' he said.

'I'll worry about that.'

'Okay, man, it's your life. Or the Duff's. He was a kid looking to die, man, he was a real crazy. Makes – made you and I look like saints. He was so crazy, even I was afraid of him. Then he started sticking that nail in his arm, and he was dead.'

'Who turned him on to smack?'

'Whoever he was dealing for.'

'He was dealing smack?'

'That's right, man.'

'Jesus,' I said. 'How long?'

'A couple of months.'

'Who for?'

'Don't know, man. Didn't want to know.'

'How'd he get started?'

'You gonna love this, man. He borrowed five grand from his sister.'

'I can't tell her that,' I said, gunning my shot.

'Don't tell me, man.'

'Christ. Where was he getting his goods?'

'He didn't say, but I can guess.'

'Guess.'

'From a cop, man. He was dealing high-grade junk, French probably, certainly not Mexican, and there ain't been nothing but Mexican junk coming through for over a year. So find the last big bust around here before they bought off the poppy farmers and look in the evidence locker and you'll probably find milk sugar instead of junk.'

'That's lovely. What's dealing have to do with killing himself?' I asked.

'Probably nothing. Just a nice way to go out.'

'You don't think there's any chance that whoever he was dealing for might have helped him? Maybe they started worrying that the kid was too crazy to deal with. Something like that.'

'Doesn't sound right, man. Whoever's controlling the junk is strictly amateur, small potatoes all the way. And this is just a one-shot operation. As soon as the supply runs out, that's the end of the junkie plague in Meriwether.'

'Jamison would be happy to know that,' I said.

'He'd be happy to know lots of things, man, that he ain't ever gonna know.'

'Just kidding,' I said.

'Not funny, man.'

'Anything else I should know?'

'How should I know,' he said, looking away from me.

'Did you see him any that last week?'

'A few times.'

'What sort of shape was he in?'

'Terrible. He took that old man's death really hard, man – I mean, he was down, way down, and really freaky at the same time. Cut his hair and shaved off his beard, threw away all his guns and cowboy clothes. He and that old man musta been tight.'

'I wonder what that means,' I said, more to myself than Reese, but he answered anyway.

'Who knows, man, and who cares. They're both dead.'

'You're a real joy, Reese,' I said. 'I'm gonna go piss and think about it.'

'You one of those guys who thinks best with his pecker in his hand?'

'You guessed it.'

When I came back from the john, all I had was an inventory of aches and pains, and all I knew was what I read on the walls. Some ambitious soul in Stone River desired sexual congress with a broad spectrum of humankind. Jews, niggers, hippies and other long-haired and/or hairy apes and freaks. A-rabs, Chinks, congressmen, the former governor of our state, and the past four Presidents. Russians, commies and, for reasons undeclared, people from North Dakota. But the writer lacked the courage of his convictions: he didn't leave a telephone number.

Mindy had finally been conquered by the machine and stood beside Reese at the bar. He didn't look as happy as he had when I left.

'What did you find out, man?' he asked.

'That I hurt all over.'

'Me too. Let's split.'

'I need a drink,' I said.

'Have mine, man,' he said, and I did.

11

On the way back to the farm, we were silent, Mindy coming off her high and Reese sunk into his own thoughts. I didn't have anything to say because I didn't know what to think. The new role I had to think of the Duffy kid playing, a heroin dealer, made it difficult to keep the various pictures of him together. The whiskey and the small whimpers of pain echoing about my body didn't help. I touched Mindy's thigh, and she leaned her head against my shoulder, falling asleep quickly. Reese glanced at her, then at me, shaking his head.

'Take what you got, man, and forget the rest,' he said as we pulled into the driveway, but I didn't answer.

In the distance, muffled by the thick cloud cover, thunder grumbled, and the rain fell steadily now on the green fields and meadows. The lower slopes of the mountains, vaguely visible through the rain, seemed massive, hinting at the weight of the peaks hidden in the clouds, and the landscape seemed fallow and patient in the sodden air, ready to burst with growth when the sun returned.

'Tell your friends I'm sorry for the trouble,' I told Reese as we parked in front of the farm house.

'Yeah. Don't worry about it, man.'

'Thanks for the information.'

'Thanks for the drinks.'

'Sure. Next time you're in town . . .' I said without finishing.

Reese nodded vaguely, lifted his hand but didn't wave, making no commitments, except to the new life before him. As he walked slowly toward the house, his head bowed against the rain and his injured hand slung into the bib of his overalls, I wondered how many new lives a man could stand.

'How'd it go?' Mindy asked shyly.

'Terrible.'

'You mean, after all that, he didn't –'

'He told me lots of things,' I interrupted, 'none of which I wanted to hear.'

'Sorry, man,' she sighed. 'How you doin'?'

'Okay. There's no need to be sorry.'

'I am anyway,' she said. She flattened her palm against my thigh and rubbed it with long, slow strokes, back and forth, as if she were polishing my pants. 'That was an awful fight.'

'Right,' I muttered. 'I lost.'

'Whatcha gonna do now?' she asked, watching her hand on my leg.

'I don't know,' I said frankly. 'Go back to town maybe. Find a new life. Who knows.'

'Maybe you oughta hit the road, man. That's good sometimes.'

'I guess I'd better go back to town,' I said, thinking about obligations I neither wanted nor understood.

'I could go with you,' she said in a bright and casual voice. 'I don't eat much.'

When I looked at her, she was grinning. I buried my face against her; she smelled of rain and stones glistening damply in a pine grove, of moss and pitch, of easy silence. I closed my eyes tightly, held her, trying. But in the dim light of my waking dream, Helen stood there, her red hair glowing like an exotic flower in a rain forest, her naked body shimmering like a white-hot flame in the faint daylight.

'I could go with you,' she repeated, her small hand holding my neck, the fingers pressing warmly into tired muscles.

'Thanks,' I said, pulling away. 'You're a sweet lady, and we had a nice afternoon, and I guess I owe you –'

'Nobody owes anybody anything,' she said quietly.

'Yeah, I guess not. Whatever, I've still got too damn many things to do.'

'Start by sleeping off this drunk,' she said, smiling.

'I'm not –' I started to say, then realized I *was* drunk.

'Hey, man, I didn't mean to bum you out.'

'That's okay. It doesn't matter.'

'Yeah, well, if I don't see you again, old man, have a nice life,' she said, then pressed her lips to mine.

'Hey, you still need some money?'

'Naw, I guess not. Maybe I'll crash up here for a few days. Guess it won't kill me to step in pigshit, huh.' She smiled once more, touched my thigh with the back of her hand. 'Take care, huh.'

'You too,' I said.

She slipped out the door and ran quickly through the

rain. In the middle of the lawn, she stopped, turned back, pointing her finger directly into the murky sky.

'It's raining, old man,' she shouted gaily, 'go to work!' A broad and happy smile lighted her face, as if she were immensely proud of remembering what she had said earlier.

But as I drove away I remembered what she had said about remembering and getting old.

Driving back toward Meriwether through the gray rain, I did another white and cracked another beer, cursing myself for a fool. The memory of Mindy's body, as smooth and clean as an ax handle, took its place among the other bruises and scrapes. It might not have lasted too long – one day she would have gone for a walk in the park and never come back – but it might have been peaceful while it lasted. For an instant, I resented Helen Duffy almost as if she were a wife, a frumpy duty between me and the fleeting pleasures of young girls. But that wasn't fair. I had made my choice when I took the case. But I didn't want to tell her that her little brother had borrowed money from her to set himself up as a heroin dealer. I didn't mind lying, but I wished I had a shot of whiskey to prop up the beer – that might make the lie more imaginative.

That was the first thing I had to do, I thought as I sipped beer and dodged traffic on the rain-slick highway. And there were other things, too, irons in various fires. Bills to pay, my bar tab especially, and Simon to feed, and queues of winos who depended on me for an occasional drink. I had to make a living somehow, which meant I had to check with Freddy and Dynamite so I could fake it with Nickie. So much to do. It seemed years since I had sweated honestly or slept without being drunk; my body seemed to have already forgotten the three-week interlude of sobriety. That was another duty, to dry out again. And fences to mend. Dick Diamond. And I had promised Hildy Ernst I would drop by, at least to say hello and good-bye, maybe, and I should find out what Muffin wanted with his odd message.

I cracked another beer, confident now. I could handle it, damn right, whatever happened, even without a shot of whiskey. Helen Duffy wasn't the only woman in the world, not by a long sight – no, there was whiskey to drink and women to love, a world of both, enough for weeks, maybe even years, maybe even thirteen years until my father's trust fell finally to me, then I could sprawl in the silken laps of luxury, loll grandly about foreign beaches finally, dawdle with expensive whores, droves of exotic dusky women, maidens with conical breasts and wide, happy mouths, and there were tall, cool drinks I'd never had, a life to live like a king, so much to wait for, so much to do, yes, and . . .

But the first thing on my new agenda was to sober up. And quickly. Find a normal voice and steady eye with which to confront the highway patrolman who was following me, his harsh blue lights whipping through the gloomy late-afternoon light. Either sober up quickly or hope I knew him.

As we both climbed out of our cars, I saw that he was a guy I had worked with in the sheriff's department some years before. I seemed to remember that he didn't actively dislike me. Once before, he had found me sleeping in my rig, parked in the interstate highway median, stinking of whiskey and vomit, and he had let me drive home without a ticket. But as he strode toward me his face seemed angry beneath the brim of his campaign hat.

'Are you drunk again, Milo? I thought you were going to drive all the way to town before you saw my lights. I was afraid to hit the siren, didn't want to wake you up or anything.'

'Sorry,' I said. 'I was thinking.'

'Well, next time drink less before you start thinking,' he said, a small smile moving about his face, so I knew I would be all right. 'Say, I just got a call. They want you in town.'

'Who?'

'Jamison.'

'What the hell's he want?'

'Well,' he said, then paused, his face suddenly still and blank, a look I remembered too well the feel of. *Dead*, his face said. 'Bad news.'

'Who?'

'Simon. I'm sorry, Milo.'

'Shit.' That was the only thing I could think to say as the blessed numbness that precedes grief settled into my guts. 'Shit.'

'Yeah.'

'Where?' I asked, thinking the old fart must have wandered in front of another car. 'When?'

'The call came in about ten minutes ago. Some address over on Lincoln, I don't remember the number, but I've got it written down,' he said, heading back to his unit.

'That's okay. I know where it is.'

'I'm sorry I had to be the one,' he said, shifting about in the rain.

'I know the feeling. Forget it.'

'Hey, I'm going the other way, but you take it easy on the way to town, okay?'

'Sure,' I answered. I tried, but it didn't help. The corpse driving my rig had a heavy foot, and we went to town like a blizzard wind, coldly cursing the old fart every step of the way.

Four uniformed policemen kept the curious crowd of old folks and long-haired kids at bay, but they nodded me through. The open front of the house looked like a stage, the curtain raised for the first act, the actors waiting for the star's entrance. Two lab men bustled about their work, moving like energetic cleaning women. Jamison and a plain-clothes cop I didn't know stood next to Amos Swift in a small arc about the body, the cloud of blue smoke from Amos's cigar hanging over them.

Simon lay on his side on the living-room floor near the stairs, his knotted and feeble hands still clutching the four-foot splinter of banister that skewered his body front to back. It had entered just below the sternum and exited beneath the right scapula. The heavy tweed overcoat humped over his back, a short stub, black with blood, exposed. In front, on the pale, varnished wood, long bloody scrawls marked his hands' futile struggle to extract the splinter. His eyes were open, his lower lip bitten through, and his shoes had left curved scrapes on the floorboards. Because of the damp, heavy air, the stench of blood and urine and feces hung in the air like dark smoke. Simon was right: I turned my head away.

Out the side window, I saw the old woman next door standing at her side window. She caught my eye, waved coyly, white fingers wriggling like grubs. In the ashen light, her gaudy mouth glowed like a neon sign. I couldn't look at her either.

'What happened?' I asked. I had wanted to be sober; now I was.

Nobody answered. A long silence flooded the room, perfected by the small crowd noises and the quiet sweep of rain. Amos mangled his cigar, his teeth loudly crushing the tobacco. He muttered something, but Jamison remained silent, not looking at me but watching the lab crew, his thumb rubbing at a short, gnawed stub of a pencil. It looked like Simon's, but Jamison stuffed it into his shirt pocket as if it was his. I looked for the red notebook, but it wasn't visible.

Finally, the other detective broke the silence.

'Looks like he was drunk, maybe looking for a dry place to sleep it off, and . . .'

Then he saw Jamison glaring at him with the hardened face he usually reserved for me and his voice ran down like a tired toy.

'Dammit, Milo, I'm sorry,' Jamison said. 'Right now it looks like an accident, but we'll make sure what it was before we say.'

'Don't make any promises you aren't smart enough to keep,' I said. He gave me a hard look too, but didn't say anything. We both knew how much time and money would go into the investigation of a wino's death unless it was clearly homicide.

'You stay out of this, Milo,' he said.

'Out of what? An accident? Sure.'

'I mean it.'

'Great,' I said. 'I mean it too.'

'What was he doing here? Was he helping you with the Duffy thing?'

'Simon was just an old drunk, Lieutenant. The last I saw of him was in Mahoney's. He was writing a letter and drinking.'

'Don't try to shit me, Milo. If I find out he was here helping you, I'll have your ass. I mean it. Don't lie to me.'

'Why should I lie?'

'Because you think you're smarter than me,' he said. It sounded like an old complaint, but this was the first time I had heard it.

'I just have more time, Jamison. That's all.'

'Milo, if you put your face into police business or withhold evidence, you won't have any time at all.'

'I'm scared to death.'

'Aw, dammit, Milo,' he muttered, too tired to hassle me. 'This won't get you anything but trouble.'

'What's new?'

'Nothing, nothing's ever new.'

'What have you got so far?' I asked.

'Not much. If it wasn't an accident, the only person I know strong enough to do that is Reese, so we've got an APB out for him. For questioning.'

'Pull it in,' I said. 'I spent the afternoon with him.'

'That what happened to your eye?'

'Sorta.'

'Told you he was a hard one.'

'You were right.'

'Did he give you anything?' he asked.

'No. What have you got here? Besides a wasted APB.'

'Where the hell do you get off asking me that? Who the hell do you think you are?' he asked, angry again, his voice booming, his face red. The two lab men glanced at him. 'Goddammit, Milo, someday –'

'Someday's ass. Either tell me what you've got so far, or I'll go down to the station and buy it, and you damn well know it.'

'Hey,' the other cop said, moving toward me, but Jamison looked at him again, and he shut up and stopped.

'Okay. It isn't much anyway,' he said, rubbing his pale face. 'No signs that the body was moved, no prints on the banister worth a damn, no evidence that anybody else was in here with him, except half the neighborhood.'

'Who found the body?'

'Two kids. Boy and girl. Said they came in to get out of the rain, but I'd guess they needed some lumber or maybe a quiet place to smoke dope and ball. At least they called it in, which is amazing. They were really scared, Milo, and still are, so I believe them.'

'They see anybody?'

He gave me a disgusted look, and I gave it back.

'All right. No. Not in the house. They said there was another long-hair on the sidewalk. Maybe he came out of the house, maybe he didn't.'

'Get a description?'

'Sure. Long black hair and beard,' he said. 'How many people you know fit that description, Milo?'

'No details, no guesses?'

'Might have been an older guy. The girl said he walked like an older dude. No, she said he didn't walk like a kid.'

'Clothes?' I asked.

'Who knows? He wasn't naked; they might have noticed that. The girl said she had a feeling as they passed him that he was a narc.'

'Why?'

'Let's see,' Jamison said, consulting his little notebook. 'She said, "Too neat to be a freak," whatever that means.'

'What about the old woman next door?' I asked.

'That's the best part of all,' he said, smiling tiredly. 'She's not only crazy or senile, she's also an illegal alien from Poland. She doesn't speak a word of English, she's been in the country forty or fifty years but she still can't speak the language. Christ. And we can't rustle up anybody who speaks Polish.'

'She lives alone?'

'No, she has a spinster daughter. The daughter used to speak some Polish, but she and the mother haven't spoken in thirty or forty years, so she forgot what she knew. Can you believe that?'

'Family life,' I said.

'Yeah. And if that wasn't enough, the daughter was drunk as a sow, and when we went to the door, she went into hysterics. Seems she thought we'd come to take her mother back to the old country.'

'Where's the daughter now?'

'Either swilling apricot brandy or passed out. Who knows? Christ, sometimes I love this town, Milo, god-damned love it.'

'Everybody's got to live someplace,' I said.

'Yeah, but they could die someplace else,' he said, then paused and took my arm, leading me over to the wall. 'And there's this other problem.'

'What?'

'You know a prof out at the college named Elton Crider?'

'I met him last night,' I said.

'So I hear. At the Riverfront. I understand that you two had a small discussion.'

'So?'

'So they fished his car out of the river this afternoon. He was in it. He was drunk but not too drunk, and there weren't any skid marks. You want to tell me what you two talked about?'

'Raymond Duffy.'

'And?'

'And that's it. He hadn't had anything to do with the Duffy kid in months, almost a year, and didn't know anything. I drove away and he went back into the bar. That's the last I saw of him.'

'That's what Vonda Kay says too, but I don't like it,' Jamison said.

'Don't like what?'

'Don't like your version, don't like the blood-alcohol count, don't like the missing skid marks. But it's in the county.' By which he meant that nothing more would come of the investigation. In our state the county sheriff is an elected official, and in our county the sheriff knew a great deal about getting elected but little else. 'Anyway, you should stop in the sheriff's office and give a statement tomorrow. Then stop in to see me.'

'Why?'

'Because I want to know what you tell them.'

'Why?'

'Because I don't like it.'

'Neither do I,' I said. Already numb about Simon, I didn't have any room to think about Elton Crider and his sad life. 'But it's none of my business.'

'And Simon is?'

'I didn't say that.'

'You didn't have to.'

We both turned to look at the body again, neither of us mentioning the missing notebook or Simon's pencil in Jamison's pocket. I knew how careful Simon had been about stairs since his accident with the pickup; his hip hurt when he climbed stairs, and he was afraid of falling down them, so he clung tightly to banisters and climbed only one step at a time. And he had been sober, I was sure, just as sure as I was that somebody had pushed Simon off the stairs, that I would find out who, and that I would kill him. And it would be easier for me if Jamison thought accident instead of homicide.

'Hey, Jamison, maybe Simon thought he was helping me. He knew I was going up to Stone River to see Reese, maybe he thought he could find something here, something about the Duffy kid. I don't know. You know how he was when he was drunk.'

'Yeah,' Jamison said, but I couldn't tell if he bought it, so I gave him some more.

'Look, I know that's Simon's pencil in your shirt pocket, and that you are wondering about his notebook,' I said, but Jamison looked blank. 'He was just about finished with his notebook, man, and maybe the letter took up the rest of the pages. Don't make more of it than necessary.'

'Yeah,' he said, but I'd blown it, talked too much, and he didn't believe me. 'Sure.' But he wanted me to think he did.

'Goddamned old drunk,' I muttered, covering my eyes as the lab boys closed their cases and the boys from the ambulance carried their stretcher in.

'Yeah.'

The attendants had trouble fitting Simon and his splinter on the stretcher.

'Hey, Jamison,' one said, 'can we pull this thing out?'

Jamison gave them his hard, disgusted glare, which they ignored.

'Well, can we?'

'Only if you want it shoved up your ass.'

'Okay, man, you don't have to get huffy. Christ, I was just asking.'

'I'm not huffy,' Jamison said softly.

'Oh,' the guy said after a long awkward moment looking at Jamison's unhappy face. 'Okay. Whatever you say, Lieutenant.'

Simon would have loved it. He stunk so badly that even the attendants turned their faces as they lifted him onto the stretcher. They put him too far to one side, and his body fell off. They cursed and put the body back on, strapping it down this time. But then they couldn't fit him into the ambulance door. They sat the load down in the rain, scratching their heads and discussing the project like two furniture movers stuck with a piano larger than the doorway.

'Get him outa here!' Jamison shouted.

They had to unstrap the body, tilt it so the splinter would fit diagonally through the door, then strap it again. There was a loud tearing noise as the wood ripped the headliner when they lifted him in.

'Watch the headliner, man,' one complained.

'Go to hell,' the other answered.

'Jesus Christ,' Jamison muttered.

Amos followed them, patting my arm and muttering around his cigar that he intended to do one hell of a good job on Simon's autopsy, then he waddled into the rainy dusk. Somewhere behind the clouds the sun found the horizon, and the long summer afternoon finally ended, night falling gently on the wet, shining streets of Meriwether.

'When the hell does summer start?' Jamison grumbled.

'Last month,' I said.

'Ain't it the truth,' he commented, then after a long pause he said, 'Say, Milo, I got some bad news for you.'

'So what's new?'

'But listen, you gotta promise me you'll stay outa this, Milo.'

'I don't have to promise you anything.'

'That's right, smart guy, you don't have to promise

me anything. I just hate to see your kid grow up with a con for a father. How do you think he'll feel about that?'

'How does he feel about having a cop for a father?' I asked.

Jamison shrugged and smiled like a man about to tell the truth.

'Like every other punk in this country,' he said. 'I'm the enemy, Milo, and you're his hero.'

'I didn't know,' I said, thinking that a man shouldn't be ashamed that his son thought of him as a hero, wondering what I was ashamed of.

'You haven't been by in too long. You ought to spend some time with him, let him see what you're really like.'

'Is that your bad news?' I asked. It had already been a long day, but the look on Jamison's face told me it was about to get longer.

'There's a warrant for Muffin,' he said.

'So?'

'Illegal possession. Two packets of heroin. Do you know where he is?'

'Goddammit. When it rains, it pours,' I said. 'How the hell did that happen?'

'Anonymous telephone call.'

'And you got a search warrant with that?'

'Milo, this town is so crazy with junkies right now that I could get a search warrant on a hunch.'

'You know Muffin never dealt smack.'

'I don't know anything anymore. Do you know where he is? Have you heard from him?'

'No,' I said. Now I understood Muffin's message and

knew where he had gone to ground. 'Not for a couple of weeks.'

'If you bullshit me, Milo, you're gonna take a fall. I promise you that.'

'Okay. This afternoon he left a message with my service that he had split for Mexico.'

'Yeah,' he grumbled, 'I got that too. What's it mean?'

'If it doesn't mean that he's gone to Mexico, or wants you to think that, then I don't know. We don't have any Captain Midnight secret codes, Jamison. I can't blame him for running. He wouldn't deal smack because it's too hard a fall and he wasn't hooked. He's not that kind.'

'I didn't tell you to adopt the kid,' Jamison said.

'You thought it was a good idea at the time.'

'Maybe I was wrong.'

'No chance of that,' I said. 'Do you think somebody might be trying to lay a bum rap on him?'

'That only happens in the movies, Milo.'

'Just like being right all the time, huh?'

'Yeah. Guess so.'

'Good thing he wasn't there when you showed up,' I said. 'I hope his luck holds.'

'Luck, hell. Whoever he owns over in robbery tipped him,' Jamison complained. 'I'll get that son of a bitch one day, and when he gets to Duck Valley, the cons'll eat him alive.'

'Good luck.'

'Fuck you.'

'How did you ever get to be a cop, Jamison? Your ideals are too high.'

'It was so long ago that I don't even remember,' he muttered.

'Remember what you said the night you found out I was on the take?'

'I remember cussing a lot,' he said, shaking his head.

'You gave me a long lecture about corruption, how it was like cancer. First, it took the man, then the police force, then the whole community.'

'That was a long time ago,' he said.

'Don't be so hard on yourself.'

'Don't be so easy,' he answered.

As we stood there, alone now, the lab boys gone, the crowd fed and dispersed, Simon's body off to the morgue to be butchered and probed, Jamison and I were nearly friends again, forgiving the distance between our lives. He reached over and squeezed my shoulder.

'I know how you felt about Simon, I'm really sorry.'

'Just another old drunk,' I said, sorry too now, trying to cover the tears.

'Reese give you anything interesting?' he asked, kneading his damp scalp.

'Lumps and pain.'

'Yeah, he's a hard one. He wouldn't give me anything either, but I got the feeling that he knew more than he was telling.'

'I thought so, too, at first, but now I don't know. He really looked like a man who wants to go straight, looked really tired of his life,' I said.

'Aren't we all,' Jamison said, patting his thin hair carefully back across his baldness. 'See you tomorrow.'

'Sure,' I said, then walked away, not bothering to

look back at him standing confused among the ruined house. The wreckage didn't amuse me anymore.

I could accept Elton Crider's death as a coincidence. He had been depressed and drinking; coincidences do happen. And from what Reese had told me, the Duffy kid had good reasons for an accidentally-on-purpose way out of his dismaying life. But nobody was going to convince me that Simon's death had been an accident. He had found out something somebody thought worth killing for, and they had pushed the old man down the stairs and taken his notebook. Not a very bright somebody, either. A smart man would have ripped out the pages with notes and left the rest of the notebook; a smart man would have known that I would take the old man's death personally. Of course, if I were a smart man, I would know how to go about finding the not-so-bright somebody who had killed Simon and set up Muffin.

The only thing I knew to do was to find a junkie and sweat him until he gave me his pusher, then sweat the pusher and work my way to the top of the dung heap. Whoever I found there was standing in shit. That was the plan.

But as I drove to Mahoney's to pick up a pair of handcuffs from my other office, I discovered that I needed Simon to talk to. Without him I wasn't sure. I could hear his gruff voice telling me what a silly bastard I was. We both knew that I wasn't mean enough to follow through. Not that I couldn't be mean when it seemed necessary in the moment, but that I lacked that abstract edge that makes violence calm and controlled, a tool for justice or vengeance. I would either get sick and quit or kill somebody before they could tell me what I needed to know.

'Dumb-ass,' the old voice said. 'Think.'

I tried, but found only confusion compounded by grief. I needed a drink. Nearly as badly as I needed the old man.

When I got to Mahoney's, Simon's wake had already taken the bar by storm, filling it with so many local drunks that they stood in line outside to get in the door. I parked in the loading zone, put the automatic and the sap and the derringer into the paper sack, then got out and tried to buck the crooked line at the door. Somebody was buying the drinks. I hoped it wasn't me.

The first wino I nudged didn't know me, so he pushed back, muttering that I should wait my turn. I picked him up by the nape of his neck and his britches, meaning to just set him aside. But I had had too much, speed or death, and I threw the old man into a parked car. He fell into the gutter, mewling curses, but he looked at me and didn't get up. If he had, I think I might have killed him. *He* thought so, scuttling away quickly. The others outside the door either knew me or had been convinced that I wanted through. Everybody either left or stood silently aside. The silence spread into the bar as I walked in, and they all stood aside.

Leo was sitting on the bar, waving his hands over his disciples, swaying gently, an amazed, drunken grin on his face. I knew who had been buying drinks.

'Fell off the wagon,' he confided happily to me. 'God,

it feels great. Makes me remember why I drank.' But then he saw my worried face and added, 'But by God, I'll be sober tomorrow, Milo, sober as a judge. Man can't stay drunk all his life, right?'

'Right,' I said.

'Goddamned old Simon,' he muttered, unhappy again. He lifted one clenched fist, nearly falling backwards behind the bar, and handed me the tiny gold star clutched in his sweaty palm. I had to peel it off, didn't have to lick it when I pasted it in the corner of Simon's picture, couldn't look at the smiling face behind the glass. Some decent soul had unplugged the jukebox as I walked over to the wall, and standing on the chair above the quietly drunken crowd, I felt as if I should give a speech, so I turned around and said, 'Fuck it.'

And they cheered.

When I walked into the cooler, they were still shouting. Somebody had plugged the jukebox back in and turned it up so loud that I could feel the bass notes thumping the floorboards, but I couldn't hear the music over the roar of the wake.

Freddy followed me into the other office and watched silently as I slipped into the shoulder holster and checked the automatic, holstered it and put the extra clips in my back pocket.

'You fixing to kill somebody?' he asked.

'If I get the chance,' I said, putting the sap into the back pocket with the extra clips.

'That ain't hardly the rig,' he said. 'It's too slow. And you ain't hardly the type.'

'It's as fast as I am,' I said, settling my arms back into

the damp windbreaker. The blood from my eyebrow had stained the left shoulder with dull brown spots and the rain had smeared them. 'And killers don't come in types.'

'Who you going after?'

'I don't know yet,' I said as I rummaged through drawers looking for the cuffs.

'You best hope he's slow on the draw, Milo. I tell you that shoulder rig with an automatic ain't for –'

But before he could finish, I had spun, drawn and cocked the pistol, and faced him in the combat stance.

'Jesus Christ,' he said, ducking. 'I'll shut up.'

'I used to practice some,' I said, finding the cuffs and hooking them over the back of my belt.

'You ever kill a man with that?' he asked, not shutting up at all. Sometimes I thought that I had to either play father or son to every drunk in town. 'Did you?'

'No.'

'Have you ever killed a man?'

'Not since the war. Haven't fired a shot in anger in nearly twenty years.'

'Hick cops,' he muttered, talking around his toothpick.

'What?'

'Milo, I killed four men and one woman. I got more time in front of review boards than you got on the crapper,' he said, taking out the toothpick and smiling. 'Why don't you let me do it?'

I looked at him. He was grinning, mean as hell, his pudgy face no longer a joke.

'No, thanks,' I said.

He shrugged, then asked, 'What about the twist I've been tailing? Want me to stay with it?'

'Oh, hell, I'd forgotten about that. Yeah, stay on it,' I said, not really caring, knowing Freddy liked the work. 'What did she do today?'

'Went shopping. Spent loads of somebody's money. Made five phone calls from public booths.'

'Catch any numbers?'

'Couldn't get that close. I can try tomorrow, if you want.'

'No, just tail her.'

'Whose hooker is she?' he asked.

'What?'

'Who does she belong to? She's a hooker, Milo. Didn't you know?'

'I should've guessed.'

'Big-city girl too. Maybe she's on vacation or something, maybe she's retired, but I know hookers, and she ain't done it for free in a long time.'

'Is she pretty?' I asked, wondering about Nickie's friend, why he had money to keep an eye on her but not enough money to come up with anything but a whore.

'She used to be. She'd turn your head till you got a good look.'

'Ain't it the truth,' I said. 'Stay with it.'

'That's some eye you've got. What happened?'

'Ran into a wall,' I said, and we grinned. 'And say, why don't you keep an eye on Leo tonight. I'll pay for the time.'

'Been watching him already,' he said, sighing bravely, a man who could hold his liquor, who could kill. 'But it's my time.'

'Thanks.'

'It's nothing. Say, you carrying a backup gun?'

'No. Why?'

'When you're hunting a man, Milo, always carry a backup gun. Anybody who would kill a worthless old fart like Simon is liable to be looking for his friends. You still got that derringer?'

'Sure,' I said, lifting it out of the sack on the table.

'Strap it to your leg or stuff it in your shorts.'

'I'd feel silly.'

'Better silly than dead.'

'Okay,' I muttered, looking for some tape, thinking I would rather have a loaded gun on my leg than in my shorts. I found some electrical tape and strapped the derringer to my left calf. 'How's that?'

'It looks okay.'

'Hell, I don't know what I'd do without all these drunk advisers,' I said as I straightened up, grinning at Freddy.

'I don't either,' he said without a trace of a smile. 'Watch yourself, Milo.'

I nodded and followed him out into the throng of mourners.

Out in the bar, it looked as if Meriwether was finally going to have a riot. A geriatrics ward had gone insane – an old folks' home in revolt, or maybe the faces had climbed down off the wall, grown flushed and grossly swollen, shedding dignity and good humor like old clothes. The air stunk of smoke and rotten teeth, cheap whiskey and thin sweat, wine puke. Lorrie – resident hooker to all the old men whose erections hadn't completely retired, a short fat old woman, nearly bald beneath her gray curls – was dancing, her skirt lifted to expose thighs once meant to drive men mad, fish-belly white, pitted, jiggling thighs rising and falling to the rock beat. The crowd made room for her dance, not to watch but to protect themselves. A shrunken Indian, wrinkled and weathered in bars, joined her in the cleared space, dancing the dance of his grandfathers, his toothless mouth wide with lost songs.

And there was Billy the dummy and Arch the railroad engineer, and Duke Meadows who had once been hairdresser to the stars, and his constant companion, Buddy Wells, who had almost been a cowboy star at Republic. And a brace of retired supply sergeants loading Army crap on Skipper, the retired bosun's mate who hadn't made chief in thirty years. And Olinger, the failed mortician who watched with a professional eye as if he still had a business. And there was Alf the swamper, who swept bars for drinks, and his ex-wife Doty who had divorced him but hadn't left yet. And they were all there but the dead, who were hanging on the walls, smiling in approval and looking like they wanted a drink.

But that was the pretty part.

As I pushed through the crowd and the grabbing hands, which offered consolation or begged for drinks to bear their sorrow, the drunken arguments and fights had already begun. Classic wino fisticuffs at the bar: one punch every five minutes until one opponent or the other could no longer rise from his stool to totter into the ring. And classic wino arguments: political discussions over men who had long since left office and died, personal grievances twenty years past. Rivers of angry tears. Leo was stretched out on the bar, sleeping and grinning like a man who meant to rise again. The drunk I had heaved into the parked car held his head at Leo's feet. A puddle of vomit, flecked with blood, blocked the doorway. As I stepped over it, a long-haired kid who was peering into the bar said, 'Them old farts is weird.' I hit him on the shoulders with the heels of my palms, and he stumbled down the street, inquiring what was wrong with me. But I couldn't tell him.

Armed and advised and ready, I headed north on Dottle searching for a junkie, until I realized that I didn't know what a junkie looked like, so I went back to the office to call Muffin to see if he knew anybody who was hooked. I thought I might need some more of Nickie's money too, just in case there was trouble. The front doors were always locked at night, so I went down the alley to the side door, all the steel hanging off my body feeling suddenly heavy and foolish.

12

They must have been waiting outside Mahoney's because they followed me into the alley and took me just as I stepped out of the light into the shadows. I must have heard something, a sole scraping on brick, perhaps, or a grunt as the one in front raised the length of two-by-four. I ducked and went to the left and back, trying to get inside the swing. The board missed my head, but his forearms caught my neck at the shoulder and knocked me into the building wall. The force took the board out of his hands, or everything would have ended right there, but I heard the wood skipping off the paving bricks with loud, flat smacks and I shoved off the wall, trying to stay close to them until I had room to run. I got one with an elbow, but the other caught me with a kidney punch, and I bounced off the wall again. The fight went on, but I had already lost; all the butting and scratching and biting afterwards just made them mad. Except for falling down, it was over quickly, as quickly as they let me fall down, which took a long time.

When I came to, they were still there, standing about five feet from me. One was counting my cash, the other wondering painfully if his nose was broken. I didn't have his problem: my nose was all over my right cheek. The one counting money paused, telling the other that there was supposed to be more money, but the other was more interested in his nose, so his partner stepped over to examine it. I watched their silhouettes against the lighted street, watched them as best I could from where I lay curled against the wall. The automatic wasn't beneath my left arm, but I didn't mind. The derringer was still on my leg, but I didn't think I could reach it. That didn't bother me either. All I wanted to do was lie very still and hope they weren't going to kill me. If they hadn't already.

'I reckon it's busted, Bubba,' I heard one say to the other, and Bubba began to breathe hard and sob, saying, 'I'm gonna kill the motherfucker.' I edged into a tighter ball, my hand reaching for my leg. 'No, Bubba,' the other said, but Bubba pushed against his outstretched arm. 'We ain't supposed to kill him,' the first one argued, but then he added gleefully, 'but we can damn sure put him in the hospital for a long time, break his goddamned leg or something.' Bubba agreed happily, but when the first one reached into the shadows to pull me out, he found the nickel-plated glint of the derringer in his face.

'Freeze,' I whispered. Maybe he heard me, maybe not. He tried to back up, to stand up and grab an automatic out of his belt. But he didn't make it. At two feet, even half blind and whipped senseless, I couldn't miss. I blew his face off.

The muzzle blast knocked him over, splashed blood and flesh all over me, blinded and deafened me for a moment. When I looked for Bubba, he was twenty yards away, streaking for the street, but I pulled off the other barrel anyway. Brick dust bloomed in his wake as he turned the corner, and the large lead slug flattened, singing across the street. A department store window exploded and fell into the display. Mannequins tumbled from their studied repose, hanging upon each other like the victims of a natural disaster. The store's alarm bell began gonging, deep and unhurried, as patiently regular as a fog horn. In the distance, sirens answered. A timid crowd formed at the window, peering inside then all around, trying to understand what had happened. Then a bolder soul moved, and within seconds, winos and freaks were fleeing down the streets with the display clothing and furniture, two wildly ambitious drunks staggering off with a wicker couch.

I knew better than to leave a gun in the hands of a dead man, since sometimes they only look dead, so I crawled over to the body, wrenching my bloody money out of his hand, and jerked the automatic out of his waistband, trying not to look at what remained of his face. But I did. When the police came to answer the store alarm, they found us eventually, heaped like garbage in the alley.

'You oughta see your face,' Jamison said when the doctor finished.

'You oughta feel it,' I mumbled.

Jamison grinned, then followed the doctor out of the emergency room. Through the open door, I could hear them arguing over where I should spend the rest of the night, the doctor insisting on the hospital, Jamison on a cell. My face didn't feel too bad, not nearly as bad as it would the next day when the Novocaine wore off. When I sat up on the table, my head was light and my taped ribs sparked with slivers of pain, but I didn't faint. I could see fairly well, out of my right eye, around the tape on my nose and cheeks and forehead, and I thought I could walk. Actually, I was fond of the pain; it kept me from thinking about the dead guy in the alley.

'He should check in for observation,' the doctor maintained loudly.

'He should check into a home,' Jamison said, 'but he's going to jail.'

'You have to clear it with the supervisor,' the doctor answered, and I heard their footsteps echo down the hall.

I didn't want to spend the night either place, so I tried standing, then walking. My shirt was too much of a mess to wear. I tossed it into the trash and wrestled into the bloodstained windbreaker, picked up the empty shoulder holster and left. Jamison wanted to charge me with carrying a concealed weapon and first-degree manslaughter, neither of which he could make stick. He just wanted me in jail so he could talk to me while I was in no condition to resist. I needed a lawyer and some sleep, and Jamison wouldn't let me have either until it was too late. I didn't think he'd be too angry if I split, particularly if I could stay away from him for a few days. And I knew just where I wanted to lie down.

Outside, Amos was waiting for Jamison, and rubbing his hands together briskly, as if he wanted to wash them again.

'Jamison in there?' he asked.

'No, he left a half-hour or so ago. Said he was going home to get some sleep.'

'He probably needs it. You look terrible too. You ought to be in the hospital, boy.'

'I been in twice today, Amos, and it didn't help.'

'I know how you feel, boy,' he answered as if he really did. 'I guess I'll go on home and catch him tomorrow.'

'Do the autopsy yet?'

'No. We're going to wait until tomorrow. I got everything ready, but I just couldn't handle it tonight. That's what I wanted to tell Jamison. But I guess it can wait.'

'Sure,' I said. 'Say, can you give me a lift to Mahoney's?'

'You don't need a drink, boy.'

'Just want to pick up my car and go home.'

'Can you drive?'

'I can walk, can't I?'

'Not too well,' he said, then helped me around the corner to his car. 'They give you anything for the pain, boy?'

'No.'

'Here,' he said, rummaging in his bag and handing me a small bottle. 'Take two every four hours, son, and you won't feel anything.'

'Thanks. I don't feel anything now.'

'Wait, boy, just wait,' he muttered as he pulled out into the traffic. He dropped me beside my rig and drove away jerkily, like a man who wasn't going to sleep much that night.

Inside the rig, I sat behind the wheel trying to sort out things in my mind, listening to that unfamiliar voice in the alley saying, '*We ain't supposed to kill him*,' and wondering what it meant. If they meant to take me out of action, they had succeeded. I was through. Helen Duffy would have to live with what I knew about her little brother, and although I was fairly certain I had killed the wrong man, that was going to have to pass for vengeance this year. If Simon couldn't rest easy with that, then that was his problem, because I was tired and old and not nearly as tough as I thought I was, and I was through. As I drove away through the bursts of pain that came in bright flashes, I could see his laughing face, but his voice was still.

Maybe she heard my rig bounce off the curb or the sound of the slamming door. Maybe she heard me stumble, cursing the rain as I stepped across the curb and sidewalk. Or maybe she had just come to the door to check the weather. When I knocked she opened the door so quickly that she must have been standing behind it, waiting. Fresh from another bath, warm and flushed and sweetly damp, she seemed draped in steam, which seeped from her body through the green robe. Curls of wet hair looped against the freckled skin of her neck. In the pale light, her scrubbed face glowed, and her mouth was slightly open, as if in passion, or grief.

'You spend more time in the water than a fish,' I said, trying to joke so she would know I was still among the living.

'Oh my God!' she breathed. 'What happened to you?'

'Hard night,' I said. But the smile I managed cracked, and I fell, tilting toward her like a falling tree.

Her arms caught me, strong arms held me upright, clutched the blood and filth to her body, her hands smooth and rubbing and holding me beneath the damp windbreaker, her lips murmuring questions and concern.

'Easy,' I said as she found a bruise beneath the tape.

'What happened?'

'Lie down,' I mumbled. 'I've got to lie down.' As I moved into the room, she still held me, her hands on my neck tugging my ruined face to the soft curve of her neck, her gentle shoulder, bumping my left ear with her chin. She felt the stiff spines of the stitches and jerked away before I could complain. 'Got to lie down.'

'Oh, no,' she moaned, 'no.'

Thinking that she meant to deny the damage, I moved against her again, heading into the room, but she pushed back.

'You can't,' she whispered. 'Oh dammit, I'm sorry but you can't. Oh God, why do things have to be like this.'

'What?' I asked, stepping back to look at her.

'My mother – she's here.' Behind her, the splash of the shower echoed from the bathroom.

'What's she doing here?'

'I don't know.'

'Oh, hell, tell her it's all right, tell her we're going to get married – my God, tell her anything. I've got to lie down.'

'Oh, I can't. Now now. Not like this.'

'Like what?' I propped my hands on her shoulders and squeezed until she flinched. 'Like what?'

'Oh, I don't know,' she whispered, her face seeming to break into painful fragments. 'Drunk and beat up.'

'Lady, I'm always drunk and beat up. That's why I need you,' I said as clearly as I could.

She looked at me for a long moment, poised in that space between our lives, hovering like a hummingbird, the breath of her confusion and compassion so strong it blew kindly on my hot, tattered face.

'It will be all right,' I said.

'Oh no. Nothing is ever all right. You don't know her,' she said, sobs laboring like stones from her heaving chest.

'I'll tell her we're in love,' I said, brushing her cheek with my thumb, wiping away tears and a freckle of dried blood.

'Not now.'

'Now's all we got, babe.'

She groaned, brushed my puffy lips with hers, whispering 'Later,' pushing at my chest with small fists as the bathroom noises gathered to some conclusion that only she understood, murmuring 'Later, I'll come later,' and she gently shoved me out the door, closed it in my face.

'Someone at the door?' I heard a strong, vibrant voice ask.

'No. Yes, Mother. They had the wrong room,' Helen answered, her voice muffled as if she was leaning against the door.

'I guess so,' I said to myself and let my raised fist fall to my side. Then I walked toward the motel lobby and the bar beyond, letting the rain wash my face.

The urbane type who had been talking to Nickie that morning noticed the sudden hush of his customers and he came around the front desk quickly, inquiring in a carefully polite voice – the sort of voice that owns things and tells people what to do and how to do it – if he might be of assistance, but I walked right through him. Nickie was behind the desk too, but he hadn't moved, his face white and his eyes wide, and he didn't move until the polite voice said his name, then Nickie rushed around the desk. As I slowed, the man behind me grabbed my arm. The tourists and dinner customers hummed with confusion, moving away from the scene. But not so far that they couldn't watch.

'Nickie, tell this fucking bellhop to get his hand off me,' I said, 'before I tear it off.'

'Jesus Christ,' Nickie pleaded, and his friend held my arm tighter.

'Look, man, I need a drink real quick and real bad, then I'll split,' I said. 'I'll even go out the back door so I don't scare the tourists.' Then I turned to the man holding my arm, but he wasn't scared, and I didn't think I could survive another fight, so I ignored him.

Nickie looked at him, his mouth moving without sound, and the man said, 'All right. In a go cup.' Then he turned my arm loose, adding, 'And I don't ever want to see you in here again.'

'Sure,' I said, shrugging, out of snappy lines and empty threats.

The man smiled blandly, as if there had been no question, a confident glaze over his face, an arrogantly arched eyebrow, but I couldn't even rise to that. If I didn't get a drink in this bar, I wouldn't make it to the next one. I let Nickie hustle me down a side hallway and through the kitchen to the back door.

'What about the drink?' I huffed; his flapping trot had worn me out, made the top of my head ache.

'I'll get it, I'll get it,' he grunted, sounding nearly as tired as I was. 'Wait there,' he said, pushing me next to the huge steel garbage hamper, 'I'll be right back.' I waited, slumped against the cold, wet metal, my hands quivering, my throat hot with sobs held back. 'Wha-what happened?' he stammered when he returned with a Styrofoam cup filled with ice and blessed whiskey, which I poured down my throat, over my chin and chest. 'You, you all right?' he asked as I gagged. The son of a bitch felt sorry for me; that kept the drink down.

'Another one,' I said.

'Huh?'

'Get me another drink, goddammit!'

'Okay, okay, right back,' he said, then left at his pounding trot.

While he was gone, I gobbled two of Amos's pills, then two more. As I waited I let my fingers finally take inventory of my face. The doctor had gotten the top half of my left ear back on my face but he suggested plastic surgery. When I touched it, it throbbed so painfully that I decided to leave it alone. The star-shaped gash at my hairline, which I had probably gotten giving a head butt, hadn't started swelling yet, so I could feel the dent and the forest of stitches. It felt as if this doctor had done a better job when he restitched my eyebrow than the first one. I didn't bother to check my nose; the doctor had set it but told me that if I wanted to breathe out of it, they would have to operate, adding that he hoped I had good medical insurance. Jamison laughed, so I didn't have to answer that.

When Nickie came back, I spit a mouthful of bloody ice cubes on the ground. He seemed to have more control over his face and voice, but his hand went back to the middle of his chest as soon as he handed me the drink.

'Wha-wha happened, Milo? Goddamn, you look terrible. Shouldn't you be in the hospital?'

'I just came from there,' I said, 'and look what happened.'

'Huh?'

'Nothing.'

'What happened? You wreck your car?'

'No,' I said, sipping the drink and rattling the ice. 'I got mugged. Right here in our fair city, Nickie, I got mugged.'

'Wha-who-wha –'

'Two guys jumped me in the alley next to the bank,' I said, not waiting for his question.

'They get away?'

'One did, yeah.'

'What about the other – one?'

'He's dead,' I said, making myself say it.

'How – Wha-what happened?'

'I shot him in the face.'

'Jesus Christ,' he groaned, looking sick, bending at the waist and belching.

'You all right?'

'Huh?'

'Are you going to be all right, Nickie?'

'Oh, yeah. Just haven't eaten yet. Goddamned business keeps me jumping, Milo, and my goddamn stomach, you know.'

'Might be an ulcer,' I said. 'You should have it checked.'

'Huh? Oh, yeah. Maybe so.'

'Nickie, I'm gonna have to take a couple of days off, but I've got somebody to cover your friend's lady friend. Is that okay?'

'Don't worry about it, you know. Take however long, you know, my friend will understand, you know.'

'I already got it covered, Nickie.'

'Okay, whatever you say, it's okay,' he mumbled. 'Hey, Milo, I heard about Simon, you know, and goddamn, I'm sorry.'

'You know what they say, Nickie?'

'Huh?'

'Nobody lives forever.'

'Oh, yeah,' he said, looking shocked. Maybe nobody had ever told him about it. 'But I'm – I'm really sorry.'

'Right,' I said. 'Check with you later.'

As I walked away he muttered something I didn't hear. A little bit of Nickie's pity and commiseration went a long way. I was too tired to stand around listening to him, so I went back to my rig and drove toward Mahoney's like a shot.

13

Two long drunken days later, after the coroner's jury had ruled Simon's death accidental, the body was released to me. Thanks to Jamison, I was free to bury the body. He must have felt sorry for me because, even though the coroner's jury hadn't ruled on the man's death in the alley, I hadn't been charged with anything. It wasn't because he couldn't find me, either, since I spent the whole time in Mahoney's, drunker than I'd been for years, too drunk to change clothes or even begin to understand the haze of pain around my head.

So I buried Simon – alone to mourn him, just as he said it would be. Leo had come along, but he was collapsed behind a nearby gravestone, too drunk to know where he was or why. Simon and I were dressed for the occasion, he in my father's overcoat, me in the bloody windbreaker. The rain had passed on, the sun returned, and the afternoon was as fresh as spring, the sky azure and cloudless, the air warm in the sun and cool in the shade. In the poplars along the road, a light breeze flashed among the crisp leaves, and the muted hum of traffic from the interstate highway buzzed like lazy bees in clover. Simon Rome had no service, no tedious eulogy at the graveside. Just the sound of Leo retching. No ceremony. I had brought a bottle of Wild Turkey to place in the grave with him, but Leo and I had drunk and spilled most of it on the drive out. I shared the rest with the two trustees from the county jail, then tossed the empty bottle into the open grave, gathered the sack of wasted flesh that contained Leo, and went back to town.

'You win, you old fart,' I whispered as I left the cemetery, 'but you cheated.'

On the way back to the bar, I dumped Leo at the hospital, glad he could afford a private room. The charity ward had been filled with drunks who had nearly killed themselves with Leo's free whiskey. Leo had fallen off the wagon, but I had fallen apart, withdrawn until I was as insensate as a stone just to hold the pieces together. The pain remained, as did the grief, as constant as a cloud of black flies. I drank, was drunk without being drunk, locked into that terrible and curious lucidity where the world has no more meaning than a movie, the colors vivid but the lighting too harsh, the focus so precise that the world seems cornered by sharp edges. So I walked into Mahoney's, shouting for whiskey and blurred definition, for drunken sleep, forsaking vengeance, forgiving love.

Later, afternoon threatening dusk, Dick Diamond woke me from the black hole of a dreamless sleep, his hand gently shaking my shoulder.

'Hey, old buddy, let's go home,' he said.

'Have a drink,' I mumbled, raising my head from the table.

'No, thanks.'

'For me, man, for me.'

'You've had enough,' he replied. 'There's no need to kill yourself.'

'Get my own goddamned whiskey,' I said, rising. When he reached for me, I swung at him blindly, but he ducked my fist, caught my arm over his shoulders, and carried me out into the neon-smudged dusk, carried me toward home and sleep, struggling uphill all the way.

In the confusion of sleep, she finally came to me, on wings in a cool throbbing wind, on her belly sinuous, angel and snake, her hair fire, her hair blood flower blooming, her hands cold, fingers ice, tears hot, her hands holding me again, to her soft breast, rocking and singing, small moans and the sound of a child weeping, hold me, held my face, my head cracked like a fallen egg . . .

And when I rose up from sleep, she came with the pain, forgiving, unlike the pain, unforgiving, that filled my body and burst out around the spike driven between my eyes, a pain more fierce than the thirst.

'How do you feel?' she asked.

'Whiskey,' somebody answered.

'No,' she sighed, 'no.'

'Yes I know yes what I'm doing I've been drunk before I need whiskey now and again to stand this,' I pleaded, crying finally, not for Simon or myself or loves lost, but for whiskey against this thirst.

She brought a bottle and a glass; foolishly, I held the bottle, my teeth rattling against the glass, and poured it into the fire inside, my stomach pleading for another, which I had, and another again. But when it came up, I couldn't find the toilet, couldn't hide the blood from her, couldn't find my hands to cover.

'Shouldn't he be in the hospital?' she asked somebody vague in the distance.

'He wouldn't like it,' a voice answered.

I croaked approval, then fell asleep. Or something akin.

'Hi,' she said when next I woke. 'How are you now?'

'Hi,' I answered, twisting in the fog, awake enough to appreciate the pain.

'You feel better, love?' she asked, gathering my hand in hers.

'Worse – but that's an improvement.'

'How so?'

'I'd have to get better to die.'

'There's a number by the phone, a doctor, call him, tell him – I've been drinking . . . but I'm sober now and need a boost . . . he'll understand . . . and next time I . . . wake up . . . food . . . love . . .'

When it seemed that the toast and tea were going to stay down, I started on the soup, but the spoon clattered against the side of the bowl.

'Let me help,' she said.

'Nope. Recovery is a matter of will. These small things count,' I said, but had to abandon the spoon in favor of drinking from the bowl. 'I used to go with a Chinese girl.'

'Really.'

'And she made the best egg-drop soup in the world.'

'I'm sure.'

'And if I had some now, I'd be up and about in a flash.'

'You just stay in bed, mister.'

'Oh, lady, I intend to. If I'd known it took all this to get you into my bedroom, I would have done it sooner. I know how, you know.'

'Just hush,' she murmured. 'And don't be silly.' But her smile glowed like a sunrise.

As I wiped the mist from the mirror, I asked the graybeard therein if he might be me, but she answered from the bedroom.

'I certainly hope not.'

'Me too.'

'You need some help?' she asked from the bathroom doorway.

'Take off your clothes and leap right in,' I said, smoothing lather over the lumps and bruises.

'It would probably kill you.'

'Braggart.'

'You'll see,' she smirked.

'I damn sure hope so,' I said, but there were sudden serious lines around her eyes, so I added lightly, 'When are we going to get married?'

'After you join the AA.'

'I don't want to hang around with a bunch of fucking drunks.'

* * *

'I just fell apart, that's all. Too much happening at once. It's cheaper than a breakdown. And if it doesn't kill you, easier to recover from. My father was a drunk, my mother was a drunk and a suicide, and my life hasn't been very pretty. I have neither character nor morals, no religion, no purpose in life, except as Simon said, to get by, so is it any wonder that I drink?'

'No.'

'At least I don't have to go to meetings.'

'No?'

'My name is Milton Chester Milodragovitch, the third, and I'm a drunk. Thank God.'

'No.'

When it became obvious that I had survived myself once again, we went out into the backyard to sun and listen to the creek as it constructed a rushing silence. We rattled our way through the weight of Sunday's paper, sipping tea and chattering as foolishly as two slightly mad squirrels. Beside her firm body, clad in a pink bikini, I felt like a suit of old clothes left in the alley for the garbage truck. But the sun worked on me, drawing a quick sweat, a greasy skim, like that of a chronic invalid, slimy with waste, odorous with my body's disgust. I went in and showered it off. The second sweat, when it came, was better, still rancid and bitter, so I repeated the shower.

'You spend more time in the water than a fish,' she commented when I came back out, then she rolled over on her stomach slowly, stretching languidly.

'Smart-ass,' I said.

'Dirty mouth.'

This time, as I lay beneath the sun, my body seemed to become flesh again instead of a sack of vile, tepid fluid, my skin tightening as old muscle rose to meet the warmth. My face still felt as hard as dried mud, and as comfortable to carry, but my limbs began to rejoice about survival. When I seemed whole, I rose and knelt beside her lounge chair, ran my hand down the small of her back, across the heated skin soft with oil and clean sweat.

'Yes?' she breathed.

'Thanks.'

'For what?'

'For coming.'

'You're welcome, but it seemed the least I could do under the circumstances. This whole thing is my fault, and I wouldn't blame you for hating me – I mean, after leaving you outside my motel room when you were half dead, I wouldn't blame you.'

'No,' I said, 'it's not your fault at all. I walked into this with my eyes open, or at least they were both open at the time, and whatever happened, it was my fault.'

'You mean you forgive me?'

'There's nothing to forgive. Just so you hang around for a while, till I get well, then maybe –'

'Don't,' she groaned, rising from under my hand, turning away with a sob. 'Don't say that.' Then she covered her face with her hands and ran across the yard to the edge of the creek.

The hand that had held her was still there, as if measuring the height of a child, and it trembled. I never knew what to do when a woman ran away, could never tell if they wanted to be alone or if they wanted me to follow. I had tried both ways, but neither worked.

'Hey,' I said, and she turned. 'What the hell am I supposed to do?'

Whatever she said was inaudible against the noise of the creek.

'What?'

'What the hell am *I* supposed to do!' she shouted, stomping her foot angrily, her fists wiping roughly at the tears. But she was smiling, so I went to her, held her against me.

'I can't have this happen,' she said. 'I have a job –'

'You better hang on to it,' I said, 'because I don't have one.'

'And I don't know what to tell my mother.'

'Tell her our children will have red hair and Cossack tempers.'

'That's not funny,' she whimpered.

'Then tell her we'll be happy because we're both too old to be unkind.'

'Don't say things like that unless you mean them, unless you're serious.'

'I've been serious from the beginning.'

'Oh God, I don't know, it's all so confusing,' she said. 'I don't know – what to say – to anybody – anymore . . .'

'Don't worry,' I said, holding her tightly, so tightly that I felt her breath sigh out. 'It will be all right,' I said, staring over her shoulder into the sun-dappled shade on the creek. Inside my chest, the stone I had placed there crumbled into white dust, and now I could cry for Simon and love for myself. Only my face was hard, scabs and scars and lumps, the tape over my nose making it seem that I saw the world from a cage or through the narrow slit in a cell door.

'I'm not what I seem,' she said softly.

'Nobody ever is,' I said, thinking of her little brother in spite of myself. 'Don't worry about it.'

'I can't help it,' she whispered. 'You don't understand – about me.'

'Do I have to understand you to love you?'

'I don't know. I don't know if anybody has ever loved me.'

'I do,' I said. And it wasn't hard at all.

She nodded, gazing into the distance, then tucked her head against my chest, and we stood there, sun-flushed skin, heated flesh, hands slowly touching each other's backs.

'Let's go inside,' I said.

'If you want,' she answered in an oddly small voice, as if she had no say in the matter, no will with which to either resist or comply.

'I need you, love,' I said, and she followed me into the house.

Against our flesh, fired in the sun, the sheets were cool, and we were as timid as children, shy and clumsy, graceless, banging noses and clicking teeth, giggling among the aching moans. Once inside her, though, I found that lovely compliance, her hips tilting toward my need, and as I knelt above her, watched her face lose focus, her eyes widen, her tiny teeth nipping at her lower lip between sighs and moans, as I waited, still, unmoving, all the sorrow emptied from me into her.

'You're lovely,' I said, 'absolutely beautiful.'

She focused her eyes, smiled slowly, saying, 'And you're the ugliest man I've ever met.'

'It wasn't very good, was it?'

'It was kind. That's enough. We're not children, we'll learn.'

'Are you sure?'

'Absolutely.'

'I didn't hurt your face?'

'Who could hurt a face like this?'

'Someone surely tried.'

It was an easy Sunday, small talk and gentle love, weak drinks dissolving, cigarette smoke captured by bars of sunlight. The delight of a new body, the tracing of design among freckles. An afternoon of touching. Waking to the pleasure of a new love.

But once when I woke, she was gone. I found her at the back door, wrapped in the bedspread against the evening chill, watching the stars perforate the sunset sky.

'Hey, what's wrong?' I asked.

'Nothing,' she answered mournfully.

'Come on.'

'Well, okay, it's Raymond.'

'What about him?'

'Every time I start to feel happy again, I think of him – and the man – whoever killed him.'

'What makes you so sure that somebody killed him?' I asked as gently as I could.

'You still don't believe me, do you?' she asked as she turned around. Her face was shadowed, but I could see her eyes, which were oddly blank. 'Do you?'

'It could have been an accident,' I suggested mildly.

'How many times do I have to tell you that Raymond was not a drug addict,' she said, her voice as empty as her eyes.

'Love, you may have to face the fact that he was.'

'Never,' she whispered. 'And even if he was, it was because somebody forced him, and that's the same as killing him. Isn't it?'

'I guess so,' I said, not wanting to argue with her stony grief.

'You know something you're not telling me,' she said, her voice trembling.

'No.'

'No what?'

'I'll tell you someday,' I said.

'When?'

'When you feel – when you don't feel so strongly about his death,' I said.

'People never understand,' she murmured.

'What?'

'How I felt about Raymond. If you understood, you'd tell me what it is that you know.'

'It's sort of – incomplete,' I said, feeling myself being pulled back into the case. 'When I know all of it, I'll tell you.'

'When?'

'Tomorrow maybe, the next day. I don't know. I'll go back to work tomorrow or the next day.'

'I'm sorry about your friend,' she said as she brushed her lips across my cheek. 'Truly sorry. Do you think there's any connection?'

'No,' I lied. 'I don't think so.'

'Dick told me his name, but I've forgotten.'

'Simon,' I said, 'Simon Rome.' Buried at county expense, his grave unmarked, his death unavenged.

And with his name, my safe world ended, my castle came tumbling down into the stagnant waters of the moat, and in confusion it began all over again, all the questions, those with no answers, those with too many.

The next morning I woke early, showered and shaved, then tried to eat, but my appetite failed me. The bacon smelled like dead pork and the eggs accused me with their fierce yellow glare. I had a piece of toast and a shot of whiskey in my coffee, drank the coffee and smoked a cigarette in the bedroom doorway, watched the lady sleep, wondered where to begin, how to keep the lady in my bed on a more permanent basis.

But I didn't know where to begin.

What would Simon say, I wondered, thinking he'd probably say *Have another drink and forget about it, dumb-ass*, which sounded good to me. For a moment. Then I realized how much I missed the old fart already. At least I was smart enough to know that. And what else did I know? The man in the alley saying I wasn't supposed to be killed, which meant that somebody didn't want me poking around. But around what? The Duffy kid's death? Simon's? Elton Crider's? Muffin's frame? Then I remembered that I hadn't returned Muffin's call, which I promised myself I would do just as soon as I passed a pay telephone.

The kid's death had to be the beginning, but I couldn't make myself believe that it had been anything other than the old accidentally-on-purpose death. Any other thing was too complicated a way to kill the Duffy kid. If somebody wanted him dead, there were much more certain ways. Still, somebody wanted me in the hospital and out of the way. Somebody had gone to the trouble to shove Simon down those stairs and steal his notebook. Maybe Jamison had the notebook, though. Then why did he hide the pencil from me? No, somebody had taken the notebook. A not-so-smart somebody. As it had occurred to me before, a smart man would have taken just the pages with notes and not the whole thing, so he had to be either dumb or excited, an amateur. And what had Reese said about the heroin dealer? An amateur. Just like me. But why couldn't Jamison come up with the dealer? Just for that reason. Which meant I was going to have the same problem.

So have another drink and forget about it.

But standing there in the doorway, watching the lady sleep, I knew I couldn't get enough drinks in my stomach to make my mind forget about it at all. My major problem, of course, was going to be the fact that I had neither training nor experience as a detective, no matter what it said on my license. For God's sake, I didn't even read mystery novels because they always seemed too complicated. As a minion of justice or vengeance, I just didn't make it. But I remembered something Muffin had told me once as I tried to convince him he should live the straight life. He told me that if I wasn't a cop, I'd be a crook, which I knew immediately to be the truth. I wasn't about to sell things or clerk in a store or teach children not to suck eggs or even bartend. But knowing that didn't help either.

Another drink, forget it.

I was just about to get mad when I heard tires crunching down the gravel of my driveway. I went to the door before whoever it was could ring the doorbell and wake Helen. When I opened the door, I saw Dick's van stopped in the driveway. He sat behind the wheel, peering through the windshield toward the house. I waved at him, and he got out. We met in the middle of the lawn and shook hands gravely, then he smiled.

'You look terrible, old buddy. Happy but terrible,' he said, which sounded strange, since I didn't feel happy at all.

'Yeah.'

'You survived, huh?'

'Looks like it. Hey, man, thanks.'

'For what?'

'Bringing me home. Calling her.'

'She called me, man.'

'Thanks anyway.'

'It's nothing,' he said, looking away. 'How's it going?'

'What?'

'You know. Everything. The two of you.'

'All right, I guess. Nothing's settled,' I said, thinking that it might be a long time before anything was. 'We haven't talked about it much.'

'Yeah, I understand,' he said, watching his feet. 'Say, man, I'm sorry as hell about – about Simon.'

'It happens,' I said, wondering why I was so cold about it.

'Yeah. I thought it was going to happen to you, old buddy. When you started puking blood, I thought it was all over. Never seen you that far gone, man.'

'Never been that far gone,' I admitted.

'What happened?' he asked casually.

Something was wrong. I didn't know what it was for a moment, then I realized that I was suspicious of Dick without knowing what the hell for. I glanced at his van. It was new and expensive, and I wondered how much he'd paid for it, where he'd gotten the money. Then I thought, *Don't be silly.* My God, the next thing would be me suspecting Jamison of being the policeman Reese thought probably had provided the heroin from an evidence locker. I couldn't go around suspecting everybody. That would be crazy.

'Well, you don't have to tell me, man. It's not any of my business,' Dick said.

'Sorry, man, but I'm not all here yet. I don't know what happened. Maybe Simon, maybe the beating . . .' Maybe Helen closing her motel door in my face. 'I don't know.'

'Feel pretty bad about the dude in the alley, huh?' he asked, a sly and nervous edge to his voice. There it was. He wanted to know what it felt like to kill a man. They always do. And it would be a long time before he could look at me without thinking about that.

'No, man, I don't feel bad at all,' I said.

'Oh.'

'I was full of whiskey and speed and had just seen Simon spitted and had just had the living shit beat out of me, so I didn't feel anything, man, it's like it happened to somebody else,' I said.

'Yeah, I guess so,' he said, not believing a word of it. 'Say, man, I want to apologize for blowing up at you – when you called me. I'm sorry. Helen – she had –'

'That's all right,' I interrupted. 'Forget about it.'

'Well, I don't know.'

'Have a drink and forget about it,' I said, smiling.

'Sure,' he said, then glanced at me, returned the smile. 'Hey, man, let's play handball sometime after – Hey, good morning!' he added, shouting over my shoulder.

Helen had come to the front door, the green robe shining darkly in the morning shade. She squinted, then waved. Watching the two of them, I waited for a rush of jealousy and anger. But only a trickle of irritation came.

'She's a good lady, man. I'm sorry for confusing things and I want to wish you two the best,' he said, almost formally.

'Thanks.'

'And, hey, I'll see you on the courts, okay?'

'Sure.'

'Take care, man,' he said, then went back to his van and drove quickly away. I guess I didn't like the exit.

'What did he want?' Helen asked as I walked up the steps.

'I don't know. Maybe he was looking for the back door.'

'What's that supposed to mean?'

'Nothing,' I said, the irritation quickly spent. 'It was a cheap shot. I'm sorry.'

'No, you're not,' she said, angry now.

'Yes, I am sorry.'

'Then why'd you say that?'

'I don't know. Hell, I don't know why I do anything. But I am sorry.'

'Well, you should be.'

'Don't do this,' I said.

'I didn't start it,' she said, then left me at the door.

When I got to the bedroom, she had hidden beneath a tangled heap of bedclothes.

'Are you going to be here when I get back?' I asked as I picked up the bloody windbreaker.

'Where are you going?' she asked, rising suddenly from the covers.

'To work.'

'In that thing?'

'It matches my face, lady. Are you going to be here when I get back?'

'I don't know,' she answered, a petty whine in her voice. 'How long will you be gone?'

'Until I get back.'

'What's that mean?' she asked.

'I don't know.'

'Then why'd you say it?'

'Oh, goddammit, I don't know!'

'Well, you don't have to shout at me,' she wailed, then fell sobbing among the sheets.

'I'm sorry!' I shouted. 'And goddammit, don't tell me I'm not!'

She looked up as if she was going to tell me just that, but the doorbell chimes rang like tin thunder.

'Goddammit,' I muttered and went to answer the door. The other plain-clothes detective stood on my porch, his thumbs hooked into his belt. He didn't look any better than I felt. 'What the hell do you want?'

'Hey, man, take it easy.'

'Sorry. What do you want?'

'Jamison asked me to drop by. He's been calling you but he don't get nothing but your answering service. He'd like to talk to you. This morning.'

'What's he want?'

'Are you kidding? He never tells me nothing,' the detective muttered. 'He thinks I'm dumb.'

'Yeah, me too,' I said, and we grinned at each other.

'He's one hard son of a bitch to work for.'

'That's what I heard.'

'I'm going down to the station, man, if you want to ride along.'

'That's okay,' I said. 'I'll take my car. I'm headed downtown anyway.'

'Whatever.'

'Hey, I'm sorry – about – I guess it's called being rude.'

'No sweat. You having a fight with your wife?'

'Something like that,' I said.

'Figures. That's the way I'm gonna get it, man, one of these days. I'll knock on a door in the middle of a family altercation and some goddamned woman'll blow me away.'

'It happens. I got flattened with a cast-iron skillet

once. Some broad called to complain that her boyfriend was beating on her head, but when I got there, they had made up. I arrested him anyway, but she got behind me. Took ten stitches in the back of my head.'

'Lucky she didn't kill you, man,' he answered sadly.

'Yeah. Hey, did you guys ever find that old man's notebook?'

'Naw. Goddamned Jamison had me sifting garbage for three days, but we never turned it up,' he said.

'Great job, huh?'

'Don't you know it. Garbage and puke.'

'Huh?'

'Aw, we found some puke at the top of the stairs, and I had to scrape up a sample to compare it with the contents of the old man's stomach.'

'Was it his?' I asked, trying not to act as if I cared.

'Naw. Belonged to some other wino. Nothing but brandy and gastric juices.'

'They make a brand on it?' I asked, but that pushed him over the line from shoptalk to nosiness.

'Ask Jamison, man. We closed the book on it.'

'Okay,' I said. 'Thanks.'

'Don't mention it. I loved being pumped,' he said, then looked worried. 'Hey, you won't say anything about this to Jamison, willya?'

'I hardly ever say anything to him.'

14

'That's a great line-up you've got there,' I said to Jamison, 'but a smart lawyer could hurt you with it.'

'What?'

'I know everybody in the line-up but the kid with the busted nose, and I'd bet money I'm supposed to know him,' I said, nodding at the line of cops and drunks. 'So even if I recognized him, it wouldn't hold up. You blew it, Jamison.'

'I'm tired,' he grunted, 'and I was in a hurry. Goddamned smart-ass lawyers.'

'That's the legal system,' I said. 'Who's the kid?'

'Cousin of the dude you blew up. Albert Lucian Swartz. They call him Bubba.'

'Makes sense.'

'Yeah, well, he and his cousin are buddies, and they were seen together earlier in the evening. They both had five hundred dollars and some change in their pockets, which is too much for unemployed construction workers. Bubba's got the broken nose, bruises and scrapes on his hands, and a bad bite on his shoulder, so we figure he was with his cousin when they jumped you.'

'Well, maybe he was, but I couldn't tell you if he was or not.'

'Or wouldn't, huh?'

'It was dark, they were behind me, and I was on the ground most of the time –'

'You stood up long enough to bite the dude, Milo. You oughta see it. I've seen some bad bites, but this one, Milo, it's terrible.'

'I wish I could remember doing it but I don't.'

'You don't recognize him at all, huh?'

'No.'

'You wouldn't lie to me, would you, Milo? Try to make this a private beef?'

'Do I look like I need a beef, private or otherwise?'

'No, you don't,' he said, sounding almost happy. 'But if you can't identify the kid, we can't go into court with it, and some people are going to be upset about that.'

'I can't help that.'

'No. You probably can't at that. That's the way it goes,' he mused, slapping me on the shoulder. 'Say, are you gonna be in your office for the next hour or so?'

'I don't know. Why?'

'I might want to get in touch with you.'

'Why?'

'Just be there, Milo. In your private office. And don't ask me why, okay?'

So I went to the other office and had another installment of breakfast, a beer and tomato juice, as I waited for Jamison. I didn't like his mood. I couldn't think of anything that would make Jamison happy that wouldn't make me unhappy. I also couldn't imagine why he wanted to meet in the other office, but as I thought about it I liked it. We could talk about things. Brandy, for instance, and vomit.

'You want a beer?' I asked him as he came in without knocking. 'Or coffee?'

'Coffee,' he said as he sat down heavily at the table. 'Black.'

'Coming right up, sir,' I said and went out to the bar and brought him back a cup of coffee. 'Why are we, ah, meeting here?'

'I don't trust you, Milo, you and your goddamned tape recorders and bugs and whatnot.'

'I'm hurt,' I said, and he smiled an odd little smile.

'Yeah.'

'What did you want?'

'Huh? Oh, to tell you that your property has been released. You can pick it up anytime. And here's your automatic, too,' he said, then took the pistol out of his belt and handed it to me. 'Be careful, it's loaded.'

'Thanks. But why didn't you tell me at the station?'

'I forgot,' he said innocently.

'Then why not call me?'

'You said you were coming over here, and I knew you didn't have a phone back here, so I walked over.' He talked like a man setting up an alibi.

'You're covering your ass, Jamison. Why?'

'No, I really forgot. I'm getting old and tired.'

'Maybe you ought to look for an easier job.'

'Yeah,' he said, watching his coffee, 'that's true. I got an offer, you know, a birdnest on the ground. A small town in Idaho. Four patrolmen and a dispatcher who doubles as jailer on each shift. I'd be the chief, Milo. Good money, an easy life. All the violence there takes place in the home.'

'You gonna take it?'

'I don't know yet. There are a few complications.'

'What's that?' I asked.

'Well, the kid's only got one more year of high school and he'd sorta like to finish here, and I'd like to get this heroin dealer busted before I leave town. So I don't know if I'll take it or not.'

'Sounds good,' I said, 'but you ain't here for my advice about your employment.'

'That's right.'

'So what do you want?'

'I wanted to talk to you, Milo. Unofficially, you understand. I want to know what you know about the Duffy kid and Simon's death and anything else that might help, such as why you lied about not recognizing the Swartz kid.'

'You got it all wrong. I don't know anything you don't.'

'Now, don't fuck me around on this, Milo,' he said, serious now. 'I've seen more dead bodies in the past few weeks than I usually see in a year and that makes me unhappy, you understand. How long's it been since you've had to watch a kid pulled out of the river with grappling hooks, huh? I didn't like watching that, Milo, and I don't want to have to think about it. It doesn't make me happy. And, Milo, I want the man who brought smack into my town. I'm giving you a break; you can tell me here, and I won't say a word about withholding evidence or obstruction, but if we go down to the station and you continue to bullshit me, you're gonna take a fall. A bad one. You're in over your head, Milo, caught between the rock and the hard place, and I'm giving you an easy way out. So you better take it.'

'What sorta crap is this?'

'Now, goddammit, listen to me. I've never broken a law in my life, not even when we were kids. I believe in the law, Milo, and the system and all that goes with it. I don't make busts outside the law, I don't make deals, but I want this dealer and I want him fast. The goddamned mayor has asked for state help, and I don't like that, bringing state boys into my town.'

'It's not your town, Jamison,' I said, and a burst of anger flashed across his face, but it ended nearly as quickly as it began, turning into what looked like resigned sadness.

'You're right. But it used to be.'

'Sometimes I think you're crazier than me, Jamison.'

'Sometimes I think so too.'

'Then maybe you can understand my side. I don't give a shit about the law.'

'What sort of world would it be, Milo, without law? Can't you –'

'Don't you understand,' I interrupted. 'I don't care about the world, man, about the law. That shit takes place on television, man, not in my life. The World. The Law. That doesn't have anything to do with my life, man, and Simon died in my life. I want the smack dealer too, but when I find him, I'm gonna blow his fucking head off and then call the Law. Understand?'

'I thought you might feel that way,' he said, coming up with that odd smile again. 'I guess I just wanted to be sure.'

'What?'

'I don't want this one to go to court, Milo, it's too goddamned important, but if I turn up the guy, I'll have to arrest him. Same with the state boys. But you might just blow him up, and if you've got a good story, you might get away with it.'

'I'm not sure I believe you, Jamison.'

'I don't blame you. I don't even know if I believe myself, but we won't know for sure unless we try. Will we?'

'That's damned slim,' I said, remembering Reese's line, 'but what the hell. Why not?'

'So give.'

'Okay. You were wrong about the Duffy kid. He wasn't just hooked, he was dealing.'

'I knew that,' he said tiredly.

'Then why bullshit me?'

'Because I thought he was the main man and that the supply would dry up with him dead. But either he was in with somebody else or they picked up when he died. Either way, there's still junk all over town. I just can't figure why he killed himself.'

'Maybe he didn't,' I said, not really believing myself. 'Somebody got pretty excited when I started poking around. Simon got killed, Muffin got framed, and I got the shit kicked out of me.'

'Are you sure about the Swartz cousins?'

'Yeah. The one with a broken nose wanted to kill me, but the other told him that they weren't supposed to.'

'That figures. And there's this other thing. Remember the vague description of the long-hair maybe coming out of Reese's house?'

'Sure.'

'Well, the Swartz cousins were seen talking to a guy who might fit that description, and –'

'And you've been turning the town upside down looking for him but can't come up with him,' I said.

'That's what I can't understand, Milo. This town ain't that big. I've busted a couple of street pushers, but they didn't know anything.'

'What kinda smack?'

'That's another problem. It ain't Mexican.'

'That's what Reese said.'

'Oh, he talked to you, huh?'

'Yeah,' I said, 'he forgave me for being a hick cop.'

'What else did he say?'

'Two things. That this was strictly amateur stuff, and that the smack probably came out of a police locker.'

'That's what I thought too, but we've checked every police force in the Northwest, and came up empty.'

'Check again.'

'We are.'

'Did you make a brand on the brandy in the vomit on the stairs?'

'How'd you know about that?'

'Where you getting your help nowadays, Jamison?'

'Huh? Okay, I see. Outa Cracker Jack boxes, I guess. But, no, we haven't made a brand yet. We sent it to the police lab in Twin Forks, but they haven't called back. Identified the soda, though. Came from the local distributor. He delivers to every bar in town that has a speed gun. You know how many bars that is?'

'No.'

'Twenty.'

'So that's probably dead, huh?'

'Yeah,' he grunted. 'And, hell, the vomit could have belonged to anybody.'

'Or it could have come from our long-haired friend. Maybe he has a weak stomach?'

'Like an amateur?'

'Right. So what else do we have?' I said. Jamison noticed the *we* and smiled.

'Well, I didn't bring my notes, Milo. I didn't know I was gonna need them. I didn't know if I'd have the nerve to do this.'

'I don't want to make you worry, man, but I don't know if I'll have the nerve to finish it,' I admitted.

'You did all right with the dude in the alley.'

'That was different.'

'Yeah, I guess so. I guess we'll just have to see what happens, huh?'

'Right.'

'So let's get after it,' he said, standing up.

'What's this, a race?'

'Sure. I'm gonna work like a son of a bitch. Just as soon as I get back from this little fishing trip.'

'You may be crazy, Jamison.'

'Yeah. You know what I was thinking about on the way over here?'

'No,' I said, expecting nostalgia.

'Evie has this cat book and she told me once what the Turks used to do with adulterous wives.'

'What's that?'

'They'd sew them up in a canvas sack with a cannon-ball and two live cats, then heave it into the sea,' he said pleasantly.

'Goddamn.'

'Yeah,' he said calmly. 'Cover your ass, Milo.'

'With both hands,' I said as he walked to the door. 'You sure we got the right man?' I asked, hoping I didn't sound as uneasy as I felt holding Jamison's hunting license.

'Oh, yeah. You should've seen the money the Swartz cousins were carrying. It was junkie money, Milo, ragged and dirty, stinking with filth,' he answered, his voice filled with disgust.

'If you say so. Say, what about Muffin?'

'What about him?'

'How about pulling in the warrant?'

'Let's wait till it's over, okay? It'll look better.'

'I hope that your boys don't decide to get trigger-happy if they arrest him.'

'Tell him not to run.'

'If I see him.'

'Right,' Jamison said. 'Good hunting.'

There didn't seem to be anything for me to say, so I nodded as he went out the door.

The trouble with sudden changes in people is that it's difficult to know if the change is real or just a moment's whim. I didn't know if I should believe Jamison. Maybe he was just playing some sort of game, using me to find the dealer. But like he said: we wouldn't know unless we tried.

I still didn't know where to begin, but I left anyway. As I passed the pay phone in the bar, I remembered Muffin, but when I went to make the call, I couldn't remember the number, so I had to go up to the office. When I got there, I called the answering service. Muffin hadn't called again, but Mrs. Crider had. Several times, each message more urgent than the one before. The last one threatened physical harm if I didn't see her right away. I called her, but she insisted on seeing me, so I promised to run out before lunch. Freddy had called too, and I called him back on the mobile unit.

'What's up?'

'We got some kinda trouble, Milo. The lady slipped the tail.'

'How?'

'Went into a café and ordered a big breakfast, then left her sweater at the table and went to the john – I thought. But she went out the back door. This lady's been around.'

'Are you still at the café?'

'No. She came back about thirty minutes later in a cab, paid for the meal, got her sweater, and went home.'

'Check the cab company, see where they picked her up.'

'Already did. The driver picked her up at a pay phone next to that tourist information booth east of town.'

'Well, hell, if she was only gone thirty minutes she didn't have time to do much, so don't worry about it.'

'That's not what I'm worried about, Milo. I want to know who dropped her off at the phone. Why don't you check the girl in the information booth.'

'Why not.'

'How you doing?'

'I'm alive.'

'Thanks to the backup piece, Milo.'

'Right, Freddy, thanks for that.'

'Well, watch yourself.'

'All right,' I said and hung up before he could give me any more advice.

I didn't care who Wanda of Wild Rose Lane balled in her spare time, but I knew Freddy would hound me for days if I didn't stop and ask a few questions. It was on the way to the Crider house anyway. And right next to a pay phone. I had a belt from the office bottle and found the telephone number of the hunting camp owned by the fence Muffin worked for. The fence was a Charlie Pride freak, and the jukebox in the camp bar didn't have any other singers on it. If Jamison only knew, I thought, how smart Muffin and I really were. At least Muffin.

The young girl behind the counter of the tourist information kiosk looked like she had been chosen for the job to make a good impression on the tourists. She had one of those lovely model faces that shouted Fresh, Clean, and Cheerful, that sells toothpaste or gives head with the same wooden sincerity. But the girl didn't go with the face: she was working stoned out of her mind, blown away and happy about it.

'Yes, sir, what can I do for you today?' she inquired as I stepped up to the counter.

'Let's fuck.'

'Wow,' she wailed, then broke out in giggles. 'Outa sight. But what would the Chamber of Commerce say?'

'What do they say about you coming to work stoned?'

'Nothing, man, my daddy is the president.'

'Great. Say, you see that pay phone over there?'

'Outa sight, man.'

'Slow down, babe. Did you see a cab pick up a woman there about an hour ago?'

'You some kinda cop, man?'

'A private investigator.'

'Wow.'

'Did you see the cab?'

'You gotta be kidding, man.'

'Yeah. Have a nice day.'

'You too, man,' she said, smiling prettily.

As I walked away, two women who looked like physical education teachers, burdened with cameras and maps, strode up to the booth to ask about the most scenic route to Canada.

'Walking, driving, flying, or by bicycle?' the girl asked cheerfully.

The counterculture revolution had done something for America: it let a lot of young people handle idiot jobs by getting stoned. As I got in the rig and stuffed the automatic under the seat, I wondered why I wasn't stoned myself.

As I drove east up the valley of the Meriwether River, past the golf course where my family home had come to rest, the morning sun exploded in my face, shattering my windshield with light. The undulations of the river, as it wound through the willowed flats, sparkled like liquid silver. An old man, distinguished and gray, outfitted out of an Eddie Bauer catalog, stood thigh-deep at the verge of a dark, shaded pool, his waders sturdy against the rushing water that thrust upon them, then divided in picturesque wakes. He stood in the shade below the cut bank, but his fly line looped and whistled in the sunshine like a burning wire. I wished him good fishing. Until I saw his station wagon beside the highway, his out-of-state plates. Then I wished him gone. And a fence built around the state.

You don't fish anymore, Simon's ragged voice nagged inside my head. *You haven't fished in years.*

Leo and I went to Idaho for steelhead last year, I complained.

Fucking tourist.

When I knocked on the front door, Mrs. Crider met me carrying a large baby straddled on her cocked hip. Over her shoulder I could see two more children and their playful debris, their faces long and sad like their father's, their eyes shining with the same lonesome hope. But Mrs. Crider's eyes were blank, clouded with anger or grief, like the sky before a snowstorm.

'I'm here,' I said lamely, after a long silence made unbearable by her eyes.

'Should Ah lead a cheer? Ah been callin' you for a long time.'

'I know. I'm sorry. I've been – busy.'

'Looks like you been damn near killed,' she said quietly, her hand brushing an errant strand of hair from her face. Then she gave it back to the child, gave him a raw, bony knuckle on which to teethe.

'That's what they say.'

'How's the other fella look?'

'I'm afraid he's dead.'

'That's what Ah hear,' she said. 'And Ah also hear you found Elton that night you lied to me.'

'I'm sorry about the lie, but lies seem to be an occupational hazard in my business.'

'That so? Like your face?'

I nodded.

'Maybe you're in the wrong business.'

'I've thought about that.'

She didn't reply, but in the silence examined my face with her hard, black eyes. I had been so busy feeling responsible for Simon's death that I had neglected the guilt festered around Elton Crider's. Her eyes took care of that, though. I doubted that his death had anything to do with the Duffy kid's, except for his grief, but under those eyes I became responsible. Before I could apologize again, the two thin boys in the living room began to argue loudly about some vague rule in their children's game, their voices rising shrilly. She turned and spat a single nasal command as sharp as the slap of stove wood against bare thighs, a flat, inchoate sound, which they obeyed instantly, falling as silent as stones, the gravely pale eyes swinging toward their mother, then away, like the eyes of small animals fleeing the rush of headlights on a nighttime country road.

''Scuse me,' she said, then stepped back into the hall. She came back with a black folder that held a slim packet of paper and handed it to me.

'What's this?'

'Ah'm not sure 'xactly. It belonged to that Duffy trash. Ah found it when Ah cleaned out Elton's desk,' she said as she moved out the door and shut it behind her. 'Let's walk a bit.' She led me across the patchy lawn; I followed like a whipped child. She wore a gray sweatshirt, clean but stained with the bleached remains of oil and grease, and a pair of faded blue pedal pushers left over from another time. Beneath the thin fabric, the muscles of her legs rippled strongly. Her bare feet had seen rough use, suffered badly fitted shoes and rocky trails, but when they touched the grass and earth, they seemed elegant in their confidence and strength, as certain of their power as were her swaying hips. And she carried her head proudly, as if she were a valuable gift. I felt a terrible pity, not for her, but for the confusions of sex.

'I'm sorry. About your husband,' I said to her back.

'Seems only right,' she answered without turning.

'What?'

'Since it was your fault,' she said, stopping and facing me.

'I – I understood it was an accident.'

'Mister, Ah may not have a fancy education but Ah ain't dumb. Elton wouldn't have it known for the world but he was pure country, and he could drive when he couldn't walk. He didn't go in that river without some kinda help. That's why Ah called you.'

'Why?' I asked, afraid of the answer, unable to lift my heavy face to meet her eyes.

'To hire you to find out who done it –'

'Oh no. I'm – busy – I haven't recovered from the beating,' I said, but the look on her long face disagreed.

'And when you find out who, Ah want you to kill them. Ah don't know how much money you'd want, but Elton had some insurance at the college, and that oughta –'

'Mrs. Crider, what makes you think you can hire me to kill somebody?'

'You owe me,' she said, then walked away into the shaded pine trees beyond the lawn, the sleeping baby riding easily on her hip.

'What?' I asked as I caught up to her and grabbed her elbow. She glanced at my hand, and I turned her loose. 'What?'

'The lie.'

'No,' I said, but she paid no attention, unwinding her fingers from the baby's fist and reaching up to touch my damaged ear.

'That there ear ain't never gonna heal right,' she said, her fingers easy and smooth on my ear as she stroked it lightly, almost as if she thought her hand could heal. 'Never. My Uncle Ab on my mother's side had an ear like that. Some fella came up side his head with a beer bottle 'cause Ab was messin' with his wife. Ab stuck his pocket knife in the other fella. Killed him dead. Ab got this funny-lookin' ear and a striped suit. He gets a letter near every week from this fella's widow.'

'No,' I said again, moving her hand away from my ear.

Bars of sunlight fell across the carpet of pine needles. Glints of red sparked off her black hair. The child stirred in the silence, his hands and mouth searching blindly for the gnawed, chapped knuckle. She let him take it, and he was quiet.

'You owe me,' she said.

'Lady, you're crazy,' I said, which made her smile benignly.

'When it's over, y'all come on out and tell me all 'bout it. Ah like mysteries, watch 'em on TV all the time.'

'There aren't any mysteries.'

'Ah'll be a-lookin' for you,' she said, then walked back toward the house. As I followed, banging the folder against my leg, I wondered if she had learned that walk on television too, or in some more elemental place, and I wondered how Elton Crider ever got up the nerve to leave her. She stopped at the front door to watch me walk to my rig.

'Y'all come back, yah hear,' she said, mocking herself. Then added in a hard voice, the accent lost beneath the mixture of command and promise. 'When it's done.'

The words felt like a rough hand on my shoulder, shoving me into the front seat, reminding me of all the sore spots. I drove away, afraid to look back.

'Look, man, don't give me no bullshit,' Muffin said after I had explained that the smack charges were sure to be dropped. 'Just come up with the bread.'

So I explained everything again, sorry now that I had stopped at the open telephone booth next to the tourist information kiosk. I had chosen that pay phone because the girl behind the counter had been the only pleasant thing that had happened to me all morning. But it had been a mistake. She was busy with the tourists, who stood around the kiosk as if they were waiting for a tour bus. Only one couple, a gray-haired man and his wife, wanted to use the telephone and they had the decency to stand far enough away so they couldn't overhear me. There were a number of small children who lacked any decency at all. I guess it was the face, but I wished that they were frightened instead of curious. It seems to take something really terrible to frighten children today, and it seemed that I was curious instead of terrible because I couldn't make them go away. I couldn't make Muffin believe me either.

'Milo, you've been a wonderful father, and I thank you, but, man, I need that mad money of yours. I'm good for it, man, you know that.'

'What is it? Don't you believe me? Don't you trust me? You think –'

'I think you're gonna fuck it up, man,' he interrupted, and I couldn't blame him for thinking that.

'Just hang on for a few more days, okay?'

'No, man, this dude up here is getting real nervous having me around, and he ain't nervous at all compared to me. I know what the slammer looks like from the outside, and that's all I want to know, man, that's all. Hell, I was counting on you for the bread, but if you ain't got it –'

'I got it,' I said, 'I'll bring it up this afternoon. Okay?'

'That's so fine, man, I can't tell you. And, hey.'

'What?'

'Don't let anybody tail you, huh?'

'Oh, shit, Muffin, shut up,' I said and hung up.

'My mother says it isn't polite to say "Shut up," ' I was informed by a little girl standing beside me.

'Tell her I said I'm sorry, okay?' I told her, ruffling her hair. She smiled as if she fully intended to.

When I glanced at the girl behind the counter, her smile was harried but undaunted, reminding me of Mindy. The Holy Light Hog Farm was a few miles out of the way but in the same general direction as the North-fork Hunting Camp where Muffin was waiting for my money. I thought about dropping by to say hello to Mindy and Reese. But when I climbed into my rig, I saw the black folder and remembered that I was supposed to be working, so I headed back to the office for mad money and a drink.

15

After I filled my wallet with my two thousand, I added a thousand of Nickie's and hoped I could cover it somehow. Then I sat down at the desk to have a drink and take a quick look at the folder Mrs. Crider had given me. But I thought about her instead. She was a hell of a woman. She had asked me to kill without even flinching. I liked that, but it also scared me. We weren't even on first-name terms yet, but she assumed because I had lied to her that I owed her a murder. Just as Jamison assumed that I owed Simon one too. Unfortunately, I didn't know who was owed what. And I began to wonder about their judgment of my character. So I opened the folder. It was the beginning of his thesis on Dalton Kimbrough and Western justice. As I had told Helen Duffy, my great-grandfather made his way into law enforcement and capital gains by killing Dalton Kimbrough, so I had always been interested.

But the thesis wasn't a simple history of Dalton Kimbrough or an estimation of Western justice. It was an examination of the difference between myth and reality in the Western hero and villain. The Duffy kid began with the distance between the Wyatt Earp created by Ned Buntline and the often too human lawman, then passed on through the careers of Billy the Kid, Joaquin Murieta, Jack Slade, et al. – the easy research – and on to the life and hard times of that infamous outlaw, highwayman and killer, Dalton Kimbrough. As it turned out, Dalton was a man ahead of his times: he handled his own public relations. The first thing he did was change his name from Ernest Ledbetter to the more heroic Dalton Kimbrough, then out of a spotty criminal career that included one arrest and one gunfight he made a name for himself throughout the gold fields of the post-Civil War West.

His solitary arrest record was for shoplifting in St. Joe, Missouri, where he had been raised. The shopkeeper had collared Dalton with a pocketful of .44 rounds and an old Navy Colt under his coat. The revolver was a paperweight with no firing pin. Dalton did his thirty days, then headed west for a life of crime and excitement in the gold camps. Dalton drank, tried mining, and probably hung around the bars more than he should have, looking for trouble. One winter, over in Montana, in a log-cabin bar just large enough for a four-foot plank bar, one table and two bunks on the opposite wall, Dalton finally found a gunfight in the midst of a poker game.

When the gunfire ended, everybody's revolver empty, there was a great deal of smoke and powder burns, but nobody had been hit. Except the bartender's dog, which had been killed by a single round through the lungs. The game resumed peacefully amid smoke and the good feelings that come with survival, only to be disturbed again. This time by odd groans from a miner sleeping off a drunk in the lower bunk. When they turned him over to tell him to shut up, they found a large puddle of blood beneath his body from a round that had passed through his thigh. He groaned once more, then died from the loss of blood. Dalton, ever ready for fame, claimed both killings as his very own, and nobody bothered to dispute his claim.

Dalton also boasted of numerous stage holdups and bank robberies, all of which either never took place in recorded history or were committed by other men, who had never heard of Dalton Kimbrough. As far as anybody knows, Dalton took part in only one stage holdup, his last one. Perhaps the gunfight in the bar went to his head. Later the same winter, he and two men stopped the Salt Lake stage as it topped the south pass into the Meriwether Valley, the stage carrying my great-grandfather to his new home, an Army wife with her young son, and a strongbox.

As the horses were blowing at the top of the pass, three armed men appeared on horseback, demanding the strongbox, which was bolted to the coach floor. Dalton fired five rounds at the lock, but it didn't open. So he went after the passengers. My great-grandfather couldn't speak English but he could count, and he was often courageously surly. When Dalton tried to open his coat to see if he carried a money belt, he met an unhappy Russian, who grabbed him in a clumsy hug. As they struggled, one of the mounted outlaws pulled off a round. Right through Dalton Kimbrough's kidneys.

He fired once more from his wildly bucking horse, hitting the frightened stagecoach driver in the chin, then his horse pitched him off. When he hit the frozen ground, he went out cold. The third outlaw, who finally decided to take control, also began to fire, but for reasons unrecorded – probably either wet or forgotten percussion caps – his revolver wouldn't fire. He cocked the hammer and pulled the trigger several times, then rode away in disgust, never to be heard of again.

After being shot through the kidneys, Dalton lost his taste for holdups and fights. He fell to the ground in my great-grandfather's embrace, where his skull was crushed by a large stone in a Russian peasant's burly hand. When the snow had settled, my great-grandfather trussed the unconscious outlaw like a pig and tossed him into the boot with Dalton's body, bound the driver's face, helped the lady back into the stage, then drove into history. As soon as his English was passable, he was hired as Meriwether's constable, then elected sheriff, and nearly appointed territorial governor. In death, Dalton Kimbrough's public relations paid off. For my great-grandfather.

And in a less obvious way, for the stagecoach driver too. He stayed around town for years, wearing a scarf over his missing chin, becoming a local curiosity and drunk. The Army wife found her husband shacked up with a Willomot squaw, which she might have forgiven if he hadn't been cashiered too, so she went back East, where people were civilized. Dalton Kimbrough's body was hung next to his partner's, the good folk of Meriwether deciding that stringing him up dead was nearly as good an example to potential outlaws as hanging him if he had been alive.

As the years passed in the usual manner, the story bloomed into heroics with the aid of imaginative newspaper editors and my great-grandfather's whiskey. According to Duffy's thesis, my great-grandfather encouraged the Kimbrough myth to further his own political ambitions, which was probably true. At the end of the typed pages, he scrawled a sour note: *A fucking klutz*. I got the impression that although he believed his thesis, he didn't especially like it, preferring myth to reality even as he cast the terrible light of a debunking truth across the years of Dalton Kimbrough's petty life.

All this was twice as sad because the truth about Kimbrough and my great-grandfather had been known for years before Raymond Duffy found Willy Jones and his papers. Even the B Western filmed in the early fifties had to invent a hero: the chinless stage driver. In the movie, he knows the truth of the Milodragovitch pose and the puniness of Kimbrough's villainy, but is unable to tell anybody. Until he is taught to write by a gentle schoolmarm from Philadelphia. Then he is able to expose the character of my great-grandfather as a cowardly and overbearing sham. In the last scene, the actor playing Milodragovitch lies sprawled in the middle of a dusty, back-lot street, the victim of unfounded pride and drunkenness. As the camera draws back, the sober, upright storekeeper, who has shotgunned the mad Russian and his knouted hand, is seen advancing like a cartoon hunter clutching a hammerless double-barreled shotgun. Then the frame widens to include the chinless hero, his eyes above the scarf suggesting a triumphant but sad smile, his hand on the schoolmarm's delicate arm. She is smiling too, but in a rather pinched way, as if the chinless wonder needs a bath. They do not embrace. Music rises. Dissolve to list of cast.

Just to set the record straight: my great-grandfather died quite bitterly sober in an old folks' home.

There is a quaintly modern notion that information will eventually equal knowledge, which is neatly balanced by the cliché that the more one learns, the less one knows. Both ideas are probably more or less accurate, but neither is particularly useful in dealing with the human animal.

As I thought of Raymond Duffy, nothing came to mind. An image remembered from a bar, his eyes as black as gun barrels glistening with pleasure above his pale cheeks. They were murderous, not suicidal. And even though Reese had said that the kid was very depressed over the death of Willy Jones, I couldn't see him killing himself. *Maybe it was an accident, pure and simple, dumb-ass, a mistake.* But I still needed a reason, if not for his death, then at least for his depression beforehand. If I knew what caused the depression, then I would be able to justify accidental death. Mistakes do happen. Like my father's death, which I had always thought of as an accident caused by the mistake of leaving the bolt open on his deer rifle, of not looking at the shotgun as he lifted it out of the closet, of not checking the safety when he put it away . . .

But as I thought of these things, an odd feeling came over me. I was missing something. And suddenly I knew and was damned sorry that I did. I remembered my father's first lecture about guns: Always keep them loaded, a full magazine and a round in the chamber, and you'll never be killed by an empty gun; keep the safety on, check that always, but keep them loaded. Drunk or sober, he had never made a mistake with a gun; he put them away loaded, the safety on. But I remembered as clearly as I remembered the bloody stain on the hallway ceiling that the bolt of the deer rifle was open, the chamber empty. I wondered how long he had planned it, that accident planted in the hall closet like a bomb.

I had a sip of whiskey, which seemed proper, but I was too tired and sore to feel any real grief. If that was the way he had wanted it, then I wasn't about to disagree with him. I wondered if my mother knew, and decided that she did. Some knowledge rises out of information, disorganized but nonetheless true. If he couldn't kill himself with a whiskey bottle, my father had to make do with guns, which made me wonder why the Duffy kid had chosen drugs instead of his pistols . . .

'Bingo,' I said to myself and sat up straight in my chair.

Even though it seemed that my father's death wasn't caused by a mistake after all, I'd bet good, or bad, money that Willy Jones's had been. If you play with guns long enough, my father had told me, eventually you'll kill somebody. And I saw the Duffy kid, drug-crazed, playing with guns, drawing and snapping the trigger in the old drunk's face, saw the round left in the cylinder by mistake, saw the old man's face explode, the back of his head hit the far wall, skull fragments and blood and brain matter all over the room. Hollywood, and quick-draw contests; that would drive him over the edge. When he saw what firearms are meant to do, when he saw the effect of an unjacketed lead round fired into a human face, that would make him throw his pistols away, cut his hair and discard his gunfighter's clothes. I knew. At that range, when a bullet enters the human head, the hydrostatic pressure blows the face up like a cheap balloon; the eardrums burst, the eyes pop out, and the head seems to dissolve in a shower of blood. Oh God, did I know, and not want to at all.

Assuming that I had had a hard day that morning, I had a long drink, then another before I called Amos Swift. He agreed that he might have missed powder burns and a gunshot wound in Willy Jones's head because the body had been so badly burnt. But he bet money that he wouldn't miss it a second time. If I could come up with something solid enough to convince a judge to sign an exhumation order. I told him I hoped it wouldn't be necessary, then hung up.

What a mess, I thought, *what a hard day*. I called Helen just to hear her voice, to remind myself why I was doing all this. She came to the telephone on the ninth ring, answered it breathlessly, timidly.

'Hello?'

'It's nice to know you're still there,' I said.

'Oh. I'm still here. I just – didn't know if I should answer your telephone – I was in the backyard – and I tripped coming in the back door.'

'Are you all right?'

'Oh yes – I'm fine. How are you?'

'I'm not in jail, anyway. I'm in pain,' I said lightly, 'but free.'

'Oh – I'm glad.'

'Are you going to be there when I get back?'

'Are you – coming home – right now? I didn't know . . . when you were coming back.'

'Well,' I said, thinking about the trip up the north fork with Muffin's money, 'I've got a few things to do yet. It'll take three or four hours, but I'll be home to take you out to dinner. If you don't mind being seen in public with me.'

'Of course not,' she answered, sounding happy instead of confused. 'It's a date.'

'Okay,' I said. 'Hey, you know it's nice to call my house and have you answer the phone.'

'Oh – oh – I'm sorry about – this morning.'

'So am I, but let's forget about it.'

'Okay – if you want . . . I'll – see you tonight.'

'Take care,' I said.

'You too,' she answered hesitantly, then we both hung up.

Whatever I'd expected out of the call to make me feel better hadn't been there, but telephones had always had some sort of curse on me anyway, so I didn't worry about it. I started to take the office bottle with me but decided to put it back in the drawer. By the time I reached the top of Willomot Hill the weight of the morning made me regret my decision. I turned into the empty parking lot of the Willomot Bar, thinking to get a couple of drinks in go cups and maybe have an unfriendly chat with the owner, Jonas. I could depend on him not to change character, not to confuse me. He had hated my guts for years, and there was something reassuring about that.

Jonas was sitting at the first table inside the door, leaning back in a chair, his tiny boots crossed on the battered tabletop, his narrow eyes watching the tourist traffic avoid his place like the plague, watching the rectangle of sunlight retreat across his dirty floor toward the doorway. Standing in the bright doorway, I assumed I must have been an anonymous shade because Jonas smiled as I stepped in. I guess the smile was too much. I lifted my foot and shoved his table. He went over backwards, thumping his head solidly against the cement floor.

Jonas was small, but stout as a stump and meaner than a sow bear, with quick hands and agile feet. He wasn't a big man but he was damn sure a handful of trouble. I had taken him before, three or four times, but that had been in the line of duty, sort of, and I had used the sap or a billy. I had a frozen moment to remember my face and all the aches and pains, especially my nose, and to regret most of my life. Two middle-aged bucks sat over shot glasses at the end of the bar, working on their hangovers, and the thick-faced barmaid stood across from them. The three heads swiveled toward the crashing sound of Jonas and furniture. One buck banked toward the back door past the dark shadow of the bear, but the other raised his glass, either toasting me or trying to hustle a drink. The barmaid simply looked away in boredom.

But Jonas wasn't bored. He rolled once, came up

ready, his feet spread, his short thick arms cocked, his head bobbing and weaving like that of a punch-drunk fighter, then he saw me and broke out in a mean grin.

'What the hell's happening, Milo?' he asked happily. 'You drunk 'fore noon, you old son of a bitch? What the hell happened to your face? Hey, man, I heard 'bout poor ol' Simon. What a fuckin' shame. He usta be a hell of a man. Did I ever tell you 'bout the time he got my old man off a manslaughter bust? The old man found two goddamned tourists cleanin' a cow elk up in that timber on the other side a the ridge and he cut down on the dumb-asses, and . . .'

As he rattled on with his favorite Simon story, he came around the table, kicking chairs out of the way with an absent-minded violence that amazed me all over again. He grabbed my arm and led me to the bar, shouting for shots and beers, shaking my hand over and over, pausing only long enough to gun his shot and half the beer chaser. By the time he finished his story, he had forgotten why he was telling it to me.

'Oh yeah. Simon. Goddamned old drunk. Goddammit, I'm sorry 'bout him. That's a nasty way to go, man, ugly. I seen a bum one time when I was a kid been hit by a train, and that was bad as I ever wanna see, but when I heard 'bout how Simon got it, man, I nearly got sick,' he prattled. 'And goddammit, Milo, you know nothing makes me sick.' Then he laughed happily.

'Wish I could say the same,' I said, but he didn't hear me through the laughter. Then an odd thing happened: I almost liked the little bastard, even after all the trouble. Of course, it had been at least ten years since we had tangled, but those times didn't count the nights when he had been drunk enough to argue with me about who to arrest but sober enough to remember that I had fifty pounds and a badge on him. When he stopped laughing, I said, 'You know it's a goddamned sorry day when I can't even pick a fight with you, Jonas.'

That made him laugh so hard that he blew beer foam all over the bar and his dark face. As he wiped his face, he said fondly, 'Goddamn, we usta have some dandy times, didn't we? Seems like ever other night you'd come in here and put knots on my head a goddamned goat couldn't climb. Hey, you still got that little flat sap?'

'Yeah, I think so,' I said, trying to remember where it had gone to. 'No, I think the police have it. Hell, I don't know.'

'I tell you, Milo, that thing was mean,' he said, as if that was the nicest compliment he knew. 'Goddamn, those were some times. Shit, somma the boys up on the reservation are still 'bout half afraid of you. You see that ol' boy take off when you come in?'

'Yeah.'

'Well, that was his older brother knocked you cold that time and drove you down to the jailhouse. Half-brother, I think it was. Anyway, he ain't near as mean. That's why he took off when you come in.'

'That was a long time ago, Jonas.'

'You tellin' me – shit, we're too old for rough and tumble, Milo, and hell, you already sewed up and taped together like a busted watermelon. Hell, you look so bad a fella'd be afraid to give you a good shot. Might kill you,' he said, and as if to prove his point, he thumped me in the ribs with a short, affectionate punch that nearly knocked me down.

'Not in the ribs, Jonas,' I grunted, trying to breathe.

'Sorry 'bout that. Heard you took a hell of a beatin'. Got that one son of a bitch, huh? Blew his fuckin' head right off, huh? That'll teach them goddamned hippies not to mess around with home folks, huh?'

'He was a construction worker, Jonas,' I explained, knowing it wouldn't make any difference.

'Yeah, whatever, he ain't gonna mess with nobody no more, right?' he said, lifting a new shot.

'Right.'

He waited for me to lift my shot, but I didn't know if it would stay down behind the memories, the new and bitter knowledge of the morning. It did but it didn't want to.

'So how's business?' Jonas asked, thumping me again.

'Not so good,' I said. 'Say, were you in here the night the kid OD'd in your john? About a month ago?'

'Don't remind me of it, Milo. The goddamn Liquor Control Board tried to take my license, but hell, that's nothing new,' he said, then laughed again. 'Why?'

'That's what I'm working on now.'

'Who for?' he asked, his eyes squinting with suspicion.

'The family. They weren't too happy with the sheriff's investigation.'

'What investigation? That old bastard can't find his ass with either hand. Hell, there wasn't anything to investigate anyway.'

'They just wanted to know what happened.'

'Nothing happened, Milo. The kid comes in, orders a drink, then goes into the john. A couple hours later somebody complains that they can't take a crap because the stall door is locked, so I climb over and find him dead, sittin' there like he's passed out, but when I seen that needle in his arm I figured he was dead. That's funny, he didn't look the type.'

'Had he ever been in before that night?'

'Hell, Milo, they come and go. I don't know. But probably not. He was such a clean-cut-lookin' kid, not like that bunch a mangy goddamned hippies in town, that I'd probably remember. He didn't look the type to be on that dope.'

'That's what I hear,' I said. 'Did he come in with anybody?'

'Well, Milo, I was busier than a one-legged man at an ass-kicking contest and I was a hair drunk, so I don't know.'

'What was he drinking?'

'A draw,' Jonas answered quickly. He had a bartender's memory for faces and drinks. 'And there wasn't nobody with him, 'cause that's all I got was the one beer.'

'Where did he sit?'

'All thc way down at the end of the bar.'

'Anybody sitting next to him?'

'Shit, Milo, I don't know,' he answered, sorry that he couldn't help.

'That's okay,' I said, 'it's not really important.' Then I thought about the guy with long black hair and a beard. 'Hey, there didn't happen to be a hippie in here that night, a guy with black hair and a beard?'

'I'll be damned. There sure was. Sittin' right next to the kid. I remember 'cause they ain't welcome here and they figure that out real quick, so we don't get many. Yeah, and 'cause he was a little old to be runnin' around like a goddamned hairy ape. He had on sunglasses too, but hell, I could tell he wasn't no kid.'

'You remember what he was wearing?'

'Milo, I could shut my eyes right now,' Jonas said, 'and I wouldn't be able to tell you what you was wearing.'

'What was he drinking?' I asked, sipping at my beer.

'Brandy and soda, no ice,' he answered quick as a shot, then motioned for another round.

Bingo. Goddammit, how could I be so dumb? Goddamned Nickie. Jesus.

'Help?' he asked.

'I don't know,' I said, forcing the thoughts and feelings out of me, retreating to hide the fear. 'Lots of people drink brandy and soda.'

'Yeah,' he said as he raised his glass. 'Sorry I don't remember more.'

'Thanks anyway, Jonas. Next time you're in town, stop by. The drinks are on me,' I said, then had a sip of beer and started to leave, but Jonas grabbed my arm.

'Wanna do me a favor, Milo?' he asked in a conspiratorial whisper so I would know it was an illegal favor. I shrugged, and Jonas took that as an affirmative answer. 'You seen Muffin lately? I got this friend on the other side of the mountains, and he's buildin' this motel. One big son of a bitch, two hundred units. But he's kinda strapped for capital right now, goddamned inflation, and he ain't got the bread for the color TVs and he can't come up with no credit he can afford. You know what I mean?'

'I'll act like I don't, Jonas. Muffin's out of business anyway.'

'That's too bad. There's a pretty penny in this deal, Milo. How 'bout puttin' me in touch with somebody else?'

'I don't know anybody, sorry.'

'Don't shit me, Milo,' he said, grinning like a small animal.

I wanted to grin back, but couldn't. Just like I wanted to rub my tired, hot face. Jonas was mean and crooked and slightly dumb, but the face he turned toward me was warm with affection. That has to count for something.

'Okay,' I said.

'How big a piece you want?'

'Nothing. I owe you, Jonas.'

'What?'

'Hell, I don't know. Maybe all those lumps on your head. I don't know.'

He grinned again, his tiny yellowed teeth nearly as dark as his Indian face, and started to poke me in the ribs. But he remembered not to.

'That don't matter none, Milo, not at all. Those were good times. Hell, you never tried to shake me down or run me in for some petty shit. You were fair, Milo, and I could count on you,' he said. 'Hey, by God, next time I'm in town, let's you an' me just get drunker than pigs in shit, then go down to them hippie bars and just kick the shit outa somebody. Anybody messes with us, we'll blow their fuckin' heads off. How 'bout it? Be like the old days, 'cept we'll be on the same side.'

'We've probably been on the same side all along and just didn't know it, Jonas, but I damn sure don't want to kill anybody . . .'

'Hey, you all right?' he asked as I headed for the john to heave it all up.

All drunks have theories, endlessly tedious arguments, both vocal and silent, with which to justify their drinking. They drink to forget or remember, to see more clearly or discover blindness, they drink out of fear of success or failure, drink to find a home and love or drink to get away. Their lives revolve around drink. Some of the theories may well be true, but because drunks lie so much, it's difficult to divide the sharp perceptions from the sorry rationalizations. Once, my father talked to me about drinking and drunks, and in my memory it sounds not at all sorry. Just sad.

I was a boy, but old enough to have already realized that even the simplest life was too complex, that my parents lived together without very much love, that I was both curse and prize in their battles; old enough to love my father without thinking that I had anything for which to forgive him. It was then, when I was old enough to be sad, that one afternoon my father and I had gone fishing. As it usually happened, we lodged in a country bar to wet our whistles before we wet our lines, and as usual, we stayed in the bar, letting the trout, as my father said, grow one more day. 'Tomorrow, son,' he'd say, 'they'll be just the right size.' Tomorrow. And every time we caught a trout, he'd hold it up and tell me, 'See, son, just right.'

But this afternoon we stayed in the bar, and sometime during the long hours of drinking, he disappeared into the john and stayed much longer than usual. I was a child among strangers, a youth to be regaled with the hopes they no longer possessed because I had a future and they had only pasts. Slightly frightened by all this weight, I went to look for my father.

He was kneeling at the toilet, his eyes fearfully shot with blood from the efforts of his retching. A long string of glutinous spittle looped heavily from his trembling lips to the stained toilet bowl.

He spit and asked how I was doing; knowing I was frightened, he was calm. 'Don't worry about me, son,' he said, 'I'm all right. I been bellied up to this trough a time or two before. You go on out and wait for me, okay? I'll be out in a minute.' As I went out the door, I tried not to hear the convulsive, heaving rasp, tried not to be disgusted by the only person in the world I loved.

But I heard and was disgusted. I went all the way outside the bar to the porch, where I watched the afternoon steal across green hayfields and pastures, the shadows of the mountain ridges reaping light, sowing darkness. After the dank, torpid air inside the bar, air more like smoke, the air outside seemed as fresh and clean as spring water, and I filled my lungs with gasp after gasp, sucking down the sobs, vowing as seriously as only a frightened child can that I would grow up and never drink, ignoring the fact that I already sipped from my father's glass whenever I pleased. I vowed, promised in innocence already lost.

He came out behind me, a huge dark man smiling tiredly, a glass of neat whiskey in his large hand. With the first swallow, he rinsed out his mouth, then spit off the porch into the dust that rimmed the parking lot. The second, he drank, emptying the glass. Then he patted me on the head, perhaps sensing what I felt. Even at his drunkest, he was kind and perceptive, at least around me. As he held my head in his great hand, I was warm in the lingering sunset chill.

'Son,' he said without preamble, 'never trust a man who doesn't drink because he's probably a self-righteous sort, a man who thinks he knows right from wrong all the time. Some of them are good men, but in the name of goodness, they cause most of the suffering in the world. They're the judges, the meddlers. And, son, never trust a man who drinks but refuses to get drunk. They're usually afraid of something deep down inside, either that they're a coward or a fool or mean and violent. You can't trust a man who's afraid of himself. But sometimes, son, you can trust a man who occasionally kneels before a toilet. The chances are that he is learning something about humility and his natural human foolishness, about how to survive himself. It's damned hard for a man to take himself too seriously when he's heaving his guts into a dirty toilet bowl.'

Then he paused for a long minute and added, 'And, son, never trust a drunk except when he's on his knees.'

When I glanced up, he was smiling an oddly distant smile, like a man who can see his own future and accepts it without complaint.

If he had left it at that, I might not have understood,

but he raised his empty glass and pointed at the vista. The fields, a lush, verdant green, grew dark with shadows, nearly as dark as the pine-thick ridges, but the sky above still glowed a bright, daylight blue. A single streak of clouds, like a long trail of smoke, angled away from the horizon, flaming a violent crimson at the far end as if it had been dipped in blood. But the middle was light pink, and the end nearest us was an ashen gray.

'A lovely view, isn't it, son?'

'Yes, sir.'

'But it's not enough,' he said, smiling, then he walked back into the bar, laughing and shouting for whiskey, love and laughter, leaving me suspended in the pellucid air.

Vomiting into the toilet of the Willomot Bar, not from the drink but from the knowledge and the dying, I felt my father's hand holding my head. He had left me this legacy of humility, and I accepted it. Where her little brother lost his life, I found mine, and understood that I wasn't going to kill anybody, except myself, and not myself for a long time yet. I remembered Simon telling me to slow down, not to drink myself to death before I had time to enjoy it. When I finished puking, I went back into the bar to wash out my mouth with whiskey.

16

When I woke the next morning, Jonas's bar resembled the field where the spirits of animals had done wild and lengthy battle with demons and ghosts, and triumphed. At least their eyes seemed glassy with victory, and their teeth bared in sneers of conquest as their heads surveyed the wreckage.

Tables and chairs had been upended, some reduced to splinters and kindling wood. Rags of clothing huddled about, some draped over the inert bodies of the slain. The floor was carpeted with fragments of glass and cigarette butts that didn't cover the drying whiskey stains. An improbably large brassiere dangled between the antlers of a bull elk, covering his eyes like a pair of cute Hollywood sunglasses. The only body I recognized in the dim morning light was Jonas's, sprawled at the feet of his grizzly bear. I had been sleeping with my face in an ash tray, and when I brushed away the ashes, I wished I hadn't. My face hadn't healed during the long night. Fresh blood had dripped from my ear onto the front of my windbreaker, and when I checked it, it felt damn funny, hot and swollen, but intact. I didn't have any scrapes on my knuckles, so if I had had a fight, I had lost quickly.

I rose carefully, checking my wallet and limbs, found them, then lurched behind the bar for a cold beer, which I drank before moving on, taking one for the road. When I walked outside into a splendid sunrise, even though I hadn't taken Muffin his money or called Helen to tell her I wasn't coming home that night, I felt absolutely great. I was still drunk as a lord.

I only hoped I could hang on to it long enough to do something about Nickie.

Helen had the front door on the chain, so I had to hammer on the chimes until she came, haggard and perplexed. She opened the door on a bare toe, and as she bent over to comfort it, she hit me in the ribs with her head. We stood around a few minutes, checking our wounds, but she recovered before I did.

'Where in the name of Christ have you been?' she growled, brushing her hair away from her face, blocking the doorway. 'Just where the hell have you been?'

'Drunk.'

'How could you do that to me?' she wailed, covering her face with her hands.

'I did it to myself, lady.'

'I think I could learn to hate you,' she said, opening her hands. Her eyes were sparkling green in the shadow. When I didn't answer, she stomped her foot and grunted, 'I could!'

'Lady, I've been playing this scene in doorways all my fucking life, and I don't have the time this morning to –'

But when I cursed, a soft ululation quivered from her throat, and she shoved me out of the way and slammed the door in my face.

'It's my goddamned house!' I shouted. After a long pause, she opened the door, smiling.

'Nobody's perfect,' she said, giggling, and we fell into each other's arms, laughing and crying and kissing, ignoring my face, trying to fill our hopelessly hungry mouths with each other, her green robe open, my pants down, we fell to the carpet like leaves circling in a light wind, leaves falling into water.

'See,' I said afterwards as our breath still gushed into the morning air. 'I told you it would be all right.'

'Ohhh,' she groaned, sighing and snuggling closer. 'Jesus, I don't – think – it's ever been – that sudden. My God – I never knew – before – why the Victorian poets – called it dying.'

'You forgive me for staying out all night, huh?'

'Right now – I'll forgive you – for anything – whewww – if you'll close – the front door.' Then she giggled happily.

'It's too late,' I said. 'I heard the paper boy fall off his bike.'

'That'll teach him – to spy on people,' she murmured, then we held each other, crushing our bodies together, as if one couldn't live without the presence of the other.

'We're gonna be all right,' I said, and felt her head nodding against my chest.

But we couldn't lounge on the hall carpet forever. Eventually, I kicked the door shut, pulled up my pants, and we hobbled into the bedroom like two old people to lose the morning in sleep. I meant to know what to do when I awoke, but it didn't work that way. When I woke, it was in the confusion of a hangover worse than a beating, with a foul mouth and a numbing depression. That old familiar feeling.

After a long hot shower, two hits of speed and two of Amos's pain pills, and a cold beer, I managed to eat a piece of toast left over from the morning before. Afterwards, I walked out to the rig to get the pistol and the shoulder holster, then went back inside to finish dressing.

'Hey,' I said, shaking her beneath the covers, 'I'm going to town. This time I will be back.'

'Where are you going?' she asked, sitting up with a wonderfully sleepy and pleased smile.

'To work.'

'Not today,' she said, pulling me toward her, 'not now.' Then she felt the pistol. 'What's that?' The smile fled.

'A pistol.'

'What's it for?'

'Sometimes I carry it,' I answered as lightly as I could. 'It makes me feel better when I've got a hangover.'

'You know,' she whispered, covering her open mouth with her hand. 'I'm scared.'

'There's nothing to be afraid of.'

'You know – who killed Raymond.'

'I think so, yes, but I'm not sure.'

'Are you going to kill them?' she asked, no longer afraid, her eyes narrow and mean.

'No.'

'Who is it?'

'Nobody you know.'

'Kill them,' she demanded, her teeth clenched tightly. 'Kill him.'

'Don't be silly,' I said. 'I can't go around killing people.'

'Don't say that to me – my mother says that. I'm not silly – kill him.'

'Love, I can't.'

'Then give me the gun,' she said, eyes blazing madly, 'give me the gun.' She tried to reach beneath my windbreaker, but I grabbed her arms. 'Turn me loose.'

'Hey, lady, settle down.'

'Do it!'

I released her hands, and she reached for the pistol again.

'Do it! For me!' she screamed, the words seeming to open the wounds in my face stitch by stitch, to pound like a stake into the center of my face, between my eyes. 'For me!'

I shook her shoulders until she stopped, fighting off her hands, which clawed at my face and chest. The back of her hand brushed my nose, bringing tears. I pushed her down on the bed, shaking her harder, shoving her against the bed until the screams became sobs, until she stopped fighting.

'Hey, I'll be back in a little while, okay?' I told her, but she ignored me, so I left her there, sobbing.

But as I opened the front door she screamed, 'I won't be here unless you do it!'

As I walked out to the rig I couldn't tell why I was crying.

Not knowing what to think, I went to Mahoney's and had another drink, trying again to forget it. But I couldn't. I still saw those wild eyes, oddly familiar, that fractured face. I told myself I just didn't understand her grief, that she would be all right by the time I went back. I did understand that I still felt terrible, so I cranked another hit of speed into my system, another pain pill, and another drink. A deep breath, then I was ready. I called Freddy from the pay phone in the bar, told him to go down to the house on Wild Rose Lane and tell Wanda that the game was over, that she had better head out.

'What's this all about?' he asked.

'Don't ask, Freddy. Just for once do what I tell you without asking, okay?'

'What the hell's wrong with you, Milo? You sound like death warmed over.'

'Apt description, fat man. Just tell her and don't answer any questions, then go back up the hill to see what she does. Okay?'

'You're the boss,' he said, and for once I believed him.

I hung up and called the hunting camp to apologize to Muffin, to tell him that I had the man.

'Let me speak to your urban representative,' I told Muffin's boss.

'Buddy, we don't have no urban representative.'

'Goddammit, this is Milo. Let me talk to Muffin.'

'Nobody here by that name.'

'What's wrong? They got a tap on your line?'

'No, Milo. I pay a creep like you good money to make sure, but I don't know about your line.'

'I'm at a pay phone.'

'Why didn't you say so?'

'I don't know. Just let me talk to Muffin.'

'Can't, man, he split last night.'

'Did he say where he was going?'

'Don't be stupid all your life, Milo.'

'Okay. Did he leave a message.'

'Yeah, lemme see, here it is. *Orphans have to adopt themselves eventually.* What the hell's that mean?'

'I don't know,' I said. 'Probably means I should have never sent him to college.'

'Huh?'

'Nothing.'

'Say, Milo, there's a problem.'

'What's that?'

'Expenses. I fronted him a grand, he said you'd cover it. Familial duty, he called it, or something like that.'

'Okay,' I said, 'it's covered.'

'When?'

'As soon as I get up there.'

'Make it sooner, okay?'

'Fuck off.'

'Don't talk to me like that, Milo,' he said pleasantly, 'or I'll have your legs broken.'

'I got the money in my pocket, but it'll take me a couple of days to get loose down here.'

'Tomorrow will be fine.'

'The day after. Hey, I gotta deal for you.'

'What?'

'Two hundred television sets, color.'

'I don't deal black-and-white, man, there ain't no percentage in that. Where?'

'I want Muffin's piece of the action.'

'Only if you deliver the sets, Milo.'

'No way.'

'Then twenty-five percent of what Muffin would have made.'

'No deal.'

'Fine,' he said and hung up before I could disagree.

As I walked back to the bar I wondered if I'd ever hear from Muffin, then decided that I probably would. I wished I had told him before he left that he and my natural son were equal heirs in my will, but then I thought better. No sense in passing on my mother's unhappiness. I leaned on the bar and ordered a beer to sip while I waited for Freddy to call back, and I saw my face in the mirror. It wasn't the face of a hero – no character, no dignity. Just the face of another drunk who had bitten off more than he could ever hope to chew, a face so battered and unhappy and bloated that not even Leo could save it with his camera.

'How's Leo?' I asked the bartender.

'They moved him over to Duck Valley two days ago. Didn't you know?' The state mental hospital was in the same valley as the prison. 'He was in bad shape.'

'Did they say how long he had to stay?'

'Six months, a year maybe. Didn't you see him?'

'No,' I said. 'I've been busy.'

'Looks like it,' he said, handing me my beer, then going to answer the phone.

It was Freddy. Wanda had split from Wild Rose Lane without looking back. I didn't want it to be Nickie, but it was, and the only thing I could find to be angry about was that he thought I would quit after a beating, and I guess I was only angry about that because he was right. Maybe that's why I intended to go after him instead of calling Jamison. I told Freddy to come on and have a drink on me.

Waiting at the end of the bar for Nickie to walk through, I sat over a slow drink, but when he came in, he didn't look surprised. Just tired and gray and drawn.

'How's the boy, Milo? Feeling better?'

'Not too bad. How's yourself?'

'Fine, fine,' he said, rubbing his stomach and mouthing a silent belch. 'Let me buy you a drink. It's a little early for me, but maybe I'll have one too.' The bartender was busy at the other end, so Nickie went behind the bar and mixed the drinks. Mine was almost all whiskey. Mama DeGrumo watched him carefully from her perch, nodding once as our eyes met.

'What is it, Nickie?' she asked.

'A Canadian and water.'

'A double?'

'No, Mama. It's on me anyway,' he answered, and her register chugged through a ticket.

'What's happening?' he asked as he slid onto the stool beside me.

'Trouble.'

'Huh? Oh, yeah, trouble everywhere these days, Milo. Sometimes I think the whole world's gone crazy, you know. Even this town. This used to be a good town, you know, I can't understand –'

'This is a different sort of trouble, Nickie. More specific.'

'Huh?' he asked, belching. 'What's that?'

'This lady you've had me tailing.'

'What's the matter? I thought you – were gonna take a few days off,' he said, then pulled hard at his drink, swallowed air and burped. 'Goddamned soda.'

'I went back to work sooner than I thought I would,' I said, 'and let me tell you, Nickie, I haven't caught this broad in the act yet, but I know she's fucking around.'

'How – how do you know?'

'It's my business, Nickie. I've been tailing horny broads all my life and I can smell it. Hell, Nickie, you've seen her, you can tell. All those bitches fuck around,' I said, trying to keep my voice sly and grimy, but having trouble controlling the speed rush that had just kicked into my nervous system, having trouble keeping from blowing his head off.

'You don't – who – Did you catch her?' he stammered.

'Naw, I haven't caught her yet, I told you that, but I will. She's been giving me the slip, but I put a beeper on her car. I'll catch her, I promise.'

'How many times did you see her?' he asked, like a man who didn't want to know.

'Five, maybe six times. Once this morning, then just a few minutes ago. This broad's slick, Nickie, she's been around.'

'She gave you the slip just now?' He finished his drink and went around the bar. 'Want another?'

'No, thanks,' I said. 'Yeah, she took off five, maybe ten minutes ago. But like I said, I got a beeper on her car.'

'What's that?'

'A transmitter. It sends out a signal so I can find her car.'

'I – I don't understand – why . . .' He couldn't finish. His hand went back to his stomach, then away, as if he could ignore the pain. 'Goddamned soda.'

'Listen, we can catch her in the act. Right now. But I need some more money.'

'Huh?'

'Money, Nickie. This electronic crap is expensive to rent. I need five bills for a deposit and another one for the rent.'

'Five hundred dollars?'

'You'll get that back. You said your friend didn't care about the money, so what the hell do you care?'

'A few minutes ago, huh?' he asked, trying to hold his face together.

'Right. Just get the money, Nickie, and we got her ass-cold.'

'I – I gotta check – be right back,' he said, then walked away toward his office, his hand worrying his stomach, his boots slapping dully on the carpet.

I wanted Nickie in my rig, wanted to see his face when I told him that I knew. I thought about what Jamison had told me about Turkish wives and cats; the image of Nickie clawed into a puddle of flesh and blood by drowning cats didn't bother me at all. I asked the bartender for another drink. He brought it with the sneer of the sober.

'It's on Nickie,' I said.

He looked at me but didn't speak.

'Are you deaf, asshole?' I asked, trembling again. He didn't answer or change expression, he just walked away when Nickie came back carrying a long white envelope in his quivering hand.

'Okay,' he said, 'damn right. Bitch.' Then he moved close to me, shielding himself from Mama D. I wondered how he'd feel if he thought his wife had been unfaithful instead of his mistress. 'Fucking whore,' he whispered. 'How much you need?' He scratched his chest violently.

'Give it all to me.'

'Huh?'

'All of it, Nickie. You don't need it.'

'Huh?'

'You're dead, you fucking creep, dead,' I hissed and jerked the envelope out of his hand. His mouth opened, lips moving vaguely like undersea weeds caught in a current. 'I'm dumb, Nickie, I'm so dumb that it's taken me this long to come up with you. The only person in town who's dumber than me is you, and you're dead.'

I guess I'll never know if I would have killed him. When I reached under my windbreaker for the automatic, Nickie's face swelled up like a frog's and his arms laced across his chest, his fingers ripping his shirt as they tried to get to the pain wired around his chest, his body leaning toward me, his face in mine, his breath shallow and hot against my skin. Then he straightened up, turned as if he was going to walk calmly away, and fell forward on his face with a thud that silenced the idle conversation in the bar.

I leaned over him, grabbed his jacket and flipped him over, shook him, telling him that he couldn't die on me. But he did. Judging from the look on his relaxed face, he wasn't all that unhappy about it.

I stood up to look around the bar. Two tourists were craning their necks from their bar stools, but they didn't get up. The bartender had come to the end of the bar and was walking toward me, not looking at Nickie. I pointed my finger at him, but he didn't stop, so I pointed the pistol, and he did. But Mama D. didn't stop for anything. She was coming like a truck, I got out of her way, she fell upon Nickie's body, screaming incoherently in Italian, holding Nickie's face and covering it with kisses. I told the bartender to stay just where he was, then holstered the piece and walked out through the crowded lobby, bucking the people who were moving toward the bar to see what all the screaming was about. As I walked out, I could hear Mama D.'s moans bursting like bombs. I understood how she felt.

I was almost to my rig when I heard the first gunshot and the crash of plate glass falling to the sidewalk. I turned, like a fool, and saw Mama D. plowing through the lobby, waving a snub-nosed revolver and shedding people like wastepaper. Her first shot had taken out one of the lobby windows. As I watched she ran into the double doors like a fullback, flinging them aside, and waddled toward me as fast as she could, the revolver held unsteadily before her. I don't think I'd ever seen her off her stool before, and certainly never in the sunlight. She was much shorter and fatter than I had realized, her mustache much darker. I didn't think I was in much danger unless she got close enough to poke the revolver into my belly and pull the trigger. I wasn't going to shoot back, so I climbed into my rig and drove away as she emptied the revolver in my direction.

She missed me, but she played hell with the tourist trade with those last five shots. She put bullets into a pickup camper and a station wagon in the parking lot and hit another station wagon in the radiator as it turned into the lot. Her fifth shot disappeared up Hell-Roaring Canyon, but her sixth found a human target – a fisherman from Schenectady, New York – in a pay phone booth half a block away on Main as he was telling his wife how good the fishing was out West.

As I drove around the stalled station wagon, I glanced into my rear-view mirror. Mama D. hadn't given up, her chubby arms pumping as she tried to run, her right hand squeezing the empty revolver again and again as she chased me out of the parking lot and into the street. Her screaming mouth looked like a large black hole in her face. She had loved the poor bastard.

Later, I heard that she had followed me three blocks west on Main before the police finally caught her. She broke one patrolman's jaw with the empty revolver, and the other had to use his billy to handle her.

17

Without thinking about it, I went downtown to the office, not to Mahoney's, not home. I wanted to be alone, and nobody would look for me in the office. I wanted some time before I had to deal with Jamison. Without counting it, I put Nickie's money in the safe along with that I had taken out for Muffin. Then I got the office bottle, propped my feet in the open north window, and stared up into the Diablos, trying to decide what I felt.

Nothing. Empty, tired, ill-used. Hung over. Slightly nervous from all the drugs rattling around in my system. But oddly peaceful too. It was over, all over but the shouting. And when that was over, I wanted to go away for a long time. I didn't care where, just out of town, away with my lady. Just like Nickie.

Poor Nickie. He hadn't wanted much. Pocket money and a smattering of respect, to be able to buy a round of drinks, to have a woman that didn't look like a hawk perched on a pig's ass. Not too much for a man to ask. But what a way to go about it. Briefly, I wondered where in hell he had gotten the idea, how he had managed to buy the heroin. But that was Jamison's worry, not mine.

I stood up and leaned out the window to see the bank clock. It had been a busy morning; it was barely noon. I sat back down, sipping whiskey, sliding gracefully into a calm sulk. Goddamned Nickie, Next Round Nickie wouldn't be promising the drinks anymore. But there wasn't too much pity for him. He hadn't meant to, but he had released about five weeks of real madness in the town he loved. And he must have been terrified the whole time, skulking about Meriwether in a false beard and a wig and wrap-around sunglasses, frightened but feeling damned important, a real gangster loose on our streets. I guessed I'd never know if he had overloaded Raymond Duffy's last fix, never know exactly how or why the kid died. Poor goddamned Nickie. Gathered up enough courage to shove a drunk old man down a stairway, then puking up his guts when he saw the result of that shove. I wondered, too, how he had gotten Elton Crider into the river. But that was Jamison's worry. For the life of me, I couldn't imagine Nickie killing anybody. He hadn't the heart for it. Any more than I did. Poor dumb Nickie. It had never occurred to me, wouldn't have in a thousand years, that he was hiring me just to get me out of the way. I believed him. But, of course, he believed me too. I didn't know what that meant. He had handled everybody else on his own, but had hired help to handle me. I didn't know if that meant he was afraid of me or thought me dumber than him. He wasn't going to rise from the grave to explain it either. Sad Nickie. I imagined him honestly amazed and disgusted when the junkies he had fathered took up crime to feed their habits. Junkies in *his* town. And dead men stacked like logs. I counted them on my fingers. It took both hands. Nine dead men. Or eight men and one twelve-year-old boy. All, except for Nickie and the Duffy kid, innocent bystanders. Jesus, I thought, never underestimate a klutz.

When the telephone rang, I expected it to be Jamison, but it was Mama D.'s resident cousin. He seemed to think that we had mutual interests to discuss. He wanted to come to my office, but I told him that I only discussed business at Mahoney's, and he agreed to meet me there in fifteen minutes. Thinking about Nickie, I had forgotten that Mama D.'s cousins were probably going to be interested in what had happened, and they weren't amateurs. I didn't think they would want a lot of trouble in a clean town, but I didn't know what they called trouble. The motel manager wasn't scared of me, so I thought perhaps I should be of him. And I imagined that organized criminals, like small-town sheriffs who have visions of being John Wayne, probably believed their own myths. That's why Mahoney's seemed like a much better place to meet than my office.

I leaned out the window to check the time again and saw the black Cadillac parked at the curb and Mama D.'s cousin, followed by the daytime bartender, walking into the bank's office entrance. They were early and at the wrong place. I checked the automatic, then locked the office door on my way to hide in the john at the end of the hallway just past the door of my cousin the dentist's office.

I peeked through a crack in the door and watched

them get out of the elevator, the executive-type in front, the bartender flanking him. He had changed out of his uniform and into a leather suit with a short jacket and bell-bottom pants, a floral print shirt and low platform shoes. He looked like a Hollywood bit player looking for work. They didn't bother to knock on my office door, but the bit player lifted a leather tool case out of his hip pocket.

'Excuse me, fellas,' I said as I stepped out of the john, 'but that door is wired into the bank's alarm system, and if you open it, you're gonna cause one hell of a fuss, and those nifty tool kits are a mandatory two-year fall.'

They stepped back cautiously, then the older one started toward me, his hand extended, his smile sincerely abashed.

'Mr. Milodragovitch,' he said, 'we just thought –'

'You want to stop right there?' I didn't want to make him angry, but I didn't want him next to me either.

'Certainly,' he answered, as if he didn't mind at all. 'It isn't necessary to be quite so nervous.'

'I'm always nervous when plans are suddenly changed without me knowing about it. So let's just meet in the bar like we planned.'

'Certainly,' he said, nodding pleasantly.

'And leave your associate in the car.'

'Whatever for?' he asked, seeming genuinely perplexed.

'Just leave him outside,' I said. My heart felt like a rabbit running wildly around inside my rib cage. Too much excitement for one day. Or one hit too many of the little white pills. The older guy looked like that was all right with him, but the guy in the leather suit didn't look too happy about being left out. 'I didn't mean to hurt your feelings, asshole,' I said to him. That was twice in one day. He started to move toward me.

'Arnold,' the older guy said.

'Arnold,' I jeered, and he took another step. 'Arnold! Wow!' I mocked, and a wonderfully violent speed rush blew into me. 'Come on, creep,' I said as his hand moved toward the pistol under his arm. 'Come on! Go for it! It's just like in the movies, mother, I'm the fastest gun in this shithole town, so go for it!'

Arnold didn't believe me, but it didn't matter. His boss didn't want to be caught in our cross fire. He was reaching out for Arnold's gun hand just as my cousin the dentist opened his office door on his way to lunch.

That did it. Luckily, the executive had a good hold on Arnold's arm. Otherwise, he and I would have blown large hunks of my cousin and him all over the hallway.

'At Mahoney's,' the older guy said, tugging Arnold down the hallway.

'Right,' I said, feeling as wasted as an old discarded condom.

'What's happening, Milo?' my cousin said, looking the scene over with round eyes. He was as big as a pro tackle but he had never played football.

'You just stepped right in the middle of a gunfight,' I told him.

'You're a card,' he said jovially, laughing and slapping me on the arm hard enough to bounce me into the wall. 'Listen, let's go to lunch, okay? And you can tell me if all that crap I read in the newspaper is true.'

'Working,' I muttered as I headed for the backstairs, and he laughed even louder.

I went in the back door of Mahoney's and took my usual booth. The older guy came in the front, moving through the early afternoon drinkers with a politely restrained force. Arnold was sitting in the Caddy in the loading zone, carefully not looking into the bar.

'Hello,' the older guy said, extending his hand again. This time I took it. 'I assume this is your usual table?' I nodded. 'Perhaps we might be more comfortable elsewhere, say, at that back table,' he said, then without waiting for my answer, he led the way past Pierre and the shuffleboard machine to a table between the silent jukebox and the shuffleboard.

'Well,' he said, offering me the chair that faced the front door so I could watch Arnold, 'I must apologize for the intrusion attempted upon your office. Events have transpired so quickly this morning, and we have never had occasion to do business with you, so at the time it seemed a necessary intrusion. I do hope you will accept my apology.'

'Sure,' I said, still standing.

'And for Arnold's unforgivable behavior also. He has been in the hinterlands too long, I fear – grown stale. I think perhaps he has much too much spare time to watch television. He is a professional, you know, and quite good, but perhaps he takes his rather limited function too seriously,' he said, his manicured hands moving like those of a well-trained lecturer to make small but significant points that I might have missed in his urbane voice. 'Won't you sit down?'

'After you,' I said. Being around him was like being around somebody who was stoned: contagious. 'Please.'

But he waited with his hand on the chair, the index finger of his other hand touching his cheek as if he was trying to think of the best way to say something mildly unpleasant.

'I hope you won't take this personally,' he said, 'but you are a private investigator and as such have access to sophisticated listening and recording devices.'

'When I can afford them, sure. A man has to keep up with technology.'

'Yes, I understand. I hope you will understand my necessary sensitivity about such devices and won't object to some sort of mechanical noise to cover our conversation –'

'Excuse me,' I said as I caught the bartender's eye. 'Would you like something to drink?'

'Thank you, nothing for me,' he said.

'You were talking about noise,' I said, nodding to the bartender when he held up a beer mug, shaking my head when he held up a shot glass.

'You wouldn't object if I were to play the jukebox?' he asked, stepping toward it.

'Of course not,' I said.

'Ah, this is rather embarrassing,' he said, turning toward me. 'Do you perhaps have some change?'

'Sure,' I said, digging into my pocket, then handing him two quarters. He found the coin slot, fed the quarters into the machine, then touched his soft fingers to the buttons, ranging across them like a piano player, playing songs at random. As he stepped back to the table he cocked his head, checking the noise level.

'That isn't quite loud enough, is it?'

'I don't know,' I said, then to the bartender as he brought my beer: 'Turn up the jukebox.'

'Go to hell, Milo,' he said as he walked away.

The nifty hood raised his eyebrow like an old maid. Nobody ever told him to go to hell.

'You make me wish I was bugged,' I said. 'Put some money in that shuffleboard machine there. No bug in the world can get past that sort of interference.' I didn't know if that was true, but he bought it.

'Really,' he said, walking over to the machine, his hands folded before him like a monk's.

'Really,' I echoed as I followed him and gave him another quarter. Like most drunks, I had a pocketful of drinking change.

'I feel I must apologize again,' he murmured softly, 'for the haphazard nature of these proceedings. Ordinarily, we have more time to plan for electronic countermeasures, but we were completely unprepared for the events of this morning. However, I hope you won't judge our organization too quickly. We really are quite efficient.' His voice was quiet, but the threat was clear.

'It isn't necessary to threaten me,' I said, just giving advice, not irritated by the threat.

'I wasn't,' he said, and that brought a small flash of anger.

'My ass is covered.'

'We assumed that, of course, but please don't

overestimate the seriousness of this affair. We have a very nice business here, but quite limited in terms of our corporate structure, or, as you might say, the larger picture. I happen to be a corporate officer, you see, and I am authorized to deal with you in whatever manner I choose. It was pure chance that I happened to be in Meriwether, a sort of working vacation, you might say. I had a small coronary accident last spring and –'

'Runs in the family?' I interrupted.

'I beg your pardon? Oh, yes. Quite humorous. As I was saying, our business here certainly isn't of major importance. In fact, our major interest is familial –'

'So I've heard.'

'But haven't understood at all. Please don't interrupt unless it is absolutely necessary,' he said, chiding me as one would a child. 'Our major interest in this affair is to avoid any embarrassment to either Mrs. DeGrumo's father or uncle, who are large stockholders in our franchise operation, and if you can assist us in any way and if you are neither too expensive nor too inconvenient, we are quite willing to settle this matter with you. Otherwise, we will seek other means.'

'I've had some hard times out of this –'

'I can well imagine, judging by the damage to your face. I understand that a broken nose is quite painful,' he said, but I couldn't tell if he was commiserating with me or threatening to punch me in the nose.

'My stake in this is personal,' I said, 'and I might be willing to be damned inconvenient rather than eat shit.'

'But you can be bought.'

'Rented.'

'Semantics. Quibbling over a word –'

'Don't condescend to me,' I said.

We looked at each other. His tanned face was impassive, but his hand moved up to touch his wide silk tie as if it were some sort of talisman.

'Of course. Please accept my apology. It is often difficult for those of us from other sections of the country to remember that the West has been quite civilized for some time. I do apologize,' he said, his voice rich with humility, cultured and phony as a tin dollar. I wanted to break his jaw, but that would have brought sweet Arnold a-running and caused more trouble than I wanted. 'Would you like to play while we talk?' he asked, holding up the stainless-steel puck.

'No thanks. I like my hands where they are.'

'I see. Arnold isn't the only victim of the media. It isn't at all necessary for you to be quite so nervous, but I suppose it is to be expected. Evil times and bad public relations, wouldn't you say?' he said, an amused smile fluttering about his calm mouth. 'Now, how does one operate this machine?'

He put the quarter into the slot, and I hit the button, and the machine clattered into life. Pierre turned his head slowly, like a large stone tilting, cast his glare across me, shaking his fist and grimacing.

'Now what does one do? What is the purpose of all those lights? Oh, I see. These are the strike zones, and one should hit the strike zones as the flashing lights cross, and that elicits the highest score. Am I correct?'

I nodded, and he began playing with some intensity, like a serious amateur golfer, talking to me as he watched the blinking lights stutter across the board and his scores register in anxious clicks, pausing occasionally to dust his hands and the cuffs of his expensive suit coat.

'You might begin by giving me some insight into what might have caused Nickie's coronary this morning,' he said, his tongue confident as it formed *coronary.* He wasn't afraid. But his hand slipped up to touch his tie again. 'And to what purpose were you carrying a weapon?'

'I told Nickie that I was going to kill him, but he collapsed before I could do anything about it.'

'Did you really intend to shoot him down right there in the bar?'

'I don't know. I don't think so,' I admitted.

'I suppose not. Why did you threaten him?'

'He killed a friend of mine.'

'Are you sure?'

'Pretty sure before, absolutely certain now.'

'He is dead, yes, so you must have been correct. But how did poor dumb Nickie ever come to kill somebody?'

'This friend of mine found out that Nickie was dealing heroin.'

'Are you absolutely sure about that?' he asked.

'Yes.'

'Amazing. We've been interested in that problem, of course, because the merchandise was of such a high quality, but we certainly never suspected Nickie. I mean, he was so *dumb*. But it begins to fit now,' he said, reaching into his coat pocket and taking out a page torn from *Time*. He glanced at it, then shook his head and handed it to me. 'We found this in his effects this morning, in a scrapbook of schemes for instant wealth – Brazilian farmland, Alaskan oil, soy bean futures, that sort of thing. He was such a fool,' he added, so much disgust in his voice that I had an odd impulse to defend Nickie.

But the clipping was sad and foolish. It explained how the Mafia was cashing in on the counterculture by cornering the supply of soft drugs and holding them off the market so that the young would move on to harder and more lucrative drugs.

'Pure nonsense, of course. Demand always exceeds supply,' he said, like a man who knew. Then he added casually, 'You wouldn't know where Nickie was getting his merchandise, would you?'

'Police evidence locker somewhere,' I said.

'Unfortunate corruption among law enforcement officers,' he intoned, smiling. 'You wouldn't know where Nickie had his merchandise hidden?'

'I can guess, but the police are going to be very interested in me as soon as they find me, and I have to have something to trade. Nickie's goods are my ticket.'

'Perhaps we could arrange something with the local authorities.'

'Too much heat right now.'

'I suppose you're right.'

'Besides, this was a one-shot deal. Nickie just wanted enough money to split, so he couldn't have much smack left in his stash.'

'You're right, of course,' he said sadly. 'Do you have any idea what Mrs. DeGrumo had in mind when she went after you with the pistol?'

'She just went berserk, as far as I know. Overcome by grief, you might say.'

'Yes, it certainly seems that way,' he said as he finished the game. 'A rather amusing device. Is that a respectable score for a novice?' he asked as the counters clicked merrily toward some mystic number beyond the ken of men.

'I wouldn't know,' I said.

'One of these might be just the thing for my family room. Do you know where I might purchase one?'

'Try Meriwether Vending.'

'Of course. Why is that old gentleman glowering at me?' he asked, nodding toward Pierre.

'He isn't too fond of the machine.'

'I see. Quite an interesting face, isn't it? And all those on the walls too. I assume those are the faces of the regular clientele?'

'Yes.'

'I don't seem to see yours among them.'

'That's right.'

'Yes. And the gold stars indicate those who are deceased?'

'That's right.'

'Very interesting. I wish I had the time to examine them more closely. I'm an amateur photographer myself, you know. But business calls. This wouldn't be quite so messy if Mrs. DeGrumo hadn't wounded that chap in the telephone booth – I take it you didn't know about that.'

'No.'

'Yes. One of her wilder shots hit a tourist in a

telephone booth. He is in critical condition. It would be quite inconvenient.'

'Hell, they don't care if you shoot an occasional tourist out here. Plead her temporarily insane. She'll spend six months in Duck Valley, then get out,' I said, giving advice again.

'We have a quite competent legal staff,' he said.

'Get a local lawyer.'

'Good point. Interesting. You're the person who told Nickie that the bar needed a brace of illegal punchboards, aren't you?'

'Yes.'

'You seem to have a rather sharp mind behind all that tape and damage. What are you going to tell the police when they, as you said, become interested in you?'

'The truth. Nickie put the dope deal together, I stumbled into it, and when I braced him to make sure, he died. Simple. Easy. Assuming Nickie was really in business for himself.'

'Oh, for heaven's sake, yes. Perhaps we misjudged him, but certainly we wouldn't have allowed him to handle anything of this nature. Perhaps we should have given him some sort of added responsibility. But, of course, every time we did, he made such a terrible mess of things. Well, you know Nickie.'

'Knew him.'

'Quite,' he said, holding the puck between his hands. He set it down. 'I suppose this is the point in the negotiations where I offer you financial remuneration, a rental fee as you called it, for your cooperation in this matter. To make sure that neither Mrs. DeGrumo nor the business is connected in any way with Nickie's lurid affairs.'

'I have to tell the truth about this whether you pay me or not.'

'I quite understand, but we would rather pay you something for your time.'

'Okay,' I said, knowing exactly what I was doing but not liking it. 'If you insist.'

'Oh, I do. We don't have a very large budget for this sort of thing, but I think I can offer you a reasonable sum,' he said, amused with himself and the way he had beaten me as easily as he had the shuffleboard machine. He took an envelope from his inside coat pocket and handed it to me, saying, 'Shall we say, a thousand now – earnest money, so to speak – and another when this situation works out satisfactorily.'

I took the envelope, folded it and stuck it in my hip pocket, and told him, 'That's not much.'

'Oh, but that's all there is, Mr. Milodragovitch. We will, of course, expect results,' he said, his hand rising to flick a speck of dried blood off my jacket. 'If this works out, we might be able to find a place for you in our local business. Provided you were neither greedy nor stupid, which I'm certain you aren't.' He smiled broadly, his eyebrow cocked again, his plump fingers finding another spot of loose blood. 'Think about it.'

'I will,' I said, thinking about it for a second, remembering what Muffin had said about me, wondering how Helen Duffy would take it if I went to work for their organization, and I found myself smiling. 'Sure, I'll think about it. Changing sides might change my luck.'

'Really,' he said, his hand reaching up to pat my cheek gently. 'You don't seem to be terribly concerned about the insidious tendrils of organized crime choking your hometown.'

'That's true,' I said, my hands moving up to straighten his tie. 'I just hate arrogant assholes.' Then I tugged on the short end of the tie, tugged hard. His smile had faded, his handsome face bloomed wonderfully florid. Then I jerked the tie, saying, 'I told you not to condescend to me.' Then I pulled the tie harder. He struggled for air, his mouth gasping loosely, his arms flapping as if they weren't connected to his shoulders.

I swung him around like a ball on a string, knocking over Pierre's table and slamming the guy into the jukebox, which went silent with a long scratchy burr, then leading him like a dog on a leash, I ran him at the shuffleboard machine and threw him down the board. His head banged into the plastic cover, then buried among the plastic pins with a fine crash.

That was too much for Pierre. He rose from his chair, walked around the overturned table and stood beside the nifty hood, raising his gnarled thick hands and bringing them down on his back, slamming heavily against the guy as he struggled to get his tie loosened and his head out of the machine. Pierre grunted like a man splitting firewood until the hood's struggles ceased.

As I looked toward the front door, remembering Arnold, heads and bodies were aimed toward the back until they heard Arnold's platform shoes banging on the wooden floor. I stepped into the aisle between the booths and the bar, and shouted 'Freeze!' at him.

He meant to, I think, but the moment seemed too perfect: the showdown between the handsome young stranger and the tired old drunk, the shared celluloid moment. He stopped, nearly falling down, but the roles had been written too long for him to change them now, and his hand went for his piece. It was still under his jacket, and he had a long instant to realize that the dying was going to be real, when I pulled the trigger. He was the wrong man, but it wasn't my fault.

18

After it was over and the echoes of the gunfire stilled, the bar emptied quickly, the afternoon drinkers fleeing into the sunshine, careful not to touch the blood-splattered doorframe or step on the fragments of bone and flesh scattered all the way out the door and across the sidewalk to the side of their Cadillac, which was spotted with bullet holes and human debris. The four jacketed rounds had gone through and into the door of their car. Arnold had managed to get his revolver out after the second time I hit him, but he didn't have the strength to pull the trigger. At least it was in his outflung hand.

'Nice shooting,' Freddy said as he walked up behind me.

'Goddammit, Freddy, shut up,' I muttered as I walked away from him around behind the bar to pour a drink. The bartender still huddled behind the bar, crouched like a whipped dog.

'It's over?' he asked, holding a bloody nose with his hand. He had banged it on the cooler trying to get down. I nodded at him, and he fled outside too, away from the stink.

Freddy checked Arnold's body, covering the entrance wounds with his hand, shaking his head like a man who couldn't believe it. Then he went to take Pierre off the other hood, sat him down, and tugged the guy out of the machine. He seemed to be alive, breathing shallowly but lying very still on the board, like a man laid out for a wake. Freddy walked over to the bar, moved my automatic out of the way, and I poured us a drink. We toasted something. When Jamison came charging into the bar in front of a squad of patrolmen, he found me hanging over a glass of whiskey, grieving and sick of the scene, acting as tired as Gregory Peck or Glenn Ford. And Jamison played the lawman well: confused.

Eventually he worked it out, though. By late afternoon he had arrested and impounded and searched to his heart's content. His boys found Nickie's heroin stash inside a water softener in the basement of the house on Wild Rose Lane. Wanda had been arrested at the airport, and when the police rushed in, the secretary in the police department who had faked the records about the destruction of a kilo of heroin went into hysterics and confessed to everything. As it turned out, she had been seduced by the Duffy kid, that gem of a young man. I was allowed to leave the police station on a personal recognizance bond, but I had to walk to the bank parking lot to get my rig. And when I got home, it was nearly sunset and the lady's mother was there.

She sat in the backyard on one of my lounge chairs, her trim legs crossed, her strong face inclined toward the setting sun, her neck arched gracefully. Helen sat on the back steps in the shade, hugging her knees and humming to herself. She heard me at the back door, rose quickly and came inside, hugging me fiercely, brushing her lips across my face, touching the stiff sutures with her soft mouth, murmuring, 'Oh, darling, I heard. How terrible, how awful, you poor darling.'

Then she tucked her face against my chest, her arms tight around my body as she swayed and hummed, childlike in the still afternoon air.

'It will be all right. I have some time to spend in court, but then we can go away. Everything will be all right.'

'Oh, no,' she whispered, stepping back from me, looking up but not in my eyes. 'She knows. She's here and she knows.'

'What?'

'Everything,' she crooned, 'she's here and she knows everything.'

'What?'

'She does that to me, you know. She insists, she always does that, you know, insists on knowing everything. I hate – hate it when she makes me tell, you won't be angry –'

'I won't be angry,' I said, silencing her against my chest, too tired to think, too wasted to really care.

'Helen.'

At the sound of the voice, her head rose and she moved away from me, her hand wiping her nose.

'Yes, Mother,' she answered the voice.

'Bring your friend outside, please. I'm sure he's quite tired, and we must hurry. Perhaps you might make the two of us a drink.' The voice was as soft and melodious as the ramble of the creek – as insistent too. 'Please.'

Helen stepped around me into the kitchen, her shoulders hunched, her hands cupped before her. She walked around the kitchen in small aimless steps, muttering, 'Damn damn damn damn . . .' Then she looked at me. 'Whadda ya wanna drink?'

'A beer. That's all. Are you all right?'

'Are you kiddin'? With that old bitch here? How can anybody be all right? She ruins everything, you know that – everything.'

'Mr. Milodragovitch,' the voice intruded. 'Please come outside. Helen is quite capable of preparing the drinks.'

'Are you sure you're all right?' I asked again.

'Oh, go outside. *She* wants to talk to you.'

As I stepped out the door, Mrs. Duffy rose to greet me, lifted herself out of the lounge chair as gracefully as if she had been borne on silver wires, and she stood there, as tall and cool and slim as the frosted glass she held lightly in her firm hand.

'I'm quite pleased to meet you,' she said, taking my hand, holding it in a dry, muscular clasp. 'Finally.'

I nodded and took back my hand.

'I meant to come much sooner, but Helen had told me that you were indisposed. From what I hear, though, not completely helpless. I'm afraid Helen exaggerated your condition. She painted a portrait of you either mewling like a baby or dying of age. I suppose I should have recognized the symptoms –'

'Symptoms?'

'Of the lying.'

'Lying?'

'I thought you knew. But I can see that you didn't.'

'Didn't know what?'

'I simply assumed that Mr. Diamond had told you that Helen is a pathological liar.'

'Oh, yeah, he did, but I thought he was lying,' I said, waving my hand vaguely.

'Really,' she said as we looked each other over like a couple of dogs about to fight.

She was slightly shorter than Helen, but slimmer, and so poised and held herself so erectly, she seemed much taller than her daughter. Her hands were aging but well tended, the nails glossy and tapered under a coat of clear polish, and the fingers that held the glass were as motionless as ice. She, too, had red hair but streaked with an arrogant gray, as if by some spell she had reversed the process by which steel was destroyed by rust. The blue of her eyes was steady, a deep violet, confident and cool. Her face might have been marked by age, like her hands, but the years didn't show beneath the smooth matte finish that covered the bevels and planes and angles of her face. Not a wrinkle marred her skin, which she hadn't exposed deliberately, not a hint of freckles. Beneath the soft sweep of her simple gray dress, her body looked as strong and supple as a willow switch.

'Have you surveyed me sufficiently?' she asked, her eyes locked on my face.

'Yeah,' I grunted.

'And what do you think?' she asked, tilting her head just enough for the sunlight to glisten off her firm jaw line, waiting with the first quivers of a confident smile for my compliment.

'Frankly?' I asked, puzzled by all this.

'Of course,' she said, straightening her head, letting the warm glow of light stray gently across her face. 'I admire frankness in a man.'

'Well, frankly, lady, I wouldn't want to meet you in a dark alley.'

She laughed. Not loudly, not throwing her head back, but deep and husky, the sort of laugh that insinuates itself through a noisy cocktail party like visiting royalty, making the women feel quite shabby and dated, making the men surreptitiously check their flies before edging toward the fount of that precious mirth.

'Well put,' she said. 'I like a man who can see beneath the surface.' Amusement wrinkled her eyes, and they sparkled wisely. Shafts of sunlight drifted within the blue and inviting depths of her eyes. 'Men are too often fooled, too easily impressed by the physical appearance of a woman, by the outer beauty. It's the cause of much grief, I'm sad to say – beauty and the inability of some men to see beyond it.'

She had confused me. At first, I had thought she was talking about herself, but at the end she seemed to mean Helen. I glanced toward the house, wishing Helen would bring the beer, come out and help me with her mother.

'Helen,' Mrs. Duffy said sharply, 'please bring the drinks.'

She must have been waiting just behind the screen door because she came out before her mother finished the command. She brought her mother another tall frosted drink, took the empty glass, then handed me a can of beer. She stood in front of us, her feet together, her hands held tightly at her waist, her head bowed.

'Perhaps Mr. Milodragovitch would like a glass, Helen.'

'Oh, no,' I said quickly.

'Then if you'll excuse us for a moment, Helen. Your friend and I have several things to discuss.' I reached for Helen to keep her with us, but she moved away from my arm, crossed the yard and hunkered on a large stone on the creek bank, doodling with a twig in a hand's span of dirt between the stones. 'Why don't we sit down,' Mrs. Duffy suggested firmly, sitting as easily as she had stood, so I took the other chair, slumping all the way into it. 'I understand from Helen that you have asked her to marry you,' she said, the tone of her voice letting me know how difficult it was to believe poor Helen. She sat on the very edge of her lounge chair, her knees together, her body and face posed as if for a portrait sitting. When I didn't answer, she asked, 'Or was that just sugar to blow in her ear?'

'No. I was serious.'

'Was?'

'Am serious.'

'Then I feel it is my responsibility as Helen's mother to acquaint you with several matters of some importance. I know that you must be quite fatigued, so I won't impose on your hospitality any longer than necessary.'

'Okay.'

'Are you a good man, Mr. Milodragovitch?'

'I don't even know what that means.'

'Are you a man with many virtues? Aside from

the obvious one of endurance, which I judge by the condition of your face. A lesser man would have found a way to quit a long time ago. But do you have any other virtues?'

'Lady, I don't know,' I grumbled, irritated, wanting to take a hot shower and lie down next to my lady.

'I hope you do. I sincerely hope so. Particularly the virtue of forgiveness, because you have a great deal to forgive.'

'Can I get another beer first?' I asked. Somehow my beer was already empty. 'I always forgive better when I've got a beer.'

'How quaint. Don't bother to get up. Helen can get it. Helen! Another beer for your friend, please.'

Helen rose obediently from her stone and shuffled across the lawn, her gnawed hands stealing toward her mouth.

'Don't bite your nails, child.'

'Yes, Mother.'

We were silent as we waited. She sat as still as a bird sleeping on a limb, but I shifted constantly in my chair, finding a new sore spot each time I moved.

'You may stay if you like,' Mrs. Duffy said to Helen when she brought me the beer. But she went back to her stone. 'I understand that you've had quite a hard time of it since Helen first came to your office.'

'At least I'm alive,' I said. 'Some people aren't.'

'Yes, so I understand,' she said, nodding her head in a brief sympathetic dismissal. 'But I must go on. We have a flight to catch –'

'Goddammit, lady, slow down. All this crap got

started, all this, a lot of people are dead, all because of your goddamned son, so don't tell me you've got a flight to catch, that –'

'Not my son,' she said bluntly. 'Hers.'

'What?'

'Raymond was her illegitimate son.'

'Come on – she's not old enough to –'

'Don't be silly. She's quite old enough. She seduced her high school band director when she was barely thirteen. I think she had had two periods before she became pregnant. I see you're having difficulty believing me. The women in my family have always been sexually precocious. We mature at an early age. Helen was a love child. I gave birth to her three weeks to the day after my fifteenth birthday. Unfortunately, unlike me, she had seduced a married man, which I could understand if not forgive, but I made the mistake of trying to atone for her mistake by adopting her son. Perhaps if she had never told Raymond of their relationship, he might have been a different sort of young man. Who knows? As it was, she told him and spoiled him terribly, and he grew up weak and effeminate, a vicious and greedy boy, full of senseless violence and hate. I tried, God knows I tried, but each time I corrected the boy, he ran to her for protection –'

'Hey, wait a minute,' I said, flat in my chair like a man who hadn't rolled with the last punch. 'This is all very interesting, but I don't see what it has to do with me.'

Her slender legs crossed with a nylon hiss, she sipped at her drink, then she looked at me with her smoothly amused smile. She said, 'As you can see by Helen's face, this has a great deal to do with you.'

When I looked at Helen, her eyes were wild again, her hands held up like a mask, and I recalled why her eyes were familiar. They were Raymond's eyes without the hate.

'I still don't see –'

'I must apologize,' Mrs. Duffy interrupted quietly, 'for waiting so long to interject myself into this affair, but my husband is an invalid while I am still a healthy woman, with, as my mother used to say, my own special needs, and I admit that I've been occupied fulfilling them. Otherwise, none of this might have happened. You see, I've been in the habit of allowing Helen to spend her summers as she chooses as long as they are spent away from home. She is quite childish about some things and she lacks my discretion. In the past she has caused me considerable embarrassment in Storm Lake, which is, after all, a small town. I had no idea that she had used this freedom to come out here to see Raymond – I'd expressly forbidden it – until after his death, and I had no idea that she had come back to hire you to investigate the death until it was too late.'

'So?'

'So this afternoon, I caught her in rather a compromising lie, and made her tell me the truth. It's a rather dreadful story, but I'm quite certain that it is the truth.'

'And?'

'Well, it seems that Helen knew from the beginning that Raymond intended to use her money for his nefarious scheme. She didn't approve, of course, but she was, as usual, unable to resist his demands. And when he telephoned her, suicidally despondent because he had caused the death of one of his vile friends –'

'One Willy Jones,' I said. 'Raymond shot him accidentally.'

'Whatever you say.'

'And burned down the hotel to cover it up.'

'That seems quite possible, yes. After his telephone call, Helen rushed out here to prevent his suicide, but she wasn't in time, and I suspect her guilt about that caused her to return to try to find some indication, however slight, that her precious son hadn't committed suicide.'

'He didn't,' Helen moaned, 'he didn't, he called me, he was coming to me, he wouldn't have, somebody killed him.' She hammered her thighs with her fists and the ground with her feet.

'Stop that nonsense this instant!'

'It may not be nonsense, Mrs. Duffy. The kid was suicidal, but somebody helped him.'

'But you don't know for sure.'

'No. And now I'll never know.'

'You don't seem angry?'

'I'm long past that,' I said, watching Helen weep with her head on her knees. Behind her the sun broke into silver ripples in the creek. In a moment, as soon as my legs recovered, I would rise and go to her. That was how it would be. 'Long past anger.'

'It is a pleasure to meet a man with your equanimity. How many men did you say have died?'

'I didn't say.'

'How many?'

'Nine men, I think, including one twelve-year-old boy. But she didn't kill any of them.'

'How many did you kill?'

'It doesn't matter.'

'My current lover is a retired military man. He says that a man never forgets the faces of the men he killed. Is that true?' she asked, boring in with a quiet intensity that made Jamison seem like a piker. 'How did you feel?'

'I can take it or leave it.'

'Don't be glib with me, young man.'

'I haven't been young in a long time, lady, and killing men makes me feel disgusted and terribly sad, but it doesn't have anything to do with Helen.'

'You don't feel betrayed? You can forgive everything? Marry in love and live happily ever after?' she asked.

'Lady, I'm more interested in being forgiven myself and having a soft place to lay my head,' I answered, and it made me feel good again, feel like things would work out. 'That's all.'

'Perhaps you are really the rarest of men, a forgiving man,' she mused, then sipped at her drink.

We watched each other again, our eyes working at each other. She smiled, but when I tried, my face was too stiff.

'Was there something else?' I asked.

'Why do you ask?'

'That shit-eatin' grin on your face.'

'You can be rather tiresome when you choose, can't you?'

'Lady, that's just the beginning.'

'Yes, well, there was one other thing,' she said, glancing pointedly at her silver watch.

'Spit it out.'

'Certainly, if you insist. I'm just afraid that you might find this additional fact rather burdensome, and I do hate to be so blunt, but –'

'I can tell.'

'Yes, well, are you aware of the fact that while you've been out doing whatever it is you do, even while you were recovering from the terrible beating you received from those thugs, that Helen and your friend, Mr. Diamond, have been, shall we say, dallying in your house – were you aware of that? Even this afternoon while you were killing that poor man?'

She allowed me a few moments of silence, allowed me to look at Helen's face, stricken with the truth, her wide frightened eyes, her fist knuckled into her open mouth.

'Strike home?' she inquired politely as I looked at Helen, my lady, my love. I found that smile.

'Fuck you, lady, and your fucking facts,' I said softly. 'Just get your shit and get your ass outa my house and my town, and take your . . .' I paused. 'Take your shit-eatin' grin with you.'

'That's clever.'

'Thanks,' I said, feeling all right now. I wasn't clever but I had endurance.

'Come, Helen, we're going.'

'She stays.'

'Oh, I'm afraid I couldn't allow it.'

'You can't prevent it,' I said.

'Oh, you poor foolish man. Helen agreed to go home

with me several hours ago,' she said, smiling lightly as she stood up. 'Come, Helen, it's time to go.'

'Then what the hell was this all about?' I asked, looking around me as if I could find the answer in the thick grass of the lawn. 'What the hell . . .'

Helen rose again from her stone, discarded her twig, and scuffled toward her mother, her hands tearing at each other under the watch of her lowered eyes, walking slowly across the lawn out of the setting sun.

'What the hell – was this all about?'

'Oh,' she answered, her smile widening. 'It seemed the thing to do at the time.' She paused, then added, 'Say good-bye to your friend, Helen.'

My lady raised her face, her pale freckled face framed by the warm red hair that flamed in the sunshine like a halo of blood and fire, but the eyes that met mine briefly were as opaque as last winter's ice, as cold and dim. I stood up, she nodded once, then followed her mother to the back door of my house.

As I stood there, the blunt shadow of the western ridge advanced darkly to the verge of the creek. I sat down, heard the sound of a car driving away. I drank my beer, and forgave her.

Turn over to enjoy a taster of

THE LAST GOOD KISS

another timeless classic from James Crumley

Meet Private Detective C. W. Sughrue.

Private detectives are supposed to find missing persons and catch criminals. But more often than not Sughrue is the one committing the crimes – everything from grand theft auto to criminal stupidity. All washed down with a bitter draught of whiskey and regret.

At the end of a three-week hunt for a runaway best-selling author, Sughrue winds up in a ramshackle bar, with an alcoholic bulldog. The landlady's daughter vanished a decade ago and now she wants Sughrue to find her. His search will take him to the deepest, darkest depths of San Francisco's underbelly – a place as fascinating, frightening and flawed as he is.

Welcome to James Crumley's America.

1

When I finally caught up with Abraham Trahearne, he was drinking beer with an alcoholic bulldog named Fireball Roberts in a ramshackle joint just outside of Sonoma, California, drinking the heart right out of a fine spring afternoon.

Trahearne had been on this wandering binge for nearly three weeks, and the big man, dressed in rumpled khakis, looked like an old soldier after a long campaign, sipping slow beers to wash the taste of death out of his mouth. The dog slumped on the stool beside him like a tired little buddy, only raising his head occasionally for a taste of beer from a dirty ashtray set on the bar.

Neither of them bothered to glance at me as I slipped onto a stool between the bulldog and the only other two customers in the place, two out-of-work shade-tree mechanics who were discussing their lost unemployment checks, their latest DWI conviction, and the probable location of a 1957 Chevy timing chain. Their knotty faces and nasal accents belonged to another time, another place. The dust bowl '30s and a rattletrap, homemade Model T truck heading into the setting sun. As I sat down, they glanced at me with the narrow eyes of country people, looking me over carefully as if I were an abandoned wreck they planned to cannibalize for spare parts. I nodded blithely to let them know that I might be a wreck but I hadn't been totaled yet. They returned my silent greeting with blank eyes and thoughtful nods that seemed to suggest that accidents could be arranged.

Already whipped by too many miles on the wrong roads, I let them think whatever they might. As I ordered a beer from the middle-aged barmaid, she slipped out of her daydreams and into a sleepy grin. When she opened the bottle, the bulldog came out of his drunken nap, belched like a dragon, then heaved his narrow haunches upright and waddled across three rickety stools through the musty cloud of stale beer and bulldog breath to trade me a wet, stringy kiss for a hit off my beer. I didn't offer him any, so he upped the ante by drooling all over my sunburnt elbow. Trahearne barked a sharp command and splashed a measure of beer into the ashtray. The bulldog gave me a mournful stare, sighed, then ambled back to a sure thing.

As I wiped the dogspit off my arm with a damp bar rag that had been used too lately and too often for the same chore, I asked the barmaid about a pay telephone. She pointed silently toward the gray dusty reaches beyond the pool table, where a black telephone hung from ashen shadows.

As I passed Trahearne, he had his heavy arm draped over the bulldog's wrinkled shoulders and recited poetry into the stubby ear: 'The bluff we face is cracking up . . . before this green Pacific wind . . . this . . . The whale's briny stink . . . ah, Christ . . . dogged we were, old friend, doggerel we became, and dogshit we too shall be . . .' Then he chuckled aimlessly, like an old man searching for his spectacles.

I didn't mind if he talked to himself. I had been talking to myself for a long time too.

That was what I had been doing the afternoon Trahearne's ex-wife had called me – sitting in my little tin office in Meriwether, Montana, staring across the alley at the overflowing Dempster Dumpster behind the discount store, and telling myself that I didn't mind if business was slow, that I liked it in fact. Then the telephone buzzed. Trahearne's ex-wife was all business. In less than a minute, she had explained that her ex-husband's health and drinking habits were both bad and that she wanted me to find him, to track him down on his running binge before he drank himself into an early grave. I suggested that we talk about the job face to face, but she wanted me on the road immediately, no time wasted driving the three hours up to Cauldron Springs. To save time, she had already hired an air-taxi out of Kalispell, which was at this very moment winging its way south toward Meriwether with a cashier's check for a retainer, a list of Trahearne's favorite bars around the West – particularly those bars about which he had written poems after other binges – and a dust-jacket photo off his last novel.

'What if I don't want the job?' I asked.

'After you see the size of the retainer, you'll want the job,' she answered coolly, then hung up.

When I picked up the large manila folder at the

Meriwether Airport, I glanced at the check and decided to take the job even before I studied the photograph. Trahearne looked like a big man, a retired longshoreman maybe, as he leaned against a pillar on the front porch of the Cauldron Springs Hotel, a drink shining in one hand, a cigar smoking in the other. His age showed, even through his boyish grin, but he clearly hadn't gone to Cauldron Springs for the waters. Behind him, through the broad darkened doorway, two arthritic ghosts in matching plaid bathrobes shuffled toward the sunlight. Their ancient faces seemed to be smiling in anticipation of dipping their brittle bones into the hot mineral waters.

In the years that I had spent looking for lost husbands, wives, and children, I had learned not to think that I could stare into a one-dimensional face and see the person behind the photograph, but the big man looked like the sort who would cut a wide swath and leave an easy trail.

At first, it was too easy. Back at my office, I called five or six of the bars and caught the old man up in Ovando, Montana, at a great little bar called Trixi's Antler Bar. Trahearne had left, though, by the time I drove the eighty miles, telling the bartender that he was off to Two Dot to check out the beer-can collection in one of Two Dot's two bars. I chased him across Montana but when I reached Two Dot, Trahearne had gone on to the 666 in Miles City. From there, he headed south to Buffalo, Wyoming, to write an epic poem about the Johnson County War. Or so he told the barmaid. As it turned out, Trahearne never made a move without discussing it with everybody in the bar. Which made him easy to follow but impossible to catch.

We covered the West, touring the bars, seeing the sights. The Chugwater Hotel down in Wyoming, the Mayflower in Cheyenne, the Stockman's in Rawlins, a barbed-wire collection in the Sacajawen Hotel Bar in Three Forks, Montana, rocks in Fossil, Oregon, drunken Mormons all over northern Utah and southern Idaho – circling, wandering in an aimless drift. Twice I hired private planes to get ahead of the old man, and twice he failed to show up until after I had left. I liked his taste in bars but I was in and out of so many that they all began to seem like the same endless bar. By the middle of the second week, my expenses were beginning to embarrass even me, so I called the former Mrs. Trahearne to ask how much money she wanted to pour down the rolling rathole. 'Whatever is necessary,' she answered, sounding irritated that I had bothered to ask.

So I settled back into the bucket seat of my fancy El Camino pickup for a long siege of moving on, following Trahearne from bar to bar, down whatever roads suited his fancy, covering the ground like an excited redbone pup just to keep from losing him, following him as he drifted on, his tail turned into some blizzard wind only he felt, his ear cocked to hear the strains of some distant song only he heard.

By the middle of the second week, I had that same high lonesome keen whistling in my chest, and if I hadn't needed the money so badly, I might have said to hell with Abraham Trahearne, stuck some Willie Nelson into my tape deck, and tried to drown in a whiskey river of my own. Taking up moving on again. But I get paid for finding folks, not for losing myself, so I held on his trail like an old hound after his last coon.

And it made me even crazier than Trahearne. I found myself chasing ghosts across gray mountain passes, then down through green valleys riddled with the snows of late spring. I took to sleeping in the same motel beds he had, trying to dream him up, took to getting drunk in the same bars, hoping for a whiskey vision. They came all right, those bleak motel dreams, those whiskey visions, but they were out of my own drifting past. As for Trahearne, I didn't have a clue.

Once I even humped the same sad young whore in a trailerhouse complex out in the Nevada desert. She was a frail, skinny little bit out of Cincinnati, and she had brought her gold mine out West, thinking perhaps it might assay better, but her shaft had collapsed, her veins petered out, and the tracks on her thin arms looked as if they had been dug with a rusty pick. After I had slaked too many nights of aimless barstool lust amid her bones, I asked her again about Trahearne. She didn't say anything at first, she just lay on her crushed bed-sheets, hitting on a joint and gazing beyond the aluminum ceiling into the cold desert night.

'You reckon they actually went up there on the moon?' she asked seriously.

'I don't know,' I admitted.

'Me neither,' she whispered into the smoke.

I buttoned up my Levis and fled into the desert, into a landscape blasted by moonlight and shadow.

Then in Reno I lost the trail, had to circle the city in

ever-widening loops, talking to bartenders and service-station attendants until I found a pump jockey in Truckee who remembered the big man in his Caddy convertible asking about the mud baths in Calistoga. The mud was still warm when I got there, but his trail was as cold as the eyes of the old folks dying around the hot baths.

When I called Trahearne's ex-wife to admit failure, she told me that she had received a postcard from him, a picture of the Golden Gate and a cryptic couplet. *Dogs, they say, are man's best friend, but their pants have no pockets, their thirst no end.* 'Trahearne has this odd affinity for bar dogs,' she told me, 'particularly those who drink as well as do tricks. Once he spent three weeks in Frenchtown, Montana, drinking with a mutt who wore a tiny crushed officer's cap, sunglasses, and a corncob pipe. Trahearne said they discussed the Pacific campaign over shots of blackberry brandy.' I told her that it was her money and that if she wanted me to wander around the Bay Area looking for a drinking bar dog, I would surely comply. That's what she wanted, so I hooked it up, headed for San Francisco, a fancy detective hot on the trail of a drinking bar dog, a fool on her errand.

I should have guessed that the city of lights would be rife with bar dogs – dancing dogs and singing dogs, even hallucinating hounds – so it wasn't until three days later, drinking gimlets with a pink poodle in Sausalito, that I heard about the beer-drinking bulldog over by Sonoma.

The battered frame building was set fifty yards off the Petaluma road, and Trahearne's red Cadillac convertible was parked in front. In the days when the old highway had been new, back before it had been rebuilt along more efficient lines, the beer joint had been a service station. The faded ghost of a flying red horse still haunted the weathered clapboard walls of the building. A small herd of abandoned cars, ranging from a russet Henry J to a fairly new but badly wrecked black Dodge Charger, stood hock deep in the dusty Johnson grass and weeds, the empty sockets of their headlights dreaming of Pegasus and asphalt flight. The place didn't even have a name, just a faded sign wanly promising BEER as it swung from the canted portico. The old glass-tanked pumps were long gone – probably off to Sausalito to open an antique shop – but the rusted bolts of their bases still dangled upward from the concrete like finger bones from a shallow grave.

I parked beside Trahearne's Caddy, got out to stretch the miles out of my legs, then walked out of the spring sunshine into the dusty shade of the joint, my boot heels rocking gently on the warped floorboards, my sigh relieved in the darkened air. This was the place, the place I would have come on my own wandering binge, come here and lodged like a marble in a crack, this place, a haven for California Okies and exiled Texans, a home for country folk lately dispossessed, their eyes so empty of hope that they reflect hot, windy plains, spare, almost biblical sweeps of horizon broken only by the spines of an orphaned rocking chair, and beyond this, clouded with rage, the reflections of orange groves and ax handles. This could just as easily have been my place, a home where a man could drink in boredom and repent in violence and be forgiven for the price of a beer.

* * *

After I had thought about it, I stuck my dime back in my pocket, walked back to the bar for another beer. I had found bits and pieces of Trahearne all along the way and I felt like an old friend. It seemed a shame not to enjoy him, not to have a few beers with him before I called his ex-wife and ended the party. Whenever I found anybody, I always suspected that I deserved more than money in payment. This was the saddest moment of the chase, the silent wait for the apologetic parents or the angry spouse or the laws. The process was fine, but the finished product was always ugly. In my business, you need a moral certitude that I no longer even claimed to possess, and every time when I came to the end of the chase, I wanted to walk away.

But not yet, not this time. I leaned against the bar and ordered another bottle of beer. When the barmaid sat it down, a large black tomcat drifted down the bar to nose the moisture on the long neck.

'The cat drink beer too?' I asked the barmaid.

'Not anymore,' she answered with a grin as she flicked the sodden bar rag at the cat's butt. He gave her a dirty look, then wandered down the bar past the bulldog and Trahearne, his tail brushing across Trahearne's stolid face. 'Sumbitch usta drink like a fish but he got to be too much trouble. He's like ol' Lester there,' she said, nodding toward the shade-tree mechanic with the most teeth. 'He can't handle it. He'd get so low-down, dirty-belly, knee-walkin' drunk, he start up tom-cattin' in all the wrong damn places.'

The barmaid gave ol' Lester a hard, knowing glance,

then broke into a happy cackle. As he tried to grin, ol' Lester showed me the rest of his teeth. They weren't any prettier than the ones I had already seen. 'One night that crazy black bastard started up a-humpin' ever'thing in sight – pool-table legs, cues, folks' legs, anything that didn't move fast enough – and then he did somethin' nasty on a lady's slacks and somebody laughed and damned if we didn't have the biggest fistfight I ever seen. Ever'body who wasn't in the hospital ended up in jail, and they took my license for six weeks.' She laughed, then added, 'So I had that scutter cut off. Right at the source. He ain't wanted a drink since.'

'Is that Lester or the tomcat?' I asked.

The barmaid cackled merrily again, the other mechanic brayed, but ol' Lester just sat there and looked like his teeth hurt.

'Naw,' she answered when she stopped laughing. 'Ol' Lester there, he don't cause no trouble in here. He's plumb terrified of my bulldog there.'

'Looks like a plain old bulldog to me,' I said, then leaned back and waited for the story.

'Plain,' Lester squealed. 'Plain mean. And I mean *mean*. Hell, mister, one mornin' last summer I come in here peaceful as could be, just mindin' my own business, and I made the mistake of steppin' on that sumbitch's foot when he had a hangover, and damn if he didn't like to tore my leg plumb off.' Lester leaned over to lift his pants' leg and exhibit a set of dog-bite scars that looked like chicken scratches. 'Took fifty-seven stitches,' he claimed proudly. 'Ol' Oney here, he had to hit that sucker with a pool cue to get him off'n my leg.'

'Broke that damned cue right smack in two,' Oney quickly added.

'Plain old bulldog, my ass,' Lester said. 'That sumbitch's meaner'n a snake. You tell him, Rosie.'

'Listen, mister,' the barmaid said as she leaned across the bar, 'I've seen that old bastard Fireball Roberts come outa dead drunks and blind hangovers and just pure-dee tear the britches off many a damn fool who thought he'd make trouble for a poor woman all alone in the world.' When she said *alone*, Rosie propped one finger under her chin and smiled coyly at me. I glanced over her shoulder into the ruined mirror to see if my hair had turned gray on the trip. An old ghost with black hair grinned back like a coyote. Rosie added, 'He don't just knock 'em down, mister, he drags 'em out by the seat of their britches, and they're usually damn glad to go.'

'Well, I'll be damned,' I said, properly impressed, then I glanced at the bulldog, who was sleeping quietly curled on his stool. Trahearne caught my eye with a glare, as if he thought I meant to impugn the courage of the dog, but his eyes lost their angry focus and seemed to drift independently apart.

''Course now, if'n Fireball can't handle all 'em by his own damn self,' Lester continued in a high, excited voice, 'ol' Rosie there, she ain't no slouch herself. You get her tail up, mister, she's just as liable to shoot your eyes out as look at you.'

I nodded and Rosie blushed sweetly.

'Show him that there *pistole*,' Lester demanded.

Rosie added a dash of bashful reluctance to her blush, and for an instant the face of a younger, prettier woman blurred her wrinkles. She patted her gray curls, then reached under the bar and came up with a nickel-plated .380 Spanish automatic pistol so ancient and ill-used that the plate had peeled away like cheap paint.

'Don't look like much,' Lester admitted gamely, 'but she's got the trigger sear filed down to a nubbin, and that sumbitch is just as liable to shoot nine times as once.' He turned to point across the bar to a cluster of unmended bulletholes between two windows above a ratty booth. 'She ain't had to touch it off but one damn time, mister, but I swear when she reaches under the bar, things do tend to get downright peaceful in here.'

'Like a church,' I said.

'More like a graveyard,' Lester amended. 'Ain't no singin' at all, just a buncha silent prayers.' Then he laughed wildly, and I toasted his mirth.

Rosie held the pistol in her rough hands for a moment more, then she sat it back under the bar with a thump.

''Course I got me a real pistol at home,' Lester said smugly.

'A German Luger,' I said without thinking.

'How'd you know?' he asked suspiciously.

The real answer was that I had spent my life in bars listening to war stories and assorted lies, but I lied and told Lester that my daddy had brought one back from the war.

'Got mine off'n a Kraut captain at Omaha Beach,' he said, his nose tilted upward as if my daddy had won his in a crap game. 'Normandy invasion,' he added.

'You must have been pretty young,' I said, then wished I hadn't. People like Lester might tell a windy tale now and again, but only a damn fool would bring it to their attention.

Lester stared at me a long time to see if I meant to call him a liar, then with practiced nonchalance he said, 'Lied about my age.' Then he asked, 'You ever been in the service?'

'No, sir,' I lied. 'Flat feet.'

'4-F, huh,' he said, trying not to sound too superior. 'Oney here, he's 4-F too, but it weren't his feet, it was his head.'

'Ain't going off to no damn Army,' Oney said seriously, then he glanced around as if the draft board might still be on his trail.

'Ain't even no draft no more,' Lester said, then snorted at Oney's ignorance.

'Yeah,' Oney said sadly. 'By God they oughtta go over there to San Francisco and draft up about a hunnert thousand a them goddamned hairy hippies.'

'Now, that's the god's truth,' Lester said, and turned to me.

'Ain't it?' His eyes narrowed at the three-day stubble on my chin as if it were an incipient beard.

For a change, I kept my mouth shut and nodded. But not emphatically enough to suit Lester. He started to say something, but I interrupted him as I excused myself and walked over toward Trahearne. Behind me, Lester muttered something about *goddamned gold-brickin' 4-F hippies*, but I acted as if I hadn't heard. I reached over and tapped Trahearne on the shoulder, and his great bald head swiveled slowly, as if it were as heavy as lead. He raised an eyebrow, wriggled a pleasant little smile onto his face, shrugged, then toppled backward off the bar stool. I caught a handful of his shirt, but it didn't even slow him down. He landed flat on his back, hard, like a two-hundred-fifty-pound sack of cement. Rafters and window lights rattled, spurts of ancient dust billowed from between the floorboards, and the balls on the pool table danced merrily across the battered felt.

As I stood there stupidly with a handful of dirty khaki in my right hand, Lester leaped off his stool and shouted, 'What the hell did you do that for?'

'Do what?'

'Hit that old man like that,' Lester said, his Adam's apple rippling up and down his skinny throat like a crazed mouse. 'I ain't never seen nothin' as chickenshit as that.'

'I didn't hit him,' I said.

'Hell, man, I seen you.'

'I'm sorry but you must have been mistaken,' I said, trying to be calm and rational, which is almost always a mistake in situations like this.

'You callin' me a liar?' Lester asked as he doubled his fists.

'Not at all,' I said, then I made another mistake as I stepped back to the bar for my beer: I tried to explain things. 'Listen, I'm a private investigator, and this gentleman's ex-wife hired me to . . .'

'What's the matter,' Lester sneered, 'he behind in his goddamned al-i-mony, huh? I know your kind, buddy. A rotten, sneaky sumbitch just like you tracked me all the way down to my mama's place in Barstow just 'cause I's a few months behind paying that whore I married, and let me tell you I kicked his ass then, and I got half a mind to kick yours right here and now.'

'Let's just calm down, huh,' I said. 'Let me buy you boys a beer and I'll tell you all about it. Okay?'

'You ain't gonna tell me shit, buddy,' Lester said, and as if that weren't enough, he added, 'and I don't drink with no trash.'

'I don't want no trouble in here,' Rosie interjected quietly.

'No trouble,' I said. Lester and Oney might have comic faces, funny accents, and bad teeth, but they also had wrists as thick as cedar fence-posts, knuckled, work-hardened hands as lumpy as socks full of rocks, and a lifetime of rage and resentment. I grew up with folks like this and I knew better than to have any serious disagreements with them. 'No trouble at all,' I said. 'I'll just leave.'

'That ain't near good enough,' Lester grunted as he took two steps toward me and a wild swing at my face.

I ducked, then backhanded him upside the head with the half-full beer bottle. His right ear disappeared in a shower of bloody foam, and he fell sideways, scrabbled across the floor, cupping his ear and cursing. Oney stood up, then sat back down when he saw the broken bottle in my hand.

'Is that good enough?' I asked.

Oney agreed with a nervous nod, but Lester had just peeked into his palm and found bits and pieces of his ear.

In a high, thin voice, he shouted, 'Goddammit, Oney, get the gun!'

Behind me, I heard Trahearne stand up and dreamily wonder what the hell had happened. But nobody answered him. Oney and Rosie and I were locked into long silent stares. Then we all moved at once. Rosie dashed down the bar toward the automatic as Oney scrambled over it. I glanced at the bulldog, who still slept like a rock, then I lit out for open country. I would have made it, too, but good ol' Lester rolled over and hooked a shoulder into my right knee. We went down in a heap. Right on his ruined ear. He whimpered but held on. Even after I stood up and jerked out a handful of his dirty hair.

Behind the bar, Rosie and Oney still struggled for the pistol.

Trahearne had sobered up enough to see it, but as he tried to run, he crashed into the pool table, then tried to scramble under it just as Oney jerked the pistol out of Rosie's hands and shoved her away. As she fell, she screamed, 'Fireball!' I gave up and raised my hands, resigned myself to an afternoon of fun and games in payment for Lester's ear. But as Oney lifted the pistol and thumbed the safety, Fireball came out of a dead sleep and cleared the bar in a single bound like a flash of fat gray light. Still in midair, he locked his stubby yellow teeth into Oney's back at that tender spot just below the short ribs and above the kidney. Oney grunted like a man hit with a baseball bat, dropped his arms, and blanched so deeply that ancient acne scars glowed like live coals across his face. He grunted again, sobbed briefly, then jerked the trigger.

The first round blew off a significant portion of his

right foot, the second wreaked a foamy havoc in the cooler, and the third slammed through the flimsy beaverboard face of the bar and slapped Mr. Abraham Trahearne right in his famous ass. The fourth powdered the fourteen ball, the fifth knocked out a window light, and the rest ventilated the roof.

When the clip finally emptied, Oney sank slowly behind the bar, the automatic still clutched in his upraised hand, and Fireball still locked to his back like a fat gray leech. During the rash of gunfire, the tomcat had come out of nowhere and shot out the front door like a streak of black lightning, while Lester had hugged my knees like a frightened child. Or a man whose war stories had finally come true.

'Goddammit, Lester,' I said when the echoes had stopped rattling the old beams, 'you're bleeding all over my britches.'

'I'm sorry,' he said quietly as if he meant it, then turned me loose.

As I handed him my handkerchief for his ear, Fireball came trotting around the end of the bar, his drooping jowls rimmed with blood. He scrambled onto the platform bar rail, a stool, then up on the bar. He worked his way along, tilting bottles, catching them in his muzzle, and drinking them dry. Then he lapped his ash-tray empty, belched, then bopped down to the floor the same way he had gotten up. With a weary waddle that seemed to sigh with every step, he wandered over to the doorway and stretched out in a patch of sunlight, asleep before his belly hit the floor, small delicate snores rippling the dust motes around him.

'I don't believe I've ever seen anything quite like that,' I told Lester.

'Goddamned sumbitchin' dog,' Lester growled as he walked over to a booth to sit down.

I went behind the bar to check on Oney and Rosie. He had fainted and she lay on the duckboards like a corpse. Except that her hands were clasped to her ears instead of crossed on her chest.

'Anybody dead?' she asked without opening her eyes.

'Some walking wounded,' I said, 'but no dead ones.'

'If you'd wait till I get my wits about me before you call the law,' she said, 'I'd surely appreciate it. We got to figure some way to explain all this crap.'

'Right,' I agreed. 'You got any whiskey?'

She nodded toward a cabinet, where I found a half-empty quart of Old Crow. I did what I could for Oney's foot, took off his work shoe and cotton sock and poured some whiskey on the nubbins of flesh where his two middle toes had been, then wrapped the foot in a clean bar towel. After I washed out the dog bite with bar soap, I went over to help Lester clean slivers of glass out of the side of his head and tattered ear.

'Ain't no ladies gonna slip their tongues in that ear no more,' I joked.

'Never much cared for that anyway,' he said primly. 'How's ol' Oney?'

'Blew off a couple of toes,' I said.

'Big'uns or little'uns?'

'Medium sized,' I answered.

'Hell, that ain't nothin',' Lester said as he gently touched his ear. 'How 'bout Rosie?'

'I think she's taking a little nap.'

'Looks like the big fella is, too,' Lester said with a nod.

I thought it unkind to point out that 'the old man' had somehow become 'the big fella,' so I went over to see why Trahearne was still huddled under the pool table.

'Are you all right, Mr. Trahearne?' I asked as I knelt to peer under the table.

'Actually, I think I've caught a round,' he answered calmly.

I didn't see any blood, so I asked where.

'Right in the ass, my friend,' he said, 'right in the ass.' Then he opened his eyes, saw the bottle, and took it away from me. 'You drink this pig swill?'

I didn't, or at least hadn't, but he didn't have any trouble getting his mouth around the neck of the bottle. Not as much as I had trying to get his pants and a pair of sail-sized boxer shorts down so I could see the wound. The jacketed round had left a neat blue hole, marked with a watery trickle of blood, just below his left buttock. I had no way of knowing if the bullet had struck a bone or an artery, but Trahearne's color and pulse were good, and I could see the lead nestled like a little blue turd just beneath the skin below the hump of fatty tissue hanging over his right hip.

'What's it look like?' he asked between sips.

'Looks like your ass, old man.'

'I always knew I'd die a comic death,' he said gravely.

'Not today, old man. Just a minor flesh wound.'

'That's easy for you to say, son, it's not your flesh.'

‘In a few days, you won’t have nothing but a bad memory and a sore ass,’ I said.

‘Thank you,’ he said, ‘but I seem to have both those already.’ He paused for a sip of whiskey. ‘How is it that you know my name, young man?’

‘Why, hell, you’re a famous man, Mr. Trahearne.’

‘Not that famous, unfortunately.’

‘Yeah, well, your ex-wife was worried about your health,’ I said.

‘And she hired you to shoot me in the ass,’ he said, ‘so I couldn’t sit on a bar stool.’

‘I didn’t shoot you,’ I said.

‘Maybe not,’ he said, ‘but you’re going to get the blame anyway.’ Then he sucked on the bourbon until he curled around the empty bottle, adding his gravelly snore to Fireball’s quiet drone.